SEP   2008

 HOW Far IS THE OCean From Here

HOW FAR IS THE ocean From HERE

A Novel

AMY SHearn

Shaye Areheart Books
New York

Acknowledgments: In recounting Susannah's story, other adventures have been evoked, invoked, and sometimes downright quoted: "The Open Boat," Stephen Crane; *Moby-Dick*, Herman Melville; *Orlando*, Virginia Woolf; *Metamorphosis*, Ovid.

Published in the United States by Shaye Areheart Books, an imprint of the Crown Publishing Group, a division of Random House, Inc., New York.
www.crownpublishing.com

Shaye Areheart Books with colophon is a registered trademark of Random House, Inc.

Library of Congress Cataloging-in-Publication Data

Shearn, Amy.
   How far is the ocean from here : a novel / Amy Shearn.—1st ed.
   1. Surrogate motherhood—Fiction.   I. Title.
PS3619.H434H69 2008
813'.6—dc22   2007033956

ISBN 978-0-307-40534-0

Printed in the United States of America

Design by Lynne Amft

1 3 5 7 9 10 8 6 4 2

First Edition

For Adam

MILLIE LAMMOREAUX: *Okay, now, what's wrong with ya.*

PINKY ROSE: *Nothin'?*

MILLIE LAMMOREAUX: *Well, there's gotta be something wrong with ya.*

—from the film *Three Women*, Robert Altman

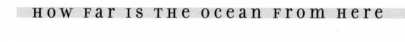

HOW Far IS THE ocean From Here

1

OTHERHOOD

Along the highway in that stretch of desert, somewhere between West Texas and East New Mexico, there was nothing
and nothing and nothing and then the Thunder Lodge. But what a
nothing! There the horizon had a weight she hadn't known a horizon
could have; a plain unvaried by cactus or tree, unstirred by lizard or
coyote, undimpled by even a shadow, only here and there the slightest
swell of hills. A house, a diner, a roadside attraction—an abandoned
gas station with leaking, ancient snouts; a gigantic plaster dinosaur;
a man in a gorilla suit advertising discounted tires—any distraction
would have inspired as raucous a *land ho* as has ever been heard. But
there was nothing, and still she moved onward, and still the desert lay
insensible to any human who entered it.

That is to say, the highway was so forgotten in those stretches that
it was difficult to believe it had ever been built. Out walking on its
dusty shoulder, her hands pressed to her belly as if it might detach in
the heat, sweat trickling between her shoulder blades, Susannah tried
to imagine the men who had done such a thing, these ghostly men
who'd installed the devolving asphalt: bending their backs in the sunlight, their lungs struggling in the grit of reddish dirt, the hides of
their legs and hands torn from arguing with the sinewy tangles that ac-
counted for vegetation. On the whole she spent entirely too much time

daydreaming—it was a weakness, she knew—picturing what it was like to be somebody else, trying on different versions of herself like suits of skin. Now she was entirely out of context, a paper doll slapped onto an unfamiliar backdrop, just any pregnant girl standing on the side of the highway twisting her spine, giving the overheated car a minute to tick time-bombishly, a chance to stop steaming from the hood.

She took stock of the landscape. The desert looked like an abandoned beach punctuated with coils of dried seaweed—no, cactusy little plants. Things were actually *growing* here. She wanted to report back to Julian, as always, to share every detail of her day, each minuscule thing she'd seen or done, the way you did when you first were in love with someone. She wanted something witty and incisive to offer him, but all she could think was, Granule. Arrowhead. Scorch. What had he said? That he had never been to the desert, that he had always wondered what it was like, who lived there, how such a horizon would change one's thinking—he'd been in one of his poetic moods. And Susannah had thought, Well, why wonder? Why wonder about a thing when one could go and do the thing? Though now that she was here, it occurred to her that maybe that hadn't been the point at all. Maybe he'd just been looking for something to say.

Meanwhile a caravan of cars drove by—the traffic on these highways always clumped together, Susannah had noticed, clinging like burrs—no, like orphans in a fairy tale. Missy Simkins, forehead pressed to the passenger-side window—she and her boyfriend had had an argument, and now he drove fast, much too fast, and neither of them was speaking—saw Susannah by the side of the road. Missy knew that they should stop but was still too angry, her heart leaping in her throat, to speak to her boyfriend—God, but he could be an ass sometimes—to say the words *Shouldn't we stop?*, and the girl's rounded belly only made her feel even stupider for ever thinking they would marry and have children as she'd always assumed, roused in her the suspicion that it would all soon be over. And anyway, the girl was going to be okay, Missy guiltily convinced herself. In the car beside hers, Bruce Londa drove mercilessly on, though his son was begging to pee. Bruce squinted through the windshield, tuning the kids out, trying not to think terrible thoughts about his shrill, girlish son, hardly even registering the woman by the side of road—seeing her only enough to miss, dimly, the days before his children were born, when the world seemed full of potential, when he could have been anyone.

Susannah watched the cars, a parade of robotic husks with blank, moony faces captured in each. *Cars seem unrealistic out here,* she would tell Julian. *They seem like something from another planet.* Everything seemed unlike itself. A sliver of moon shone in the sky like a bit of showing seam. The highway roared like an ocean. After the initial herd, no cars passed for some time, and Susannah swallowed the metallic fizz of dread—if the car didn't start again, how long would it be before someone rescued her? What were you supposed to do—dig for water? Slice through a cactus? Because it was easy, too easy, to see how these remnants—the road, the leaning telephone poles, the Thunder Lodge and the gas station down the way, and everyone in them, Susannah Prue and all the others—might disappear entirely one day, how no one would know to miss them.

HOW THIS HUGELY pregnant girl named Susannah Prue came to settle at the Thunder Lodge, a godforsaken fleabag motel in the middle of truly-not-exaggerating nowhere, was this: She'd been driving for four days, a distance that ought to have taken three or even two but for her frequent stops to use bathrooms in sordid truck stops, traveling in a car that did not approve of the plan, heading southwest the whole time (eating cherry licorice until her head rang with sugar) while the heat and dust bore down upon her, while the too-redness of the ground and too-blueness of the sky made her eyes ache, their usual palette being that greeny gray Midwestern sort of affair. She drove with the windows down, because the air conditioner was busted; she drove mummified in the grit of the desert, blasted by inhumane heat. She opened the glove box and as she drove she threw things out the window, things she had taken from home, things she no longer needed, reaching in and extracting them one by one: the key to Julian and Kit's apartment, a lavender hair ribbon, a plastic stick with its pink plus-sign, a locket without a picture inside, a ticket stub from a movie she hadn't wanted to see anyway, a paper cup—embarrassing to think of it now—that she'd washed out and kept, because Julian had bought the tea for her. One by one she held the things out the open window, fighting the wall of wind, and released them into the current, picturing the hair ribbon flinging out on the breeze and winding itself into a jaunty bow tie around a cactus's throat, the paper cup dying a long, drawn-out death pulverized by a century of truck wheels. The pregnancy test tucked away by insects, the ticket shredded and woven into a snake's nest. Ha! Susannah patted her stomach, said to it soothingly, "What? Am I having a nervous breakdown? Me? Of course not, don't be silly. I'm fine! Everything's going to be just fine, just completely fine. Don't you worry about a thing," then cupping the baby, palming it like a basketball, and laughing at herself a little, because of course it was crazy, crazy, crazy of her, crazy to be skipping town, crazy to be talking this way and laughing because otherwise she would probably cry. The car had been coughing something blackish for almost all of Texas as she passed the turnoffs for the interesting cities and even the Gulf, willfully bypassing anything that seemed remotely appealing or refreshing, until finally the car's tubercular heaving began to concern Susannah, really concern her, but it was too late to head toward Midland or Marfa or Mexico. And so she continued to drive, and was humming a nursery rhyme whose singsong had begun to clang uncomfortably around her head when she saw, at the dusk of the fourth day, in the matte light of one streetlamp fluttering against the quick nightfall of the desert, a billboard peeling with paint.

It featured a fearsome Indian chief, arms akimbo and glaring into the eyes of what appeared to be Zeus wielding a thunderbolt—presumably in the midst of some interdenominational skirmish?—and anyway it wasn't the most *welcoming* sign she'd ever seen, but it read THUNDER LODGE 1 MI in zappy, lightningy letters, and a moment later she was skidding into the strip of parking lot, which was not nearly so well lit as the sign. She stepped out of the car. Heat crackled across her skin. Above the motel a rain cloud and a zigzag of lightning flickered in neon. Susannah looked toward the car, whose hood emitted a fine mist like a perturbed skunk. Then she stepped into the office.

It was a dingy box of a room noisy with two small TVs stacked on the counter and a dripping air conditioner bulging from the only window. Two plastic chairs with seats molded in approximations of butt shapes were pushed against the wall across from the door. The walls were bare, the floor swept clean but somehow still unsanitary-seeming, everything gone soft-focus beneath a permanent layer of grit. Beside the televisions on the counter was a spiral notebook with a Persian cat on the cover, and beside the notebook was a plastic cup in which floated a set of teeth.

The notebook, the teeth—everything seemed like a clue to something else. Susannah thought of the things she had thrown out her car window and suffered a sharp twist of regret. Part of her wanted to race back down the highway. But at a certain point you made your bed and you had to lie in it, wasn't that the saying? And she had made a certain kind of bed for herself—it was unpleasant, but at least it was hers. So she stood there a long time, too long, but she could hear someone rustling around just behind the counter, beyond the back door that yawned partially open, leading to some kind of living quarters in which another TV was muttering, and she kept thinking the person would pop into the office, and she didn't want to be loudly saying "Excuse me" or something to a person who was about to be right there. "Oh yes you *are* taking a bath, mister," a woman was saying.

Susannah took a step forward, then back, faced the door, returned to the counter, simultaneously embarrassed for having interrupted some domestic scene and annoyed at being made to feel embarrassed when all she wanted was a room or maybe (as she looked around the office and saw the room keys lined up on hooks—all eleven, all there), maybe just to use the phone. She stood paralyzed, hands protectively on her belly, listening to some kind of yelp from the bath refuser, and, afraid of hearing more or of being caught eavesdropping, she left the office, shut the door, opened the door again, and reentered the room, this time shutting the door behind her more resolutely and walking heavily up to the counter, hoping to thereby summon the proprietors. But this time there was only a louder "Dammit, Tim!" and a door slamming, followed by a long silence in which Susannah noticed what was on the two TVs: a local news program ridged with static and, above, an antique Mighty Mouse cartoon, both murmuring as if trying to communicate with each other. "The ATM bandits strike again in Las Cruces," the newscaster told Mighty Mouse. Mighty Mouse shook his head and extended a fist, lighting out into the sky.

Finally an old man stuck his head into the office from the back door and bugged his eyes at Susannah. So his wife had been right—there *was* someone waiting to check in, and he hadn't heard the door! It was awful to be getting old, to not hear the door, to snap at Char only to realize she'd been right all along, to come out into the office and see a pitiful, dusty-looking girl with large, sad eyes. Not the kind of guest they usually had, no. Then again, they hadn't had anyone at all for days, for so long that he'd started to wonder, as he did from time to time, whether something terrible had happened that they hadn't heard about—nuclear explosion, oil spill—but Char said he worried too much. Here was a guest, a young mother-to-be, waiting to check in. Marlon still remembered their very first guest, that first night they were open for business; he still remembered his name—William Schultz—and the way his angular signature had pressed into that first

6

page of their guest registry, leaving an indentation on the next five sheets of paper. But he couldn't remember what William Schultz had looked like or where he had been headed. Oh, it was awful to be getting old—he'd have to ask Char, she'd remember about William Schultz—with no money to retire, with Tim, their boy, to think about, to be getting old and a little deaf and not to hear the door, not to realize until a little too late that someone was waiting.

Marlon Garland pushed open the door and left it wide behind him, revealing a disheveled living room that struck Susannah, as she tried to look at it without looking like she was looking at it, as being impressively orange and brown. She thought she knew that it smelled like tomato soup and dusty potpourri, that she knew there would be a pile of decrepit *Ranger Rick* magazines somewhere, and needlepoint with homey sayings on the walls. A stale, air-conditioned breeze wafted from the living room into the office. The man sat on the stool behind the counter—hurriedly, as if responding to a soundless *Places, please! Places!*—and then fished the teeth out of the cup and popped them into his mouth, twisting around his jaw to get everything settled in before saying, "Well, hello there, miss!"

He was maybe sixty-five or seventy, possibly older, although Susannah always found it difficult to distinguish degrees of oldness and melded together everyone from about age fifty on as just generally oldish. And going by the way he was squinting at her, she knew he had the same problem but reversed, and was trying to decide if she was a runaway teen or an ordinary wife. She tugged at her ratty, oversize T-shirt, an old favorite she had chosen for luck but which she now worried revealed the bottom of her engorged belly, making her look like a fat man at the county fair. The motel proprietor tapped his nails on the counter. "One?" he said helpfully. "A single?" How could she answer a question like this? How could she say anything of the sort to him—I am alone, or I am not alone—when she wasn't even planning on spending the night? But something in the way he spoke was convincing enough. He was certain that she was there to stay, and someone had to be certain of something. He looked her up and down and smiled and said, "Or should I say a double!" winking gym-teacherily at her and chuckling.

"Well," she said, then cleared her throat—realizing she hadn't spoken in a long time and hoping the voice that emerged sounded okay—"I'm not sure. I think my car's sort of dying. How far is the next city?"

The man put both his palms on the countertop and guffawed. "I'll put you down for the night," he said. It wasn't until later that Susannah realized how important this had been, that if he'd let her try to go even the next hundred miles or so in that junky car, she would have broken down on even a bleaker strip of highway than this one, and it might have been a day or two before someone passed. "And tomorrow I'll take a look at the car, if you like."

"Oh," said Susannah. "How nice of you."

"Where you coming from?" He flipped through the spiral note-book, searched around for a pen.

"Chicago," she said, which made him laugh even harder.

"Chicago! Kind of a roundabout route you're taking, isn't it? You've gone and driven yourself right off the map." Though he couldn't have known where her destination was, since she didn't even know her-self, and therefore who was to say whether or not her route was really roundabout at all? She was trying to figure out how to address this, what to ask him, what a person did in such a situation, when he offered, "Vis-iting relatives or something?"

"Something like that."

"What are they, snakes?" he said, chuckling.

"Scorpions," she said.

He became suddenly serious. "Just sign your name and address here."

She thought briefly of using a made-up name, and she certainly should have, but she didn't have one ready and was afraid he would notice her hesitation. "I'll be paying in cash," she said. "How much is the room?"

"Marlon Garland," he said, extending a hand. "But you can call me Marlon Garland."

"Oh," she said, "okay," while he chuckled at himself. "And, sorry, how much is the room?"

"How much you willing to pay?" Marlon said, and Susannah patted her belly the careless way you'd pat a friend's arm and said, "I'll give you my firstborn child," and again his laugh dissolved and he pressed his lips together. As an appeal she added, "My name is Susannah Prue."

"Well, pleased to meet you, Susie Q." He winked.

Susannah flushed and shook her head and said, flustered, "Oh, no. Call me Susannah."

He half turned then to holler, "Char," and just as he did so, a woman with her left arm crooked in a sling appeared behind him, giving Susannah a look that was both a frown and a smile, or maybe neither. "Tim won't take his bath," the woman announced. Shut the door behind her, perched on the stool beside Marlon Garland. She was about his age but more nimble, and her sundress and white-streaked braid lent her a youthful appearance. The sling was periwinkle, rimmed with white plastic piping; the arm within pale and inert as a caught fish. She looked at the bottom TV for a moment—the weather now—and scoffed, waved her good hand at it, and only then did she say to Susannah, "Hot night, isn't it."

Susannah nodded. She extracted from her pocket a deformed lozenge of saltwater taffy and picked off the waxed paper. Lately she'd been starved for sugar, nothing but sugar, only the sweetest and chewiest of foods, foods that seemed to have emerged fully formed from factories, that had nothing to do with the earth. She'd been this way as a kid, too, had managed to buck it in adulthood, but since she'd become

9

pregnant, just the word *candy* could make her salivate. She chewed, welcoming the tingle in her teeth, the welling-up in the back of her jaw. "Tim is your grandson?" she said, still chewing. It seemed like an okay thing to say, friendly and expressive of interest, and they were too old to be anything but the grandparents of the little boy she pictured—a slippery five-year-old pouting in a bubble bath. But the woman grumbled something under her breath. Marlon said to her, "Oh, Char, be nice! Can't you see we've an expectant mother here?" and again winked at Susannah, who looked around the room, eager to do anything but meet his gaze or that of the woman and trying to seem in fact expectant and wide-eyed and generally ready to rock, but the woman just cackled back at Marlon—"Showing off, are we?" Meanwhile he had selected key number 11 and slid it across the counter toward Susannah, saying, "This here's my lovely wife, Charlotte Garland," as if Char had just entered the room. He meant it, too. Char was still his lovely wife, still the dancing girl with the long braids he'd seen at the bar and fallen in love with, still the girl he'd gone drunkenly up to and said, "I'm going to marry you one day;" the girl who'd laughed in his face and knocked back a shot of some of the toxic stuff she drank in those days, whiskey or scotch or whatever it was—God, it was awful, made kissing her like sucking on a tube of gasoline. "Nice to meet you," said Susannah, and Char half smiled at her and said, "Be sure to check out the Grotto," moving her head as if pointing backward with one ear. Susannah looked past Char toward the living room. Marlon shook his head. "Out the way you came," he said. "Go through the office door and make a left—it's out back." Which was the only way one *could* go, since through the office door and to the right would have led straight into room number 1—the motel was shaped like a long, languid L, with the rooms parallel to the strip of gravel parking lot and beyond that the highway, and the office—the Garlands' rooms attached—as the stubby end. Susannah, impressed by her luck—a *grotto*—nodded.

Leaving the office, she noticed the sign by the door that said AMERICAN OWNED, stopped to blink at it. "It's so you know we're not 'Injuns,'" called out Char. Susannah looked at her. Marlon was shaking his head again. "It was there when we bought the place. It's a relic." But Char leaned against the counter, staring straight at Susannah, daring her to say something, something cityish and inappropriate, something to betray how little she really understood about Life in the Desert, about Things Out West. Susannah raised her eyebrows and managed a kind of smile and shut the door behind her.

Before her stretched the rooms, a long block of building punctured by doors and closed windows. Talking to the Garlands had exhausted her, made her feel foolish and uncertain all over again. Why did there have to be *people* everywhere—even here? Why couldn't she just have stopped at the motel, let herself into a room, and lay there breathing for a few weeks? She stumbled on the pebbled drive, righted herself, ponderous as a barge. Maybe there would be no other guests. That seemed hopeful. She became flustered quickly around people these days, giggling and trying to joke and not saying things exactly right, wound up and embarrassed by herself before it even began. She thought that people could tell just by looking at her that something was very wrong with her, that she was the kind of person who did terrible things, the kind of person who made trouble—not that she meant to! she never had meant to!—for everyone around her. In the city she'd walked around seeing the way people looked right through her; she'd moved down the street wanting to grab people's arms, wanting to say, *Listen! I am here! I am someone! Why won't you look at me?* But you couldn't do a thing like that, not really.

The Thunder Lodge was crumbling stucco in an unremarkable shade of beige, the doors were flesh-toned—a kind of Vegasy approximation of adobe—and each room, Susannah saw as she walked along the thin strip of pavement that inched between the building and the pebble drive (which itself faded out at its edges, dissolving into the desert), was named for a saint. The names were hand-painted onto whitewashed strips of wood that had been clumsily hammered to the wall between each room's door and window, lit by furious spotlights. ST. CHRISTOPHER. ST. VERONICA. JOAN OF ARC. Beneath each room's window languished a flower box of parched dirt and strawlike stems. The neon sign that towered above the office buzzed noisily. ST. CATHERINE. ST. BARTHOLOMEW. ST. BRIDGET. Susannah was almost to her room—the farthest from the office—when she realized she should have pulled her car around, should have parked in the patch of dust in front of her room. Even though there didn't seem to be anyone else around, this was the way it was done, wasn't it? Why was she always so *off*, so confused by the most ordinary of human events?

And that was her state of mind when she turned to face the expanse of land, to squint into the shadowy distances—harder to see because of the bald bulbs outside each room's door and the haze exuded by the motel's neon sign—the sky sinking into cobalt blue, the air taking on a certain nighttimey weight as it settled on her skin, draping over her shoulders, dusk laying itself across the barren terrain, arranging a picnic of nothing. So she was startled, actually flinched, when her eyes finally found the figure on the opposite side of the highway.

It was a smallish child—a little boy of perhaps ten years old. He stood there on the other side of the road and did not move. Susannah tightened her fist around her keys. Was it the Garlands' child, run from his bathtime? It must have been. The child raised a hand to her and waved. Light tipped his curly head, his extended fingertips. Susannah looked around, waved uncertainly, turned away, took a step, reconsidered, turned back—because it was not safe for a child there, at any instant a semi might speed past—and she could not think what to do, but the child had turned toward the swallowing dark of the desert, and so Susannah called, "Wait! Hey! Come back!" and then turned toward the crunching footsteps on the gravel nearby. Char had come from the office with Susannah's receipt, which she had forgotten. But when Susannah called out, Char stopped, then knit her brows together and said, "Beg pardon?" and peered into the distance. "You with someone?"

Susannah gestured toward the boy. "Oh, no, it's only that . . . ah, there's a kid over there. I thought it might be your boy"—the old woman peered toward where the boy had been—"or he *was* over there."

"Well, it wasn't Tim; he's in his bath, finally." She frowned at Susannah. "You feeling all right?" Susannah nodded vigorously, nodded in a way that made the idea of nodding feel ridiculous. Was this what people did? Did they nod? And it meant something? "I was just bringing your receipt," said Char. "And I was gonna say, y'all should pull around your car. Or I guess your husband'll do that?"

"Oh. See. No, I . . . I'm traveling alone."

Char scanned the horizon, maybe for signs of the phantom boy, and sighed and said, "I didn't realize. Well, good night."

That first night was not a pleasant one, but then it never is. Susannah had always been bad at this kind of game—with whom would you want to be stranded? what book would you bring if you could choose only one?—she never could decide on any one thing, and even now as she locked the door of her own desert island, it struck her as a pointless joke, a cruel way to pass the time, because when it actually happened, of course you couldn't choose any of those things at all, now, could you? She thumped her suitcase down on the carpet, left it yawning there. The ominous drip of the sink, the suggestive flicker of the bathroom's light. The portent of polyester bedcovering, the moldering smell of skin flakes and perspiration peppered with carpet deodorizer. She was in Francis of Assisi, which meant a frightening oil painting of crows (gory with paint so globby it seemed alive, intestinal) and a medal hung over the bed depicting a creature who resembled a hobo. She might have been anywhere. She found herself looking for something to read, anything, a Bible or at least the Yellow

Pages—in her haste to leave, she hadn't brought anything remotely entertaining, just an unfamiliar, thumbed-through paperback of *Robinson Crusoe* she'd discovered buried in the trunk of her car—and in the room she found nothing but a few faded brochures advertising the local attractions: HAUNTED CAVE, 100% REAL HAUNTED SINCE 1974; FOSSIL BED HISTORIC LOOKOUT POINT; BIG JIM'S "MODERN" TRUCK STOP.

And here it came, the regret rupturing beneath her ribs like a used-up appendix. From the very first moment of the pregnancy, she'd been fighting off this searing, seething regret. Regret! *Regret* wasn't even the word for how desperate she'd felt when she saw the test, when she knew she was pregnant, when it became real, when she realized what she had done. It was as if she'd jumped from a window only to change her mind a split second later, only to realize on the way down, as the wind whistled in her ears and pavement roared up to meet her face, that no, no, she didn't want to die, that she'd made a mistake and that it was entirely, irrevocably, utterly too late. She was pregnant. She'd signed the papers. Up roared the pavement. The feeling had to be buried, tamped down into thin sheets and stowed beneath her organs, left to dissolve in the landfill of her body. "Everything's fine!" she told Julian and Kit. "I'm so happy I'm doing this," she said to her mother; to her best friend, Rose; to anyone who would listen. Meanwhile her heart screamed in her chest. The pavement, it screamed. The pavement is coming up fast.

The pavement swallowed everything, swung wide its monstrous mouth, gobbled up everything she had. She had thrown away too much—too many things that she suddenly wanted back. What an idiot she was, honestly, what a complete moron. "Hey," she said to the empty room. "Way to go, you fucking idiot. You've really outdone yourself this time." The lavender hair ribbon of Rose's that she'd carried in her wallet for years and years—what kind of person let this flutter into the hot wind? For so much of her life, her entire childhood, it had been Susannahnrose, Rosensusannah; they had been so much a part of each other that Susannah hadn't known who she was without Rose. Rose was drooping hair ribbon, she was red jelly bean, she was a stick thwacking at a wasp's nest; Rose had always been reckless, too charming for her own good, charismatically amoral. Then they had a falling-out in high school, and by the time they came back together, the magical quality of the friendship had died. And now Rose was an adult, the wife of a mind-numbingly dull hedge-fund manager, the mother of two grubby, charmless toddlers; all that was left of the Rose she'd loved was a filthy lavender hair ribbon.

And the illegible movie ticket from her first date with Aaron, Aaron whom everyone thought she would marry, Aaron who was cigarette smoke and car leather, who was the flavor of popcorn in a movie she hadn't wanted to see, anyway. Aaronnsusannah, Susannahnaaron. With Aaron she'd felt herself fading, dimming—she was the quiet girlfriend, the agreeable sidekick. Because Susannah had always had the sense that she was a supporting character in her own life, and it was awful, awful, awful to know such a thing, to have always been part of someone else's story, to flail for a way to escape it, to have to work so hard so late in the game to discover what she was on her own. What happened when she finally did something as reckless as Aaron running off to India, as risky as Rose thwacking at a wasp's nest (why had she done that? pretending to think it was a piñata, screaming about candy), what happened when Susannah struck out on her own? She was doing a terrible job. She knew she was doing a terrible job, but it was too late now. Here came the pavement; up it roared.

She lay on the bed, sucking at a Starlight Mint. She would have liked to call someone. She blinked at the black rotary phone, its cord coiled as if about to strike. There was no one in the whole world she could call. Not her mother, who had said, "Well, dear, maybe it's for the best," about Aaron; who had listened to what Susannah planned on doing with Julian and Kit and had looked away, shrugged, replied in a monotone, "Whatever you want to do, dear. Whatever will make you happy." (Why didn't her mother ever take her by the shoulders, give her a good shake?) Or Julian, she could always call Julian: "Hi, it's me, I just wanted to say hello, sorry I disappeared, please don't look for me." The thought was absurd. Julian, unreadable as an ocean. She picked up the phone, listening to the dial tone until it became a kind of song. Hung it up again. The stranger gurgled inside her, rolling around as if trying to get comfortable in an unfamiliar bed. She looked down at her belly, told it, "Come on, now." Then she picked up the phone and dialed Julian's number and hung up before it rang. Lay back in the bed, set about to decipher the pattern in the ceiling's popcorn tiles. That ceiling is about to break into pieces and rain down on me, she couldn't stop thinking. This whole ceiling's about to fall.

THE RACKET OUTSIDE was what probably woke her, but in that early confusion Susannah imagined she'd seen a man peeking in the window and that the heat of his gaze had woken her. She sat up in bed, looked around. She'd slept in her clothes and now felt shrink-wrapped, stiff. Light edged the curtain. There was what sounded like the old man lifting the hood of her car and exclaiming a stream of curses.

"Morning, Susie Q!" Marlon saluted her when she stepped into the sunlight, the sour film of sleep still pasting her mouth shut. Filaments blasted off in her ears, twanging like guitar strings. Her nose and eyes felt unsettlingly dry, everything that had once been liquid solidified into an immobile crust. The man was bent over her car's exposed engine, his lips moving as if he were telling it stories. "Good morning," Susannah managed, the heat of the day spider-walking across her skin. She was starving for something sweet. Where would she get things to eat? Hers was the only car in the gravelly lot, other than a truck she assumed was the Garlands'—a hulking Ford with gruesomely rusted wheel wells—parked at a haphazard angle near the office. Susannah bowed out her back in an awkward stretch, looked left down the string of rooms toward the office and the Garlands' and somewhere beyond the Grotto; looked right, into the expanse of desert. Nothing but horizon in any direction.

"This thing is dry as a bone." Marlon tapped at the knobby landscape under the hood.

"Oh, that. Well. You know, at a Jiffy Lube near Amarillo, I had them fill it with sand. Instead of oil. Much cheaper that way."

He blinked. "Terrible thing to do to a car."

"Yes, sir." Susannah bit her lip. "Er, just a joke." Something giddy rose galloping in her stomach.

When Marlon Garland wiped his wrench on a rag and said seriously, "Right. So this engine's done. I mean, look at it—it's about to split right in two. We'll have to order a new one. When did you need to take off?" and Susannah answered, "Oh, well, as soon as possible, please," because after all, the baby was due in under a month, and she supposed an answer like that was in order, and when he shook his head and said, "I don't know what to tell you, Miss Prue," what should not have surprised Susannah was that she ducked to hide her smile. It should have come as no surprise, in fact, that she would stay at the Thunder Lodge for as long as she could, that she wanted to be stranded somewhere until her decision was made for her, until there was no more decision to be made; even she could have probably guessed that she was only pretending to hate the desolation, only convincing herself that she would soon press on. Really, she was tired; she was already so tired. Really, this was what she had come for, to be hot and tired and stranded and alone. And the car had done the stranding for her. She hadn't had to decide anything at all. The effect was quite satisfying. She calculated how long it would take for Julian and Kit to realize she was gone, for them to start trying to track her down, for them to actually find her. There was time; there was still time.

Then Marlon left to fetch a tool or something, and she sat on the curb in front of her car, just kind of staring into the fender, watching the grisly specks of fly bodies decompose in the sun, the light glinting back at her and dazzling her eyes into confusion, the way a word loses its meaning when repeated again and again—it had been a game she and Rose played as children, saying a word over and over *(water, water, water)* until it dissolved into nonsense, until it seemed impossible that anyone ever said a word called *water,* that it meant anything to anyone—until she wasn't sure what she was looking at, and when her brain suggested, *Fender?* she thought, Fender? What on earth is a fender? And it was this defamiliarized state that she was startled out of when someone tapped her on the shoulder. Susannah looked up, blinking.

There Char stood, Hun-like, sun haloed behind her. "Girl, what *are* you doing? That can't be good for the baby." Clucked her tongue. "How far along are you, anyhow?" And, "Shew, I think the heat's gotten to you!"

Susannah shook her head, unable to speak. It wasn't! It hadn't!

There was so much she didn't know about this place she had come to, and when she saw in that moment the man lurking there near Char, of course she didn't know, there was no way to tell immediately that anything was . . . not *wrong,* you weren't supposed to say *wrong,* but different. She hadn't known that anything was *different,* or even who he was; another guest at the motel, she thought, perhaps.

Really, when she first saw him, all she thought was, Anchor. Mast. Swell. The flickering breeze ran salty and cool. His skin, if licked, would be salty and cool. He looked up, a frayed length of hair obscuring his eyes. Sun flensed her eyes, daggering beneath her skull.

Anchor. Mast. Swell.

"You all right?"

Char was leaning so close, her weathered, frowning face too dark a thing to see in all that light—and then Susannah scrambled up and looked at the boy and said to Char, "Yes, thank you." Feeling a bit dazed, a bit unreal, unable to stop staring at the handsome boy—

because she saw now that he was maybe seventeen—standing arms dangling in the sun. Who was *this*? He answered her with an even gaze, saying nothing. Char looked from one to the other and furrowed her brow and muttered to Susannah, "Just don't want you getting sun poisoning or anything," as she turned and went back toward the office. Char didn't much care for the way the girl looked at him, felt her hackles rise all down her spine. Marlon said she didn't trust people. Well, why should she? They'd been robbed, cheated, swindled, they'd been victimized plenty of times, just a couple of old fogeys ready to be taken for a ride, with no one around to help them. Why should Char trust a living soul? She let the door slam shut behind her.

The boy said nothing to Susannah, an inchoate smile mumbling at his lips. She walked a few steps as the heat smacked its palm at the back of her head, ducked into her room to change into her swimsuit. She stood in the blueness of the room, smiling at her reflection, soured as it was by the yellowish mirror. Her face had transformed, too, everything about her gone cartoonishly rosy. Pregnancy had agreed with her. She knew she looked lovely.

When she reentered the heat of the day, the young man was still there, now squatting on the gravel, turning over a pebble in his hand and humming to himself. Her first thought was, Oh, great, why did I have to look him up and down like that? He's some weird kid, one of those trying-to-be-different kids, and he's going to hit on me now, and with everything that's happened, I don't think I could stand it. Because it was, wasn't it, always the most offhand things that got said to her, like the other day in a gas station in Oklahoma when a trucker had said to her why did she look so sad, darlin', and she'd gotten back into her car thinking, Look so *sad*, what is that supposed to mean? People were always telling her she looked sad, and when she remembered this, she tried to assemble a pleased but not clownishly grinning expression.

So she worked at not looking at the beautiful boy as she passed.

He had one of those faces that momentarily confused the eyes, it was so unusually well made. And he really was more of a kid than a man, she saw when he moved closer, a lanky and muscular kid with brown skin and this beautiful face. She braced herself for the stare, for the brazen comment. There should be a test for such things, a Popsicle stick of plastic you could pee on within moments of seeing someone, with an indicator that would show up pink for love at first sight or blue for mere infatuation, the simplest of crushes. This seemed like a funny idea to Susannah, and it seemed too bad that she had no one to tell it to. Would Julian think it was a funny idea? Would anyone? There was really no point in having a funny idea if there were no one to tell.

She watched the boy plunk himself down on his butt, sitting cross-legged and humming tunelessly as he lined up his collection of rocks. Still she didn't understand and thought, Oh, God, I know this one, I've seen this all before. Oh, God, he's one of these I-picked-this-dandelion-and-wrote-you-a-poem kind of guys, a free spirit, ugh. He looked up at her then, and didn't smile. She stood frozen a few feet away, tried to look determinedly toward the Grotto. A lock of hair drooped in front of his gray eyes. She held up a hand in an open wave, and he squinted unresponsively back. Finally he said, "Horses."

Horses? Susannah looked into the desert. Looked back at the boy. "Horses?"

He laughed—a strange, one-noted, expressionless laugh. "Huh. Horses!" Pointing at the horizon. Susannah looked again—willing herself to see a herd of wild horses thundering along in the sand, and though everything was perfectly still, something electric passed through Susannah Prue, some prickling along her scalp. A magical boy, an invisible herd. She wanted to say something, to say an important and true thing. She stood there, biting her lip. Anchor. Mast. Swell.

They were very still, watching each other, there in the moat of gravel wet from air-conditioner drips and humming with the sound of the building. Then Char bustled out and said, "I thought you were right behind me," and the boy looked at her, holding a pebble very close to his eye, and said flatly, "I got lost"—though he hadn't in fact moved an inch since Char had been standing out there with him. Char said, "Dammit Tim, I told you to come with me. You know you shouldn't be bothering the guests!" and glared at Susannah, and when Tim didn't move, Char came close and grabbed his sleeve and half dragged him back toward the office. Susannah watched without a word. That was Tim? She thought, Mast. She thought, Swell.

IT WaS PrObaBLY because she'd been there a night and a day and another night already and now for a whole morning sitting on the bench outside the motel's office with strips of moldered paint crackling at her thighs, her belly balanced in her lap like a pile of blankets, waiting, just waiting for someone to say something, for something to be said, and because of the heat that formed an immobile slab over everything, leaving her gagged and depleted there in the uninterruptible desert, that Susannah felt herself starting to slip. She gritted her teeth, clamped her hands onto the seat of the bench, riding out the bout of terror. The Garlands stood inside the office, gazing stupidly at the fan and once in a while commenting on the weather. All anyone ever wanted to talk about was the weather. Oh, the weather! It had been a feverish 103 for days. And Susannah Prue had been moping around the Thunder Lodge a night and a day and another night already, and perhaps the Garlands were becoming tired of her presence.

The Garlands were becoming tired of her presence? The Garlands, those sweating pigs, squinting into the hot turbulence stirred up by the fan! The Garlands should have gone out of their way to make Susannah happy! The Garlands should have been apologizing for the unreliable air-conditioning in the rooms, apologizing for their godforsaken desert that was not even the pretty kind, rainbowed with igneous stripes and many-pronged cacti or soaring with buttes or sandy expanses, not a desert worth painting or black-and-white-photographing for inspirational posters or even really driving through—just a pebbly, moony terrain, an endless driveway of dirt. Couldn't they see she was a woman in the family way, that she was a delicate specimen, that she could use a little goddamned special attention? She wanted them to offer advice, to tuck her under their wings like a wounded baby chick, and to tell her there, there and here is what to do about it, but no one seemed that interested. She'd formulated all sorts of answers to the questions that never came, explanations as to why she was carrying this child, reasons that sounded solid and respectable, that could be held up to the light and examined for cracks. Hadn't her mother sent her away when she became inconvenient, holding her always at arm's length? And hadn't the boy everyone thought she would marry up-and-left her, gone off to study in India, of all places? And hadn't she been casting about for something to do with her life? Or couldn't it be blamed on Susannah's eternal, grinding lack of money? Hadn't she been in love, a little, with Julian and Kit, with the version of herself that she was around them? There were lots of reasonable explanations, she felt, for why she had done what she'd done, explanations that didn't make her sound like a monster, and any of them might have been true. But no one asked! It was terrible. She'd miscalculated everything, as usual, and now she was stuck here with the Garlands, who didn't pry, who had trained themselves to be incurious, who worked hard at not seeming nosy.

"Doing all right there, city girl?" Marlon stuck his head out the door.

Susannah nodded, gave him a thumbs-up, as if they were astronauts or deep-sea divers and could not speak normally, bound by unbreathable atmosphere.

Marlon peered down the highway in one direction, then the other. Susannah sat lifting her thighs and picking paint chips off the bottom of each leg; one, then the other.

She should have left that day and headed back home.

But she still hadn't decided what she'd come here to decide. And what would have been the point of it all—the dayslong drive from the green-gray guts of the Midwest through the reddish grit of Texas to this crater of a place; the nights on the merciless mattress of room 11, the Francis of Assisi room (farthest from the office and the Garlands' abode behind, and between them a string of empty rooms like a mouthful of cavities); the half-friendly banter with Char about her troubles with Tim—what would have been the point of it all if Susannah were to give up now and turn around, to retreat? She had come here to think, goddamnit, and so she hunkered down on the scabrous bench, working a hunk of watermelon-flavored bubble gum with her jaw, her belly making itself felt in her lap, and she shut her eyes against the horizon and tried to think, to really think the thing through to its end.

"Hot out," Marlon said, puncturing the inaugural attempt.

"Yep," she said.

Marlon retreated into the office then and plunked his teeth into the cup of water on the counter beside the spiral notebook they called the guest register. Susannah could hear Char sighing loudly, turning up one of the televisions. "Well, it's a hot one!" the television was saying, like the establishing shot of a film.

After sitting a little longer on the crackling paint of the bench and trying to think and finding herself unable, she went back to her room to change into her bathing suit and tiptoed childlike across the burning asphalt back past the office, in which Marlon and Char argued noisily about something, through the gate in the concrete wall around the pool that Char called without any hint of irony the Grotto—that rectangle of brackish water rafted with bugs and guarded by a few dead houseplants, each hanging its head as if unable to look away from its wads of whitish earth.

But Tim would be at the pool.

And certainly Tim had a right to be at the pool, more of a right than Susannah herself! Tim was young, after all, so young that Susannah knew she should think of him as a child, and he was stranded at the dingy lodge with his taciturn parents, being by some cruel trick of nature unable even to drive, as a boy his age would to the gas station that burned fluorescently twenty-five miles down the highway, where kids were sipping stolen liquor in the parking lot. Tim had nothing but the sun-warmed swimming pool, his collections of pebbles and vegetation, his imaginary animals, the slime of aged chlorine on his skin. Susannah sat at the edge of the pool and dangled her feet into the water. The boy was crouched in a corner by the wall, gathering dead leaves that had somehow migrated in the windless air from the potted plants. She studied his suntanned skin and the fine bone structure and lean ripples of strength.

Tim stood up suddenly and came over to her. They'd gotten to be friends, in a way. They seemed to have a certain understanding. "Leaves," he said. "Leaves."

Susannah looked at his cupped palms, at what seemed mostly to be the shells of expired insects. "Yes, Tim. That's very nice." His hands were too white, the nails too long, and he often kept his fingers all pressed together like the claw of a plastic doll, and this was the first thing one noticed about him—that is, the first sign that something was wrong, no, *different*. This had been what explained things to Susannah.

The smile stayed uncertainly on Tim's face, dimples piercing his cheeks, and he kept his eyes pointing downward and clarified, "Yeah. Leaves." His skin, his lean boy's body, the dampish hair swinging before his eyes. The grayed pallor of his teeth gave him the look of a ruined prince. He stood there at the edge of the pool, smiling blankly as

Susannah slipped in and did what she imagined to be the breaststroke. "Yeah," she heard Tim saying through the roar of water in her ears, "Leaves." He giggled again, that giggle that seemed joyless and shrill because it didn't crinkle his eyes the way a real smile did, that giggle that was more like a default, the way Susannah's aunt would say, "Dum-da-dum-da-dum," if ever there was a silence in a conversation, an airless unquiet. Oh, but Susannah was trying not to think about her aunt, about her mother, about her boss, about anyone left behind who was likely starting to worry, no, that was not what this was about, no. She liked the way she felt with Tim. She didn't feel as if Tim was molding her into any particular thing, impressing his idea of her upon her skin, the way it was with others.

She resurfaced at the other end in time to see Tim dropping the handful of leaf shards and roach remains onto the surface of the water. "Hey," she said. Tim looked up, squinting one eye at her through the falling, lank hair, his expression unchanged. "Don't do that," she told him. But she felt better already, the water a relief from the brittle blasts of heat, and she continued to swim her un-skilled laps while Tim stood at the edge of the pool throwing leaf remnants in.

Finally she lifted herself clumsily from the water and sat on the too-hot plastic-strapped lawn chair striated from sun. Tim giggled, staring at the leaves dispersing across the water's back. "What is it, Tim? What's so funny?" Susannah spread the worn bath towel from her room across the chair—they hadn't offered her any other towel yet—and stretched out, although already the heat had become too much to bear. She felt Tim's eyes on her, her belly, her swollen breasts. Dazed, she said, "Do you know any secrets?"

He stared at her.

"Tim," said Susannah, "do you have a girlfriend?"

Tim smiled, but his eyes didn't change. His hair tangled with his eyelashes and moved when he blinked. "Yeah."

"You do? Who?"

"No!" With that neutral giggle, he made his way to the corner nearest Susannah's chair and knelt again, this time at a small pile of sand and faded potato-chip bags. Tim's bathing suit strained against his butt. Susannah looked away. Her heart slammed against her chest, stupid as a bird flying into glass. Swell. Swallow.

"So you don't know any good secrets?"

Tim stopped, crouched there in the corner, and then said, "Yeah."

"Yeah you *do* know good secrets?"

He nodded.

"All right, then, what are they?"

Tim giggled, nervously now, she imagined, though it sounded the same as always. He held up a forlorn Doritos bag and squinted at the whiteness of sun on the foil. Susannah opened her eyes, sat forward slightly.

But why couldn't Susannah see, or how could she will herself so convincingly *not* to see, that waiting for things to happen was her greatest weakness? After all, she had fled from the city in order to wait, here, for an answer to come to her. They would be expecting an answer, not that they knew there was any question yet—as far as they knew, everything was as settled as it had been the week before—but soon enough they'd realize that Susannah had gone and that there was a question after all, and they would be expecting an answer. Either way they would be unhappy and wounded and would never quite trust her again, and in a scenario that demanded such blind and burning trust! Maybe she would stay here forever. Maybe she would just stay here forever and hang out with Tim and keep the baby after all, teach it to swim in the pool, breast-feed it on the bench while watching the highway, squinting out toward the horizon.

She went back into the pool and did six more laps.

Then she stood, resting her palms flat on the lid of water, and demanded, "Tim, tell me your secret."

Tim was hunched over his newest pile of debris, facing away from her, his spine a ladder. That same atonal giggle—*giggle* maybe wasn't the right word; it sometimes sounded more like a wheeze, a measure of hyperventilation. Tim said, "Yeah. You're not supposed to."

Susannah smacked lightly at the water. "Of course not. That's why it's a secret."

Tim said, "Yeah," thinking. Then, "Dad's teeth are fake."

"That's not a secret, Tim. That's obvious. Everyone knows that." After all, the teeth spent most of their time doing the dead man's float in their cup on the office counter. She wanted to speak to Tim as she would any adult and not in that high-pitched wheedle his parents used around him, not in that cloying way people talked to babies or dogs when trying to convince others that they were good with babies and dogs. It seemed unfair to treat him like a child.

"Yeah," he said with a giggle, as if answering her thought. Then, "I get in trouble."

"For what?"

"Peeping, yeah," he said.

"For *what?*"

"Watching people do nasty things."

Now Susannah really was interested. She tried to remain very still so as not to distract him from saying more. These were more words already than she'd yet heard from Tim. She sensed there was something to be drawn out in him, some part to his mind that so far had gone unplumbed, a thoughtfulness that would surface like a toy flung into a pool. His eyes would spark now and then, signaling something that was in there, something that had been ignored, something that she thought she could get to. "Who, Tim? People who come here? Guests at the motel?"

Tim giggled. "Yeah. Doing nasty things."

"Nasty things! Like what?"

Tim looked at his hands and slowly spread out his pile of leaves and bug shells and chip bags, began lining them up neatly. "Yeah."

"You're not going to tell me?"

"Yeah. Nasty things. Like moms and dads. Like making a baby."

"I see. That's a pretty good secret."

"Yeah."

"Maybe I'll tell you my secret sometime."

Tim shrugged noncommittally. "Yeah." Which was pretty much the response she'd been getting lately. Here she'd done something brave, something bold, something unpredictable, and the world had responded with a shrug. It turned out no one was paying any attention at all.

Susannah stretched out onto her back and thought that she felt him looking at her gleaming there in her bathing suit and floating and didn't know quite how to feel about it. Still floating and looking into the sky through the ache in her eyes, she said again, "Tim, do you think you'll ever get to have a girlfriend?" It was an academic question in her own mind and not quite a proposition.

But it was Tim's question, too. His posture stiffened, pigeonlike. After a long pause, he got into the pool. He stood near the edge without moving or swimming or even splashing, just stood here staring nakedly at Susannah, his arms limply by his sides. Susannah reached the far edge and turned and floated back toward him.

"Yeah," he said, finally, slowly, and Susannah thought that he knew this was important and that no one had asked him this before. His skin was brailled with goose bumps, and the fair hair stood up on his chest and shoulders. There was part of her that wanted to say oh-fuckit and just touch him, just to feel lightly the smoothness of a seventeen-year-old's nipple, just to give the poor boy a thrill or herself a thrill—to say to him, *I want you to know that you are okay, that everything is okay, that you are loved*—but a larger part of her was aware that she would not do this. He was standing very close to her now, a wall of water between them, and there was a sudden heat in the way he glowered at her. She thought, A boy who doesn't know his own beauty is more dangerous than a boy who doesn't know his own strength. He said, "A girlfriend?"

"Do you want to?"

"Yeah."

"You know, Tim, I think you probably can."

Tim didn't look at her. "With kissing?"

"Probably. Someday."

"With the nasty parts?"

"Nasty parts?"

He giggled, an unsmiling *Huh. Huh.* "Yeah. You know. You know." Susannah did know. "Nasty parts that make a baby."

She didn't want to lie to him and thought about what to say, then lost track of her buoyancy somehow and fell from her float. "Probably not. I guess that would depend."

Tim considered this, said, "Okay."

Susannah saw through the water that his swimming trunks had tented around an erection, and, ashamed of herself, she stepped out of pool and wrapped the wisp of a towel around her body and went through the gate without a word to Tim and walked across the seethe of sun-scorched parking lot to her own room, where she drew the curtains and bolted her door and then, increasingly angry, opened the curtains and peeled off her bathing suit and lay naked on the unmade bed, a hill of bone-white flesh.

THEN SUSANNAH PRUE would fall into one of her states of melancholy. Maybe it was the sight of a car, lean and flat as a hammerhead shark and as slowly deliberate, finning down the highway and passing the Thunder Lodge without slowing down; maybe it was that her phone's battery had finally died, and with it the record of the 246 missed calls, which she'd been carrying around as a kind of a talisman; or maybe it was simply the hormones tidal-waving through her gut, her cells swelling with this child that wasn't hers, while she wondered what it was to really be held, to really be made love to; or maybe it was nothing all, just a moody girl indulging herself; but the melancholy would grip her in its colorless fist and shake her to and fro, and she would walk along the gravel strip, squinting into the sky. The sky stared baldly back. She knew there was something childish about this habit of hers, this seeing everything as a sign. Sentimental, Aaron had called her. On first arriving she'd thought this unblinking sky was an omen, that it would lend her some clarity, some bright revelation, that decisions would come easy under such an open sky, but already she was starting to see in it the blank stare of an idiotic beauty. She tried to remember things, to remember as much as she could, as early as her memory reached: sitting on her father's knee as he sang "Oh! Susanna"; finding a robin's nest for the first time and smoothing a fingertip over a blue egg; her mother crying in the guest room, which she'd just cleaned out, painted blue; the smell of the carpet in nursery school. How far back could she remember? It didn't seem to be enough. It was as if a large part of her own life had been hidden from herself. What sort of childhood had she had to turn out the way she did? A person who sometimes felt nothing, a person who didn't think anything through, a person who hurt people? She wondered if it was the sort of thing she would blame on her parents—their early divorce maybe, or her being an only child. She did not want to think it was all her own fault. I need a cloud, she'd say to herself. If a cloud appears today, even just a shudder of a wisp, even a whitish shadow, then it will mean I should stay, no, it will mean I should go back, yes, a cloud will mean go back. Obviously there would be no clouds. So she walked. This is how a restless mind recruits the body, how the body betrays the mind. Susannah walked up and down, up and down, counting the doors of Thunder Lodge. One, two, three. Char poked her head out after the fifth rotation and clucked her tongue, but that was all; then

she ducked back into the office. Nine, ten, eleven. It was too hot out
to scold.

SHE DEVELOPED CERTAIN habits at the Thunder
Lodge. After sitting in the office, watching distant news beamed from
El Paso and half in Spanish, she would go outside and sit on the
bench and read the classifieds in the county newspaper, musing over
offers for used pickup trucks or free saddles or what was mysteriously
described as a well-loved mule. She'd struggle through a crossword
puzzle in red pen. That's all there was at the Thunder Lodge—felt-
tipped red pens—as if a caravan of math teachers had passed
through, leaving detritus. Then, if she completed the crossword puzzle, she let herself go to the vending machine and buy a strawberry
Charleston Chew, and she'd stand there and cram it rapturously into
her mouth.

Marlon would come out to tinker with her car—an engine had
been ordered—or Char would shout something at her from inside
the office, so that Susannah had to stand up and enter and say,
"What was that?" and Char would say, almost reluctantly, "We were
going to make some chili for dinner. I suppose you could have
some" (and Susannah would hungrily accept and then eat out of a
paper cup, sitting on one of the chairs in the office, staring into the
air conditioner) or, "Have you seen Tim? That boy needs a bath and
he knows it." There was something suspicious in the way Char
spoke to Susannah, narrowing her eyes, as if she couldn't quite figure her out.

But Susannah was a paying guest, and she didn't cause any particular trouble and was always polite—why should Char mind her? Susannah called her ma'am and avoided her eyes, feeling young and
flushed in her presence.

Or Char would step out, squint into the empty highway, and

exclaim, "Woo-ee!" Soaking in all that air-conditioning made a coolness reside under her skin like a layer of blubber, so that she was cool to the touch. Susannah, who was starting to feel like a native there in her good-luck T-shirt and cutoff jeans unbuttoned beneath her belly, peeled back slightly as if she were an orange someone had started for someone else to finish; Susannah, soaking in the sun, explained to Char that it wasn't so bad once you were used to it.

"It's a dry heat," Susannah told Char.

Char glared at her and went back inside, turned up the volume on the yellowed cartoons she was watching. The Betty Boop theme dissolved in the desert air.

So Susannah changed into her swimsuit, the two-piece, the not-quite-a-bikini. Her belly bowed out—the skin striped with whitish marks, a dark line tracing the front as if the spine's shadow had become visible, her navel a grotesque new shape like a vestigial toe. And yet it was easy, her little trick—easy to think of the burbles as gas, the insistent kicking as a large and anthropomorphic indigestion, to forget that someone was in there. A stranger. She didn't even know this kid! That was what killed her! She'd formed an unhelpful habit of picturing the baby as a stranger come to town; there he was, sitting on the edge of a motel bed, rubbing his forehead with his palms, tired after the long drive from Poughkeepsie, his hat and sample case on the floor. Sometimes he drank too much at the roadhouse down the way; sometimes he stayed up late watching this new state's local television, and these were the nights she had the worst of the heartburn. This tableau kept her from thinking of the baby as a baby, something alive and still unformed, something lovable and cute, something that might, once born, hoodwink her into accidentally loving it. She could not conceive of giving birth to the stranger, touching his tiny, pinkish toes. No, he would just pick up his sample case and hat and leave one day, waving as his train left the platform.

She swam, that is, from one side of the pool to the other. When she emerged at the shallow end, there was Tim, perched on the edge.

"Ah, hello," she said. The sun was beginning to slant across the roof.

Tim crinkled his nose at her. "Hosannah."

Susannah treaded water, her toes scraping the pool's rough bottom. "What?"

Tim laughed. "Hosannah!"

"Where'd you get that one?"

"Hosannah Prue." He pointed at her and closed his eyes, pleased with himself.

"Funny. That's just great. Where did you get that from? You were watching the ministries again?" It was all that came in some days on the television sets. The swell of the choir would crackle unfluently into the air.

Tim nodded. He sat with his spine curved like a sickle. A lock of hair fell over his eyes. He blinked at Susannah and laughed his flat giggle. "Pretty."

Susannah pushed off the wall into a clumsy backstroke. It was strange to be pleased by such a thing, and anyway the other day she'd heard Char admonishing Tim for peeping in her window, for pestering her at the Grotto, so she set her jaw, determined to be appropriate about the whole thing. After all, if any of this was going to work, she was going to have to be a goddamned grown-up for once, and she repeated this to herself, rolling it over in her mind as she completed her splashy lap. Still, no one had said anything so nice to her in a long time. When Tim slipped into the pool, they swam side by side. Soon it became a game they had wordlessly agreed on. He scrambled to the side and stood up in mute glory, and she swam over and splashed him, and then they turned to swim to the other side, laughing and breathless.

The game ended as quickly as it had begun. Tim stood near the edge. She pushed a wave of water toward him, and it splashed up into his face, and he blinked at her and giggled. "The champion swimmer of Thunder Lodge, Timothy Garland!" she crowed.

But this was how it was with a boy like Tim. "Bye," he said suddenly, unsmiling, something dark brewing behind his brow. He climbed from the pool—his skin erupted into goose bumps, but his posture didn't change—and walked without expression, without moving his arms, toward the office. Susannah closed her eyes. The stitching of her legs through the water. She could hear Char shrilly scolding Tim about what, about staying out too late, about spending too much time with the guest, about why couldn't he just leave her alone, and no looking in windows, goddammit, how many times had they been through this already? Then she heard, "Get your *hands* off yourself, Timothy, and you leave the door of your room *open*! None of that!"

Inside, the stranger turned over stiffly, tangled in rented sheets.

THAT AFTERNOON a new guest arrived at the Thunder Lodge, rendering Susannah redundant. When she came out from her room, she saw the eighties-era Chevy, dully metallic in the sun. Tim was standing behind it, slightly stooped, sprinkling sand onto the trunk. Susannah read the plate aloud, "Florida," and Tim startled and looked at her and then dropped his shoulders and smacked his hands on the trunk, hard, with an angry new stiffness to his posture, upset perhaps about the visitor or maybe about a pebble— his moods were as uncharitable as weather—before he turned and walked away.

She sat back on the bench where she usually spent the morning and drew her fingers through her pool-tangled hair, and once again she determined to think the thing through, to rehearse just what she would say to them when she got back. Tim walked down the parking lot, turned right past room 11, and disappeared behind the building. The dust-covered Chevy looked like something recently unearthed from a long period of neglect, the evidence of an empire in decline. Susannah closed her eyes, rested her hands over her belly, let the sun bake into her skin. In the office Char turned down the two TVs, and Marlon was cracking his unfunny jokes for this new visitor, this upstart from Florida probably feeling very proud of herself and eager to get on the road in the morning, no doubt headed to California or, at the very least, Phoenix.

When really, who was Susannah Prue to ridicule this fellow traveler for having a *plan,* for being able to decide one way or another—what was so great about being paralyzed, stalled in transit, reduced to a waxy facsimile of oneself? In the office the woman was saying, "Yes, thank you, just the one night." She had a nice voice, Susannah allowed; she spoke like a kindergarten teacher reading a story. The Garlands scurried around. "Room number five," Marlon was saying, "St. Catherine, you'll like that one, and two beds like you said"—he had put his teeth in, to impress her!—and Susannah could hear the key ring rattling, but she would not turn around, she would not seem nosy, and Char was explaining about the vending machine and the Grotto ("Oh!" said the new guest) and riffling through the guest register's pages.

Susannah had it all figured out before the Floridian had left the office: The new guest was thirty-five or forty, blond and tanned and healthy, and on her way alone to visit friends, or a man, or a hometown, thinking herself brave and irreverent. But when the Floridian appeared beside the bench, blinking in the sunshine and holding the limpish hand of a sexless seven- or eight-year-old child with a face creased from a nap in the car, Susannah knew she had to revise her story. "Gol*ly,*" said the Floridian to Susannah, "is it ever hot."

"Isn't it hot in Florida?" Susannah said.

The Floridian, who looked younger than Susannah had imagined, with one of those faces that seemed perpetually apologetic, swiped self-consciously at her wispy hair, blinked, said, "Oh, honey, we're not from Florida. We're only borrowing the car."

"I see," said Susannah, disappointed. "Hi there." The child stuck its tongue out at her. "What's your name?"

The Floridian—the not-Floridian—gave the kid's hand a squeeze and then tried to extract herself from the grip, wiggling the kid's noodley arm. "Sorry, I guess Frankie's feeling a little shy. She's tired; we've had a long drive."

"Oh." Susannah was trying to remember what one said to a child. "Aren't you cute," she finally said.

Frankie scowled, pulled away from the Floridian, and went to their car, disappearing into the backseat. She was the kind of kid Susannah had been fascinated with as a little girl herself—a tomboy with blunt hair and crinkled shorts, unimpressed by adults but likely capable of holding great sway over her peers. Soon her sneakers appeared in the backseat window, smacking the pane with rhythmic thumps. The Floridian sat on the bench beside Susannah and sighed. "My sister's child. I'm afraid she's not very happy about how everything's turned out."

The Floridian was from Alabama, her name was Dicey, and she was taking Frankie to Frankie's father's place in Arizona. Frankie was currently not speaking to her, though they hoped to work this out in the near future. The woman, Dicey, wore her worry close to the surface, hot as a rash. Dicey, who seemed to feel like talking, did not ask what had brought Susannah to the Thunder Lodge, and Susannah did not offer.

THE HOURS MELTED together, gone runny from the heat. Susannah woke up from a sweaty nap (the Floridians were outside, talking noisily) with parts of her dreams lingering in the room like extra furniture. A baby squalling in the armchair, a basket of blank papers on the counter, horses galloping by outside. There had been some argument—Julian shimmered soapily by the window, went glassy and rainbowed, then popped and disappeared—and in a few moments she couldn't quite remember what the dream had been or what he had been shouting at her about.

She made her way through the film of dream residue to shower again and then dress and go out to find Tim. She opened her door and started—he was waiting there at her doorstep, just standing, a pile of pebbles in his cupped hands. "How long have you been standing here?" she said in a flush.

He giggled. Tim held out the pebbles toward her. "Yeah," he greeted her.

"Tim," Susannah said, trying to sound motherly. When would she get that voice that said things in an unignorable way, that voice that could convince you of anything? Kit had that voice. Char had that voice. Susannah just sounded plaintive and uncertain. Susannah couldn't even convince *herself* of anything.

And here was Tim, standing before her. Here was Tim, someone she could trust, someone she could (she admitted it to herself once quickly and then pretended not to have thought it) control. Tim, without guile. "Tim," she said, "didn't your mother tell you not to spy on me?" But even Tim could see through this, could hear the waver in her voice, knew that a smile would disarm her completely. "Excuse me," Susannah said, motioning for him to step aside, "let me by. Tim."

He ignored her, crinkling his brow, dropped the pebbles at her feet—a dry rain shower crackling through the morning heat—showed her, with that toneless giggle, the single pebble he'd kept tucked under his thumb, like a magician revealing a trick. He smoothed one finger over the pebble and then, looking at Susannah, stealthily popped it into his mouth. "Tim!" she cried. His posture crumpled. He spit out the stone, held it glistening in his palm, and handed it to Susannah.

Susannah looked past him, across the dirt driveway and the

empty road. The little boy stood squinting toward the sun as if he'd always been standing right there, just waiting to be noticed, a spot cut into the horizon, more like a space missing than like something extra. As Susannah watched, the boy turned back toward the expanse of the desert and, in a moment, disappeared.

Who knew what was going through her mind? She took the pebble from Tim, put it in her mouth, and swallowed it. Which caused him to look at her as if he'd never seen her before, as if he were recognizing an old friend.

Stone. Anchor. Salt.

susannah prue was noticing things like this: that there are different kinds of deserts, though she hadn't before thought of it this way. She had always pictured the deathly moonscape of the Gobi or the parched crackle of Death Valley or maybe, just maybe, the cactus-dotted land of westerns, the saguaro-heady hills of Arizona. Susannah had never been to the desert before now, hadn't really known what to expect. She had simply been feeling parched and desperate and like getting lost. And to the amateur, like Susannah, a desert is an abstraction, a metaphor, a Hollywood soundstage for hatchet-faced cowpokes and horses in symbolic colors, a cartoon involving a parched rider on a knobby-kneed horse and palm-treed mirages that rise shimmering from the sand.

But here at the Thunder Lodge, there was a different kind of desperateness. The earth wore a colorless skin of dust, rashy with outcroppings of low-lying, dead-looking shrubs. Even tumbleweeds were a novelty, and when one did scrape against Susannah's door, like a stray wanting to be let in, she was surprised to see how ugly it was up close, how thorns and strands of discarded paper were wound in its belly, and what looked like vertebrae—yes, tangled in its midst, delicate as the filament in a lightbulb, was some tiny animal's spine.

IN THE EVENING, with nothing else to do, Susannah went again to the Grotto.

It wasn't entirely clear why Char Garland had so dubbed what was, after all, a very ordinary rectangle-shaped, six-foot-deep-at-best, aggressively chlorinated motel pool. One imagined that it had to do with some idea she'd had of improvement, of spicing things up, a decorating show she'd seen revealing the transformative secrets of draped cloth and houseplants and the right lighting; some future plan, some dull hope. A grotto in its most ordinary sense is, after all, a small cavern or cave—though there is something dampish about its name; it doesn't necessarily include water, either sitting or running. The name seemed meant to imply a cool, protected place—a respite from the desert air—perhaps the oversize ceramic pots at the crotch of the wall had once held ill-fated palm trees that gave the place a tropical, near-refreshing feel. Or perhaps she had in mind the religious grotto, a concatenation of shrine, sculpture, and geology—like the famous Cave of Apparitions in Lourdes, France—one of those man-made miracles.

Susannah had no way of knowing that Char had visited such a grotto as a little girl in the Midwest, an elaborate garden of rock assembled by an eccentric priest as a shrine to the Virgin—that six-year-old Charlotte had gotten separated from her parents wandering through the seashelled paths, running fingers along the walls made of rocks from all over the world, pausing at quartz, tigereye, shingles of malachite. It had been a hot day in the fields of Iowa, and a scorched wind, smelling vaguely of Jiffy Pop, came tumbling across the prairie, whipping Char's yellow hair in front of her eyes so that she saw everything in a striped squint—a gaggle of Mennonite boys with their black hats and tanned necks brushing by her, their index fingers knuckle-deep in their noses; a pale, poetic-looking invalid limping by on one crutch; a bespectacled couple laughing noiselessly at some secret joke—and when she whirled around trying to locate her parents, she found instead the rose-quartz path. At the path's end, she saw, in a shaft of sunlight spangled with dust, a recess in the wall of rock—an oval punched in and blued with paint—the plaster Virgin, who nodded and winked at Char.

It wasn't something Char spoke of often. But there was, in the cement wall around the Thunder Lodge pool, an indented oval in which was set a glass window, and behind that a plastic Mary, her robes faded, her throne dusty and littered with insect bodies. Susannah either had not seen it or had not thought twice about it. She would not notice it, in fact, until much later. She lay on the lid of water, describing to Julian in her head everything that had happened so far, all about Tim and the Garlands. *And these new guests have arrived, too—a woman and her niece. I'm so glad they've come. I love children, and the little girl seems sweet.* She would never tell Julian how grumblingly she accepted the new guests into her private little world. It made her sound too mean.

Tim had disappeared, and the Floridians had driven off to find hamburgers (they would have to settle for the gas station's microwavable turds of meat, miles down the road, Susannah decided to let them discover themselves), so she did long, lazy laps while the sun did its best to abate. Around eight, the sky still vaunted with light, she heard the Garlands switch off the televisions and lock up the office. Then the Chevy roared up the highway—you could hear it a long way off—and into the parking lot. Susannah emerged from the end of a lap to see the Floridian, Dicey, toeing the water.

"It doesn't look too clean," Dicey said.

Susannah churned at the far end of the pool, treading water. "It's not. But it feels nice." Staying in the water relieved the weight of her belly against her spine and hips, the crushing gravity of the stranger. Staying in the water, Susannah almost felt okay sometimes, almost like a normal kind of creature.

Dicey wore a bathing suit with a little skirt like an old lady, which did nothing for her pearish shape; she had pulled back her hair, and her ears stuck out from her head in a jaunty twin salute. She struck Susannah as being a strange accumulation of parts left over from building other kinds of people—her reddish face didn't match the flawless white of her arms; her doughy hips and thighs seemed to have nothing to do with her stalk-thin legs and delicate, bone-ridged hands and feet. She moved as if she were aware of not being beautiful, as if she wanted to sneak past without bothering anyone with her plainness, walking lightly, her shoulders slightly stooped. She sat at the pool's edge and dipped her bony feet in. Behind her, the child appeared at the gate.

"Hello there." Susannah waved, causing Dicey to turn around and see Frankie and start beckoning frantically. "Oh, yes, come here, Frankie baby, come take a dip!" Dicey cried, lowering herself into the water and spreading her arms. She had a funny twang to her voice that Susannah didn't think she'd ever heard before, not the southern accent she imagined from movies but some other, softer thing. Frankie, who was still in creased, boyish overalls that Susannah guessed were result of having won some battle, took a step backward and said, "I only like to swim in the ocean."

Frankie didn't know why she would say a thing like that, except that she was feeling cranky, and sick and tired of grown-ups and their inane ideas about things. She wanted to express somehow to her Aunt Dicey that she was brave, that she was fearless; she wanted Dicey to know that she knew she was being betrayed. But the only thing she could think to say, like a total dork (but it was true, a little) was, "I only like to swim in the ocean."

"The ocean!" said Susannah, eager to prove that she could talk to this child. An ache simmered beneath her breastbone. "I've never even been swimming in the ocean! I'd like to sometime."

Frankie frowned. "You'd probably be scared. There are sharks and jellyfish."

41

"Oh, Frankie!" said Dicey.

"Well, there's some pretty pinchy bugs in this pool. We could pretend it's the ocean!" Susannah cried, a bit hysterically.

"It's not a long way till the ocean, butterbean," said Dicey.

Frankie waved a hand dismissively and disappeared. What sort of child preferred the ocean, with all its bottomlessness and black water, to a shallow motel pool, Susannah could not imagine, and she considered that maybe she had been mistaken about the kid, too.

"Frankie!" Dicey called, and a shout bounded back, resonant against the concrete walls: "Omina watch TV," and then the door to room 5 slammed shut.

Dicey gave Susannah a knowing look, as if they were partners in something, an assumption Susannah felt like protesting, but the woman had gone and started meandering around the pool, just walking very slowly like she'd never heard of swimming. Susannah tried to do some laps the short way so as not to run into the wading Floridian but soon gave up. A few locusts from God-knew-where had started wheezing away in the corner most concentrated with houseplants. The water tinkled with the movements of the women, reflecting the neon sign buzzing above in long strands of light, playing off the wavelets. Susannah knew by now that the heat, which had made its presence felt all afternoon, was about to drop out from under itself, leaving them shivering and blued with dusk.

Dicey was looking down at her own arms, slick with pool water, when she said, "So when are you expecting?"

Susannah hooked her elbows behind her over the gutter ringing the pool, letting her legs and torso float out in front of her. Ah. What was this heat that swelled in her throat? I'm going to scream, she thought. Up rushed the pavement. God, she thought, I hope I don't scream. When was she expecting, when was she expecting? *What* was she expecting? was more like it. She watched her toes bob in the water—tiny, distant planets—and for some reason she told the truth. "I have to say, that's sort of complicated right now."

Dicey laughed. "I see," she said.

"I mean, just over two weeks. Or wait, I guess, just under two weeks."

Dicey emitted a low whistle. "Well! I guess you'll be skeedaddling home soon, in that case. Your husband's in your room, or . . . ?"

Susannah swallowed the panic that rose as brightly as vomit. "What happened to Frankie's parents?"

Dicey laughed again, a labored, hollowed-sounding laugh. "That's complicated, too."

"I see."

The dark was collapsing upon them now.

"Poor thing," Dicey said, "she's never even known her father, and now she's going off to live with him. Hard on a kid. I considered just taking her in myself, not that she's so crazy about me these days, but my sister, her mother, you know, thinks she should get to know her father."

"That makes a certain amount of sense."

"I guess." Dicey shivered. She hugged herself and held on to her upper arms, gripping the mottled flesh. She did not look at Susannah but stared thoughtfully at the Thunder Lodge sign, at the flickering bolts of lightning. "What do you think?" she said suddenly. "About a kid and a father, I mean. I mean, I don't mean to pry, but your husband . . . or . . . No, sorry, it's none of my business. Here we don't even know each other, and look how nosy I'm being."

"The baby's father is my boyfriend," said Susannah, "and he's absolutely thrilled. Absolutely ecstatic. He will totally be involved, a hundred percent." She didn't even sound like herself. These weren't words or phrases she would ever really use. "I'm just here on a little vacation, before the baby comes along!" Each word sounded worse than the last—misshapen as a botched surgery.

"Not a bad idea!" said Dicey. "You're going to be awfully busy pretty soon!"

Susannah nodded, then pushed off the pool wall and dog-paddled across to the far end again, the water splashing against her lips. "They're fun, though," Dicey continued, sailboating her voice along the water's surface. "They are fun. I don't have any of my own, just Frankie, you know, and of course she's not at her best right now, but sometimes you just love them so much you think your heart will break of it. You can't say they aren't fun, sometimes." Susannah didn't answer, dog-paddling to and fro. After a pause, Dicey got out of the pool and pulled her towel—a proper beach towel with colorful stripes—around her waist. "Do they always leave it lit up like that?" she said. "All the way out here?"

Susannah looked up toward the neon sign and saw that Tim was standing in the open gateway. Dicey shifted her weight, gripped her towel, and beamed at Susannah. "Oh! Is this your boyfriend?"

There was no moon, just a violent spray of stars and the flicker-flick of the sign, and shadows fell across Tim's face, and Susannah couldn't make out his expression but knew he was glowering at her. He still wore just his swimming trunks, and his muscular chest and stomach looked impossibly white. In that light he was just a handsome young man. He could have been anyone. A truck droned along the highway, roaring like an ocean, as enormous and distant as the flap of a wave, the gut of a tide currenting throughout the night.

"Yes," said Susannah, before disappearing beneath the water again. "That's him."

2

EXPECTING

When Julian Forsythe looked at his wife, she made his mind sputter, inarticulate and grasping, and this, he thought, was why he loved her. There was no choice in it.

When Julian looked at Susannah Prue, he thought of lights in buildings, black against gray sky. All winter he'd dreamed of her moving soundlessly through a sunken ship, swimming quiet and blue as a shark in and out of ruined life preservers, wakeless. He had touched her skin: smooth and firm as a whale.

How the body betrays the mind. Outside the doctor's office— a few dandruffy flakes of snow migrating lazily through the sky— after they'd all huddled around those first images of the baby, that screen with its plotless story, its one idea the shadowy image of the baby's bones curled in the dusk of Susannah, as she lay in the chair weakly smiling up at everyone—as they were leaving, Julian had pulled Susannah in for a hug, pressing his body against hers a little too closely a little too long. Just the other day, when they'd gone walking in the park, they'd embraced, hugging, unable to stop. He couldn't get enough of her, couldn't press her closely enough.

Neither of them mentioned it, of course. It was nothing a person could really put into words.

AND IF HE AND KIT could have gone back in time and done it all differently—but of course wasn't that what everyone thought? and somehow thinking the same thing as everyone else, not being able to lay claim even to one's own seethingest regrets as original, this, too, seemed part of the tragedy to Julian—they certainly would have, though, done it differently. They would have screened them more carefully, considering not just whether each had a strong back and a healthy complexion but asking more probing questions, the way Julian did for a staff interview—he gave potential filing clerks more rigorous interviews than he had Susannah, he saw that now—setting up perhaps an invented scenario involving a conflict with another employee, or a time you had to make a difficult decision, and even though they would say what they thought you wanted to hear, you could tell something about them from the ways their eyes flickered, couldn't you? They could have gone through one of those goddamned agencies, one of those places that set it all up for you. Everyone had said you were supposed to go through one of those goddamned agencies. You were supposed to find a woman who already had children of her own, but they had ignored the logic of this, because all the mothers they met seemed so bored by the idea, so businesslike or so starved for the money that Julian and Kit would leave the meetings feeling freaked out and defensive and like they had to check to make sure their wallets were still there, or else the women were overweight and unwholesome-seeming, or else self-righteously religious and do-goody—but of course. That was what one wanted, what they should have known they wanted; they should have known that it didn't matter that Susannah felt so perfect, assured them she didn't even want kids of her own—she'd known just what to say, hadn't she?—that she seemed as excited about the proposition as they did, that they had a "connection." Oh, what hokum! You weren't supposed to find someone so appealing, so lovely. It was a business transaction. It was meant to be just business. Julian tried to think he blamed it all on himself. Meanwhile Kit wept into the couch cushions.

Or better yet they could have simply had children earlier. Kit had believed she wanted to work until she had, you know, her own office, her own assistant, until she *was* somebody, but look how happy all *that* was making her. Or Julian could have married younger—of course he would never say this to Kit, and of course he felt a twinge at even thinking it—but there were instants in which he wondered what would have happened if he'd married, say, Evvie Saunders from college and they'd had piles of rosy babies in their firm and youthful twenties. But Evvie Saunders, as cute as she was—he always pictured her Rollerblading around a lake on campus, although upon considera-tion he wasn't quite sure he'd ever seen her in such a setting or that she'd ever Rollerbladed at all; had anyone even Rollerbladed back then?—had had that thickness to her wrists and ankles, and by now she would have been fat and the children grown. No, it was better with Kit. It was better to marry a woman who already had some sense of herself. Standing at the window watching a pair of nannies pushing strollers languidly down the street, Julian wondered once again if any of it was even worth it, why anyone would even want a baby so badly.

"We could always adopt," he said lamely, for the third or fourth time.

Kit sat up, pressing the backs of her hands into her eyes. "But it's too *late,* Julie. It's *done.*" She sucked in a phlegmy breath.

She was right. It was too late. It was done. Somewhere was the woman pregnant with their child, their mucus pile lovingly stirred in a laboratory, their scientifically blessed immaculate conception, their carefully baked little Kitty or Jules Jr. It made his skin crawl to think of it, as if he'd been unfaithful. This girl—she was lovely, was the worst of it; she was so young—carrying his child, their child. At times it had seemed incredible, an incredible sacrifice the girl was making for them, for needy strangers—giving birth, she would give birth (or that was idea anyhow; who knew now? all bets were off now) to their child. A guilty part of Julian thought of her birth canal stretched out like the elastic band of old boxer shorts, torn open from him, as if it meant he were taking her virginity, but no one else seemed to think of it that way; even Kit seemed not to see any reason for jealousy or worry—and all the while Kit, his trim and beautiful wife, would stay undamaged, her belly smooth and markless, her birth canal unperturbed. And then he'd remember how very much, how very fucking much money they were paying her. How it was double the going rate for this kind of thing. More than that. And how, because she'd asked, he had paid her half already. What had they been thinking? Had she had this in mind the whole time?

"Dear," he said, sitting beside her on the couch. "Kitty, dollface, please don't cry."

Kit looked at him. "Are you kidding? Don't *cry*?"

"Sorry."

She wasn't even crying anymore, had just gone generally soggy. "What should I do? *Laugh*?"

"Sweetie."

"Oh, ha, ha, ha! Oh, tra la, tra la! I've never *been* so happy!" Kit's smeary brightness was terrifying. Then she collapsed again into the pillows. "Ha, ha, ha!" she sobbed.

Julian put his hand on her shoulders and then took it away after a few mindless swipes. Kit formed a fist and smacked it into the couch feebly, as if she were moving through water. "How could she do this to us? That cunning little bitch," she said without conviction, and Julian stood, pocketed his hands, walked again to the window. "Maybe it's all a mistake," he tried. There had been longer spans of time before when they didn't speak with Susannah, after all. Of course, those had been before the pregnancy. "Maybe she's gone to visit relatives for a few weeks and forgot to leave word."

"Oh, I'm sure you're right. I don't know why I didn't think of that. You're right. I must be a complete idiot."

"Kit, please."

"You know what? Who wants a baby, anyhow? Let's just redecorate the kitchen. It'll cost less and will never talk back to us!"

Julian squared his shoulders. He expected the sarcasm but not the breathless, heaving sobs, and he felt impatient with Kit for weeping into the sofa when what they needed was to take action, to contact their lawyer and do what it took to find the girl—and their baby, if it still existed.

The worst part of it was their neighborhood, a section of the city they both loved, where two years ago they'd purchased their condo in a gleaming new spire of a building, where they strolled on Sundays to the lake where Rollerbladers (maybe this was where he'd gotten the image of the muscular, grinning girl) skidded over the slabs of limestone, where squat brown families fished off the rocks for whatever deformed species swam in the lake, where high-school kids smoked near the scrawls of graffiti painted with the telltale grace of art students rather than thugs, but mostly where couples in shorts paced along the shore, heads bent in private conversation. Kit and Julian would stop for iced coffees at the bright café and watch mothers fuss over SUV-proportioned strollers. There were bars with zinc counters where they met their other couple friends, all of whom had their own children already, these unfailingly precocious kindergartners who attended the public school down the street, said to be excellent, inside its chicken-wire-ringed playground some series of boys always playing basketball, always. That is, the neighborhood was crawling with kids. So that it would be impossible—now, for example—to say to his wife, *Say, Kit, should we walk down to Tusky's for some pancakes and tea?* as she liked to on weekends, and to step out onto the street without dodging three or four buggies in that first block. The mothers were all toned and tanned and traveled in packs during weekdays, or with their white-toothed husbands on weekends. The kids never seemed to have fits or even colds. These brilliant specimens of family. Maybe it was just the neighborhood that had given them the idea in the first place. Had they ever once spoken of children in the loft downtown?

"Let's get breakfast," Kit said, standing up and rubbing her eyes. "Let's go to Tusky's."

Julian shook his head.

"No, really. We can see some horrible children eating their own scabs and give dirty looks to the parents and congratulate ourselves on our luck. No kid for us! Hurrah!"

Kit *would* insist on breakfast out, like any other couple on any other weekend. She ordered the blueberry pancakes and a pot of green tea, as he had known that she would. He couldn't remember what he had ordered, and even when it arrived, it didn't seem familiar. He poked at the food with his fork, his stomach churning at a low boil. "Maybe this is just part of it, like the uncertainty any expecting parents have, right?" Kit was saying, not quite sincerely. Who knew how long she'd been talking! "You never know how it's going to turn out, if your baby will be okay, if you will be okay. Maybe it's just always like this. We're supposed to feel . . . you know, uncertain."

Julian cleared his throat. "We'll call Michael"—their lawyer, Kit's cousin—"we'll find her. This is just . . . it's just not right." He slammed his hand suddenly on the table, causing the entire restaurant to skip a beat and earning a grimace from his wife. She wouldn't look at him but sliced her pancakes into slimmer and slimmer strips, her neat fingers grasping the silverware like an imitation of eating. Our baby, Julian's brain kept saying, our *baby*. "Where did she say she had relatives?" Kit finally said, in a conspicuously calm voice.

"Tulsa?" Julian said uncertainly. "Tampa?"

"We could look for her. Or! Get a private eye," said Kit, waggling her fork at him. She seemed entirely recovered, completely on top of things, probably because they were in public. She was always at her best in public. They could have been talking about anything. A mystery movie, a news article. "Or you know what? Let's just start over. We could get a new surrogate with you know, no legs. Or someone on house arrest, someone with one of those ankle bracelets."

"Ankle bracelets?"

"We could track her movements via radar. We could set up a control room in the nursery."

Julian smiled weakly, though the word *nursery* had struck them both dumb with renewed grief. The tiny room off the office, they'd both thought privately without daring to say it even on their first look at the place, the Realtor waiting with a prim smile and folded arms, that could be the nursery. Now in the room, which they had painted butter yellow the day they found Susannah, impossibly heavy boxes containing the unconstructed crib and changing table leaned against the walls like opaque windowpanes. Kit hadn't wanted to set up the room yet, not until the baby was actually a baby, and now and then she'd peer into the empty little room and declare it as barren as she was or some awful thing. She couldn't turn it off, this wanting to be clever, this trying to be funny, and sometimes the strain of it made Julian cringe. So Julian had to say, "Try some of my oatmeal. It has peaches in it."

"Peaches."

"Yes. Peaches."

It was exhausting, trying to keep away from it, from the dread that washed up in the blanks between conversations. And it had been only—what? a few days, really, maybe a week?—since they'd tried to reach Susannah, phoned her cell a thousand times, called the doctor, and now the understanding had welled up in them that their baby had split town—or, worse, maybe Susannah was lying dead somewhere, on the street or in her apartment, sprawled and strangled, maybe she'd been mugged or kidnapped or killed or whatever. Maybe their baby was hurt. And then wouldn't they feel awful for blaming her! Maybe her phone had broken, or something had happened to her e-mail, and even though they had been in constant touch the whole time, maybe this could all be chalked up to technical difficulties. Yes! She was just out of minutes on her phone—that must be it. And she had just happened to be out each time Julian stopped by her apartment—that could happen. And her coworkers at the bookstore were mistaken when they said she hadn't been in to work. Because they couldn't keep thinking this way, could they? They had to quell somehow the panic rising in their throats, they had to say, as Kit did, "That kid in the booster seat—he looks just like Nixon!" or "Ugh, my pancake is grinning at me," making Julian look at the ghoulish arrangement of blueberries in the remaining shred of dough. They had to keep up somehow, to keep away from it. Our baby, our baby, our baby, he had to stop thinking.

The waitress came up smiling. Julian hated her. She had what she didn't even know she had: youth, its particular shine.

"You want anything else?" she said.

Kit smiled. "Just true love and eternal happiness."

"Oh, but you have that with me, darling," said Julian, and the waitress laughed. It was their little show. They left Tusky's with their arms around each other, passing into the squint of sunlight. Julian thought that if they stayed in the sunlight, walking down the east side of the street past the park and the drugstore and into the lobby of their building, that as long as they stayed in the light, it would all be okay, and as soon as he thought it, a bank of clouds enveloped the sun and everything softened.

Julian remembered the doctor, yesterday, frowning in a rather undoctorly way: "No, no, I'm sure she was in for her checkup last week. Yes, quite sure. Everything's progressing normally." He continued to frown as Kit raged on— Normally? No, not quite normally, no, she wouldn't say that, she really couldn't say things were totally normal right then. How could she just *disappear*? The *nerve* of the girl! They had to *find* her! To find their *baby*!— And though Julian was just as upset as she was, for some reason he found himself sitting on the doctor's plastic sofa with his legs crossed, engaged in the feature article of the office's complimentary copy of *Bassmaster* magazine. It occurred to him that he had never been fishing. Here he was, practically half a century old. Never even once had he been fishing! Was it possible? The doctor looked hopelessly from Kit to Julian and back again.

"Well, I assure you, we will do what we can to help."

"Help?!" Kit stood, blinking. "Help what?"

Dr. Kilgore cleared his throat, wiping at his glimmering forehead. It was always a little too warm in his office. "We are terribly sorry for your inconvenience. Of course, it's a matter for your lawyers now."

Julian looked up and nodded. Kit cleared her throat. "So that's *it?*"

"We feel for you. I mean, I'm sure she'll turn up. Her psychological tests seemed entirely normal."

"Oh, well, *I* certainly feel better. So she's sane. She's just run off with our baby. That's terrific news. Can't we get . . . I don't know, a little more than that? I mean, all the money we've paid for all of this, what was it for? I mean, our baby is missing, and no one *cares?*"

Julian could feel the doctor looking at him for help. He riffled through the back of the magazine for the rest of the story. Bass fishing! He'd have to arrange something. The doctor sighed deeply and said, "Mrs. Forsythe, I have to remind you that the two of you, and not I or this hospital or anyone associated with this hospital, were the ones who found the surrogate and reached your agreement. While the baby's needs are of course foremost in my mind, it's not as though we have—heh, heh—a private detective employed on our staff. . . ." He trailed off, waiting for a chuckle.

Kit threw herself onto the sofa beside Julian. More hysterics! But no, she just sat there, breathing. "Isn't there . . . ? I mean, what do we do?" Julian didn't know if she was talking to him or to the doctor. He was almost finished with his article and turned the page, only to find that the final paragraph had been torn out. He held the magazine up to show the doctor, who shrugged. Julian exhaled, closed his eyes.

On the way home, he said to his wife, "How about Aldo?"

She was driving. Her knuckles went white. She didn't look up. "What."

"For the baby. Aldo. My grandfather's name."

"What is wrong with you? I'm just asking. What is *wrong* with you?"

Julian put up his hands in surrender. "You can just say you don't like the name if you don't like it."

Kit gunned through a yellow light. The move was unlike her. She was usually a very cautious driver.

"That's right, Julie. Right. I just don't like the name Aldo, that's all."

MAYBE IT HAD been that first night they had Susannah over for dinner. It had been a little weird, Julian registered at the time and felt especially now. After the formal interview and after they'd decided on her—but before the contract and the lawyers, before the actual procedure, before the actual impregnation. Kit had bought two very nice bottles of wine for some reason, maybe to impress upon Susannah their willingness to spend money on fine things, but also as a kind of a test to see how much she would drink and how she would behave, and Julian had opened one of the bottles while sautéing the scallops in the late afternoon. For some reason they wanted to impress her, *her,* this bookstore clerk without a boyfriend or a husband or anything better to do than to carry some strangers' child. This girl who had leaned forward and said so earnestly, "I want to give back. I want to do something to help others." She had been talking to a doctor about selling some of her eggs—a few thousand dollars that she really could use, for some sheddable part of her body she really couldn't use just now—when the whole surrogate thing had come up. So she said. She'd known all the right things to say, to them, to the lawyers, to the doctors. After a few glasses of wine, Julian paused in front of the CD player, wondering what he could play that would be inviting and impressive and, in the back of his mind, he didn't quite think, seductive. He kept forgetting exactly what was going on. There was a nervous excitement that accompanied his confusion (as he downed his third glass, Kit walked by cradling an armful of linen napkins, disapproval radiating from her in waves), as if he were going to make love to this girl, as if tonight, after their delicious and tasteful and just-fancy-enough-but-not-intimidatingly-gourmet dinner, he was going to lay her down on the bed and—in the most businesslike of ways, but tenderly enough—impregnate her. But that was only how it worked in movies, wasn't it? And who ever heard of a girl getting pregnant on the first try, unless you really *didn't* want her to (which explained what had happened with Evvie Saunders), and then of course it would be his child, his and Susannah's (even just thinking her name bolted a kind of shock through his mind, bringing him back to reality), and not his and Kit's. And that's what this was about, his and Kit's baby, the baby they deserved, after years of miscarriages and fertility treatments and tests and timed romances. After years of Kit leaping onto the bed and crying, "I am Robot Wife, and I am programmed to screw right now or else," while waving around that unsexy scrap of paper monogrammed in charts and little blue X's, meaning that yes, this should be the day. After the month or so when they'd convinced themselves—sure, Julian himself had been adopted, why not adopt?— to flip through brochures of serious-looking Chinese babies, a prospect that had made Kit—who was usually quite politically correct, who advocated at her company for recruitment of minorities and all that— particularly nasty, saying things like "Oh, Mommy, mo' flied lice, prease"—Julian knew she was just trying to be funny, convinced himself it was just the frustration, and nerves, and hormones, and whatever else he could think of. And finally they'd agreed on the no-longer-strange-seeming idea of the surrogate, and here she was, Susannah, at their door, offering a cheap bunch of carnations. "Thank you for having me," she'd said. The carnations dyed in garish hues! She'd actually gotten the fluorescent blue and green bunch they always laughed at. Thank God Kit didn't say anything, only, "Well, thank you for having *us*," graciously accepting the flowers and laughing. This was their joke—they'd already planned out the card they'd send Susannah after the baby's birth, with a picture of the baby and a bubble coming from its mouth saying, THANK YOU FOR HAVING ME. I HAD A LOVELY TIME.

Julian had grinned and lifted his glass. He was still pondering the shelf of CDs.

Kit waved a hand at him, the carnations cradled beauty-queen style in the crook of her elbow. She touched Susannah's arm and led her inside, a series of motions that Julian found fascinating. How capable she was! How good she was at being a host, when she set her mind to it, how gifted at putting people at ease, at being simply herself! He had to remember to tell her sometime how wonderful it was, how good Kit was at being Kit. "He's drunk," Kit stage-whispered to Susannah, gesturing as they passed him. "I don't know how it happened. We don't drink much, I guess." Julian was speechless. "He's like a sorority girl. Soon he'll be dancing on the table." Susannah laughed.

Here I am, thought Julian, with these two beautiful girls. His wife he still thought of—would always think of—as a girl, though she was forty this March. Kit was smaller than Susannah, with sharper edges, and standing beside the younger woman—who looked soft and simple and gracious with her brown ponytail and makeupless face and plain white shirt, though she had clearly tried to dress nicely, as if it were a job interview—Kit looked *too* put together; her smooth hair and angular face and crimson lipstick looked forced, too stiff, too something. It was only a moment, though, and it passed, and in what he thought of at the time as his extreme clarity, Julian saw Kit's superiority. Kit was smarter and shrewder and wittier. Kit had an answer to direct questions—where Susannah seemed to try to guess what should be said, to swim tentatively through conversation, and never remembered to ask questions back. But they were not in competition. The thought was absurd. He pressed PLAY, and an Al Green song came mellowing through the air, and Kit shot him a look.

So maybe that had been unnerving to Susannah—the dinner, his attention to her—and more so as she thought about it. At the time, though, she seemed to be enjoying herself. Julian tried to be attentive but not *too* attentive. Kit was better at this. She talked about normal things, like it were any dinner party, where Julian would have blurted out right away, *But don't you mind not having sex for nine months?* or, *Wait, are you going to not have sex for nine months?* or, *What if you meet a guy and have to explain you are pregnant with my child?* or, *How could you give up the occasional glass of beer or clandestine cigarette or even morning coffee for us?* or, *Will you? Can we be sure you will? Please promise you will.* "Susannah," Kit said, and Julian imagined that any young girl would want to hear her name spoken in just such a way, "Have you seen that new movie—the bank-robber thing?"

"How funny—I have. Usually I never see movies like that, but I did see this one."

"Tell me you thought it was awful." Kit served her more steamed greens without asking. The way she did it reminded Julian of something. Kit mock-furrowed her brow. "Tell me you thought it was awful, or we simply can't go on."

Susannah laughed, maybe nervously. "Oh, I don't know. It was pretty to look at."

"Exactly." Kit replaced the dish of greens and searched around for the wine bottle, located it by Julian's plate, poured herself another glass. "And that's all. The whole time I kept thinking, Gosh these movie stars are pretty."

"That's true," said Susannah, sounding relieved, perhaps at the realization that Kit was going to carry the conversation. "You never think of them as people. Just as prettiness."

"They *are* pretty," Kit agreed. "What are you reading these days?" They sounded like old friends catching up. Julian thought he saw something flicker across Susannah's face—why was Kit asking all these silly questions, and how was Susannah to know what answer was wanted, and what difference did any of it make? It all felt too important if they thought about Susannah as what she was, as the birth mother—no, the surrogate mother of their child. It was only a business transaction. This he kept repeating to himself. It was only business, just money. Still, he was fascinated by Susannah, by what she was signing on for. In the days that followed, he found that he couldn't stop thinking about her. He didn't yet know that he would take to calling her every day, writing her letters, stopping by her apartment, loitering around like a young man in love. She glanced up at him then and smiled. He looked away. Kit offered more greens, and Julian realized what it was that he had been thinking: Kit looked like a fairy-tale witch fattening up a child to devour. Of course he didn't mean to think that his wife was a witch, only that there was that same starved intensity in the way she watched Susannah eat.

Susannah had answered appropriately, listing familiar titles about health and nutrition during pregnancy, a pamphlet the doctor had provided on being a surrogate. Kit beamed. "Sounds gripping, darling, very exciting. Perfect for the beach," she said, laughing. Susannah had passed that test at least.

Maybe if one of them had had a sister, or even a sister-in-law, who could have been the surrogate—but they were the tail end of a pair of dwindling families. Kit had no siblings. Julian himself had been adopted by an aging couple. The thought of asking Elizabeth, his one cousin, was absurd: She was a chronic drug user—nothing serious, but nothing she would give up, either and, he was pretty sure, a lesbian, besides—not that it mattered, only in that it seemed to reduce the chances she'd say yes. For an afternoon Kit had been toying with the idea of asking the secretary at her office—a big-boned Scandinavian type, though it was an exceedingly odd thing to ask of a secretary, no matter how long and faithfully she had been employed there—but then the secretary had announced her engagement, and Kit guessed that would mean no. Where were all the women in the world? As soon as the need arose, they disappeared. Every woman Julian passed on the street seemed exquisitely unsuited to the task—the girl on the El wearing a neck brace, the woman in line at the museum with fused-together toes. Horrible! They had spent weeks walking in their own bizarrely fertile neighborhood, eyeing women balancing children on their hips. "We'll just sneak in one night with a syringe and impregnate Brenda," Kit said of an acquaintance of theirs down the block. "And someday we'll snatch the kid at the park. She'd never even notice!" It was true that Brenda had somehow fitted into her slim town house four enormous boys, their strapping father, and a pair of wolfish dogs, all of whom seemed to be perpetually running in different directions. Since Kit had brought this up, Julian felt strange pang whenever he passed Brenda's boys on the street—the younger ones spent endless hours racing up and down the block on flimsy-looking scooters—as if they might have been his own sons.

So they'd talked to their doctor and asked around and placed an ad, and here she was—they'd met her once before in a room at the hospital, one of those rooms that was clearly meant to feel *homey* but was so very unlike anything they thought of as home: plastic sofas and orange and brown flowered curtains of immobile material and home-and-garden-themed magazines fanned out on a wooden coffee table—and it was different to see her here, among their own things, to catch her browsing the bookshelf (Julian felt a twinge of embarrassment at the USED—CAMPUS stickers still visible on the spines of all the classics that he hadn't touched since college but had moved in and out of five—no, six, wait, seven—apartments over the past twenty-odd years), smiling at their framed wedding photos, her hair catching the light of their own flickering candles. And now the Al Green CD had ended, and Kit sent him a warning look, and he paused a long time over the stereo trying to find something innocuous but appealing and finally selected a sampler of Blue Note Jazz.

"Susannah," he said, her name dusty in his throat, "What kind of music do you like?" even though he'd already selected a CD and pressed PLAY. The whole thing was so backward! To meet a girl who agreed to carry your baby, *then* to get to know her. He wanted to know everything about her all at once. He wanted to know her favorite song, her favorite color, her middle name.

Susannah shrugged and said, "Oh, anything's fine." She's trying to figure out who we want her to be, Julian registered dimly. I have to tell her it's okay.

"Okay," he said.

The whole night Kit had been watchful, it seemed, and whenever he looked up, there she was. And after Susannah finally left ("Oh, no, honey, let us pay for your cab"), Kit turned on him almost immediately. "What was *that*?" she said. "What *was* that?"

"What?" Julian started to clear the table. The dessert plates were runny with melted ice cream that he concentrated on not spilling.

"Al *Green*? Are you in*sane*?"

Julian ran water into the sink and dribbled the jewel-green dish soap into the steam.

"What were you going for there, Julie, a three-way?"

"The things that come out of your mouth," he said, but she didn't hear him over the water. She was floating wineglasses in the suds in a way that made it clear to him she wasn't really angry, was only teasing to see if she could strike a nerve somewhere. "Do you play Al Green at all your work meetings, too? At your employees' yearly reviews?" Kit laughed. "She said she's never been to the ocean. Did you hear that? I was telling her about when we went diving in New Zealand—I don't know why, it makes me sound like such a rich old lady to say things like that—and she said she's always wanted to swim in the ocean but she's never been, unless Lake Michigan counts, which I guess was a joke."

"I'm sure it was."

"She's a little strange, though, isn't she? I like her, don't get me wrong. She's lovely and somehow . . . I don't know, sexless. She reminds me of a health teacher. Did you get that sense? Someone who could tell you about reproduction in a completely boring way. Or like someone who would be a tollbooth operator. These people you see and think, 'Who *are* these people?'"

"She was probably nervous. It's kind of a weird situation."

"Well, sure, with some old guy practically drooling over her. I'm kidding, darling, don't be grumpy. Just the Al Green was a little over the top. And the very soft, 'That's a nice shirt.' That was a little weird, too. You might as well have just said, 'Those are lovely tits.' I'm not saying I care—I just mean how awkward for her. But don't feel bad, Julie, she probably didn't even notice. Is it weird that I feel very motherly toward her? I kept wanting to tell her to sit up straight and to stop playing with her hair and to look for a better job. Do you think it's my mothering hormones revving up? They're, like, dragging themselves out of this dusty cave somewhere and shaking themselves off."

"Kit."

"Oh, relax. Here, let's finish this bottle or it'll have been a waste." They were hand-washing the delicate china plates now, Julian washing and Kit drying and sipping from the bottle on the counter. They had washed dishes together so many times that there was no need to discuss how it would be done, what went into the dishwasher and what didn't. Julian ran a sponge over the toothy knives. Kit continued, "Do you think maybe some of her will rub off on the baby, I mean, with her carrying it for so long? It might be a good thing. It'll be this kid who's just like us but then very sturdy and never gets sick. Doesn't she seem like someone who never gets sick? She's like something out of *Little House on the Prairie,* isn't she? I like her. I'm glad she's the one." She paused. Julian didn't say it, but he thought she was wrong about Susannah. She wasn't sturdy and sexless at all—she was warm; she was sparkly; she was bright and vivacious; she was everything he would have wanted his own mother to be, had he gotten to pick. "Do you have a *baby shower* when there's a surrogate mother? And does the surrogate come? How weird! How weird will that be?"

Julian wiped his hands on the dish towel and took Kit into his arms and pressed her to him. "Oh, my," she murmured, only half joking. He felt the need to tell her something, to communicate something important, but the wine had rendered him voiceless. In the same way that he thought of Evvie Saunders in a strange, invented tableau, he remembered seeing Kit for the first time in a scenario he was sure hadn't really happened—he remembered her sitting on a park bench outside his office building, reading the newspaper quite calmly, ignoring the thundering sky and threat of certain rain. She was so small that she looked like a child until he saw her face, and of course the way she dressed, very competent and put together. He wanted to say to her that she was his little girl, his baby, no matter what happened, though she wouldn't like that, she had worked so hard to be cool and distant and professional, to be a formidable woman. Still, when she was sleeping or crying or making love, she was his little girl. His baby. He held her close and smelled her hair and felt his heart beating through his rib cage, as if trying to escape into hers.

"Katherine Forsythe," he said. God, how he loved her. "I am now going to perform my marital duties," which had been a joke with them for a long time after what the pastor had said at their wedding, and he knelt down there in the kitchen and started caressing her backside and thighs through the thin slip of her skirt until she pulled him up and said, "Jesus, Julie, your knees" (they did crack disconcertingly on the way up), and led him to the bedroom.

3

THE JACKALOPE

Susannah sat in the car, her belly pressed against the steering wheel. She'd packed up her suitcases—not that she'd ever really unpacked; each morning she'd dissected some clean item of clothing from the suitcases' tousled entrails, thinking, I really ought to unpack; I'll unpack and get things organized soon—so that the process that morning was as simple as slamming the cases shut and tossing them back into the trunk of her car. Runaway packing. But then she couldn't remember whether or not she'd already paid for the night before—it was really as if she were losing her mind—so she got out of the car and left an envelope of cash on top of St. Francis's bureau— she had enough money; for once in her life she had money, at least there was that—and then surveyed the room one more time before getting back into the car and revving its emphysemic engine. She sat in the driver's seat, deciding on the next move. Where would she go? Where on earth did she go from here?

It reminded her of a game they'd once played, she and her old friend Rose, sitting in Rose's father's parked car, pretending to drive. (Rose was lucky; Rose still had a father, when Susannah's had gone and moved far, far away, marrying a series of younger and younger women.) They must have been thirteen or fourteen, too old for a game like that, but Rose never cared what anyone thought. Rose decided they were headed to California. It sounded magical to them, impossibly far away, all Technicolor and movie-set. Rose had been there on vacation and reported that it was the most glorious place she ever had seen. That was so like her, using a word like *glorious* at age thirteen, unafraid to say it instead of *awesome;* Rose had always been the keeper of secrets, of special knowledge that Susannah lacked access to. They had been playing the game, driving to California in the driveway, when Susannah told Rose about the summer she was seven and lived with her aunt and uncle and cousins at their home by the lake. She hadn't known why her mother was sending her away, but she'd been happy all summer, insanely happy. She told Rose about sleeping in her cousin Becky's trundle bed, running around dressed in Becky's hand-me-downs; about how it had seemed there were no rules for her, how Becky and Scott let her do whatever she wanted, let her ransack their rooms and cherry-pick their toys (so it was true, as she'd always suspected, that children with siblings had a much better time of it); how her aunt let her eat anything, anything at all, sugar cereal in chocolate milk followed by coconut Snowballs washed down with orange soda sucked through cherry-licorice straws; about lying beneath the boardwalk and inventing a game of stacking pastel-colored miniature marshmallows on top of bits of beachy debris—an earlike shell, a toothy bit of white sea glass, a finger of driftwood—and thinking, this was it, she was alive, she was a person, and she was alive, and she was happy. She was not Becky, swimming out to the sandbar, or her aunt, eating sandwiches under the umbrella—she was she, she was herself, she was a pistachio green marshmallow balanced on the jawbone of a fish. She told Rose about her cousins' huge, hairy dog, a sheepy mutt called Cooper that terrified her. About how her aunt always described that summer as "the summer Cooper ran away," but that Susannah didn't remember anything happening to Cooper at all and assumed that her aunt was mistaken about the timing of things. Rose finally interrupted her: "God, you're a dunce." Susannah had blinked. She'd been talking too much. She bit her lip, embarrassed. "No, no, I just mean . . . well, I mean, don't you know why your mother sent you away? Haven't you guessed?" Susannah, honestly, had never really thought about it. Rose shook her head knowingly. "Oh, silly. My mom told me about it ages ago. Don't you know she had a miscarriage, your mother? You would have had a little baby brother." At that, Susannah's heart dried into sand. Rose thought she was so smart, but she didn't know anything, not a thing at all. Rose was a stranger, impossibly distant and separate from Susannah. Suddenly they weren't Susannahnrose anymore. They were two girls, each with secrets. And soon they'd be in high school, and Susannah would overhear Rose saying, *Who, Susannah Prue? She practically stalks me, is all. I can't get rid of her!* "She had a miscarriage, and then she lost her mind, and that's why your dad sent you away. That's probably why everyone was being so nice to you, dingbat. Your mom was at home, lying in her bedroom with the shades closed, that whole summer. Everyone thought she would kill herself. That's what my mom says, anyway."

But everyone knew that Rose exaggerated, Rose told stories. Wouldn't that have made Susannah's mother hold her close, love her harder, cradle her all summer and call her baby, instead of forgetting she existed? Rose was such a liar! Susannah left the car, walked home in a huff, sat sullenly at supper, studying her mother for signs.

Susannah had thought of calling her cousin Becky to ask her if it was true, thought of asking her cousin Scott, but she knew she wouldn't even be able to say what it was she needed to say. She knew it was probably true, acknowledged that it did explain a lot. And now it was much too late; things were different between her and her cousins. Only a month ago, largely pregnant and without a date, Susannah skulked in a corner at Becky's wedding, mortified, as relatives passed silently by. So it had happened. So she had finally really become invisible. And here she'd thought being a surrogate would have the exact opposite effect! It turned out everyone had liked her better when she was with Aaron—Scott would poke her in the ribs, demanding,

"So when are you two getting hitched?"—and now she had slipped off the track of things; now there was nothing they could ask her, nothing they understood about her. People liked when you did things the predictable way (she realized at the wedding, mooning over the punch bowl). People liked when you graduated college, began a career, got married, had babies, all in the right order. No one knew what to make of her now. Becky had defended her, had come to her aid, had said, "And have you met my cousin Susannah, the surrogate mother? Isn't that amazing? This isn't even her child! She's such an angel, right? Can you imagine?" Susannah knew that she was only trying to help, and it was awful, awful.

Now she sat in the car in the motel driveway, playing the same old game of deciding where to go, hearing Rose's decisive voice: "California!" Just because Rose had gotten conventional and dull didn't mean *she* had to, now, did it? She would head west, drive to California, of course she would.

This was the way she was in her new life, or anyhow this was what they all thought of her—the Garlands and the Floridians and Tim. She was reckless and free-spirited; she lived by a different set of rules. She would keep west, heading toward the coast, and Julian and Kit would never find her in all that fog. She would rent an apartment by the sea and always wear black. She would be just another single mother. She would never see Tim again.

She would never see Tim again? Susannah welcomed the surge of pain, like the throb announcing the end of a dentist's anesthetic spell. What a relief to feel something so unequivocally, to have something hurt. She sat there watching the sun wink in the rooms' windows. The stranger elbowed Susannah's spine, a guy nudging another guy, a reminder of something. She concentrated on ignoring this. She strove to be as cool and inscrutable as an adulteress in a French film, the way (she imagined) they all imagined her; she put on a pair of oversize sunglasses. The plastic was hot on the bridge of her nose, baked from its days on the dash. Now what? She was tired, tired, tired of being Susannah Prue. She wanted to believe things that didn't make sense. She was trying to be the kind of person who believed things that didn't make sense.

The car started shuddering in an alarming way, and she stopped the engine to let it rest. It was probably her complete lack of technical skills that caused her to be so superstitious about machinery, to assume that cars needed patience, that computers craved well-wishing, that getting things to work was a matter of will and luck. She opened the door, wanting to give the vehicle time to think and, still sitting in the driver's seat, planted her feet in the dust.

The Floridian's child had materialized at the end of the gravel drive. Susannah lowered the sunglasses and over their rims watched the child bounce a red rubber ball, the kind procured from truck-stop gumball machines. The lipsticky red was the only colorized speck in the whole brownish earth. The kid was wearing last night's overalls and no T-shirt, her tangled hair swinging in front of her face, and she seemed not to have noticed Susannah. Her tongue played in the corner of her mouth. Susannah felt as if she had known Frankie her whole life, or maybe it was only that the kid reminded her of someone. *Chuk, chuk, chuk.* The ball landed dully in the dirt and each time projectiled up at a slightly skewed angle. Frankie leaped this way and that. Susannah stood up to stretch out her legs. In that same moment, Frankie's ball ricocheted off a stone and rocketed away from her, bouncing toward the highway. Frankie yelped in panic, and then saw Susannah. "Teacher! Teacher!" she cried. "I mean, lady! My ball!"

Susannah watched the ball settle into the ditch that guttered alongside the road. "Stay there," she told Frankie. "I'll get it."

She made her way cautiously into the ditch. The ball had rolled nearly all the way to the lip of the highway. Mindful of invisible traffic, Susannah knelt on one knee, her belly pitching her forward. She grabbed the ball and secured it in her pocket, launched herself back to a standing position. Frankie greeted her beside the car, pumping a fist. "Yesss!" She held out a grubby palm.

Susannah twirled the ball between her fingers, hefting its small weight instead of passing it to the child right away. "What do you say?" The child's mistaking her for a teacher had made her something of a teacher, had made her feel like teaching the child, like being one of those formidable adults who demands politeness and decorum.

Frankie squinted at her. "That's my ball."

"Oh, really?" Susannah smiled and threw the ball lightly up into the air, catching it in her cupped palms. "What do you say?"

"Excuse me, please, and thank you," said Frankie, rolling her eyes. "Duh."

Susannah paused for a moment, unsure if this counted, before dropping the ball into Frankie's hand. Frankie blew a breath up toward her bangs, spraying hair from her sticky face, and went right back to bouncing the ball. "Whatcha doing? You leaving?" she said, her eyes trained on the little red planet.

"Um, yep. Gotta get going," said Susannah. She sat back down in her car, keeping her feet on the ground.

"Where you going?"

Susannah shrugged. "California?"

"Wow. Not me," said Frankie. "I *wish*."

"You like California?"

"How should I know?"

Susannah tried to think. She didn't talk to kids very often and wasn't sure what kinds of conversation topics they had at their disposal. "So," she said finally. "What's your favorite subject in school?" There it was. School. They went to school.

Frankie set the ball off on an errant bounce and ran to catch it again. "None of them. Gym."

"Ooh. Gym." What else did kids that age even do in school?

Susannah couldn't quite conjure it up. Penmanship? Fractions? Playing with blocks? "That sounds like fun!"

"Um, you think?" Frankie tossed the ball from one hand to another. "I think it's completely lame. Anyway, none of my friends will be at my new school. I think that sucks."

She studied Frankie's splay-legged posture, her belly pouched out in front of her, the careless way she shoved her stringy hair behind her ears. The tiny fingernails were bitten to the quick, like a stressed-out accountant's. She had a puckish face with a turned-up nose and round eyes with dark fringes of curled lashes, the only really girly thing about her. She had the particular look of a motherless child—the stickiness, the unwashed hair, the guarded way she peeked up at Susannah now and then. "My neighbor was pregnant, but we didn't even know, because she was already so fat."

"Well," Susannah said, "that's not a very nice thing to say, is it?"

"But it's true! And Mom said you can't really ask fat pregnant ladies about their babies, because what if there isn't one?"

"I guess that's true."

"But you're really pregnant, aren't you? You really have a baby in there."

"Yep. Baby in the tummy." Susannah patted her stomach.

"In the *uterus*," Frankie corrected her. "If I had a baby I would name it Sparks. My fat neighbor has a dog that's called that. I think it's cute. Sparks!" Susannah laughed.

Inside the office Marlon shuffled about, stopped by the window to watch the two girls talking to one another. He started the coffeemaker, checked to make sure the Vacancy sign was on. He hoped she wasn't planning on taking off—she wouldn't be getting far in that car. He doubted she'd make it down the drive. Not that he would have been sorry to see her go. (He fitted his teeth in his mouth.) She seemed like a sweet girl, but there was something unsettling about her, about having a very pregnant person around. He felt like they should all move very cautiously around her, try very hard not to touch her or upset her in the least. Marlon was the first to admit that he mostly preferred things to stay the same. Like Tim, he appreciated a routine. He respected the steady pace of the status quo. So he was ready, more than ready, for the unsettling girl to leave. Look there, the little one's ball had rolled under that rattletrap of a car. He turned away from the window, tried to remember if he'd already checked the Vacancy sign and the coffeemaker.

"I guess it's mine now!" Susannah said brightly when the ball rolled beneath her car.

Frankie shoved her hands into her pockets. "Nuh-uh."

"But it's under *my* car." Susannah pushed her sunglasses back up on her nose, two dusky shields. She meant it to sound joking, but everything she said was just sounding sort of mean and creepy. She would never have thought she'd become one of those sorts of adults. Finally Frankie said, like a director of a play, or a cop moving traffic, "Can you please move your car, lady, so I can have my ball?"

The car only choked its way a few dusty inches before stalling to a stop. Susannah leaned forward against the steering wheel, describing circles into her forehead with her fingertips. Frankie waved a hand. "Don't worry about it!" She slithered under the car and in an instant appeared out the other side, holding up the rubber ball with one hand and with the other swiping at her back. "Hot!" Then she pranced off, tossing her hair one way and another. Susannah stayed behind the wheel for a few more moments before getting out and going back into her room and shutting the door behind her.

Maybe she'd known she couldn't really leave, not yet, not alone. Things were getting too interesting at the Thunder Lodge. She'd just started calling Tim "the jackalope," which amused both of them. For days now he'd been collecting thorny blossoms, schist chips, the occasional arrowhead and leaving them at Susannah's door. She spent more time than she would have admitted fingering through the piles of dirt, seeing in them things she'd never noticed before—flecks of light, grains of varying color (not all beigey brown like she would have assumed), tiny fragments of plant or bone. It was as if her eyes had been adjusted, cranked by some inner optometrist. "Why, I don't believe anyone's ever brought me such a . . . um, lovely bouquet before," she'd said, watching Tim deposit a handful outside her door. "It must have been a strange creature that did it—a jackalope or something." He had only smiled and loped off, leaving her in the doorway with the pile of grayish debris at her feet.

She thought she knew that a boy like Tim just wanted a nickname the way anyone did, but as soon as she had uttered it, as soon as she had finished saying, "I think I'll call you the jackalope," she regretted it; she knew that she would forget to use the nickname, and she hated to be the kind of girl who invented nicknames only to never use them. Oh, it was disgusting!

Later, when she was curled on the bed with her eyes shut, riding out a wave of heartburn, listening to a rerun of *Dallas* on the ancient television in her darkened room in the too-hot afternoon, she heard another deposit rattle onto her doorstep and cried, "Tim! Tim! Um, Jackalope, wait," pushing herself off the bed. "Freeze!" Tim stood blinking at her. "Good. Thank you. I'm going nuts in here. Walk with me." She stepped over the rocky wreckage he'd left, walked slowly alongside him, pressing a hand now and then to the small of her back as he knelt to gather treasures.

It wasn't that Tim was unintelligent, was it? Only that he was hidden in a kind of fog, or this was how it seemed to Susannah. Now and then there was a certain flicker in his eye or brow that bespoke real wit, real compassion. She should have known that she wouldn't leave now, that she couldn't say good-bye to him just yet, not when she felt on the precipice of something with him, so close to breaking through to him. She liked talking to Tim more than anyone else she'd ever met—it was so much easier than with Aaron, who challenged and mocked and put her on edge, or with Julian, who made her feel like a charming but very silly girl; these men who were too smart, too clever, with an intellect that, if you let your guard down, could run through you like knives. She could have told Tim anything, and he would have responded with a knowing nod and a giggle. So they walked, starting from the back of the Thunder Lodge and heading straight into the desert, sidestepping the eruptions of brush.

Tim clapped his hands suddenly, and Susannah jumped a little. "Rocks," he announced.

"Oh, yeah?" Susannah felt that she understood in some elemental way.

"Find some rocks," said Tim.

She watched him finger through a palmful of dirt. "We should go into town someday. Would you like that, Tim? Where's the nearest town?"

He didn't respond. In the contrasty sunlight, uninterrupted at noon, beads of sweat rolled down his high cheekbones like an Indian's.

Susannah trudged on through the dirt. The sun made her woozy, made the stranger churn in her stomach, kicking toward her belly button black-belt style. Hi-yah! She should have taken water, she knew; one needed to plan these things out. "You know, I like towns. I'm from a city, you know, and it feels funny to me out here. I mean, where are all the people? Where do your things come from? Where do you buy your food? It all seems so difficult here. Have you ever been to a big city? Tim?"

He stopped walking and shrugged.

"No?"

Tim shrugged again.

"Would you like to go to a big city someday? Tim? Yes or no. We're having a conversation here."

He surveyed the land, as if trying to imagine such a thing. "No."

"No?"

"Yeah, probably not."

"We could go together—to a big city. Somewhere with water. Near the ocean, or a lake. Do you know what I mean, Tim? We could take a little trip! Me and you. Maybe we could borrow your dad's truck. And we could just take off, and be alone together, and go different places. Right?" She closed her eyes. It *could* work, really. It wasn't any worse an idea than coming here in the first place, was it?

Tim giggled. "Yeah. Probably not, yeah." He dropped down, suddenly, gripping a dusty stone and holding it close to his eye and then presenting it to Susannah.

"Oh, honey," she said, "it's only dirt!" She dissolved it between two fingers, but when she saw the way he blinked and turned away, she wished she hadn't. He was punching at his thighs with his fists, his biceps contracting beneath his T-shirt sleeve. "Tim, come on. Don't be upset." She reached out to touch his shoulder, brushed his skin lightly, her fingers registering a kind of elemental shock that sent heat all the way down her arm.

He gave her a funny look. "Susannah Prue, want to come in my room?" he said, nodding his head as if to convince her of it.

"Sure. I'd love to." Susannah was so relieved about Tim's regained calm that she would have done anything to maintain it. He turned and walked stiffly toward the back door. She followed him, laughing a little—it was all so strange!—into the Garlands' tidy box of a kitchen.

The room was cool and dim, wallpapered in a faded olive green jungle theme. Something simmered beefily on the stove. A pair of Tim's sneakers sat squarely on the kitchen table. To the left was the living room, which Susannah recognized—it was visible from the door to the office. Char and Marlon snoozed on a corduroy couch in front of a blaring game show. To the right were two doors. Susannah peeked into the first—Marlon and Char's bedroom was carpeted in orange, outfitted with matching bedside tables, wood-grain frames displaying photographs of Tim, a smallish bed made neat as a pin, a white Marcella quilt snugged around it like a layer of skin. For some reason

Susannah tiptoed. She felt that she shouldn't be in there but at the same time couldn't think of a very compelling reason why not. She followed Tim through the doorway directly beside the Garlands', into his own little room.

He sat on his bed, giggling. "My room," he said, clapping once. He spread his hands out very flat on his thighs, rubbed once, twice, thrice. It seemed so strange to have Susannah Prue in there! It made him giggle, rub his thighs again, once, twice, thrice.

The room, lit by only a tiny window and a single light fixture, was full of the smell of Tim. She breathed it in, the very essence of boy: outdoors and sweatsocks and mushroom and soap. His bedspread was a child's, patterned in primary-colored trucks. And on the walls—the ocean. Susannah wheeled around. He'd covered every inch of the walls with cutouts from magazines, drawings and watercolors, glossy motivational posters, and reproductions of famous photographs. On one wall was the sea, on the other a limitless herd of horses. "It's . . . amazing," she said. Tim giggled. "Huh. Yeah. Thanks." As much as she'd liked Tim, she hadn't expected this—had expected something more teenagerish—hot rods and bikini girls, or the tanned monsters of wrestling.

"Tim! How did you do this?"

He shrugged.

"I mean—why horses? Why water?"

"The ocean," he corrected her.

Susannah sat gingerly on the edge of his unmade bed—her back was squealing at her, and it was the only place to sit in the room. They sat there side by side, looking at the wall of water. Susannah felt very cold suddenly; her skin erupted in goose bumps. Then Tim sprang up, started pointing at different sections of the wall. "A tidal wave," he said. "A whirlpool. A deep-sea vent." He turned to the other wall. "A quarter horse. A Shetland. A Kentucky Derby horse."

"But, Tim," Susannah said. She stopped. Char stood in the door, hefting the weight of her slinged arm in her good hand, as if it were a weapon she might fling at Susannah. "Hi," Susannah said.

"What are you doing in here?" Char said. She swung the door open wide. "What are you doing in my son's bedroom?"

Susannah pushed herself up off the bed. "We were just . . . playing." She cringed. That hadn't come out right at all. But how could Char accuse her of anything? Had she failed to notice how completely . . . you know, pregnant she was? Still—Susannah groped for words, feeling her face go red. She looked at Tim, who watched his mother impassively.

"Get out of here," Char said, with terrifying calm. "Please, stay out of my son's room."

Susannah inched past her. "I just want to be his friend," she mumbled.

"I'll bet you do."

On her way out ("Timothy Garland, what *could* you be thinking!" Char was shouting), Susannah took a fork from the kitchen counter and slipped it into her shorts pocket. Once outside, she stopped by her car, threw the fork into the glove box, and leaned against the door to think a minute, to recover, to let the sun soak into her skin.

THE arrival OF Dicey and Frankie had destroyed her routine, working a crack into her momentary peace. They were only staying the night, supposedly, but day two, half past checkout time: Dicey still lolling in the Grotto. Susannah, after her run-in with Char, sat on the bench with a crossword, chewing the end of a red pen, when the child appeared beside her, again—or maybe still—bouncing the rubber ball in the dirt. Susannah didn't look up yet, close to remembering the name of the character from *M*A*S*H*. . . . Got it, though it didn't seem to fit. She frowned at the puzzle, forcing two letters into the final square, and looked up. "Hello, Frankie," she said. So she'd failed with Tim today. Maybe this was another chance.

But the ball-rescuing heroism of the morning had apparently been forgotten, had created no private little bond. Frankie shrugged non-committally, kicking her legs. Now she was wearing only boys' swimming trunks, dark with fluorescent splashes of vicious-mouthed sharks, her ribs countably visible, her sexless nipples sloe-eyed and rabbity pink. She stared straight out into the highway. "That's some outfit!" said Susannah brightly. She'd gotten it into her head somehow that one had to be cheerful with children.

Frankie shrugged again, her bobbed hair swaying. "It's just a swimsuit."

"That's true. That's true."

Frankie leaned toward Susannah confidentially and said out of the corner of her mouth, "I'm really a boy, you know."

"Oh! Is that so!"

"Actually, yes." After a pause she added, "Aunt Dicey doesn't get it." She paused again. "That's part of our problem."

"I see."

Now and then a bird with the demeanor of a delivery van would barrel through the air above the Thunder Lodge, cawing excessively, and one was doing so now, swooping in giant, lazy loops. Susannah was no good at identifying things like birds. She would have liked to point out the beast to Frankie but was afraid that it might be a vulture or something equally grim, and she didn't want to be the one to frighten a child in this way, to be seen as one of those misguided grown-ups with all the wrong answers. She preferred to think of the things as eagles or hawks, something noble and uplifting, not so ominous as a carrion bird circling their heads. Then suddenly she was incredibly thirsty. She wanted something sweet to drink so desperately that she could easily imagine dying of it—yes, they would all starve to death, and the great bird would devour them—and as the stranger rolled around in her belly, Susannah felt a wave of panic. But the child was still talking, being downright friendly, and this demanded Susannah's presence. She mustered herself up to say, "How interesting. Do your mother and father know that you really are a boy?"

Frankie crinkled her brow, lifting her blunt-cut hair from her shoulders. "Mom knows. That's why she and Deke thought I should spend some time with Dad. She couldn't get off work, though, so she got Aunt Dicey to take me."

"I see," said Susannah. "Deke?"

"Her boyfriend. He's a real Deke-head. Excuse my French. Ha. You get it? Deke-head? Anyway. I don't like him."

"I see. Sweetheart, could you do me an enormous favor? Could you please please please go to the vending machine and buy me a Coke, anything?"—holding out a palmful of coins.

Frankie acquiesced, returned with an orange soda. "All that's left," she said, waggling it at Susannah. Susannah took the soda can, speechlessly thankful and surging suddenly with love for the child, or maybe it was only the thirst making her joints feel overheated, and opened it—they watched a spray of fizz darken the dust below her feet—and drank gulpingly, the bubbles stinging her throat, the cloying flavor coming unattached in her gullet. "I think I need to lie down," she said.

Frankie sat beside her again, this time closer, their thighs touching. "Okay." They sat there, each staring at the horizon. "My dad doesn't know I'm really a boy, either. But I don't think he'll mind."

"Sure, all dads want a son, right? You can play sports and things, right?"

The child nodded. "I have to admit, I'm really good at soccer. I don't mean to sound conceited, but everybody says so. Deke even says so, and he hates my guts."

"Oh, I'm sure he doesn't hate your guts."

"Yeah, he hates my guts. But it's okay. Someone should be allowed to hate someone else's guts, if you ask me." Frankie leaned back philosophically, only to dart forward again when her bare skin met the sun-heated siding. "What is it?"

"What is what?"

Frankie poked at Susannah's belly.

"Oh." Susannah paused, licking her lips. "It's a boy."

"Cool. What are you going to name him?"

But Susannah didn't answer, sipped at the too-cold, too-sweet drink that burned down her throat. How could someone name a child when they hadn't even met yet? She felt as if she might be sick but made no effort to move. Shrugging, she said, "Sparks?" Frankie's face betrayed no flicker of recognition. "Ha. Um. Maybe Jackalope. Jack for short. Maybe that. I haven't decided yet, actually. There's just so much to choose from, you know?" She wished Julian could see her now, could see her getting along so well with this child, could see what a wonderful mother she would be, what a kind person she was at her heart. *See, I'm not so bad!* she wanted to cry to the world. But the kid only shrugged and ran off again, leaving Susannah to the heat and deafening quiet.

Not that the quiet of the desert was a real quiet, not a peaceful kind, anyway. Once her senses had adjusted, she began to register the scrape of wind against the ground; she thought she could hear the far-away rustle of a coyote loping toward the mountains, the appliance-like hum of the earth spinning on its axis. Sitting on the bench outside the office, Susannah could hear everything—the amble of a roadrunner a half mile away, the wet-lashed blink of a sad someone in the next town over. So the hollering that came unfurling from St. Catherine was at best extremely disruptive—vibrating uncomfortably around her eardrums. She rubbed her face and looked toward the Floridians.

Muffled by the door came Dicey's crying, "Frankie! *Frank*ie! There's no choice here! It's not a choosing matter! I said one more day, and that was today, and now we are getting on the road tomorrow, so help me God! You hear me? We are leaving tomorrow, if I have to pick you up and throw you into that car." But even Susannah could hear the falter in her voice, the plaintiveness, the give.

Frankie was answering in modulated tones that Susannah couldn't quite distinguish. Oh, Aunt Dicey—can't you see you're giving the child the upper hand? Dicey's voice shrilled. "Baby, what do you want me to do? I need to get back to my job, and my cats, and your father is expecting you— But he *is*, Frankie, and he wants to see you." After a few more rounds, Dicey rushed from the room, slamming the door behind her. She didn't see Susannah at first and stood there with her face in her hands, and Susannah sat uncomfortably, an arm outstretched as if to shush her, wanting to say something to identify herself but not wanting to startle, because she was already embarrassed for the moment when Dicey would see her and be startled, so she tried to alert Dicey gradually to her presence, murmuring, "I . . . Hey . . . You . . ." and finally had to give up and sit there mortified and waiting.

"Oh! Oh, I'm sorry!" Dicey cried when she saw her. "You don't have any idea! It's just so difficult!"

Shh, shh, said someone the next county over. Susannah was sure she could hear it: *Shh, shh.*

By that afternoon Susannah had been voted referee, though she wasn't feeling well and sat at the edge of the pool somewhat wilted, for the Frankie and Tim Ultimate Race. Frankie had named the affair and dictated the rules. They lapped up and down the pool, and at each end, Frankie—still in her shark-patterned swimming trunks—erupted from the water, a tiny, competitive sea serpent, screaming, "Ha, ha! Gotcha again!" at Tim, who surfaced with a scowl. Susannah sat with her hand on her belly.

The sun on her back paused, and then Dicey sat beside her. They watched their feet dangle in the water like meaty, knuckled fishing lures.

"Nice day!" said Dicey brightly, though every day there was the same. It wasn't so bad to spend an extra day at the Thunder Lodge, not that she would let Frankie know she thought so. She'd seen

Frankie smile so infrequently lately that she felt desperate to hold very still now, while Frankie was playing and laughing, reaching out, drawing in; she would have done anything, anything, to keep Frankie happy. In truth she dreaded leaving her with Skip, a wincing man she'd never thought much of. Here she'd practically raised Frankie herself, and Jean was sending her away, and Dicey had the terrifying sense (especially at night, when she watched Frankie sleep, her baby face softened and sweet) that once she dropped Frankie off, she would never see her again.

And then there was this Susannah Prue—she reminded Dicey of something, or someone. From the window Dicey had watched her talking to Frankie in the morning, seen her being so kind and gentle, rescuing Frankie's ball, humoring the poor kid. She was a cocoon, a hive, a bud about to bloom. Dicey couldn't stop looking at her, trying to memorize her face. Anything could happen. Anything at all. But she had to reach out to Susannah, to draw her in. "Hot out!" she tried again.

"Mmm-hmm."

"Hope you've got sunscreen on. I have some if you need it."

"Mmm."

But Susannah was determined not to engage in this conversation. Because she had come here to make a decision. Because her money would run out eventually, and her time. Because there was a very inflexible deadline coming up. Because there was something about Dicey. Because Susannah had come here, in part, maybe, to get away from all these *women,* all those knowing smiles on the subway, all these concerned strangers, all those coworkers asking with creased brows was something wrong? was there anything they could get her? and then behind her back gossiping about her billowing body. They weren't interested in whose baby it was or why the young and single Susannah was pregnant so much as how much weight she was gaining and where. She must be carrying a boy, they'd shriek, laying their hands on her belly like it was public, like it was a pet, like it was a crippled leg that their palms could heal—look at how low she was carrying! At this, Susannah felt herself go dead, felt her emotions lie down and press their eyes shut. No, no thank you. And her mother, oh God, her mother and her aunt, always leaning forward, always touching her arm, with that glint of pity simpering around near their pupils. Was there anything they could do for her? Was there anything she wanted? And worst of all, naturally, was Kit: Kit calling every day to remind her of this thing or that; Kit with her vitamins and supplements and exercises; Kit with her CDs of Mozart and headphones for Susannah to press against her abdomen, rocking her intestines to sleep; Kit stopping by with flowers and tea and that energetic, crushing concern; Kit imposing her vision of the world so oppressively that Susannah felt she could hardly see straight after talking to her; Kit with her perfect life, Kit in her little bubble that only Susannah had the power to puncture, though she didn't want to, though she'd tried so hard, until now, not to. And now there was this Floridian, in what had been Susannah's one time of peace in a year of aggravations, sitting beside her, crinkling up her beady eyes, cooing at her—"Feeling all right?"—and touching her, always touching her. Susannah stiffened, opened her eyes.

"Hmm?"

"Feeling okay? You look a bit pale, or something."

"Just tired," Susannah said, a little more snappily than she'd intended. Because even her *asking*, even just the way she'd *asked*, vexed Susannah into shuddering. Why couldn't people just leave her alone? Why wouldn't anyone ever leave anyone else alone? "My sister was sick all nine months with Frankie. Poor thing," the "poor thing" seeming universally to apply to the sister, Frankie, Susannah, anyone, everyone. As if they were friends, as if they shared some, any, degree of closeness, as if Dicey knew Susannah better than she knew herself; and maybe that was it, that Dicey had the plain face and knowing voice, the general yellowish tint of one of those women who always thought they knew you so well when you'd only just met, one of those women who would say, *Oh, that's just like you,* or, *It made me think of you.* Something in Susannah would buck against the assumed intimacy, because the woman, because Dicey, didn't know her at all, didn't have any right to ask was she feeling okay with that look of sickening goodwill. Susannah knew herself, or thought herself, to be particularly unknowable. Wasn't that what Aaron had always said—that she was unknowable (as if it were an indictment of her, and not just evidence of his own failings)? In any case, Dicey was a stranger, a Floridian or whatever, just another guest in a roadside motel. What need was there for them even to talk? Their lives had nothing to do with each other.

"Ha! Gotcha!" Frankie geysered out of the water near where the women sat and splashed Tim when he finally reached the pool's edge. The swimmers exchanged a sportsman's glance and then pushed off in the other direction. Susannah had lost track of the score, but it was turning into a different kind of game, anyway.

"I hear Frankie's really a boy," Susannah said to Dicey. She was feeling ruthless and like saying something to needle her.

"Oh, yeah?"

"That's what I hear. She says you just don't understand."

"Right!" cried Dicey a little too loudly, forcing out a laughlike sound. "We just don't understand! That's it. Of course, it's hard to play along when she runs into the men's room at a McDonald's on the side of the highway in the middle of nowhere, and you worry yourself sick about what will happen to her, disappeared in there with truckers and God-knows-what." Dicey's voice had taken on a changed, greenish hue.

"I see."

"I mean, I'm all for games and pretend and kids being kids, but it gets tiring."

Susannah's stranger spasmed, burbling, spinning into a fierce kick—*Hi-YAH*—like a pang of remorse. She shifted uncomfortably.

"Sorry," said Dicey, "it's not your problem."

They were quiet a while. Susannah felt the heat of Dicey's side boring into her arm.

Finally Dicey said, "Can I ask you something?"

"Sure."

"Why did you say Tim was your boyfriend?"

Susannah tried to gauge Dicey's expression, but she had turned away, her strawish hair parting around her ears, which glowed opalescently where the sunlight shone through. Susannah looked back toward the pool and said, trying to laugh, "Oh, I was just making a joke, I guess!"

They were supposed to have left in the morning, the drifting Floridians, and then it wouldn't have mattered at all. Still, it had been reckless of her, she knew that. Stupid. Like the month before, when she'd run into an old friend in the city and invented suddenly some story of a lover who'd been killed overseas, told how after hearing the news she'd discovered she was pregnant with his child—casting herself as this tragic single mother—and telling the whole thing with a weird half smile twitching at her lips, because she was not ever any good at lying, hoping that the whole thing would get back to Aaron somehow. The friend had been wide-eyed, nodding. And Susannah realized only afterward that this meant that she could not see the friend again, that with the unpremeditated lie she had made it impossible to refold the friend into her life, because then the lie would be revealed. She threw away the phone number the friend had given her. The distance between them was splayed open now. She made reentering her old life impossible. Stupid.

Now she was spangled with nerves, as if Dicey were saying they all knew that something was wrong with her, something wrong with her love for Tim—no, not a love exactly, just that she loved to look at him, just that she enjoyed his company, found him interesting, was all. But she thought she saw a complete appraisal of the situation in the twitch in Dicey's eyelid, like the change in Char's posture when she saw Susannah touch Tim's shoulder, and Susannah thought, my God, my God, I have got to get out of here.

"I see," said Dicey. A pause. "Do you really have a boyfriend?" Dicey seemed to be holding something large and hot in her chest, sucking in her breath as if to force whatever it was from bubbling up into her throat. Her voice was as orangey and single-noted as spray-on tan.

"Well, I must have gotten pregnant somehow, right?" Susannah knew she was being cruel but couldn't stop it. She almost believed herself.

"I guess so!" Dicey agreed. "I'm sorry. It's none of my business." She reached over and squeezed Susannah's hand—though her own hand trembled, clammy, as if this weren't the kind of gesture that came naturally to her. "You let me know if there's anything I can do for you."

"Ha!" Frankie screamed at the end of the pool. "Gotcha!" Tim bellowed in protest, like a sea lion, "No!"

Susannah looked up the Thunder Lodge sign, at the crudely wrought lightning bolt and furrowed thundercloud and neon raindrops that—had she noticed them before?—glimmered in the fading daylight and slid off the sign, puncturing the dusty ground. She watched this for a moment, unable to speak, until she realized that real raindrops were falling on her, too, and that Frankie and Tim were scrambling out of the pool, standing side by side in deflated swim trunks like funhouse versions of each other. That the sky had darkened, lowered, gone stewy with viscous, purple clouds. That the rain sluiced down, transforming the entire crew—Susannah, who was looking at Tim, who was looking at Frankie, who was looking at Dicey, who was looking at Susannah—into emaciated creatures the consistency of wet sand (Susannah thought of the beach with her cousins as a child, sitting on the shore and squinting in the sun, wet sand glopping through her knuckles to make a gnome's castle there by the lake; Becky and Scott laughing over some joke she didn't get), that this was—oh, it was a thunderstorm, that's what this was.

Tim clenched his fists with an inarticulate cry. Frankie and Dicey were laughing—it had all rolled in so quick—but the rain had started to hurt. "It's hail! It's hail!" Frankie shrieked. Now the darkness collapsed in closer, a rain cloud beard, a veiled and terrible Neptune come to punish Susannah, who stood there unable to stop staring at Tim, at his swimming trunks plastered to his crotch. Hail bounced across the pavement like Ping-Pong balls, looking senselessly light, absurdly fun. The pool churned with the invented current. Frankie, laughing, grabbed Tim's arm, and they ran toward the office.

Susannah would stay, would let the sky bruise her shoulders and back, would go icy and wooden as the sky landed in clumps all around. This was a sign, a miracle, a punishment. But Dicey had to go and ruin it—she threw her beach towel over Susannah and squeezed an arm around her waist, leaned in conspiratorially, cried, "Let's go!"

Then they were shivering in the climate-controlled office. Char sat at the counter, looked up from a crossword. "Hail season," she greeted them. Dicey was laughing and wiping hair off Susannah's face with motherly concern, and Susannah was trying not to look at Tim, who was tugging at his trunks, releasing hailstones like another storm. Marlon came in and took one look at them and started bellowing his Santa Claus laugh—"Ho, ho! Get caught in a gale? What a sorry bunch of sailors!"

In a few minutes the sky was back to blaring sunlight like a bullhorn. The motel's gravel skirt remained dark a moment longer. Susannah watched from the doorway. "Look, Frankie," she said, "it's like it never happened at all." Frankie crowded beside her in the doorway, touching her leg absently, looking without commenting, then went back to stare at the television programs Char had on—the cartoon stacked on top of a revival meeting beamed over from mid-Texas. Char shook her head, made a sound so sour it took Susannah a moment to identify it as a laugh. "It's just that season," Char muttered. "It's just how it goes." Marlon, perched on stool beside his wife, sighed at this, and popped his teeth in and out of his head, like a teenager fiddling with a new retainer. Susannah turned around, and there was Tim, having changed into sweatpants and a too-small T-shirt, standing too closely behind her. They looked at each other like that until Dicey said, "Does anyone want to go for a drive? I really feel like going for a drive. Anyone feel like going for a drive with me?"

Susannah looked away, about to say no, but then Frankie and Tim shouted, "Yeah!" as if in response to a silent one, two, three. Char was saying, "The new gas station up the road is just beautiful. Y'all could go up there, it's not too far. Tim likes the pinball machine by the bathrooms." She rested her weight on her slinged arm in a way that made Susannah wonder why the arm was in a sling at all.

"Yes," said Dicey, generously, carefully, "that does sound like a treat. Frankie and I went there last night, and you're right, it's real nice. Only I was thinking . . . well, this *is* a kind of vacation for me and Frankie. Isn't there anything . . . fun to do around here?"

Char shrugged, flipped her ropy braid, went back to her crossword puzzle. But Susannah remembered the flyers in her room—wasn't there a haunted cave somewhere nearby? Wouldn't everyone like to go to a haunted cave? If there was a haunted cave nearby, shouldn't they see it? When was the last time she'd done something for fun? Or, really, done anything but paddle her bloated body around that infernal swimming pool? "Of course!" bellowed Marlon, touching Char's elbow in a quick, proprietary way. "You kids should go see the haunted cave! Tim's never been, and it might be fun for him. Oh, come on—" This to Char, in response to some protest inaudible to the rest of them. "They might think it's fun."

The whole thing was so labored, so forced, this strained seeking of fun in the desert, this invented mission while Susannah was trying to just, Jesus, get away from all that—already she was tired of the idea, her enthusiasm leaking out, oil-spotting the pavement as she walked to her room and dressed quickly, afraid they would leave her behind.

Char stood in the gravel drive, glaring them off on their journey. Dicey drove, and Susannah fidgeted with the radio, and Dicey laughed and touched her arm like they were old friends. Frankie leaned forward in between the front seats, and Dicey kept saying, sit down, sit back, put on your seat belt, like a real mother. Tim sat woodenly behind Susannah, his hands flat on his thighs, his forehead pressed against the window. "Horses," he said as they pulled onto the road.

Susannah turned to him. "Horses? You said that when I first met you. Do you remember that? Horses . . . what are you talking about, you jackalope?" Tim giggled at this.

"Maybe he sees horses," Frankie said.

"That's right—maybe he's been to a rodeo down this way, or horseback riding."

"No, Aunt Dicey." Frankie rolled her eyes and collapsed into the seat. "That's not what I mean. I mean, maybe he sees horses *now,* like, only we can't see them."

Dicey frowned into the rearview mirror. "Is that true, Tim? What an imagination!"

Frankie rolled her eyes again, an eye roll expressing this time even greater and more delicately variegated layers of disgust. Meanwhile Tim was scowling, his fingers braided. "No. No. *Horses.*" And then he seemed to remember some private thought and giggled, rubbing his hands along his thighs, rocking back and forth.

They drove along the road that bowed across the barren plain like the spine of the earth. Cool air wheezed through the car. As the Thunder Lodge shrank behind them, Susannah's stomach turned. Because here they were in this gunmetal lifeboat, with only its thinnish mechanical skin between them and the elements. They hadn't brought water, cell phones—life vests of any practical sort. Soon Tim and Frankie were dozing guilelessly in the backseat, trusting in the munificence of the world. Dicey looked over her shoulder at them, then smiled at Susannah, who sat blanketed by an unfurled map she was pretending to study. Here they were, a mistranslated family, a foreigner's half-heard version, close to the real thing but not *quite,* and (Susannah squirmed in her seat, too big for the seat belt that bound her back), like a family, blind to the dangers around them, to the scorching, uninhabited weight of the world. An imitation of life, that's what this was.

The signs to the caves started early and with an enthusiasm out of all proportion to the attraction itself. GAS AND HAUNTED CAVES AHEAD! The wobbly, hand-painted wooden billboards were nearly illegible with age, screaming in blood-drippy letters, GHOSTS! GHOULS! GAS! 8 MI and THE GHOST OF JESSE JAMES'S MISTRESS SEZ, "GAS THIS CHEAP IS A CRIME!" Finally they neared the two-pump station, an inauspicious hump of shingles leaning away from the road, as if trying not to impose itself on anyone. Dicey pulled into the drive and stopped, squinted through the waves of dust eddying around. "Is it still open? Seems kinda . . ."

"Deserted?" said Susannah.

"Exactly."

They roused the children and went single-file into the station. A cluster of sleigh bells on the door sounded their entrance. They found themselves in an ordinary if dusty gas-station mart. Behind the counter a man in flannel sat dozing, his arms crossed in front of his chest, his bald head drooping at an alarming angle. Tim giggled as they entered, and said too loudly, "Caves! Yeah!" and the man sucked in a long strand of drool but didn't awaken. On the counter before him was a sign on folded cardboard like a dinner-party place card: HAUNTED CAVE OUT BACK FREE WITH PURCHASE OF GAS. Dicey shrugged and led the group through the back door, beneath an arch of microwavable-soup buckets and a lintel of wiper blades. The screen door slammed listlessly behind them.

There was a little swell in the earth behind the gas station, a six-foot-high rictus ratcheted open mid-yawn. A sign plunged into the ground read, ENTER AT YOUR 'OWN RISK.' So many signs ordering them around! Susannah squinted at the opening. "I don't know that I'll fit," she laughed, rubbing her belly. Tim frowned, tightening his fists. "Susannah in the caves," he said. "The caves!"

"Okay, okay, calm down, I'm coming." Tim's shoulders relaxed, and he followed Frankie, who had already entered the dim lobby of the cave.

It was just an ordinary cave, opening into an area the size of the Grotto. The cool air enveloped Susannah, swallowing her in one soppy gulp. "Ooh, it feels good in here," said Frankie. Moisture gathered on the tips of stalactites like sweat on a nose, dangling for instants before dropping. Dicey walked cautiously around the perimeter of the cave, one palm flat against the wall. Susannah saw Tim fisting his hands, straightening his back, dimly registered the underlying *uh-oh* of his posture, but she said nothing, peered into the zigzag of deeper warrens.

What was so terribly *haunted* about it, anyhow? It was haunting the way any landscape will be if you let it, or if you are tired, or have traveled a long way, or have something so ponderously on your mind that even the landscape seems to be thinking the same thing, but not really any more haunting than that. Susannah's eyes adjusted in jerky, clicking strides, a manual camera gone sticky. It hadn't occurred to her before that their whole desert landscape had beneath it these lacy organs, this intricate veining of hollowed-out spaces—the way human bodies were mostly water, the way atoms were mostly empty. The cool air pressed at her skin, perfuming her hair with must. Dicey followed Frankie deeper into the cave, while Tim squatted, brushing his fingers over the smooth ground. The dark parts of the cavern came surging up again, dazzling in the edges of Susannah's vision. She went hot all over, then hollow as the cave. I am hollow as the cave, she thought. There is no anything inside me. There is nothing.

Then three things happened.

First, the haunting of the cave began, which is to say there was a recorded volley of gunfire, and a wooden cutout of bandits, ghosts, apparently, albinoed with age, cranked out on a creaky set of chains, and presumably (if the delighted cries of Frankie and Dicey were any measure) a similar thing happened in the next chamber—oh, *that* kind of haunted cave!

The arrival of these ghosts caused the second thing, which was that Tim began to panic. Anyone who knew Tim, or anyone like him, knew how troubling such a scene might be. Somehow Susannah had not really believed it, had assumed that he was essentially just like anyone. Yet here he was, hunkered down on his haunches, cupping his hands over his ears, producing a wail as high-pitched and one-noted as a tornado siren, rocking back and forth and punching at his own head now and then. The punching at his head was what really frightened her, and she stared at him, unable to move.

Tim's screaming surely caused the third thing, which was the hurried arrival of the gas-station attendant, who had been roused from his nap by all the commotion and who burst into the cave crying, "Now, what in the hell?" (You fell asleep for an instant and look what happened! Still, a secret part of him was pleased. Just the other day, hadn't James been saying that the Haunted Caves were stupid, were a joke, wouldn't entertain a child? And look, here was a whole family, losing their minds over it. But when he'd heard screaming, he'd had to check—you never knew, in today's world. You didn't want to get sued.)

Susannah didn't faint, exactly—she didn't fall, anyway. Her eyes rolled back, and she took a few swoony steps backward (inside, she was hot and blinded and shimmering), and the gas-station attendant grasped her elbows, staggering under her weight. "Christ Almighty," he said, struggling to hold her, "what in the hell is going on down here?" Susannah's distress caused Tim's keening to take on a newly intense pitch. Dicey and Frankie rushed forward from the shadows, startling the gas-station attendant into nearly dropping the pregnant woman whose head lolled back onto his shoulder, and as Dicey was saying, "Get *away* from her," Susannah was blinking dozily and saying, "Who?" She turned to see the now-slack-jawed man shaking his head.

"See here. Uh, can't anyone get him to shut up?" he jerked his head toward Tim. But when Dicey knelt beside him and put a hand on his back, he clenched himself into a tighter, screamier ball.

Frankie matter-of-factly pattered over and said loudly enough so that her voice carried above the wailing, "I saw the BEST PEBBLES just outside here. I'm going to go get them ALL." Tim stopped crying, unstiffened cautiously. Frankie turned on her heel and left the cave. Tim stood and, grunting quietly now, dampish and snuffling, followed.

Which left Dicey to rush to Susannah's side and take her arm, and before she could say anything, the gas-station attendant stepped back with his palms shown in surrender, saying, "I just heard hollering and came running and saw the pregnant lady faint. I thought the boy maybe did something to her." Dicey grasped Susannah's elbow as they moved slowly into the light. "Oh, you poor dear," Dicey cooed, pawing at Susannah's head, as if the dishevelment of her hair were some serious sadness, "My goodness, did Tim try to touch you? Did he try to hurt you?" As they left, the cave sounded with another volley of canned gunfire, another set of ghastly cowboys rushing forth, swinging on their hinges.

Susannah shook her off. "God, no. Tim would never hurt a fly. Jesus, he got scared, was all." She waded out into the caramel muck of sunlight, tangibly gooey after the gray damp of the cave. "I just need . . . something to drink, I think. Something sweet." She was still light-headed, the darkness still bubbling in the edges of her vision.

Dicey nodded, dutifully followed the sighing attendant into the shop. In the gravel by a lone park bench, Frankie was counting pebbles as Tim watched.

Dicey soon reappeared by Susannah's side with a can of strawberry

soda. "I . . . we used to have this exact kind, all the time. I loved it," Susannah said. Dicey smiled, her whole face brightening.

Susannah drank thirstily. It was her cousins on the beach; it was
morning under the boardwalk. It was a darkish pink that clung to the
back of her throat. It was the exact flavor of homesickness—a too-
bright, sentimentally sweet version of itself, an unforgettable, irre-
sistible falseness. She looked at Dicey and thought, Pink. Neat. She
thought, Sea glass. Though she didn't know what to do with these
words yet, she bundled them up like a handful of stones, weighing the
heft in her hand, thinking, I might need these later.

Back in the car, the tank groaning with the gasoline the attendant
had forced them to buy, Susannah pressed her forehead against the
passenger-side window. The weight of their excursion clung to her
skin like sunscreen; she dragged a fingernail across her thigh as if to
scrape it off. She'd never fainted in her life. God! The whole thing had
been so *pregnant* of her. And Tim—he stared straight ahead in the
backseat, his face returned to normal but for his swollen eyes, his
lashes tamped into damp clumps. Tim was a boy. Tim was a troubled
boy, a boy with troubles. He giggled emptily, then muttered, "Caves.
Want to see the caves. Yeah!"

Dicey patted Susannah's thigh once, quickly. "You okay, hon?"

Susannah looked away. "Yeah."

Because, pressing her forehead against the glass, half blinded by
the eddies of sun-salted dust, she *was* okay. She saw clearly, now able
to grasp hold of some truth that had once been obscured—maybe the
faint in the caves had cleared her head—but there it was, as if it had always been there, waiting for her to notice it: They belonged together.
She saw it the way someone would see it from across the street—her
hair tangling prettily in the wind, the baby strapped to her chest in a
cozy sling, Tim walking straight and tall, Frankie between them holding on to their hands. Frankie calming Tim, and Tim calming Susannah. They could be a little family.

Because poor Frankie and poor Tim! Poor baby, to have to grow up in the unimaginative world of the Forsythes, under the conventional eye of dull Kit, dull Julian. Poor all of them, surrounded as they were by people who didn't know them. Julian didn't know what Susannah needed, not really, and anyway, he was utterly and irrevocably unavailable to her; the Garlands were made confused and ashamed by their son, and in this same way Dicey didn't know what to make of Frankie—she didn't really understand her, Susannah thought dozily, not the way Susannah did. Frankie couldn't go to her father's—she'd be eaten alive at some new school. Susannah and Frankie and Tim. Only all together did they make sense, and wasn't that what love was? Making each other make sense? Because what was this tingling in the back of her throat, this ache in her jaw, like a bubble had opened between her mouth and her spine? It was home—of course—that was it. It came cresting down her gullet like the too-sweet soda, as if she'd started to think it a thousand times before but only now really uncovered what it was—home was people, was these people. They could see her. She was a part of this.

At the Thunder Lodge, Marlon was out tinkering with Susannah's car and started waving as soon as he saw them on the road. "How was it?" he called. Dicey helped Susannah out of her seat.

"Oh, it was fine," said Susannah before anyone could say any different. "Fun! You ever been?"

Marlon laughed, wiping a wrench on a rag. "Nah. You like it, boy?"

Tim presented his father with a handful of pebbles. "Yeah." Marlon wordlessly extended a palm for Tim to fill with the stones, then slipped them into his pants pocket.

Dicey steered Susannah toward her room. "You wanna lie down?" Susannah could only nod. But Dicey knew what to do. Dicey was an expert when it came to comforting those with lives more dramatic than her own. She knew to say quietly to Susannah, "That's your idea of fun?"—making a joke of it but still acknowledging the lie, her complicity in it, her faint disapproval. She knew to take the key from Susannah's trembling hand and push open the door. They walked into the dim of the room. Pink. Neat. She pulled the door shut behind them, led Susannah to the bed. Sea glass. Susannah lay mutely down, unable to protest. The stranger had been silent for some time. In fact, he did not seem to be moving at all. Numb, biting her lips, Susannah leaned back into Dicey's lap. Dicey laid a hand on Susannah's belly, and Susannah felt heat mizzle through her limbs. It felt good to relax in this way. It felt foreign and new and good. "Can I feel?" Dicey asked, her hands passing over the belly.

"He's moving around, right?" said Susannah. "He's okay, right?"

"He's fine, just fine," said Dicey. She laughed. "So he's a boy, then?"

Susannah nodded. It was difficult to remember why she'd found Dicey so annoying earlier in the day—except that maybe she just wasn't used to people being so nice. How ridiculous, how absurd. She was allowed to be with people like Dicey, people who were kind, of course she was. She didn't have to be around people who were always testing her, always pushing her, who knew themselves to be superior but who still made everything a contest, every conversation, every interaction. Everyone wasn't Rose, Aaron, Kit. It was okay that Dicey was nice to her, was stroking her hair, saying there, there.

"Will you tell me a story?" Susannah said. She laughed at how childish it sounded. "Anything. I'm just tired of myself. I'm so tired of myself, and I want to hear about somebody else. Tell me about Frankie's parents. Tell me about Alabama." As she said this, she saw three coins slip out of Dicey's jeans pocket, and when Dicey wasn't looking, Susannah pushed the coins under her palm. She would start restocking her glove box. Stone. Fork. Coin.

Dicey smiled. "Well, I don't know if it'll make you feel any better, but I'll tell you whatever you want to know." Susannah lay there a long time, listening to Dicey, before drifting into sleep.

4

THE ACCIDENT

Throughout the pregnancy Susannah saw them mostly at their place and by night, like a mistress. Or she would meet them at the doctor's office or, in the beginning, at the lawyer's, their faces rendered unreadable by the formality of the setting. Julian and Kit had no real idea of what her life was like, had only the vaguest understanding of what she did at the bookstore (though, to be fair, Susannah had only the vaguest interest in the job herself) or of how little she was paid or of her massive student-loan debts; they didn't know that she was an only child, a Pisces, a failed vegetarian, that she was afraid of flying, that she secretly loved musicals, that she'd always wished she were left-handed; that she had recently declared herself— in a bar, reunited with some old college friends, giddy from having drunk too much too fast and being around so many people—to be a virgin, as she'd been fucked before but never *made love to* (a declaration she'd thought very witty and biting but which no one had heard over the wail of the jukebox); that though she lived a mile from her mother, they spoke maybe once a month, *maybe;* that she wanted to do something interesting, something reckless, something to differentiate herself from others; that she suspected she didn't really matter much to anyone; that she, like anyone, was capable of terrible things: Julian and Kit suffered no knowledge of the recent, bitter breakup with

Aaron and the painful crisis of faith, of something, of whatever, that had led her to this, to this answering of an ad in the paper. (They'd argued about this, she would find out later from Julian—Kit had insisted no one looked in actual newspapers anymore, but Julian had prevailed. Julian specifically wanted the kind of person who still looked at ads in the physical newspaper. He wanted a woman who would consider their offer while rubbing her fingers together to release the smudgy smell of the ink.) They didn't even know that she hadn't really answered the ad in the newspaper at all, that she had seen them hunched over their sugary coffees, parsing the verbiage of what would be the ad, right there in the winking fluorescence of the bookstore; that she had watched Julian watch Kit try not to cry; that she had turned back toward the shelves when Julian excused himself to use the men's room; that she was the girl he'd walked by, the softly curving hips he'd noticed, for a split second, not even realizing he was looking, as she knelt down to reach a low shelf and her jeans strained against her skin.

Throughout the whole process, Julian came to her apartment occasionally, and always alone. She knew not to mention this to Kit. She would be attempting a crossword at her kitchen table, actively thinking, This is a stupid waste of time, I need to get up right now and clean up or do *something*, but unable to, sitting there stunned by her own inertia when the buzzer would bark through the air. Ugh! She was irritated by her own skin, angered by the air around her. And who was *this* now? No one she knew was the visiting-unannounced type, so this must be someone with the wrong buzzer, someone who should just go away and leave her alone already! But no, that would be Julian leaning on her bell, looking ridiculously well defined, sharp-edged, there in the shabby entryway, exuding his air of certainty and cleanliness, his scent of shampoo and chestnuts and something expensive, maybe leather car seats. Something would leap in her chest—some ill-conceived thought she immediately tried to bury, because it wasn't right to look at him and think, Why couldn't I have someone like that? I want to have someone like that.

"Oh. Hey," she said with a nervous laugh, standing in the doorway of her building. He took hold of the door but made no move to enter. The irritation subsided, a tide in her throat.

Bulb, thought Susannah. Minnow. Snail.

A neighbor brushed past them, hurrying out into the street.

"You're probably busy. I'm sorry if you're busy."

Or not snail, exactly, but the brittle crisp of its shell, the sheeny moment of panic after crunching one underfoot, before realizing what one has done. The glittery trail that is left.

It was maybe four or five months in.

"It's okay."

"I was in the neighborhood. Kit's out of town for the weekend, and I've been wandering around like a maniac. I don't know what to do with myself." The unsaid *Can I come in?* hung in the air a moment before plinking to the ground, valuable and lost as a dropped coin. Susannah leaned against the wall, some twang spasming in her spinal cord. The entire street gathered at Julian's back—all the energy and heat and bustle bundling itself into a mass that Julian alone protected her from. This whole world that we carry around with us, Susannah was thinking, but she was already tired by the thought. Julian shifted his weight, and for a horrible, beautiful instant, Susannah thought he was leaning in to kiss her. Finally! She knew that if he tried, she would kiss him back, that she would lead him into her apartment, that she would let him do whatever he wanted to her, that her body already belonged to him anyway, and that all he had to do was to stake his claim over the rest of her, and that then she would be done for.

"I don't know where I'd be without Kit," said Julian suddenly. "I'm a mess without her! She's only gone a few days, and I just . . . I just don't know where I'd be without her."

"Me too!" said Susannah, too loudly.

"She's such a rock," said Julian, "so strong," standing there with his weight evenly divided between his legs, back straight, like a drawing of a man.

"Oh, yeah." She tangled her fingers together behind her back, trying to keep still. "Though I was . . . well, I mean, I sort of was kidding. I mean to say, I don't know what I would do without her, because, you know, well, I certainly wouldn't be, that is, like this. I mean, I guess not. Ha." She gestured toward her midsection. It had become a part of her body that got gestured toward a lot lately, this alien length of her. She would point it out to people the way she'd point out a train station to lost tourists, this part of her that no longer belonged to her but to its tenants, Julian and Kit. She had become the landlord of her own biology. (Maybe after this she'd fashion a sign to wear around her neck: WOMB FOR RENT! She'd never have to shelve another book again, never have to haggle with customers over the expiration date of their coupons or the policy on returns!) Or—she wasn't even the landlord so much as the groundskeeper. She kept explaining it like this, anyway, to people who asked questions. Because people— at the bookstore or the Laundromat, there was nowhere quite safe from it—asked a lot of questions. This part of it she actually enjoyed, in what she knew was a sick way; she enjoyed stoppering inquiries with answers like, "Oh, this baby's not mine," and watching the confusion play on people's lips. She savored the final, "What a good person you are. What an *angel,*" in whichever permutation it came, and it always came. "I could never be so brave. You're a hero. And she would answer, "Oh, no, no, don't be silly, it's not like that at all. It's just business; it's all business. Do you know how much money I'm making? I don't even have to *do* anything!" She'd even convinced herself that this was true, or she'd tried to, anyway. She really had tried.

Really, she had become her own planet, with her own atmosphere. She carried with her at all times her own weather, a temperature she invented herself; she was always overheated, the engine of her belly emitting waves of warmth like the breeze from a space heater, crackling around her vast interior spaces. Since becoming pregnant, since being implanted, injected, whatever, Susannah had come to feel that she was living in the world without quite being of it; she was bobbing along the earth's surface, being blown across the plains of the globe as ponderously as a hot-air balloon. Loosed entirely from whatever life she'd once had. She found herself avoiding friends, throwing away Aaron's letters unopened, not answering Rose's calls—she didn't have to deal with any of that anymore, wasn't that the joy of it? She was a new breed now, entirely distinct from the world they inhabited. As for human contact beyond conversation with strangers, as for a smile or a hand on her wrist, she surfaced only occasionally, like a whale sipping in air, sucking in an afternoon with her mother or a lunch with a coworker before slipping back into her self-contained airlessness. She stopped calling her mother back (her mother had been strange about the whole thing, anyway, had shrugged and said, "Whatever you want to do, dear," when Susannah had first brought it up, and hadn't said much about it since), she stopped going to meet friends, stopped answering e-mails—she didn't feel like interacting with anyone but the stranger riding around on her hipbones.

Susannah had, of course, expected none of this. She had thought, silly as it now seemed, that she was doing a simple good deed and that her body would take over, that she would scarcely notice the pregnancy, that it would be like sticking another fern in an overcrowded greenhouse. That it wouldn't change anything. That she was doing it to help. That she was doing it for the money and for an interesting change of pace. That it was, as she kept saying, all business.

"Well," said Julian, when neither of them had spoken for a few beats.

"Well," said Susannah.

The baby bobbed, a drip of mercury poisoning a length of glass.

"Would you like to get some coffee . . . er, tea . . . or, you know, decaf, whatever?"

"Sure! Let's do it." Oh, *God.* She went back to her apartment for her things and met him back in the street. When she saw him, she noticed he had missed a sliver of stubble when shaving. The tiny silver studs stung in a scythe shape near his ear. He looked old in the sunlight. He looked his age. It seemed unlike him to have missed a strip while shaving, and her discovery of this made Susannah feel embarrassed.

She watched him as they walked. His was a face that would always be agreeable, even as his skin started to slacken ever so slightly with exhaustion from being alive so long, from suctioning to his angular bone structure, his hawkish nose, for fifty years or whatever. Forty-five. Half a century! His eyes were startlingly blue, the kind of blue that was so bright and clean and unexpected, somehow, that Susannah usually forgot that his eyes were blue at all, and each time she saw him, she was surprised by them. His graying hair curled softly at his temple. As they walked down the street, chatting mindlessly about Kit's weekend away—or pretending that that's what they were talking about anyhow, as if neither of them noticed the true direction of the conversation, the way Kit was a red herring, a dummy URL redirecting to what they needed to get to—it occurred to Susannah that someone might think they were any married couple expecting a child. She looked at Julian differently then as if he were her husband or a man she loved or was interested in, a man she might sleep with. She had slept with men before, but none as handsome as Julian—Aaron would have looked ridiculous beside him; scruffy and childish—and she allowed herself for a moment to wonder what that would be like.

Because he dressed himself impeccably. Because he wore tailored suits on workdays and too-perfect blue jeans and crisp shirts on weekends, and an oddly stylish leather coat. Because his teeth were straight and a shade too white. Because he never ran his fingers through his hair or laughed out loud, really; because of that close-lipped chuckle. But, thought Susannah with something like relief, he could never be my husband. No, of course that's ridiculous, and of course he wouldn't leave Kit—they're perfectly happy together and will make perfectly great parents—and no, there is nothing between us but money, and flesh. Well, it was settled, then. There it was.

So they traveled down the street, not a married couple, not even a couple, and at the coffee shop on the corner Julian swung the door open for her with a grand sweep of his arm. The bells tinkled to sound their arrival. Everyone in the coffee shop looked up, the glow of their laptops illuminating their pale faces, a sea of tiny moons.

Susannah sat, and he brought her herbal tea that was much too hot, handing it to her in a way that made it impossible for her to reach the handle, so that she had to press her fingers to the steaming rim. She tried not to wince at the beads of pain in her fingertips.

"Well!"

"Well!"

"How are you feeling? Kit said you'd been queasy."

"Ha. For about five months now, yeah. The age of nausea. But I think it's getting better." She'd been feeling better for months but for some reason stuck with the nausea bit, which tended to inspire sympathetic cooing.

You could tell that Julian had been a husband for some time. He glazed over instantly, staring into the recesses of the coffee shop, nodding. "Mmm-hmm." The mmm-hmm wasn't uncaring; on the contrary, he managed to express a lot with it—sympathy, empathy, interest, a healthy dose of "I'm listening to every word." This was how you could tell that he was no hobbyist, but an experienced husband. He couldn't seem to get situated in his seat on the low-slung couch, with its malleable cushions that slopped to the sides like batter in a bowl. Susannah watched him from the armchair he had offered her. He and Kit probably frequented proper establishments with proper chairs. He soon dropped the pretense of listening to her at all and twisted around in his seat, trying not to move too much while readjusting his entire body, leaning forward and tugging jerkily at the cushion beneath him, squatting above the couch as if to mark his territory but then only pushing the cushion into place again and sitting heavily upon it and starting the whole process over again. Finally he leaned back, seemingly exhausted. Now and then he tried to shift the cushion as they spoke. His face became flushed with the effort, his eyes taking on a distant sheen. He would say something and then spasm bizarrely to one side or the other. "The most beautiful girl in the world," he said, as if choosing a topic in a game show. Susannah's spine went hot. The stranger slammed around her midsection, moshing today to some unhearable rock music. "Kit," Julian went on. "The first time I saw her, I thought, 'This is the most beautiful girl in the world.'" Oh. Susannah stared into her tea. Right. Yes. Oh, what a woman.

Julian pressed ahead. Yeah, he was a husband, all right. No unmarried man would have gone on like that to a woman, even a woman in her particular situation, which was maybe too particular a situation to be a kind of thing at all. It was only the thing itself. Susannah looked around the coffee shop, struck dumb by the world. What was going on here? She was carrying Julian's child? But why on earth? . . . She sipped at her boiling-hot tea and burned herself; her tongue became a pink eraser, heavy in her mouth. Julian said, "Kit thinks the world of you, she does. We both do."

"Oh," said Susannah. "Well. Thanks."

"Listen, she asked me to ask you this. Er, the baby shower. You know?"

Susannah looked at him blankly.

"We're having a baby shower, some of her friends are, anyway, I mean, our friends. In a few months. We'd love for you to be there."

As if it hadn't been enough, everything she had done! "Oh," and it came out strangled, and she looked away. "Oh, God, but I hate parties."

"But this wouldn't be bad. It would be fun! You'd be, you know, the guest of honor." Julian smiled apologetically. Susannah understood that Kit had fed him the lines, probably word for word. What a farce it all was.

"Yeah," was what she could manage. She squeezed her injured tongue between her teeth, twisting it one way, then the other.

"Just show up and smile and let everyone ooh and ah over you—that's probably what usually happens to you at parties, anyway, right?" He forced an awkward, avuncular laugh. "And Kit opens a bunch of presents. No big deal, right? And then you go, 'Oh, God, look at all that stuff! Oh, wow! Julian and Kit won't get a good night's sleep for years now! They'll be changing diapers while I'm out partying!'"

Susannah's eyes stung. "Yep!" she squeaked out. Partying!

A long pause passed between them. Julian shook his head. "Don't you ever find that you can be told about something a million times and still be surprised by it? Like with falling in love—you can hear a million love songs, see a billion romantic movies, but when it's happening to you, it still feels surprising and unbelievable and new."

Susannah nodded. God, she loved when Julian got like this, when he said things that seemed so true, things she wanted to go home and scribble down, to carry with her and reread every day. He continued, "I know people keep saying we're going to love this baby so much we can't stand it. That the feeling will be like nothing we've ever felt before. And I can imagine it, of course. I already love it in a way—but I don't *feel* it yet. But I know that I will, and that it will be entirely unlike what I'm expecting, but that once it happens, I'll describe it the same way it's always been described to me, only now it will mean so much more. You know?"

"Exactly!" said Susannah. Could she tell him—he would understand, wouldn't he?—about how she felt? About how people had said she would start to feel something for the baby, about how it would be hard to think of it as someone else's, about how she'd thought they were being silly, melodramatic, but now how she knew they were right, how she felt it? No, she shouldn't, probably. She sipped at her tea.

"Anyway. So here I am, about to be someone's dad—not just myself, not just an ordinary person, but someone's dad, doomed to years of children's birthday parties," Julian said seriously, as if the truth of this had only just sunk in. "Children's birthday parties! Some life I'll have."

"Oh, come on. It'll be fun."

"My God. Clowns and balloons and crying kids." He laughed. "I really don't know if I can handle that." He grabbed Susannah's shoulders in mock terror. "What have I gotten myself into?" When the Forsythes were together, they presented a unified enough front, but once Susannah and Julian were alone, he spoke as if the baby had all been Kit's idea, something he'd been hoodwinked into. Susannah smiled. It was too easy to join forces with him, to implicitly exclude Kit, to blame her.

"Aw, it'll be all right. I like kids' parties. I mean, I guess I haven't been to one in a long time. But come on, they're fun."

"Okay, you go. We'll call you every time the kid gets an invitation, and you can take him. I'll be at home, drinking martinis."

"No, you'll have to come! You'll run the balloon-animal stand."

Susannah could see the whole thing: She'd be bustling across the room with a toddler on her hip, catching Julian's desperate look as he swiped at a puddle of spilled ice cream, a ribbon adhered to his head. "That's just it!" Julian said, "I can't do balloon animals! I can't do anything!"

"Well, you can clean up the wrapping paper and things."

"Oh, thanks. Think I can handle that much responsibility?"

"I'm sure you're good at something! I mean, a man as old as you has to have struck on something he can do."

Julian laughed. She was proud to have made him really laugh, not just a polite chuckle but a genuine laugh. "Ouch!" he said. "A man as old as me! Well, you'd hope so anyway, but honestly, I'm useless."

"I love all that kid stuff," Susannah said. "Birthday parties and playgrounds and zoos and amusement parks." She saw herself pushing a stroller through the entrance of the city zoo, Julian's arm slung around her shoulders.

"I bet you do." He said it admiringly. "I bet kids love you. I bet you'd get crazy and silly and dance around and invent songs and games—I bet you'd get down on your knees and dig in the dirt and build snow forts. I worry about that. Kit would never do anything like that."

Kit's name landed on the table like a length of lead. Hearing it made Susannah go hot all over. What were they *doing?* Imagining this life for themselves, fantasizing about being parents together, about their nonexistent family? She didn't remember, suddenly, how any of it had started, how they had ever let themselves start talking this way. Julian refused to meet her eyes, busily examining his own hands. Her mortification was complete.

"Kit will be a wonderful mother," Susannah managed to say.

"Of course she will. I shouldn't have said that. I didn't mean to say that," Julian mumbled, without looking up. Susannah thought she might be sick. She rubbed her hands over her belly, nervously straightening her shirt, pulling her sweatshirt smooth, patting obsessively at the wrinkles in the fabric.

Julian leaned back in the couch and then forward again and then back again. His face passed behind a cloud. "Think what great practice this all is," he said, his voice changed. He was moving away from her, toward Kit, toward real life.

"Ha. Yeah."

"What an experience to have had. So interesting."

"Oh, very."

"Do you think you'll ever have kids?"

The woman reading the paper at the other end of sofa looked up sharply at Julian, then to Susannah's bulging stomach and back to him again. Susannah put her hands on her belly, patting the stranger's head. "Oh," she said laughingly, "who knows? I don't think I want to."

They went walking then, and it seemed to her that Julian walked too close to her. Their arms bumped again and again, and he'd laugh and pat her back or arm. But maybe it was just what it seemed not to be, simply this man expressing how friendly they were, how they were such pals that they could touch without the possibility of misinterpretation. Then he slung his arm around her shoulders but, catching himself, quickly extracted it. They talked about nothing in particular, which was better than talking about the baby, which made Susannah's chest flare and sizzle in a crippled display of heat, an amateur fireworks finale. They posed hypothetical questions to one another in the way of people who don't know each other at all, or of people who know everything about each other and therefore have nothing else to talk about. They asked each other questions like, "What would you bring to a desert island?" And, "Which would you rather bite into, an underripe tomato or an orange with the peel still on?" And, "Would you rather lose a leg or an arm? All your teeth or all your hair?" Susannah was saying, "Oh, here's a good one: Would you rather eat mud or dirt?" Julian considered this one carefully. "Mud would go down quicker I guess. Now you, would you rather drown or burn to death?"

She wanted to tell him things, to tell him everything that had ever happened to her, to tell him about the summer her mother had sent her away, about her baby brother who was born dead, about the months she'd lived with her cousins and the dog, Cooper, that ran away, about the games she played with Rose, about stacking marshmallows on top of shells and realizing that she was really alive; she wanted to tell him everything that popped into her mind. *Today I saw a half-smashed bird getting pecked at by another bird,* she wanted to tell him. *I saw a man riding a very tall bike.* And she wanted to know everything that had happened to him all day, everything he had seen;

she was hungry for every detail. She blurted out, "Tell me everything about yourself!" and then looked away, embarrassed. But he only laughed and said, "Well, where to start . . . ? I was adopted when I was six months old. Can you imagine having your baby for six months and then giving it up? Six months just seems like a long time to be with a kid and then give it up, but what do I know? Maybe I wasn't such a charming kid. My parents are old, almost ninety—they got the idea to adopt pretty late in life. I never did the whole trying-to-find-my-birth-parents thing. Just—ach, no thanks." Adopted! It was fascinating. Everything about him was fascinating; everything he said was the most fascinating thing ever said. And just listening, just walking alongside him, made her feel fascinating, too. She wanted to give him everything, everything. She found herself talking about Aaron, saying things she'd never said to anyone, about how he'd always made her feel ordinary and boring and depleted—and the way Julian looked at her when she said it made her feel like it was impossible she'd ever felt ordinary and boring and depleted. She was beautiful! She was enchanting! She was fascinating! All because of the way Julian looked at her. He reached out and squeezed her hand; she laughed and touched his arm. Their movements were jerky with the strain of holding back. He told her about the first concert he'd ever been to, the first instrument he'd ever played, the things he wanted to do.

"If you could go anywhere in the world, where would it be?" she asked him. She had a million more questions like it. Everything, everything!

Julian considered this. "I've never been to the desert—to the Southwest. I guess I'd like to see it. What about you?"

Susannah couldn't think of a thing she wanted in the world more than walking like this with him. They were by the lake, on the path in the park. She glimpsed the lighthouse on its little island. "I'd like to see the ocean," she said.

Julian laughed. "We're opposites, then! Complete opposites."

This seemed fascinating, too. But—the desert and the ocean, weren't they kind of the same thing? Susannah wanted to know. They talked and talked and talked.

When he dropped her off at her door, he stood facing her and patted the outsides of her arms as if fluffing her for an embrace that didn't come, obviously. Obviously all they could do was stand there and look into each other's eyes for a few seconds at a time before looking nervously away, heat rocketing between them. The baby seemed to swim toward Julian. "It's going, 'Daddy! That's my daddy!'" she said, and Julian laughed and gently moved aside her open jacket to pat her belly. "Hey, kiddo," he said, "Hey, keep cool in there, man. Sit tight," and then he pulled his hand away and said to Susannah, "You know, when this baby is born, it will be my first blood relative I've ever known. Isn't that funny? I've never been related to anyone before." Susannah smiled, not knowing how to answer. He had told her all this before, but maybe if she held very still, rabbit-in-the-open still, he would tell her again. "I can't wait to meet this kid," said Julian, and she said, "Me neither," and they laughed. The heat from his hand glowed through her shirt, and after they said good-bye, awkwardly shifting around and deciding at the same time to hug instead of shake hands, a back-patting, loosely wound and friendly hug, Susannah went upstairs into her apartment and pulled up her shirt and could have sworn she could still see his handprint, the fingers burned into her skin, pulsing like stigmata.

THOSE LAST FEW months, then, the three of them met weekly. This seemed to Susannah like an awful lot—still, and maybe it was a function of her youth or maybe it was a glut of empathy, but she didn't know how to say no—and to Julian and Kit like hardly ever. The Forsythes wanted her to stay with them always. It was easier to pretend this way that the process was something organic, something easily shared, passed between them like love, or a tangle of knitting. So Susannah trotted over, a child indulging Grandma. They showered her with gifts and books and treats, offered expensive delicacies, fed her chocolate-covered lychees and starfruits and other things she'd never heard of. If Susannah felt ill, Kit suffered along with her, pressed cool hand to damp forehead. If the baby started kicking, Kit felt his little heels with the palm of her own hand.

When Kit was around, Julian hardly looked at Susannah, as if he didn't trust himself to—and as soon as his wife left the room, he would rush forward with some question or private joke. It was strange to see him with Kit. He seemed more like himself when they were alone together. Of course neither of them mentioned his visits around Kit—Susannah somehow knew not to bring it up, even though it wasn't like they did anything wrong. They only talked and talked and talked, but still Susannah knew that it wasn't what they were supposed to be doing, that Kit would be upset if she knew, and the idea that Kit would be upset made it seem all the more illicit and delicious. Julian winked at her behind Kit's back, patted her hand. He'd call her, later, deep in the night, just to share some ordinary detail, something he'd wanted to tell her. He knows what he's doing, it occurred to Susannah. But . . . what *is* he doing?

With just under two months to go, they had Susannah over for breakfast on a Sunday. Kit drank two mimosas and started speaking recklessly. "I had another one of those horrible moments last week at work."

Susannah looked at her. "Oh, no. What happened?"

"It's happened a million times, and I still hate it. It's the old, 'Yes, we're expecting a baby in two months,' and then the blank look. It just blows people's minds, like you've actually injured their brains by saying it. And the stuttering, 'Oh! Um, wow. You look . . . great.' I mean, what are they, retarded? How could I possibly be seven months pregnant?"

As she watched Kit mock-pat her own flat midsection, Susannah felt outrageously huge and fleshy and fat. Still, she could see how it would be awful in a way. Kit didn't want to be strange. Kit didn't want to injure people's brains by doing something so out of the ordinary. Which was why Kit waved a hand and said breezily, "So then you say, 'There's a surrogate carrying the baby,' and they kind of laugh and say, with such fucking relief it's unbelievable, 'Oh, of course, of course! How wonderful! My old boss had a cousin whose neighbor had a surrogate,' or something ridiculous like that. God, it's annoying." Then she took another sip of her mimosa and blurted, "Oh! And we've named him! We've decided on a name" (They knew it was a boy by then. On hearing the news, Julian had felt a long, low surge through his gut, an internal sigh of relief. Susannah meanwhile felt both like she'd known all along it was a boy and like it couldn't possibly be right that it wasn't a girl. She had told her mother she thought it was a girl, just felt it was a girl somehow, and her mother had clapped her hands together and exclaimed, "A granddaughter!" "No, Ma," Susannah'd said, her stomach shipwrecking against her chest, "Not yours. Not ours. You're just not getting this." Her mother seemed to think Susannah was hiding something from her, seemed to keep thinking that Susannah had gotten pregnant on her own and was giving the baby to the Forsythes for adoption or something, still thought there was some chance of keeping it as Susannah's own. She just didn't get the whole concept and was trying to be nice about it, to not ask questions or get involved, in a way that was driving Susannah insane. When the whole thing was so impossible.)

And here was Kit, pointing at Susannah with a folded slice of bacon. "Oh?" said Susannah, looking at Julian. "You named him?" With a friendly, casual pat to her own belly.

Kit was waving the bacon around, saying breezily, "But of course we're not telling anyone. We've decided not to tell anyone, because you know how it is, darling, one person finds out someone else knows and then everyone has to know, and you know how people get, they get so *judgmental* about this kind of stuff, and we don't want to start questioning things, because it's such a big decision after all, and we're pretty sure this is the one, and you know, we were talking it over half the night, how if you just name the baby and *then* tell everyone the name once it's here, they can't very well tell you they hate it, can they?"

Susannah blinked, laughing a little. She'd gotten used to Kit by now and just dabbed at her mouth and smiled at Julian. He shrugged evasively.

"So you see we can't very well tell you and no one else, now, can we? My mother would just die if we told someone else and not her." Kit rolled her eyes, as if her mother were there at the table. Then Kit jumped up, went to the kitchen to pour more coffee for herself and Julian, more orange juice for the surrogate.

Susannah looked at Julian, her smile fading. "So you're not going to tell me?" She tried to make her voice sound light, imitating that way Kit had of never sounding too serious about anything, never overcommitting to the gravity of a statement, but the trick didn't work for her, and she just sounded plaintive and shrill. In so many ways, she was still a child.

Julian pressed his lips together. (What an uncomfortable morning! He tapped his fingers on the table, waiting for breakfast to end. Could he read the paper? He eyed it, still tidily folded there on the extra chair against the dining-room wall. Susannah was part of the family, right? And he always read the paper when he and Kit were having breakfast together. He had never read the paper while having breakfast with anyone before Kit, with Evvie Saunders or Janet Weiss or any of the women he'd ever lived with or dated, and this was how he'd known that they really were married, he and Kit. Reading the paper at breakfast was such an intimacy, wasn't it? So couldn't he? Wouldn't it be a sign of familial love and trust toward Susannah, an extended arm of friendship? Proof that he was comfortable enough around her not to need to prattle on about work or the baby, about

this thing or that? That he was leaving everything up to the ladies—
wasn't that what they ultimately wanted? But he couldn't upset Kit,
and he couldn't upset Susannah.) Finally he mumbled, "Would you
like to go for coffee sometime? Might be easier to talk then," just before Kit came back to the table.

"What are you two lovebirds whispering about?" Kit emphasized
the word *love* mockingly. She could be the meanest person in the
world sometimes.

Susannah went red. "What!"

Kit laughed. In the back of her mouth, a pair of silver fillings
glinted like eyes. "You've gotten awfully cozy, haven't you? You're two
peas in a pod. It's adorable, really."

Julian just looked at Susannah and rolled his eyes teenagerishly,
but Susannah had seen the look that flashed across Kit's face, the truth
in it, the edge. It was a look that made Susannah blurt out an ill-
advised, "What are you talking about?"

"Oh, Su, don't get upset now. I think it's sweet, I really do, how
Julian has his old-man crush on you—you should hear the way he
talks about you! It doesn't bother me in the least. I mean, I sort of
picked you, you know, for all of this, so it really makes me proud more
than anything. See, Julie, I told you I'd pick a good one!"

No one called Susannah "Su" but Kit. Susannah liked it despite
herself, or at least couldn't resist the intimacy it forced upon her. She
studied Kit's face. Her features were intensely bright and sharp, as if
chiseled out of marble. You could cut your hand on the tip of her
nose, nick your fingertips with those cheekbones. Her eyes looked desperate and hungry, and Susannah knew that Kit was only trying to get
a rise out of Julian, that Julian was gently deferring this particular re-
quest for attention. He cleared his throat and refolded a section of the
newspaper. The paper clattered like thunder.

"God, we could have saved so much money, Julie. You could have
just fucked her."

Susannah excused herself to use the bathroom.

It was horrible, horrible. When they'd done nothing wrong; they'd been so careful to do nothing wrong. There she stood in front of the sink, trembling, hot prickles all over, feeling poisoned by the gory pulp of the orange juice, the tang of bacon, the salt in Kit's voice, the acidic afterburn of the whole thing. She could hear the rumble of Julian piping in too late, the even replies of Kit like little underlines to his sentences. Susannah felt suddenly like such an *accessory*, just another thing for a married couple to squabble about, as helpful but as essentially superfluous as the doctors and nurses and manufacturers of baby clothes—just another hired gun committed to this little family, just another satellite drawn to the orbit of the Forsythes, sucked in by the gravitational pull of their money, oh, their fucking money. They drew in so many people with their money that it functioned like a kind of warmth, an extra layer of skin—her and the doctors and yoga teachers and masseuses and nannies, and, Jesus, that was right, they were probably going to hire a nanny. Why hadn't Susannah thought of this, that Kit couldn't, wouldn't, leave the career she'd worked so hard for and would hire a nanny, wouldn't even raise the kid herself, and after all Susannah's work! Everything she'd done for them! That they wouldn't even tell her the name of the baby, the creature spreading throughout her whole body like a poison. The stranger. Who were Julian and Kit, anyway? How had Susannah ever talked herself *into* this? It was a thing you heard about other people doing, not a thing you actually did! This was her life, her youth, the only one she'd ever have! And whatever she'd imagined she shared with Julian—whatever special bond that linked them, whatever attraction he had for her—it was as ridiculous as Kit had made it sound.

She closed her eyes, let the faucets run.

In the dining room, Kit kissed Julian's cheek in reluctant apology ("Oh, I was only joking—don't be so grouchy at me"), picked up the front section of the paper, commented on the top headline. The ordinary patterns of their life, their breakfasts, oozed over Susannah's absence like wet sand filling a footprint. Julian spoke through gritted teeth, "And why did you tell her we named him if you weren't going to tell her the name?" Kit peered at him over the edge of the paper, as if he were a stranger on a subway.

"What?"

"Nothing."

SUSANNAH PRUE WAS not much given to making scenes, but what Kit had said lodged in her gut and festered there. She spent the afternoon at work reshelving a stack of baby-naming manuals as thick as dictionaries. They had been left sprawled across a café table in the bookstore by a gaggle of teenage girls, whose whipped-cream-capped drinks had powered them through an entire lifetime of browsing—from fashion rags to bridal magazines all the way to the baby-naming books. Susannah's smock rode up over her belly as she reached for the highest shelf.

Or she went to the aquarium alone. She stalked down the pier like a prisoner walking the plank, past the planetarium to the puddley park. The lake splashed up around in fishy, unclean eruptions. The sky draped around the city. Was it always gray here? Had it always been gray? Inside, light filtered from the water boxes dreamily into the empty aquarium rooms. Susannah moved through them without looking very carefully at the fish, at the bright crabs and captive sea horses. The muted light, the hush of the carpet, the burble of the tanks, the underlying hum. The tanks like watery eyes. She stood in the center of the shark room and tried to think.

She found herself calling Julian, something she almost never did. Why should she have any contact with them at all, other than for doctors' visits, other than for official Baby Business? And why did she feel so nervous while waiting for him to answer, as if she were calling a boy she liked? "Yes, yes, yes, everything's fine, just great!" she said.

"I was just going to call you," he said.

She walked around the tiny kitchen of her apartment, speaking too loudly into the cordless phone, because as usual her connection was burred with static. On the fire escape out the window, pigeons moved around as if socializing at a party.

Julian guessed immediately. He said it in such a way that made Susannah deny it at all costs. "What? Oh, I guess she did say that. I'd forgotten. Oh, of course I'm not upset!" She lowered herself into a chair. Sickly light trickled greenly through the trees.

She had reached Julian on his cell phone and so didn't know where he was, which she always found unsettling. She was always afraid that she'd caught people at a terrible time, in a terribly inconvenient place, and that they would be too polite to tell her, and so now she tried to guess from the way he spoke, from the ambient sound shimmering around his voice. "And we haven't even really decided on the name, not a hundred percent," he was saying. "Kit spoke out of turn. You know how she gets."

Susannah did not know how she got. Susannah hardly knew them, really, at all. She was so suddenly and intensely upset that the only thing she could say was, "I don't even know why you'd think I'd be upset! Of course I'm not upset! I'd forgotten all about it!" He was crossing the street, maybe, there was the up-and-down of the voice, and yes, honking, the crescendo of motors. "Of course it's *your* baby. No one's ever said it wasn't *your* baby."

Julian paused, gave Susannah a second to register how very strange what she had just said sounded. Heat quicksanded up her neck. The kitchen went dapple bright and shifting.

Maybe he was heading to meet Kit for lunch, or for shopping. Kit was a great shopper. "I mean," said Susannah, "I just mean, you can do whatever you want."

"I know, but like I said, we haven't decided on a name yet."

"If you need any help . . ." but it guttered in her throat.

"What's that?"

"Nothing."

"I just don't want you to feel left out or weird about anything. We want you to be happy. It's important to us to keep you happy."

Susannah shifted her weight. "Mmm-hmmm," she said. Tactically, he meant. Practically. She had been wrong to call him.

"What are you doing?" he said.

"What do you mean?"

"I don't mean anything. I just mean, what are you doing right now?"

A bus lumbered down Susannah's street, setting off a car alarm that always went off when the bus went by (every twenty minutes on weekdays). She wouldn't have even noticed it—never noticed it anymore—but this time it swelled in her ear through the phone, Siamese-twinned with the sound in the street.

"Because I was in the neighborhood," Julian was saying.

"I'll be right down." As soon as she hung up, Susannah started to doubt herself. What if that hadn't been what he meant? (She scurried around, searching for her bag, her keys.) What if he'd only meant to ask about a place in the neighborhood, did she know a Thai food place nearby, something? But then—he had no reason to be in her neighborhood. Of course he had come wanting to see her.

He was waiting on the stoop. She rewarded him with a smile. They wordlessly embarked into the street, a tiny school of fish. This meant they were friends, didn't it? That they could wordlessly embark into the street? But Julian didn't smile at her. His face had a kind of stiffness to it, as if he were trying not to be recognized.

These were the things Susannah walked by a million times a day, the things she had loved so much when she rented this apartment three years ago, the things that she was now so tired of she could barely stand to see. She looked around, trying to see them as Julian must see them. The beautiful old church at the end of the block emitted a single bat from its spire, spiraling out into the dusking sky. The brownstones along the avenue had windows striped with bars. From midway down the block, you could smell the lake—its saltless, gasoliney breeze settling in your nostrils like silt. People had sailboats moored along the muddy piers. The convenience store in the lobby of the retirement complex looked uncharacteristically inviting as they passed, its yellow light brightening against the dull of evening. Inside, a child overfilled a Slurpee cup. Susannah looked away as the mess spilled in gruesome, cherry red globs onto the floor.

And in the same way, Susannah started to see the version of herself that Julian saw (it always took a few minutes to soak in); she started to become this version of her that would be a wonderful mother, that would kneel in the dirt and sing silly songs, the version of her that was a cheerful and earthy foil to Kit. He talked about her in ways that didn't sound familiar to her—he would say something about how happy she was, how young and bubbly—he actually used the word *bubbly* one time, and it struck Susannah as being so inaccurate that she panicked, wanting to live up to what he thought of her but unsure of how to do it. She became superbly vivacious whenever he was around. She really couldn't help it—it came on like a rash, Jekyll-and-Hydeing across her skin, until the old Susannah was buried in some deep place while Julian's Susannah bounced along the city streets, cheerily exclaiming things, making charming observations, inventing silly games. "Ooh, let's go!" she cried, ridiculously, pulling his arm, tugging him toward a group posing for a wedding photo in the park so that they could sneak into the background at the last minute and then collapse into giggles as they scooted away. Who was this girl, and why did Julian like her so much?

They walked toward the park, their arms bumping and twanging like guitar strings. Once he had inquired about her work and her health, Julian said, "Sometimes I think you're lucky. After all this your life will still be the same. For us everything is going to change. Already I think Kit loves this baby more than she's ever loved me."

Something bucked in Susannah. "But, I mean, *everything* isn't going to change, right? It'll be different, but, you know. You'll both still have the same jobs and everything. The nanny will take care of a lot." As soon as she'd said the words, she wanted to reel them back in. This was not the right version of Susannah, not the bubbly sweetheart that Julian had come to see. He looked wounded.

"Did Kit talk to you about that?"—so Kit had questions, too, so Kit was considering whether it was worth all the hassle, for a baby she would hardly ever see—well, all right then! Susannah felt a flood of warmth, and of regret for thinking poorly of them, for questioning the kind of parents they would be—and anyway, who was she to judge, people with nannies still raised their own children, of course they did, didn't they, and it was good that Kit had the money for help, that they had the means to make this happen, despite everything. Kit would be a good role model to any kid, that was good wasn't it—and sure Kit had been cruel to say what she'd said but it wasn't entirely un-true that Susannah and Julian had spent a lot of time together, that there were things they had said and done that they wouldn't necessar-ily want her to know about, and though nothing serious had happened you couldn't entirely blame her for being annoyed and snappish— "Because," Julian continued, "we're looking for a good nanny. If you know of anyone."

Susannah's face burned.

"No one who could love this kid like you could," she said, despite herself. She'd meant to accompany this with a rueful laugh but choked on it and looked away. Julian didn't say anything. Something had cooled suddenly between them, and they both felt it, a change in weather. "Where are we headed?" Susannah said finally. "You want coffee or something?"

"Sure. I don't know. Actually, no."

"It's okay. We can just walk."

"I feel like walking. How about you?"

"Sure, of course. I'm supposed to be walking a lot, anyway," she said. She rested a hand on her belly, gave it a proprietary pat. Julian smiled at her, dismissing the tension of the moment before, and already she felt better, the anxiety of the day neutralizing in his presence. He had an earnestness to him, or maybe it was an air of authority—you could tell he was used to being the boss—that made Susannah's stomach settle, made the muscles around her eyebrows unclench, or at least become suddenly aware of having been clenched. Julian would tell her the name of the baby. Julian would bring her back, would draw her in, would help re-create what had been (she now realized, in its absence) so important to her all along, the forbidden imagining of the family they might make together, the shortcut to that perfect little life. She looked at him and not the street as they walked. He looked at his feet, she saw. There was a whole city brisking by, and he looked down at his feet.

Julian glanced up, conscious of being watched, and, as always when saw her, he registered a kind of shock. She was so young, and so very sweet. How did they all go around pretending to be adults, when she was so very young, when even Julian felt like he'd been alive for about fifteen minutes for all he knew of the world? He tried to see Susannah as if he'd never seen her before. He would fall in love with her, he thought, if he'd never met her. He would catch a glimpse of her on the street and have one of those one-second love affairs that happened, living in a city. He wanted to tell her things, things like, "When we found out Kit couldn't get pregnant, I just really didn't want to adopt. My parents—my adoptive parents—are great people and were wonderful parents and all that, you know, and I feel like I am their son, of

course, but for once in my life I want to know someone I am really related to. You've"—it was difficult to say, his throat cemented over, but
he had to, he forced himself to—"you've given us a great gift."

She flushed. "I'm so glad."

They walked. He kept forgetting to move slowly, the way she now
moved slowly, and would be talking to her and realize she'd fallen a
few paces behind, or rather that he'd moved a few paces ahead. It took
up most of his energy to match her pace, so that he hardly even knew
what he said or if it made any sense at all. "So have you thought about
the shower?" he finally said. They were waiting for a light to change.
Susannah squinted at the stoplight, her hair whipping across her face.
"You know, the baby shower? You're coming, right? We'd really like to
have you there."

Kit had sent him on this mission, of course. As much as Kit tried,
she knew Susannah would respond better to Julian, the way girls without men in their lives always responded to men who paid them attention. It would be weird to have the baby shower without the baby
around, Kit had complained, pretty pretty pretty please. She appealed
to his vanity. Susannah was *in love* with him, she was *devoted* to him,
she would do absolutely *anything* he asked, so could he just ask, please?
And here was Julian, awkwardly broaching the subject while crossing
the street a few steps ahead of Susannah because a truck barreling toward the intersection didn't seem to be slowing down fast enough, and
though he knew it would, he couldn't keep himself from moving a little quicker, as if he wanted to hustle them both out of the way in time.
He wanted to protect Susannah from every inevitable thing when they
were together, though he forgot about such things as soon as she was
out of his sight and she and the baby nestled in the back of his mind
as generally safe and protected from the world. So he was saying, "It
would mean so much to me," and then almost immediately resorted to
pretending to beg. "You can't leave me alone with those women!
They're crazy!"

This made Susannah laugh.

Aha! He was getting somewhere. "Kit's friends have basically been planning this for decades. Since practically before you were born. My coworkers attack me daily. These women, Susannah, they're hungry for blood!"

They had crossed the street and now stopped on the other side of the road. Julian put his hands on her shoulders. She was taller than Kit, sturdier. Her shoulders felt animal, horsey, strong as knees. "You look," he said with great effort, ". . . so lovely." Oops. It hadn't been what he'd meant to say at all, but it was too late to take it back, to unsay it, and maybe he didn't want to, maybe he wanted her to know that it was okay, that everything was going to be okay, the poor thing. But all he'd been able to manage was to stutter out, "You look . . . so lovely." It was a bad idea, both of them knew it, but he'd already started, so he figured he might as well pull her in close to him, wrap his arms around her (there, in public! in the middle of the city, where anyone could see them—it was terrible! he had to stop it!), and it was so good to touch her, to hold her, to feel her heart thumping against his, as if knocking, waiting to be let in (she made a feeble effort to pull away but didn't mean it, not really, not with her limbs all hot and liquidy, a deep, oceany blue rising in her chest and in her throat—it was the boardwalk on the beach, it was Rose's lavender hair ribbon, it was water and darkness), and they were both made so lazy and drugged by the heat of it that they held each other a little too closely, a little too long. When she finally tried to pull away, she couldn't. But no, she really couldn't—her hair had gotten tangled around the button of his shirt. Susannah felt her face go bright red. "I got it, hold still," Julian was saying, laughing, pawing at her hair. Susannah's head was stuck at a horrible angle. She stared at a blackened heart of chewing gum on the sidewalk, laughing, laughing, unable to stop. Of course this would happen to her, of course it would.

Julian finally unwound the hair, and she looked up, and he

opened his mouth. But instead of words, a metallic screeching tore through the air, a sickly skidding and a scream and a crash. Julian whispered, "Shit." This was the first thing Susannah registered, that he had whispered, "Shit," and for a second she'd thought, Whatever does he mean by *that*? But he was walking quickly back toward the intersection they had just crossed, where a boy on a bike had been struck by a car.

In the seconds since the impact, a crowd had gathered. Where had these people been an instant ago? Susannah hadn't been noticing anyone around, had felt without thinking, she now realized (her limbs and chest and groin still spangled, still purpley blue, still hot and liquid), that she and Julian were the only people left in the world. But here they were, clumped together like wet lashes. Julian was the one who went to the boy. People were shouting about ambulances. The driver of the car, an elderly man, was standing by his open door gesturing toward the streetlight. He looked stunned, his face stroke-stiff, and he was shaking his head, not looking at the boy, but he was right, people were murmuring, the bicyclist had run the red light, and they were never obeying the traffic signals, those bicyclists, and here was one not even wearing a helmet. The whole day had irrevocably changed. The air felt muddy. One needed to obey the traffic signals. It took Susannah a long time to find a way through the crowd, to see Julian kneeling. It still seemed to her that she was alone, that the figures around her were as inconsequential as set dressing. She was the ball in a vast and narcotically slow pinball machine. There was no sound but her breathing and the echo of the crunch.

Of course Julian was the one who would kneel by the tangled semaphore of the bike. Of course he was the one directing people to step away. Like in a movie—how did Julian know so many things in so many different situations? Was it the wisdom of age? Or just having seen enough movies? She would have to remember to bring this up somehow. As she neared the scene (people suddenly remembering their manners, sweeping out of her way and directing knowing smiles at her belly or, in the case of one woman, a palm on her shoulder as the crowd shepherded Susannah toward the front), she told herself not to look and then immediately caught a glimpse of the crumpled body, the blood pooled in the street. The boy's head had been broken. Shards of color dazzled around her peripheral vision, a darkness welling in the center. Her body was shutting down, folding inward. The boy's head was broken, was not the shape a head should be, was cracked open on the pavement. His body was not at a healthy angle. It was difficult to imagine that he might have ever been a young man, lean and strong and capable of moving around the world, that he was that way only a few minutes earlier. An ambulance came shrieking down the street.

Susannah had to step back, had to take the arm of concerned stranger just for a moment, to steady herself, the woman peeking her owlish face into Susannah's and saying, "Are you okay? Hon, you okay?" and Susannah nodding and staggering back. What was it about pregnant women, Ellie Piersol was thinking, that made her sympathies rise to the surface, when usually she found the city such a drag, such a drain—usually she walked around trying not to make eye contact with anyone, grumbling at people who brushed by her, who stood too close on the train. This poor girl, her older husband who'd rushed to help the boy—they both looked so frightened and stunned, and Ellie wanted to say to them, *Oh, babies.* She wanted to say to them, *Before it gets any better, it will only get worse.* She patted the girl's back. *Just be good to each other,* she wanted to say to the couple. Their whole lives were ahead of them! Why should they seem so nervous and scared, so guilty and tired? Susannah looked gratefully at her, thanked her, and moved away. Behind them someone was saying, "I was right here. I heard his head go under the tires. I heard it pop like a melon. It sounded exactly like a melon being crushed." (Three days later he'd be in a diner at midnight, unable to sleep, still saying this to anyone who would listen—"It sounded exactly like a melon!")

Susannah broke from the crowd and moved into open air, feeling like she was leaving an overheated room. She found a bench half a block down, where the traffic ended and the park began. She sat and rested her forehead in her hands. Her face was so hot. If only he had made it to the park, the bicyclist, just half a block away, where things were safe and green, where you would fall into manicured grass, hit your head on a dandelion, make the sound of a peach, lie happy that you'd fallen. The wind shuddered by, releasing dandelion spores. The tiny, furred sails moved toward the lake, toward who-knew-where. The park made a rustling music.

Eventually Julian found her. The ambulance had come and gone, the crowd dispersed. The driver still stood looking lost, talking to a police officer. Even from where they were, they could see the large, dark shadow left on the pavement. So that was all it took. A knock to the head, and it was over. Susannah basketed her hands over her belly. "You okay?" was what Julian said first. She gathered her hair in one hand and lifted it from her neck. Was *she* okay? How she loved Julian, just then. Fuck, she thought. Fuck, do I love him sometimes. No, no, it wasn't love. What did love have to do with it? Ha! Wasn't that a song . . . who had sung it? The raspy voice. Oh, stop, Susannah told her brain. Please don't go crazy right now.

"I'm fine," she said, "thank you." She fanned at the back of her neck. "That was . . . weird. Yeah?"

It *had* been weird. It was wrong of him to hold her, to want to hold her, to respond to this twitching electricity deep within his muscles; another few seconds and he would have kissed her, and that was something you could never take back. The sky went very, very blue, the sounds of the lake rising noisily toward them. Everything became a little more than it was. Julian nodded, gathered up his apology, his appeal—God, if she mentioned any of this to Kit!—but then chickened out, decided to assume she was talking about the accident. She watched the scene, as if hypnotized by the man who'd been driving the car, the old man who stood there shaking his head. Of course, of course, it was only the boy, only the accident—and it was a relief, because that at least had not been his fault. "Awful," he said. "What can you do?"

"He's . . . ?"

"Dead. Probably right away."

"I heard people talking about his head," Susannah said. "They said it popped like a melon."

Julian grimaced, a face that had some sliver of a smile hidden within it. "How descriptive."

"How can things like this happen?" Susannah could hear her voice going up a pitch. "I mean . . ."

Julian was not looking at her but just past her, at the water. Gulls scraped through the sky, circling something. "It's awful," he agreed, "but it's not like there's anything we can do about it. It's too bad. You move on." Anyway, there was nothing to tell Kit. He'd done nothing wrong.

"Like a melon!" said Susannah, shuddering. She couldn't stop herself.

Julian put a hand on her arm. "Susannah, please."

"Sorry. Just . . . ugh! I was eating melon this morning. Cut-up honeydew. Jesus, why did he have to say melon? I feel like I'm going to throw up."

Julian didn't shift his gaze from the scene of the accident but took his hand away. She didn't get the hand, she guessed, if she was going to throw up or talk about throwing up. She stopped, willing the hand back. Its gentle weight had been pressing something good into her arm, the sense of being alive, being well. But no—he returned it to his pocket. His cell phone was vibrating, and he answered it. "Hi, Kitty," he said. "No, not doing anything in particular. Nope." Susannah flushed, looked away. There was a reason he didn't tell Kit where he was, or whom he was with. The whole thing made her feel as shamed

as if they really had broken some rule, as if he really had taken her upstairs and laid her down upon her bed, as if they really had talked
about running off together. Which they hadn't. Which they wouldn't.
The regret—oh, God—came roaring. What had she done? How had
she thought this would work out okay in the end? Now she was falling,
and up came the pavement. And there it was: There was nothing between them. He was talking to his *wife*, was all it was. His *wife*. Susannah studied her own palms, bewildered. What a joke it had all been. It
wasn't like this was their baby. It wasn't like the baby had anything to
do with them, like there was any *them* at all. She realized this with a
kind of a shock. Maybe it was because he kept appearing the way he
did, sneaking around behind his wife's back, the way he leaned forward and smiled, or maybe it was what Kit had said—why *hadn't* he
just fucked her?—maybe it had tricked her into thinking, somehow,
that this was their baby. When she was the hired gun, that was all it
was. Hadn't she told herself this a hundred times, in a hundred different ways?

But the version of herself that Julian knew—that he had, possibly, invented entirely—was someone who wouldn't stand for it; she
was a girl who wanted everything, and she was the one, this grabby,
gregarious beast, who leaned forward and whispered in Susannah's ear
exactly what had to be done. Susannah watched the old man at the
scene of the accident, waiting for a sign. If he shook his head, slowly,
like a mournful cow, three more times, then she would go. She would
take off, keep the baby, never see Julian again. If he kept shaking his
head after three, she would lean forward and make Julian kiss her.
Those were the only two options she could see. The old man's hair
stuck up in places, tousled as a toddler's. The police officers moved
closer to him. He shook his head. One: Susannah's muscles tensed,
willing him to stop. Two: "Sure," Julian was saying, "we haven't seen
Sarah and Dan in a while—that should be fun." Three: Then a police
officer took his arm, led him gently to the ambulance. Susannah

stared. Holy shit—he'd shaken his head three times. Then he'd stopped. She felt like laughing. What the . . . ! Why hadn't she picked hand-wringing? He was still wringing his hands! But those weren't the rules. And Julian was talking to his bright and capable wife about their perfect little life, and Susannah had nothing. She was invisible, she was no one. The sky flared with brightness. The sounds of the street roared like an ocean.

She was too hot, but when she tried to unzip her sweatshirt, it stuck halfway down. She yanked the zipper up and down, examined the flap of fabric bitten by the zipper's teeth. Julian didn't offer to help. He didn't seem to notice, and she certainly wasn't going to ask, not now, and so she gave up, shoved her hands into her pockets, and waited for him to stop talking. Finally Julian clicked his cell phone shut, weighed it in his palm before returning it to his pocket. A child stopped in the street, identifying the pool of blood with an excited hop. His mother dragged him away. Nearby a crow pecked at a soppy mess of bread crumbs. *I really better be going,* Susannah practiced saying in her head.

On the lake, people were taking out their sailboats. It was the season for such things.

Julian extended his left arm along the back of the bench, his hand flopping toward Susannah's left shoulder, and with his right arm he reached out and patted her stomach. His knees bowed apart from each other. Everything about his posture said, You Are Mine. So they were back to this old game. Susannah wriggled away as politely as possible and stood up.

"Wow, I just remembered. I have to go." She'd go to the desert—that was it. She'd go somewhere very, very far away, somewhere she'd never been, somewhere where no one knew her, where she could think things through, where she could figure out what she was when no one was watching. Julian frowned. "A thing," she said brightly. "I have this thing. A thing I just remembered. With friends. I better get back and get ready and all that." Something panged yellowly in the back of her throat. A thing with friends. Wouldn't that be something?

Julian's face puckered. "I'm sorry to talk your ear off all afternoon." He had been wrong to start talking about himself, about having been adopted, all that crap that had nothing to do with anything. Susannah looked pale. "I'll walk you back to your building?"

"No, no, no." She waved a hand in a pantomime of breeziness. "Oh, no. I'll be fine. You just enjoy the day and whatever." She smiled and then turned away and then looked back at him when he said, "The shower! What about the baby shower? You'll come, right?" "Oh! Sure, yeah, we'll be in touch," she said, and then she was gone.

An ice cream truck pulled up, its tinkly song virusing throughout the park. Julian watched children appear from nowhere, their parents straggling behind. All that was done in pursuit of those runny-nosed miniature people, those tiny men and women, out of their minds for sugar, tugging at their parents' sleeves. What sense was there in any of it? Didn't he and Kit have a good life? Didn't they have everything they wanted?

The truth of it was that he had asked his parents about his biological mother—you had to say *biological*, not *real*—when he'd been a teenager, when he was told what he'd always suspected. His adoptive parents were a pair of neatly pressed older people given to quiet pursuits like bird-watching and canasta, who loved their son but always wanted him to please quiet down, quiet down, please, who weren't much given to heart-to-hearts. They were ruffled by his questions. And only now, he thought, did he get it. If he and Kit were to adopt a child, raise it as their own, like a little foundling, knowing all along that the kid would someday ask about its *real* parents, to whom it would have some deep, mostly imagined bond . . . well, it was precisely why they had gone to such great measures to have one themselves. Which wasn't to say that Julian didn't feel impressed by his parents, especially now. Taking another's child into their lives—it changed one's view of the world. It made the whole world seem a smaller, kinder place—he was able to think this only now, when he considered it philosophically, and when he was well rested and in a good mood and not annoyed with his parents about one petty thing or another—it meant that the world was a civilized place, where adults had tacit understandings, where adults did not need to say to each other, *If you come to trouble, I will help you; if you abandon your child, I will care for it, and send it to meet you when it is grown and everyone is ready.* Not that his parents had done that. They had said his birth mother disappeared. Had been in the city, had arranged the thing through lawyers, et cetera, had been in touch at first, then disappeared after a while. She had been nineteen, was all they knew. She had handed over, when she handed him over, a tiny stack of baby pictures, but many of them included her, so Julian's new parents hadn't really wanted them. They'd kept only one of the photos of her, a desaturated Polaroid. From it squinted an angular girl with long, dark hair, a baby that could have been any baby. Somehow Julian had never cared for looking at it, particularly now that she seemed like such a child to him, like any teenager he'd see on the street, glowering into a cell phone or laughing with friends in matching jeans or kissing a boy on a park bench. She was a stranger, like anyone.

All of which was to say he was glad, so glad, they had found Susannah, that they would have a baby of their own. That the world really did operate under his parents' code of kindness sometimes, that he and Kit had been in trouble and a stranger had swooped in to save them.

The sun left its perch on the clutch of leaves he'd been staring at, and just like that, his powers of concentration left him. What was this sense of dread? Oh, right, Susannah was still upset about the baby shower, of all ridiculous things. His left foot erupted in itchiness on its sole, where he could not reach it without removing his shoe. That would have to wait. What would Kit want for dinner? She would be home from work soon—he had taken the afternoon off; it was Friday, and almost summer, and he was in a holiday sort of mood—but Kit was never that kind. She would want to keep working, of course. Should they have already found a nanny? His friend Robert spoke so highly of his nanny, an islander called Sweetie. How could someone name a child Sweetie, knowing it would someday be a grown woman? He and Kit had been talking of nothing but names, names, names and had really come to a standstill over the whole thing. No, he would have to take off his shoe and scratch—it was becoming quite unbearable. Then he would walk back to the El, take the train the four stops home, or maybe he would walk home, but by now he didn't have time if he wanted to get there before Kit. He unlaced his shoe. It turned out to be the kind of itch that wasn't easily solved by scratching. He rubbed through the slightly moist sock. That poor kid on the bike. It had been a blip in their day, like the sun on the tree, that now for them was over but for someone was seeping away into sadness; someone's life would never be the same. He hoped the kid—he must have been Susannah's age—had been in love, had been happy. The itch began to subside. Maybe they would ask Susannah about the baby's name. Of course she wanted to know what they were thinking, and maybe it would please her, and she would come to the shower beaming, and that would please Kit. Maybe Susannah could be the tiebreaker. All right (he laced up his shoe again and stood), he would talk to Kit, and they would call her tonight. Tonight they would get it all sorted out.

5

THE MIND BETRAYS
THE BODY

It was a place like the face of the moon, though it had once been inhabited by people, animals, things. A track mark snaking through the ground might have been an ancient snail's path. Nearby roared an oceany sound. Looking hard enough, you could see the evidence of the world that had been, and you did look, and hard, like a dog surveying a park for another dog, because you wanted to see something of yourself in the desiccated landscape; because you wanted to believe that the world had a pattern, an order to make sense of. The sun's heat searing your neck like nuclear fission.

She'd discovered an abandoned structure along the ruined highway. A warehouse? No, a series of rooms, doors facing into the gravel clearing. Some sort of command center. And at the end of the long building, a pit in the ground, a tiny statuette, mysterious seating accoutrements. Could the pit be full of water, after so many years on this dry and distant planet? It was, and what there was of it glittered. Water, water, water. Command Control would want to hear about this. "Come in, please, Roger," Frankie said, but the sound of her own voice broke something about the morning, and interrupted her unpopulated fantasy.

Frankie had gotten up early and snuck out to the Grotto, where she was crouched near the edge of the pool wearing only swimming trunks and peering into the water. "Command Control," she whispered into the reflected world. But everything had become normal again, and she couldn't recapture the things she had imagined. Here was the real world, the toothless universe. She floated her red rubber ball out onto the water, watched, disappointed, as it sank to the bottom of the pool. "Come in, please." She tapped at the imaginary headset. "Command Control. We need your assistance." Most of her games involved being stranded on some distant, hostile planet, a control center lodged into the ocean bottom, mysterious forces gathering against her.

She was watching the faint stripes at the bottom of the pool waver back and forth, her ball quavering like a lost sun, when she heard a car door slam in the parking lot. Feedback crackled through her ear, her imaginary equipment always on the fritz. "Trouble with the natives. I'll have to get back to you, Commander." She tapped once more at the microphone of her headset before she forgot about it and it dissolved into the heat of the morning. She padded across the Grotto's paved path and across the gravel in the parking lot, expecting to see Aunt Dicey finally making good on her threat, getting ready to go. Frankie was surprised that her stalling had worked his long, had worked at all. It was amazing what a good temper tantrum could do. It was amazing how much more aunts let you get away with than mothers.

Susannah Prue's hair glinted in the sun. Frankie visored a hand above her eyes. "Whatcha doin'?"

Susannah straightened up slowly, as if she were in possession of a new body, a rental she didn't quite know how to work. "Frankie. You startled me."

Frankie frowned, hiked up her swimming trunks. "You going to California again?"

Susannah's suitcases were lined up alongside the car—a little one, a bigger one, and a biggest one, like a family. Frankie watched Susannah decide what to say. Susannah was so pretty, Frankie thought. Her hair wisped down from a ponytail, her breasts and belly strained against her T-shirt. There was a kind of calm to her, a kind of glow, the kind of okayness that Dicey never had. Dicey was all angles and dark shapes and worry. Susannah was softer, slower, malleable as honey. Frankie therefore preferred Susannah and in fact had been thinking that when she grew up and was finally a man, she would fall in love with women like Susannah. Susannah was sand; she was sugarcane. Frankie had tried sugarcane with her class in school and been extremely impressed—the proud, adult way she felt upon discovering how anything familiar was actually made—and had craved it ever since, the sinewy scrape against her teeth, the juicy, fleshy sweetness.

Frankie knew two things about the world so far, in her abbreviated experience of it: that her own mother was a distant force, as abstract and inhuman as a current, and that she, Frankie, was not like other kids. The former would be confirmed when she never did end up going back to live with her mother, when her mother from then on corresponded with her strictly though Dicey's letters or curt e-mails sent to mass mailings: *Deke and I have broken up, and I'm looking for a place to stay*, or, *Nursing school is going well! Come visit, everyone!* Frankie knew from an early age that she had been an accident—she had heard the story enough times: how her mother was in high school, had missed the prom because of Frankie's being born, how (this she heard from her grandparents arguing late one night) the family had wanted to give Frankie up for adoption, but Jean wouldn't, seemingly out of spite (Frankie would think later) or because the boyfriend, a rangy kid called Skip, had wanted to keep the baby and name her for his grandmother Francine, et cetera, only to join the military for no reason and leave and never quite exactly return, and here was Frankie, her mother's little orphan. It was a funny sort of thing for a kid to know. And could anyone blame the teenage mother (Frankie would think this later, much later) for not being exactly the most attentive when it came to changing and cleaning her tiny child, to ignoring or conceivably not noticing the unusual arrangements of bits between the sausagey baby legs, for simply lacking the wherewithal, the something, to point out to her own mother or a doctor, *Look at my little girl. Doesn't she seem to have . . . er, a bit extra down there? Are you certain that my baby girl is . . . well, a baby girl?* At any rate, Frankie's mother had never said anything about this to anyone, or to Frankie, and for a long time Frankie had thought this was just the way things were. And the thing that people called her—a tomboy—seemed related to playing soccer and disliking dolls, and nothing to do with the extra parts in her panties.

The latter piece of knowledge—that she was not like other kids—would be confirmed a few weeks after the trip into the desert, when she was settled in Phoenix and her father first took her for her checkup and the physician identified the issue. Her father, now a rangy salesman named Skip, a colorless ex-marine who played a key role in his bowling league, would pat Frankie's arm and thank the doctor while rubbing restlessly at some foul-smelling suppurations behind his ears, only to start punching the steering wheel with surprising vigor as soon they got back into the car. Frankie, frightened of the angry stranger, would say nothing, would sit there as he punched—punch, punch, punch—staring out the car window into the parking lot of the strip mall—pain gestating in her stomach.

DESPITE ALL THIS, Frankie did mostly try to act like a normal, carefree child. She felt that it helped the adults around her. So now she kicked at the gravel as Susannah chewed on her lips, and said, "Are you leaving for real this time?"

Susannah swallowed, working against the knot in her throat. "I think so," she said.

But there wasn't anything Susannah could do there, any way she *could* go. Marlon was still waiting on the parts ordered over the telephone from a catalog that Susannah wasn't entirely convinced was real, or anyway current, and she imagined the parts being shipped to them from twenty-five years in the past, zooming toward them like the light of a star that no longer existed. Ordering over the *phone*! From a *paper catalog*! Though her car would start, sort of, she had no reason to believe that it would get her anywhere. And she had to, but had to, leave. The baby had reached such a heft that it almost seemed greedy of him to still be residing inside her; the pregnancy itself was starting to seem redundant, to take on the feel of overmothering—of course not mothering, no, of course she didn't mean that, exactly—overprotecting, or something. Overdoing it. Enough already. Though she knew she needed to get back to the city, back to the doctors with their bland smiles, the very idea of it filled her with such shuddering dread that she thought she might die of it. Instead, she wanted to drive as far as she could in the opposite direction from Julian, from the weight of her entire life and everyone who knew her, from the Susannah that existed back home in Chicago. Besides, Julian and Kit would be coming to get her by now. She'd been so stupid, but she'd called, so of course they'd be coming to get her. Maybe part of her had wanted to set this into motion, was wondering what on earth was taking them so long to give chase. She'd called them the night before last, had given them a day's lead. Now all she could think of was driving, driving, driving, hitting the road, skipping town, heading west.

Susannah Prue squinted out toward the horizon for a long time—a cowboy movie on freeze-frame. Frankie shuffled back and forth. Susannah said finally, "You wouldn't mind staying here a little longer, would you?"

Frankie's posture changed. She studied Susannah's expression. "What do you mean?" She was accustomed to tricks from grown-ups.

Susannah dropped into the backseat, feet on the dusty earth. When she spoke, Frankie had to move in close to be able to hear.

Susannah was trying to speak calmly, spackling her words across the cracks between them, smoothing each out one as she formed it. "I need to go somewhere," she said. "But my car won't make it."

"Okay."

"But I bet your aunt would let me borrow her car."

"Really?"

"Well, I don't think she'd mind *too* much, do you?"

Frankie shrugged. It was impossible for her to say. "It's not even really her car. We borrowed it from Monica."

Something about this caught in Susannah's ear. A wind scalloped down from the sun.

"Frankie." Susannah reached out, and Frankie scooted closer obediently. She put her hands on the child's arms as if molding the warm skin into longer and thinner arms, rubbing her palms forcefully down. "I need to leave here today. I need Aunt Dicey's car keys."

For an instant something bucked in Frankie. She determined to play dumb.

"Please, Frankie. Please," Susannah said, leaning very close to Frankie's face. Her intensity was frightening to both of them. "I'll only be gone for a short time. Dicey won't mind! Do you think she'll mind? I don't think she'll really mind." She switched tactics, dropping her arms suddenly, collapsing into the seat. "A man is coming to get me. A man is going to come and take my baby." It was the first time Susannah was aware of having said those words out loud. My. Baby. And as soon as they had spilled out of her mouth and lay there soaking into the ground, she realized what she had said, or what it meant that she had said what she'd said, and something sour leaked into her gut. The baby kneed her spinal column in rebuke. She had gotten this all wrong, entirely all wrong.

"What d'you mean?"

Susannah sighed. "It would take a long time to explain, but there is a man who thinks this baby belongs to him. We made a kind of arrangement, I guess, is why. But now I want to keep the baby. You see what I mean? And he's angry, and he's going to come get me." As she said it, it seemed reasonable enough. It even seemed a little true. Julian and Kit had misunderstood, or maybe Susannah had. Maybe she'd had this in mind the whole time, it occurred to her suddenly, as the words tumbled out, easily as air—maybe she'd always known it would end this way. Maybe this was the little brother she'd almost had, the baby her mother had lost. Maybe the baby was a gift to her, was meant to be hers. She knew this wasn't a good thought and tried to unthink it.

"Ooh," said Frankie, her eyes wide. "Is he dangerous?"

"I suppose he could be, yes. Any man could be, really."

A tumbleweed shuttled down the road, due west.

Frankie scratched at her stomach, found a crust of sand curled in her belly button, examined it, yawned. "All right. Fine. I'll get the keys," she said finally. Anyway, she had already been stalling for days, trying to avoid the inevitable. The thought of being left at her father's worried her, roiled in her chest and knees and elbows, bubbling up acidly now and then, an arthritis of fear. How was it that the grown-ups in her life would abandon her so? How could she, a kid without power, without options, avoid being dumped with some strange man in Arizona? This seemed as good a way as any. "Don't cry. I said I'll get them."

"I wasn't," said Susannah waterily.

Frankie rolled her eyes.

SUSANNAH HAD DONE something stupid the night before last, sometime around midnight when she couldn't sleep, when the night seemed so quiet and shatter-thin, when she'd finally figured it out what it was that she wanted to say to him. She wanted to say, *See, Julian, you said you wanted your normal life back. You said you didn't want any birthday parties or diapers or spit-up.* She wanted him to still love her, despite what she'd done; she wanted there to be a way she could come out of this looking okay, looking at least uncruel. She had picked up the phone in her room and dialed Julian's number. It rang twice. Kit, shrilly: "Hello? Hello? Hello?" Idiotically, again and again, as if each attempt might accomplish something different. Then Julian had taken the phone.

"Hello?" The voice was so thick with sleep and confusion that she doubted it could even be him. The man on the phone, the hello, sounded like any person in the world, like any man. She was suddenly terrified. She meant to have hung up by now.

"I . . ." Her finger hovered over the phone, ready to plunge into its Adam's apple, to force it into silence. "I think I have the wrong number."

But before she finished saying it, he'd begun, "Susannah? Susannah? Is that you? Listen, Susannah?"

Her throat closed. A faulty connection.

"Susannah."

"I'm sorry," she said. "Don't worry. Everything's okay."

She hung up, heart pounding. Waited until morning. Spent the day lazily swimming laps with Tim. Somewhere Julian and Kit were looking grimly at each other. Somewhere Julian was thinking this was all his fault, was setting his jaw, sending an e-mail to work, sipping bitter coffee, packing a bag while saying to his wife, "I'll go. I'm going to bring her back." "Dead or alive," agreed Kit. Susannah and Tim lolled in the water until their fingertips pruned, until the prunes on their fingertips pruned; Julian was peering at the MapQuest screen, the coiled hieroglyphs of direction. "I'll be back in a week." Susannah and Tim circled one another like orbiting stars. They spent the whole day together and did not speak. "Right," Kit was saying, and only then did he realize she was packing her own bag, and she was saying, "I'm coming with you, of course," and Julian, who had wanted to be the hero, who had been somehow looking forward to a dramatic flight alone to the desert, but knew his wife well enough by now, nodded his head. In the late slant of afternoon, Tim nervously kissed Susannah's hand, then he furrowed his brow, as if about to ask her forearm a question, and stuck out his tongue and licked her sweat-salty skin. He giggled. "Mmm!"

In the evening Susannah sat in her stalled car, looking through the glove box. Pebbles from Tim, the Garlands' fork, Dicey's coins. Frankie had left a sopping sock on the concrete beside the pool, and when she was sure no one was watching, Susannah had wrung it out and taken that, too. She touched everything, arranging the items, before closing and locking the box. Then she went into the lobby to ask Marlon about her car, to pay with wadded bills for one more night. Instead she found Char staring unfocusedly at a newspaper that Susannah saw was a week old. Char looked up, silently acknowledging her presence. Susannah leaned against the counter. Char scooted her stool back an inch. She had in front of her a halved pomegranate hinged open obscenely on a plate. Susannah watched Char pick the seeds from it one by one, each bloodred as the eyes of some supernatural rodent. It was difficult to imagine where she would have gotten such a fruit, but then, there at the Thunder Lodge, any food seemed miraculous. Susannah slumped in the folding chair by the air conditioner, pressing her hands to her belly in the international sign for Have Pity, I'm Pregnant. Char watched her wordlessly, sucking on a crimson bead of juice.

"Staying through the weekend?" she finally said, working the pulp between her teeth.

If only we could really communicate with each other, Susannah thought, I bet we would have so much to say to each other. Susannah watched the way Char managed with her one arm snugged in the sling like a baby in a carrier, maneuvering around Marlon's cup of teeth. They weren't so different from one another. They had all had their bodies fail them.

"Oh," said Susannah, "actually, I think I'm leaving . . . oh, tomorrow. Or the next day. I mean, if the car's ready." Char fingered through the carnage of fruit. "That's what I came to ask. About the car. Is Marlon around?"

"There's a crafts fair coming up. We get awfully busy round then."

"Oh. Well, I won't be here then, that's for sure."

"A lot of the craft people stay here. Crazy bunch," Char said. Now Susannah was beginning to feel suspicious. This was as forthcoming, as friendly, or anyway as not-unfriendly, as Char had been since she'd first seen Susannah talking alone with Tim, since before Tim had taken to waiting outside Susannah's doorstep with an armful of pebbles and sticks, waiting for her to get up, to come out. (Susannah didn't know it, but there were mornings when he stood there for hours, just waiting.) And anyway, why couldn't Char be kind to her, or at least friendly, or at least not unfriendly, Jesus? Why shouldn't they communicate? Here was Susannah, a girl with a goddamned condition! The most the shriveled-up old woman could do was squint at her and say, "Last year we bought some handmade pottery."

"How nice," squeaked Susannah. Maintaining the conversation had become a challenge.

"I suppose. But then Tim broke it all, you see, when he got upset about something or another."

"Oh."

"He's . . . like that sometimes. You know how he gets. Or maybe you don't."

Susannah wasn't sure whether she was meant to respond to this, or how. It was a challenge, wasn't it? A cloaked version of, *You don't know him like I know him,* or, maybe worse, *You don't know him like you think you know him.* Wasn't it? Susannah didn't say anything. She would let this be Char's project. The office swallowed their silence, working it into the air conditioner and spitting it out into their faces again, cold and chemical.

Char reached her good hand into her sling and scratched. "That boy. He can be so much trouble sometimes you just . . . it just makes you wonder, is all." She didn't look at Susannah. And here it was: They were really talking! Char was really spilling her guts! Susannah remained still, so as not to break the spell. She breathed shallowly, trying to use only part of her nostrils. Char continued, "I know everyone thinks he's great at first. He's a charmer, he can be. When he was little, we'd take him to the grocery store in town and we'd be there hours, he'd be so busy waving at people, showing strangers his watch or some collection of rocks. But now, you know, nobody wants to wave back anymore. Nobody thinks it's cute, coming from a grown man. We just don't know what's gonna happen to him."

"Well," said Susannah, "isn't he happy here?"

"Sure, I guess. But you know, Marlon and I aren't as young as we used to be. Ten years from now, twenty if we're real lucky, we won't be able to take care of him, let alone run this place. And I just wonder sometimes what will become of him."

"Couldn't . . . can't he live on his own someday?"

Char sighed like she'd sprung a meaningful leak. "The boy can hardly bathe himself. He has no concept of money. He heads out into the desert, brings no water, no nothing, comes back hours later looking peaked and scared. He eats cigarette butts and coffee grounds and dirt. He can't read."

"Okay."

"He has the mentality of a child."

"Well—"

"We sent him to a school, did you know that? A special boarding school for kids like him. Everyone said it would be best." Char gestured around the empty office, indicating "everyone." "We took out loans to do it, sent him out of the state, because we thought it would help, because the schools around here have nothing for him. I told them to lock his doors at night, but they wouldn't do it. They looked

at me like I was this horrible person, like I'd suggested they beat him
every hour on the hour. So of course he'd sneak out of his room every
night. They'd find him looking in girls' windows, sneaking into the
bathrooms, touching himself. He got into one girl's room and stole
her panties. She woke up with him just sitting there staring at her, his
hand down his pants. I don't know if you can know how awful this
was for us. Marlon—I thought he'd die of shame."

Susannah wasn't looking at her anymore. "I had no idea."

"I know what you must think of us," said Char. "Don't think I
don't know."

"I don't think anything of you," said Susannah. It hadn't come
out sounding right—she'd only meant to say that she didn't think
about them very much at all, which she truly didn't—and she sucked
in a breath, embarrassed.

Char raised an eyebrow and then, unexpectedly, laughed. "You remind me of me. You know that? You remind me of me at your age. I
thought the whole world would rearrange itself to accommodate me. I
thought the whole world was just furniture."

Susannah blinked, too surprised to deny it.

"I mean it. I was having a grand old time, drinking and dancing
every night. I sang in a country band." Smiling rendered Char's face
unrecognizable. "Can you believe that? I sang with the band each Sat-
urday night! Gosh, I must have gone dancing with every man in Las
Cruces before I settled down with Marlon." It was true that youth
was wasted on the wrong people. Char had never had that simpering,
sorrowful look that painted Susannah's face. She had been tall, angular, possessed of rough-hewn grace; she would walk down the street
and feel it all collect, contract, suck in toward her. She controlled people's eyes with transparent lines of fishing wire, cranking them toward her wherever she went. Where had it gone, the ballsy confidence
of that lanky girl in trousers and long, straight hair tumbling all down
her back? When Char thought of her life, that was what she thought

of. Not this life at all. She'd never been the kind of girl who'd get
stuck, who'd be prematurely old, a rattly sack of bones in a cotton
sundress, the mother of a damaged boy, alone out in the desert. It
wasn't how she saw herself at all. And Marlon had gotten old, had
gotten doddery and equally unrecognizable—transformed from the
boy who'd flicked cigarettes from car windows, who'd kissed her at
the bar and then poured whiskey down her throat as if trying to
drown her. This place did something to people. This place dried people up, laid them out flat.

"But that's not like me at all," Susannah blurted out.

Char didn't seem to hear. "I married my high-school sweetheart,
young, too young, and we left Iowa, and we traveled all over. He was a
door-to-door salesman, if you can believe that—you're probably too
young to remember those—and by the time I found myself dumped
and alone in Las Cruces, I was twenty-three years old and feeling just
about done. I figured I was an old lady and had nothing left to lose."

Susannah had realized that it didn't matter what she said, as long
as it was something. "Freedom's just another word," was what surfaced. Char nodded. It was almost as if she'd gone into a trance. Susannah considered sneaking out of the room, getting a soda, then
coming back in time to say something in response to Char's next
pause.

Char resumed, on cue. "Then I met Marlon, and we got married
at the city hall and just up and left town without telling anyone. We
needed a new life, and we needed it right then and there. I think you
know what I mean. Sometimes something just snaps. Something
about your old life doesn't fit anymore, like shoes that pinch your
feet." Susannah realized she was nodding ridiculously and made a con-
certed effort to stop. "We drove around for a few weeks before we
found this old place. It was a wreck, needed to be completely gutted,
and so we rehabbed it ourselves. Must have been, gosh, thirty years
ago now. Hard to believe. And then just when I'd thought I'd never

have kids of my own, along came Tim. And let me tell you: There's nothing like motherhood to take a girl down a peg."

"Mmm."

"All I'm saying is it never happens how you think it will."

"Mmm?"

"I mean, they told us to give Tim up. Can you imagine? They said to send him to an institution. But we kept him. Of course we had to keep that boy."

Only now did Susannah see it—the worried new parents, the expressionless, too-small child. The ache of it. "I had no idea."

Char shrugged. "How would you? You don't know us any better than we know you."

"Beg pardon?"

Char's good hand was busy straightening the things on the counter, throwing away a half of the carved-out pomegranate rind, stacking a pile of papers, refolding the newspaper into a rectangle, lining up the guest register and Marlon's tooth cup. She looked slyly at Susannah and said, "Bet your boyfriend misses you."

"My boyfriend?"

She moved her forehead toward Susannah's midsection, as if pointing with a unicorn's horn.

"Oh. Yes."

"You look about ready to pop."

"Yep, feels that way."

"Feet swollen? That was the worst, I remember, with Tim. But I was a lot older than you are, and maybe that made it worse."

"I guess. My whole body feels like it's gone insane. It's like it's trying to do its best imitation of a Macy's float."

"Ee-yup."

"It's a boy, you know."

"A boy?"

"It is."

"That so?" Char bit into a bitter seed, made a face, spit it at the garbage can. She dug her finger into the remaining half of the fruit. Elmer Fudd tiptoed through a cartoon desert an inch from where she leaned.

Susannah closed her eyes. Now it was her turn. How she hated these conversations between women—Char's confessions meant that now Susannah owed her something, needed to tell her something in exchange. It was a contract, she knew. And also—it was exhausting to have one's defenses up all the time, up so high you could hardly see over them, and anyway, she thought she knew that Char would hate her a little less if she knew what had happened to her. *You shouldn't hate me,* she wanted to say to Char. *Honestly, I don't think you should hate me.* So she said, "I'll tell you something, Char." And what was that? "I don't have a boyfriend. In fact, this baby"—she inflected the word *baby* in a dubious way, as if it were encased in air quotes—"isn't even mine."

Char formed her lips as if to say, *Oh,* but didn't make the sound that accompanied it. There was a long silence. Bugs Bunny erupted from a rabbit hole, shrieking with laughter. Elmer Fudd's legs swirled impotently in the air. The air conditioner whirred, then rested.

"Hon," Char finally said. "How in the hell can that baby not be yours?"

"What if I told you it was a virgin birth?" She meant it to sound like a joke.

Char squinted, unamused. "I'd tell you there's no such thing."

Maybe it was just that she wanted to tell someone; she hadn't said the words out loud in a long time and needed to. Or maybe she wanted to see what she could get from Char—wanted to melt what was flinty and distrusting in her, wanted to win her over. She wanted Char to clutch her hand, to tell her that everything was okay. What was it about this place that made her feel stripped raw, as if she didn't have any skin at all? "Well, it's not my baby. I mean, I'm the surrogate. A couple is paying me. It's theirs."

"Oh, sweetheart. Oh, you baby girl," Char muttered, wiping her fingers against a handkerchief. She looked very sad, suddenly, and very tired.

"And I've run away. And the parents don't know where to find me."

"Girl," said Char sorrowfully, "you are up shit's creek." She said it as if she regretted having to say it. But she didn't touch Susannah's hand again, or look into her eyes. Susannah could feel her cooling, quieting, drifting away, like a spot of sun leaving a rock.

"I know."

"Without a paddle."

"I know. I said I know that already. Thank you. I know."

Char opened her mouth to take a breath in, then changed her mind and turned around and disappeared into the Garlands' living quarters. Susannah waited a minute, two minutes, a little too long, expected her to come out and say what she was going to say or offer her something or threaten to turn her in, but Char didn't come back and didn't come back, and Susannah was about to leave the office when finally Char reappeared. She had a plastic cup of water. She did not offer any to Susannah.

She offered this: "What you are doing is a sin."

This was not what Susannah had expected, and she hooted out a laugh that caused Char to narrow her eyes. Char knew she'd been right about the girl. She looked forward, in a funny way, to telling Marlon—see, she'd been right all along! Marlon thought she judged too quickly, but it was only that she got a feeling about people immediately, and it was almost always right. She'd recognized the kernel at the center of this girl. She knew, of course, because she'd once been exactly the same way, profoundly selfish without knowing it, a selfishness so solid it was like an extra organ lodged in one's body. It protected you, this selfishness, but it was also dangerous—it disguised itself as other things, so that you never quite recognized it. Char was sure Susannah didn't know she was selfish, and there was something glorious about it, the sturdy egoism of a young girl, especially when the girl was pretty enough to get away with it, to get away with awful things. Whoever had trusted this girl with a child must have been afflicted with the same grinding, blinding ego—to have missed the desperateness in her pupils, legible as a street sign! Joseph, Mary, and Jesus, what a world. Maybe it was better that Tim was what he was, that they could keep him close to them, safe from the universe.

Char continued, "Look. I don't know what you're doing here or why you been hiding out here so long. People come here for all sorts of reasons, and we try not to pry. It's none of my business whose baby that is or isn't. But what is my business is the very real fact that there's not a hospital for miles and miles, and you're about ready to pop. Where's the daddy? Where's your people? You gotta get back to all that. You sure aren't having any baby in my motel."

Susannah hunched her shoulders a little and assembled a mournful face. The only way to survive this was by shrinking, like when you were being attacked by a bear, wasn't that right? With a bear you played dead, and with a mountain lion you fought back? Or was it the other way around? "I'm not ready," she said. She knew she sounded whiny, that it was too late to get Char on her side, anyway.

"You don't have time not to be ready," Char snapped. "That baby's coming whether you're ready or not. Nobody's ready. You think I was ready?" Then she changed tactics, softened somewhat. "It's just nerves. Everyone gets them. But you get through it. Everyone gets through it. Every person in the world is proof that someone got through it." She suddenly became busy with the bottom television set on the noisy tower, turning the dial from static to static to louder and yellower static. The noise tinted the room an uncomfortable shade, like a wash of light from a fluorescent bulb. "Think about those poor people. The parents. If they lose their baby. That is not a thing you get over."

Susannah said, a little peevishly, as if she were talking to her mother or aunt, "I'm going to give them their baby. I mean, of course

I am. I just . . . needed some time to think. Some time to have him to myself."

Char snorted. The friendliness, the earlier trance that had compelled Char to talk to Susannah as if they might be friends, whatever it was, dissolved just like that. "You won't be able to do it. Don't you get it? You ruined it the first time you thought of that baby as yours for even a second." The stranger nudged at her belly button as if in agreement.

"Excuse me?" said Susannah. "Ex*cuse* me?" She sounded like her least favorite kind of woman. She stood there a moment trying to collect herself, trying to gather something barbed and witty and undeniable to shoot back at Char, but then it was too late, the moment had passed, and she sputtered there before finally rising and turning on her heel and waddling out of the office with as much dignity as she could muster. The worst of it was that she knew Char was only trying to help. She knew that Char was right and that now she was more trapped than ever before. She could not stay and she could not go.

So she left the office, running right into Marlon. He chuckled. "Where's the fire?" Susannah couldn't look him in the eye (he was holding on to her arms) and mumbled toward his feet, "Oh, I just remembered I've got this meeting."

He laughed, letting go of her arms gently, as if setting her down on the ground. "Oh, of course. In the boardroom, isn't it? I saw them getting ready for you."

Susannah smiled. "I made this amazing presentation. I think I'm going to get that big raise I've been gunning for." It felt good to joke around with someone. There was something sweet about Marlon that she admired, a basic, unfettered sweetness. He went on, "You know, I had a funny phone call last night."

Susannah froze, her stomach sinking. "Oh? From top management?" Hoping there was a chance they were still playing around.

Marlon shook his head. An odd smile twitched at his colorless lips. "Well, no. From a man in Chicago. A man who said he'd just gotten a phone call from our motel."

"Must have been some mistake."

"I guess so. That's what I told him. Only . . . well, tell me what I should make of this, Miss Prue. He said he'd been looking for a girl. A girl who was pregnant with his child, who'd run off and scared the bejesus out of everyone. Said everyone was real worried about her. And that he'd just gotten a call that he thought was her. And that she'd called from here. And that if she was here, then he was coming to get her."

Susannah opened and closed her mouth. Blood crashed in her face, welling hotly beneath her eyes.

"Er, what do you make of it?" Marlon scratched his head.

She could tell he was trying to be kind. She could tell he was giving her a chance to make it all okay. But something in her stalled, stupidly—her mind as dry as her car's engine, and as likely to split right in two. "It's not what you think," she managed.

Marlon shrugged. "I suppose it's none of my business. I only thought you might like to know that he planned to leave early this morning, so seems like, hmm"—matter-of-factly, as if she'd just asked for directions to town—"well, I'd guess he'd be here by tomorrow afternoon, or maybe the next day. Sounded like he really missed this girl. Like he just wanted to make sure she was okay. Nice guy. Jerry? Jonathan? Something Forsythe." Susannah clasped her hands over her belly. Marlon shrugged. "He didn't even ask to make a reservation. Funny kind of call to get. Guess there's room for him, anyway," nodding his head toward the string of empty rooms. He shrugged again and said, "Well, good luck with that meeting," and went into the office.

Char didn't look up at him. He hadn't mentioned anything to her about the phone call, since she'd slept right through it last night. There was no sense in getting her all worked up. He didn't know why he'd even mentioned it to the girl, except that there was a terrible scene coming, and he hoped it didn't happen on his watch; he wanted, in some strange way, to protect her. Perhaps the boyfriend would come and collect his girl and baby and none of it would be Marlon's problem anymore. Or perhaps she'd decide to go back home. Her damn car wouldn't be fixed until next week, but he could offer her a ride to the bus station in the next town. That's what he'd do. That car was nothing anyone would miss; he'd buy it from her for parts, and tomorrow he'd offer her a ride to the bus station. Anything to move her along, to set things into motion. Marlon missed the easy rhythms of their life before Susannah. He plunked his teeth into the cup of solution, kissed the top of Char's head, went into the living room.

Susannah locked herself in her room. It seemed like the thing to do would be to hurl herself on the lumpy bed and cry, but that sounded too tiring. There was no comfort here. The air conditioner spit musty air. The pine green flocked walls and furniture made to look like dark wood, the ineffective television set, the leprous mirror, the trickle of eggy water from the crusted shower spout. The scrapey bedclothes. The too-thick curtains. The room clung around dampish and too dark. She wondered what had become of her studio apartment near the lake. It seemed she had been gone for years. It seemed possible that her building—though it was prewar brick, shamelessly solid—might have leased to exist at all, that the passage of time must have eroded it away. That if she did ever go back, she would find the city swallowed by the lake, her neighbors fossilized, the Sears Tower impotent as a shipwrecked mast, the Harold Washington Library a reef. Julian and Kit in their perfect home, long dead, bones plucked clean by kissy-faced fish.

There was a knock at the door.

Susannah jumped, and the baby jumped, too, doing one of its little karate moves out of sympathy.

It was only Tim, clutching a jagged bit of quartz. "Come in, come in," she said. He stood in the doorway, shaking his head, giggling—he'd been warned not to. "Come on, Tim." She plopped down on the bed to wait. Tim stepped an inch into the room. His hands were joined at his breastbone, engaged in crumpled prayer. "Come on," Susannah soothed, as if talking to a cat. He giggled, took one step farther. He extended his hand.

"I brought you a sparkly," he said, thrusting the piece of quartz toward her.

She felt like crying. "Thanks."

"Yeah."

"Hey, Tim?"

"Brought you a sparkly," he repeated, weaving his white fingers together. "Brought you a sparkly, brought you a sparkly."

The door was still open. Behind Tim the sky was doing its evening calisthenics.

Susannah took the stone from him. She rolled it over in her palm. It might have been a particularly weathered and opaque bit of glass. She closed her hand around it. She wanted it to be whatever Tim said it was. She felt a surge of love sweeping over her like nausea. Tim!

"A sparkly," he reminded her, giggling.

"Yes, I have it now. Thank you very much."

He nodded and then didn't stop nodding, looking around the room, twisting his fingers, nodding.

"Are you nervous about something? You seem nervous about something."

Tim giggled. "Huh. Yeah."

"Yeah you are? You are nervous?"

"Yeah. You're nervous."

"No. No, not *me*. You. You, Tim Garland."

"Yeah! Tim!" He slapped himself on the chest once, quickly, like a gorilla.

The surge of love subsided, soured. Jeez, he was exhausting.

"Okay. Forget it. You know what? I don't even know why I try to talk to you. It's impossible. This whole thing is so fucking stupid."

Tim stopped rocking, stopped twisting his hands, and stared at her.

"Go home. Go back."

His smiled faded.

"I mean it. Go, Tim. Can you please go?"

"Susannah Prue," he said. Because this was how it happened with him. He'd seem so distant, so lost within himself, so strange and confused and dim, and then there would be a moment of clarity, some instant when the true him seemed to peek out, when he seemed sweet and real and normal, but better than normal, as if there were some supernatural connection between them. He reached out and touched her face. With one cold hand, he stroked the top of her head, twice, very gently. Then he turned and left the room.

So she couldn't sleep. All night she heard him crunching up and down the gravel until Char hollered for him around ten. Everyone had forgotten about her. There were no interruptions from him, from Dicey or Frankie. The night was so quiet behind Tim's footsteps. She could disappear into that night and never be heard from again. No one would know to miss her. She lay on her side, glaring at the wall, bubbled as a diseased face. The baby was restless. He was a contrary one, you could tell, and as soon as she wanted to rest, he started practicing his moves—it was like he was training for some sort of dance-off in there, some sort of cross-country-runningish thing—and as soon as she was awake, he was as still as the dead. Had her little brother just stopped one day, stopped moving, and that's how they knew that something had gone terribly wrong? Her mother had changed after that summer, had taken to sleeping alone in the guest room painted blue, walking around like a ghost in the house. They had never talked about it. Susannah's mother wasn't the talking-about-it type, and neither was Susannah. Susannah hoped Kit wouldn't be that kind of mother, the kind who made one feel alone, the kind who made one feel irrelevant. She hoped the kid would be okay with Julian and Kit, though Kit could be mean, though Julian could be dense.

She dreamed.

She would carry him in one of those slings, like a little monkey. In the streets people would ask to peek in, they would baptize the baby with stranger-germs. Susannah would stop in a café for tea in a paper cup. She would stroke the downy fur on the baby's scalp. The baby would reach out and curl his hand around her finger, he would squint into her eyes with myopic adoration when she breast-fed him in public restrooms. Everywhere they went, people would smile. They would exude that vanilla-y sense of well-being that steamed off of mothers and their children, equal parts love and exhaustion. Susannah would always smell like milk. He would crawl around while she tidied up, on the phone with her mother; he would bob in her lap while she wrote letters. She would write letters to the Forsythes her whole life. She would write, *We are both doing fine.* She would write, *He took his first step.* She would mail the unsigned postcards from roadside mailboxes in various cities. It would be a life like that. It would be lifelike.

No, no, no, no, no! No.

It was much too late for any of this. Behind the burka of curtains, the mountains went modest and black.

Of course the Forsythes had caller ID, the way everyone did—they'd looked up the Thunder Lodge and called back and spoken to Marlon. God, she was stupid. They had left already, setting sail into the airless morning, and now they were coming for her. The most she could hope for at this point was that they didn't take her to court. It would be in the papers. Her mother would read it. Everyone she'd ever known would know that she was crazy, that she was a terrible person who did horrible things. Then she would finally be completely invisible, thoroughly shunted to the side. They probably didn't even have to pay her the rest of her money now, with all that she'd done. She knew what she'd signed.

When Susannah closed her eyes, she heard the pounding of horse hooves, thundering across the desert.

AND A FEW hours later, she was standing outside, waiting for Frankie to come back with the keys. The car gave off its own heat, like the flank of an animal.

How far could the ocean be from there? A day? Two days? How could it be that Susannah had lived this long and never been to the ocean? It went quickly from being an idea to an imperative. She would smother if she stayed in the desert, at the godforsaken Thunder Lodge, for an instant longer. She would go, and if she saw the ocean before the baby was born, it would be a sign. Aaron had always teased her about her signs, about how she'd make decisions this way—*If that squirrel leaps to the next tree, let's get pizza; if it climbs down to the ground, let's get Chinese*—but then he'd always teased her about everything. Well, maybe she didn't think it was such a bad way to make decisions. She didn't know any other way to think right now besides this, besides, *If we get to the ocean before the baby is born, that will mean I should keep him. If not, I'll give him up to Julian and Kit.* The sky scorched in her vision, huge and low, draped over her head and shoulders like an enormous blue blanket. She felt as if she were watching herself from a great distance. The whole world seemed like someone else's idea, like a movie she only remembered having seen halfway through: very familiar, and very distant.

The sky darkened suddenly, preparing for a morning storm. Susannah leaned against the car. The Thunder Lodge sign flickered down at her, its glow given currency by the suddenly darker sky. She was tired already. Her legs felt like water balloons, sweating swollenly into her cutoffs; perspiration rivered down her back. Her lucky T-shirt emitted a sour smell. And across the street (Susannah squinted) was the boy she had seen her first night there.

The boy? He stood still against the gathering storm. He lifted one arm and waved with the slingshot that dangled from his hand.

"Okay," said Susannah. "Okay."

Somewhere nearby were Marlon and Char, still sleeping side by side through the early morning, Marlon's leg draped over Char's bottom. Somewhere was Tim, touching himself quietly in bed. Somewhere the drowsy gas-station attendant checked the hinges and pulleys of the ghosts in the haunted cave. Somewhere was Susannah's mother, waking in that film of dream panic, realizing that Susannah was still gone, unaccounted for, and that that part hadn't been the dream. Somewhere in the world were men Susannah had slept with, men she didn't care about, men whose faces she could scarcely remember, men she would someday sleep with, men she would never meet. Somewhere was Rose, making coffee for her husband as her babies wailed in the next room. Somewhere was the friend Susannah had encountered and lied to. Somewhere was her apartment near the train tracks, furred with dust, a fire-escape pigeon at the window wondering what had become of the crumbs he'd once found strewn on the sill each morning.

FRANKIE DISLODGED THE key ring from her aunt's purse.

Dicey stirred in her sleep.

FRANKIE RETURNED TO the car, key ring in one hand, suitcase in the other.

"Oh, no, Frankie," said Susannah softly. "No, you stay here. I'll bring the car back soon, I promise."

"I only like swimming in the ocean," said Frankie. "Don't you remember?" She stood sturdily, her legs splayed out and belly thrust forward. "That's where you're going, right?"

"Are you kidding me?" Susannah scanned the motel for signs of stirring. "Absolutely not," she hissed. "Are you nuts? I can't take you with me. Dicey would kill me, for one thing."

Frankie waved the key ring in one hand. "Do you want the keys or what?"

Susannah rubbed at her forehead, laughing a little. "This is crazy."

Because Frankie had run out of excuses and time with Dicey, and there was no way she was going to live with Skip. She was an old hand at running away from home for an afternoon or so at a time. It was usually fun, too—though a little less fun, somehow, when no one noticed. And now she was headed to California with beautiful Susannah, who she knew loved her, and who never said no, and who, besides, always had candy. She rattled the keys again, as if teasing a dog. "Do you want 'em or what? It's a package deal." (She had heard the phrase on a television show and felt very pleased to have a reason to use it.) "I wanna come with."

Susannah sighed. "Fine. You know what? Fine. But no whining."

They creaked open the car doors, packing Susannah's suitcases into the backseat as gingerly as three enormous eggs, because Dicey's trunk was already jammed with Frankie's things, her gear for Life with Dad. "If we're only going to the ocean and back," said Frankie across the backseat, "why do you need all these suitcases?"

Susannah didn't meet her eyes. She would bring Frankie back, eventually, after Julian and Kit had given up. Of course she would. It would be fine, maybe even fun, to have Frankie along.

The air thickened around them, fat with the impending storm.

"Hallelujah!"

They both stiffened, turned to look over their shoulders. Tim stood in the doorway of the office, moved toward them as stiff-legged as Frankenstein's monster, his tousled hair sticking in his eyes. He wore a pair of jelly-caked sweatpants and a white T-shirt too small for him.

"Hallelujah Prue," he said in his flat, one-volumed way. "Going to the caves? The Haunted Caves?" And he would wake Marlon and Char, and the commotion would stir Dicey, and what a scene *that* would be.

"Shhhh!" A part of Susannah that she hadn't seen in a while, or maybe never had at all, bubbled to the top, rising through the silt of personality she had created for herself—through decisions she had always made to be quiet, to be nice, to let others decide—through all that came this purpley force, this veiny, thorned mass—this powerful unpleasantness. It stirred in her gut like an engine. The baby leaned hard against her spine, as if experiencing a sudden gust. She grabbed Tim's arm, his skin still cold from the air-conditioned night. She extended her index finger in front of her lips. "Shhhh. Both of you, hush."

Frankie said to Tim, "We're going to the ocean! We're going to go swimming!"

Tim looked at Susannah. "The ocean! Yeah! Definitely the ocean. Definitely." He jumped a little, clasping his hands together. He looked so out of his mind with excitement that it made Frankie laugh—"Yesss!" he said. He had an unignorable smile; he giggled a little faster than usual. "Go to the ocean with Susannah Prue! Go to the ocean with Susannah Prue!"

Despite herself Susannah laughed, felt something releasing in her neck that she hadn't even realized was tensed. "Shhh," she said again. Frankie and Tim now raced around, Frankie tiptoeing exaggeratedly, trying to mime something to Tim, who laughed at her. "You nut. I'll see you later."

Tim stopped short, his face clouding over. "No."

"Timmy," Susannah said quietly. "Please. We have to go now. Please, just be quiet."

"No!" He said louder. "Go to the ocean with Susannah Prue!"

"Be *quiet.*" Susannah stole a look toward the office. This was ridiculous. But then, she considered, they wouldn't be gone long, and if Tim had a fit now, they wouldn't be going anywhere at all. And anyway, weren't they a perfect little family, made for each other—hadn't she felt that? Tim opened the car door and plopped himself down in the backseat. Frankie tumbled into the passenger side, standing on her knees and facing Tim. "Okay, here's the game we're playing," she said. "Put your hands down, like this, and I put my hands here, and— Oh! I got you!" She slapped Tim's hands, and he flinched, looked at her with an injured expression. Frankie giggled. "It's a *game*—you're supposed to move your hands." Tim slapped her hands suddenly. "No!" Frankie cried, but she was laughing. "Let me show you."

Susannah sighed, smiling, rubbing her forehead. "All right, you guys. Fine. Let's get going. Tim, if there's anything you need, go get it now, *quietly*, you hear me? This is a top-secret mission, okay?" Tim nodded and headed toward the office. She leaned back in the driver's seat of Dicey's car. Adrenaline ricocheted around in her body, twitching each toe, each hair, each nerve ending alive, alive, alive.

She wanted to gather them close, Frankie and Tim; she wanted to squeeze them until they screamed. They would head across the desert, the sun at their backs. If Julian and Kit called the motel or actually arrived . . . well, the Garlands wouldn't be lying when they said they didn't know where she'd gone.

Frankie was making a nest in the front seat—a pillow swiped from the room, her navy blue sweatshirt, a soccer ball Susannah had never seen. "Do you need that?" she said, pointing. Frankie nodded seriously. The morning heated up by the minute. The rainstorm had passed without erupting, blown farther down the road. They could see the clouds hanging there, a few miles away, waiting, suspended in the enormous clear sky like a mobile over a crib. All of it had become so familiar—the neon sign crackling in the sky, the dust of the parking lot, the parched tangles rooting the sand, the highway dissolving into the sky. The sky blindingly blue, the sun impossible to look at, even now, so early. Susannah had never before felt so viscerally that it was a planet she lived on—a sphere of dirt precarious in the universe, a slave of the sun.

She moved the front seat back as far as it would go to accommodate her belly. The pregnancy and baby-care books had all been left at home, but she was pretty sure she shouldn't be driving or whatever. Her spine squealed when she sat. She had Frankie take the thin, disinfectant-scented pillow from her room and cram it behind her back. In one more minute, they would leave, Tim or no. In fact yes, it was better without.

Then Tim appeared, clutching a backpack.

He had this way of seeming totally normal, totally reasonable, that was the thing. He could have been any young man, throwing his backpack into the car, squinting at Susannah, straightening and surveying the horizon one last time before climbing in and clapping his hands together. Ready. Set. It was going to be fun. What an adventure!

"Tim, will you be okay? We're going to be in the car for a long time. We're not going to see Mom and Dad for a few days," Susannah said. She sounded like a doctor, like a principal, some noxious authority saying *Mom and Dad* like that—ugh. But Tim was nodding, even smiling—that half smile that looked so knowing. He was ready. He was set. Away from his parents, he would start to unfurl, he would become the boy she knew he could be. He wasn't stupid, he wasn't crazy. He was the sweetest man she'd ever met, he was so gentle—bringing Susannah offerings every morning, giving her the kind of undivided attention she had never gotten from anyone. It was impossible to look at his chiseled face, his eyes, the lock of hair falling at his brow, and be suspicious of his mind.

Of course, if she'd been honest with herself, she would have seen that there was something unsettling about this voyage with these two unknown quantities, these people that she really hardly knew but who would be an irrevocable presence during every moment of the trip. But when a person suspects any wrong, it sometimes happens that she tries to cover up her suspicions even from herself. It was this way with Susannah. She said nothing and tried to think nothing.

Dicey's car was one of those enormous American things from the eighties that navigated like a ship. They coasted down the highway, away from the storm that finally erupted, concentrated (it seemed) in an axis just to the side of the Thunder Lodge. Frankie bounced in the passenger seat. "Now, I'm serious, if we meet anyone, tell them I'm a boy. I'm ready for that. Okay?" In the back Tim sat stiffly, still sleepy. "The ocean?" he said. "Are we at the ocean yet? Are we almost at the ocean?"

"No, you dingbat," Frankie told him. "It's not for a long ways."

"Oh," said Tim. "Now?"

"Are you kidding me?" Frankie laughed.

Tim laughed, too. "Yeah. Are you kidding me? Yeah. Heh."

"Jeez Louise. What a spaz."

Susannah looked up sharply. "Frankie. Don't use that word."

Frankie rolled her eyes. "So-rry. I meant, what a retard."

"Frankie!"

Even Frankie could hear the edge in her voice. The smile dropped from her face. She turned to Tim. "I'm sorry. I didn't mean it."

"Thank you," Susannah muttered, shaking her head.

Tim looked blankly at Frankie, stared out the window for a minute, then turned back to her. "*Now* are we at the ocean?"

Frankie pointed at him. "You see what I mean!"

Dread fizzed beneath Susannah's breastbone, stung across her belly. She already had to pee. They headed west, the rising sun whitely at their backs. No one spoke for a long time. Then, "Is there something wrong with the windshield?" The windshield made everything look yellow. Susannah squinted out through it. "Does it seem kind of yellow?"

Frankie gave her a sympathetic look.

Here was the world, dumb and bare. They careened past the gas station and the caves. The ridge of mountains puffed itself up like an adder. Wind came tumbling from the plains, palpable and powerful, nudging the car this way and that. A tour bus jammed with senior citizens lunged at the rear of the car, then lurched into the empty left lane, sped up, and passed. Susannah concentrated on the back of the bus as it pulled ahead, shrank into a lozenge in her field of vision. The seniors must have been heading somewhere to gamble. Susannah could respect this.

"Seriously, Frankie. Is there something funny with the glass?"

"I don't get what you mean."

"I feel like everything is yellowish." Stained with iodine, drips of bloody dye. The world looked as jaundiced as an old photograph, with the sepia hue of nostalgia. For some reason it made Susannah long for things she'd always hated: the auditorium of her high school with its nubby blue walls, the smell of ammonia when her mother cleaned the house, the clumpy sound of Rose gnawing at her fingernails, the sickly tint of food dye seeping into a mound of dough. Why did the liquefied yellow look like blood? Her mother was always getting clever with her baking, staining sugar cookies into mini hamburger stacks or Rice Krispies into wreaths. Everything always had to be something else. A cookie couldn't be just a cookie. Susannah had always been repelled by this, had always sworn that it would not be the way she was, and here, miles away from any kind of cookie, months since she'd been within burning distance of a stove, with the baby treading water, she could already feel it revving up in her, the mother she would be (potentially, might be, someday), the irrelevant fusses she would make about things like cookies. She already knew what would annoy her children about her. The things she had said and done already, the kinds of things she said and did every day. She was glad this child wasn't hers. She was glad it was

Julian and Kit's. She was glad she didn't have to be as exposed and adored and despised as a mother was, a celebrity to a very select cult following. All of this would end someday, and she would be just a normal girl again.

But for now—everything was fleshy and peeling. The sky had some sort of problem. The people in the car were quiet. Tim slept in the back. Frankie slept in the front. By 10:00 A.M. the car was baking despite the wheeze of the air-conditioning. It was the kind of heat that just nudged the cold air to the side, swirling it in its moist mouth, spitting it out as a warmish sludge. The unfiltered light of the day shoved at the roof of the car. In Susannah's back the pain was not a thing she had known before. It daggered into her cells, excavating each nerve ending. There would be nowhere to stop for a long time, no one to take a turn driving. She shot a glance at Frankie, at Tim. This was something she had done to herself. Pain poured down her back like syrup. Dust crescendoed around.

Along the side of the highway, a turkey vulture hunched over an unidentifiable pile of meat.

Tim leaned forward sleepily. Susannah looked at him. He manufactured for her a listless giggle. "Huh."

"Hi, Tim. Good morning."

"Breakfast," he said. He pushed his hair from his eyes with his fingertips.

Susannah's gut sank. She'd been driving about an hour. There was no way to turn back. Dicey would surely be missing her car, her niece, by now. "What do you mean?" she said, stalling for time to think.

"Pop-Tarts and a orange," he said. "Yeah."

"How about let's try something different this morning? Since we're doing something new. How about, in a little bit we'll stop somewhere and get some bacon and eggs? Yum! Right?"

Tim stiffened. The look on his face was familiar to her from . . .

what was it? Oh, from the caves, the moment before he had erupted. She was desperate to avoid such a scene. How could she have been so stupid? It really was amazing. He said, his face flushing, "Pop-Tarts. A orange."

"Tim," tried Susannah. "Jackalope."

He punched his hand into his thigh. "Time for breakfast!"

Frankie blinked sleepily, looked at the two of them. Her hair was matted to her face in a way that reminded Susannah of the first time she'd ever seen her. It was difficult to remember what the child had looked like to Susannah before she'd known her the way she knew her now, which was at least a little. Frankie had seemed like such a baby to her then, an overalled infant. Frankie rubbed her eyes and then reached into a plastic bag Susannah hadn't noticed before. Tim was punching his thigh with some regularity now, as if revving an engine. The baby seemed to get upset, too, twisting suddenly to sock an elbow into Susannah's spine. Sometimes she suspected that the baby perhaps knew what was happening and was angry, impatient to get to his real parents, frustrated with Susannah's indecisiveness. Tim opened his mouth, his eyes flashing around, and Frankie said, "Cool your jets," in the pseudononchalant way of a kid repeating a phrase from someone admired. (Who said, "Cool your jets?" Susannah pictured Frankie's mother—a young, sultry version of Dicey—stubbing out a cigarette and saying, "Cool your jets.") And then she took from the bag a package of Pop-Tarts. Susannah breathed out. How had Frankie remembered to bring food and Susannah had not? It was simultaneously relieving and disturbing.

Tim took the silver package and considered its heft in his hand. "A orange," he reminded her. Frankie shook her head no. There weren't any. He set his jaw, tore open the Mylar envelope, took a bite of the cardboardy sweet.

Which seemed like a good sign.

WHEN IT CAME to the ocean, they had a long way to go. The New Mexico highways were largely uninhabited, governed by forgiving speed limits and listless police enforcement. The clean, open landscape helped Susannah feel that her mind was wiped clean, too, uncluttered by consideration or thought or worry. But it also meant there weren't many places to stop along the way and that Susannah did a lot of awkward peeing into dust, squatting in some cases right beside the car so she could steady her top-heavy self. Now and then she pointed something out to the kids as they sped through the state. An outcropping of scrubby cacti blooming a single red fruit. The abandoned hull of a car. A roadrunner sprinting in the distance. Frankie was disappointed with the roadrunner—it was nothing like the cartoon! Shouldn't it have been blue, jovial, tall as a man?

They stopped for breakfast in a grubby little town one block long. Frankie and Tim had been lobbying for the McDonald's on the side of the highway, but this seemed wrong to Susannah, tawdry and too bright; eating in a fast-food restaurant on a sunny summer day was the kind of thing that exposed your life for the sad series of mistakes it was. Susannah was after a bit more atmosphere and happily found a run-down diner in the center of the town, across the street from the inevitable abandoned-looking hardware store. Here there would be wisecracking waitresses with sad life stories. Here there would be actual food made by actual people, and this was what they needed right now, she'd decided. They needed a little nourishment.

A white-aproned man stood behind the counter, swiping at it listlessly with a rag. He nodded them toward the booth by the window. Sun filtered through the painted-on letters, through the dusty pane. All her life, Susannah thought, she wanted to be sitting across from Frankie and Tim at a booth by a window, watching the light play on Tim's hair, catching Frankie's foot when it flung out in a kick, holding on to the foot as Frankie laughed and squirmed. The diner made a clanging music—white strips of bacon sizzling on the grill, a waitress emptying the dishwasher below the counter and noisily stacking the plates, customers clinking forks and murmuring. Susannah studied the menu and said, "Tim, they have a fruit cup," still worried about the orange.

Frankie stacked plastic creamers and frowned. "I want pancakes. Do they have silver-dollar pancakes? I want silver-dollar pancakes. They're like regular pancakes, only smaller."

Tim handed her a creamer and watched her add it to the stack. "Me, too. Pancakes."

"You both want pancakes?"

"*Silver-dollar* pancakes." The creamer tower toppled down. "Can you just order for us already? We're kind of busy now," Frankie said, flustered.

Susannah rubbed her belly. Poor baby. She'd eat something really healthful and nourishing. She'd get back on track. She'd been so good in the beginning, with all her vitamins and soothing music. Now she'd order . . . what? She was suddenly ravenous. A cheeseburger and a salad—it would be iceberg lettuce and some diced unripe tomato, she was sure of it, but it was worth a shot—and she'd get cottage cheese and a scoop of tuna salad and a chocolate milk and apple pie. God, she was starving! It was only ten or so in the morning, but it felt like they'd been traveling for ages. She ordered, and the waitress laughed. "Eating for two, I see!" she said, taking the menus.

"At least!" Susannah answered.

Frankie and Tim were racing towers, but after balancing one creamer on top of the first, Tim inevitably knocked his over with a clumsy hand. A child sitting with her grandfather in the next booth hooked her elbows over the back of the bench and watched for a minute before offering Tim some pointers. Soon the waitress was involved, too—she stopped by with a tray of water glasses and said, casually, "You could build something together, instead of racing." And just like that, changed the whole tenor of the morning. Now, *that* was an excellent mother. The child in the next booth agreed—"A castle!"—and donated the blue Equal packets from her table as roofing material. Frankie directed Tim to construct the castle wall out of sugar cubes while she built up the infrastructure. Susannah offered her straw as a periscope for the lookout tower.

She wanted to show it to Julian—the castle, the kids. She wanted to freeze the moment and deliver it to him, a skin sliver on a glass slide, to say, *See! See, this is what I am made of!* They had gone to a diner in the city one night, when Julian couldn't sleep and snuck out and called her; they had ordered egg creams and then argued, teasingly, about what egg creams even were; they had recruited people sitting nearby, had finally asked the waitress, demanding to know what the hell egg creams even were. Drinking egg creams in the middle of the night by a reflective window, like kids on a date in 1950. They had fun together, that's all it was. What was so terrible about that?

Now Frankie wanted to make a moat, was threatening to pour ketchup onto the napkins they'd spread out on the table, surrounding the castle. Tim started shaking his head when she opened the bottle. "No, no, no," he told her, shaking his head more furiously and waving his hand in front of his nose. "No!" Raising his voice, causing people to turn and look.

"Frankie," Susannah said. "He doesn't like the way that smells."

Tim nodded. Frankie looked from one of them to the other. "But! It's not fair! It would make a cool moat," she said, putting down the ketchup bottle.

"You should clean that up, anyway. Look, our food is coming."

Tim rubbed his hands along his thighs. "Moats aren't red," he said finally. He sounded offended.

Susannah raised her eyebrows. "He has a point, Frank."

Frankie glumly collected the pieces of the castle. It had been an impressive structure. They could agree on that. "Well, it would be red after the enemies came, and attacked, and it was all full of blood."

"That's gross," said Susannah, but Tim burst out into a hooting round of laughter. Frankie stifled a smile, trying to seem still upset. They were a funny little group, thought the waitress as she delivered the plates of tiny pancakes, and the mother too young, too permissive, letting them make ten kinds of messes—but there was something magnetic about them, something in their presence that changed the feel of the diner ever so slightly. If the mother ate all the food she'd ordered, it would make a funny thing to tell Nell, the pregnant waitress who worked weekends—she'd tell her, *Pickles and chocolate milk, just like you.* When they left, thought the waitress, the diner would seem a little too quiet, a little too still. Now the kids were laughing about something else, and the pregnant woman, shaking her head and smiling, confiscated the ketchup bottle, said, "Just eat your pancakes, you maniacs."

For the rest of the morning and into the afternoon, they were one big happy family, on a pleasant and leisurely drive. The only problem was that Susannah had forgotten about the state of Arizona. The trip would take one or two days longer than she'd thought. And Tim, though a handsome and in many ways a fine boy, simply did not have it in him to be flexible; he survived the morning but became increasingly agitated throughout the day. She found him standing in the center of a truck-stop convenience store, grinding his jaw.

"Time to go to the Grotto," he told her mournfully. That was his life. Every day he woke up and received two untoasted Pop-Tarts and an orange cut into four fat wedges. He visited the Grotto, touched his hand to the head of the Virgin shrine in the concrete wall, swam until he tired. He walked around looking for pebbles. He took a bath, maybe, when his mother made him. He went into his bedroom at ten o'clock at night and masturbated under the covers. What else should he do with himself?

Susannah tried to tempt him back toward the car. "Tim-my," she cooed. Everything was so difficult, like moving through glue. "Frankie just bought a big package of beef jerky. Would you like that? Want to try it?"

He looked at her in a way that said, unmistakably, *Please stop being such an asshole.*

Truckers with bodies shaped like Susannah's brushed past. A dusty family in shorts squabbled nearby. A teenage son was gesticulating with a package of Cool Ranch Doritos. Muzak blared. *What's love got to do, got to do with it?*

Susannah put her hand on Tim's shoulder. She tried to look into his eyes, but he avoided her, giggling nervously, muttering, "Yeah. Yeah. Yeah."

"Tim," she said, moving her face close to his so that he couldn't help but look at her. "Tim"—and she put her other hand on his other shoulder, and her belly pressed against his—"I need you to roll with the punches here. Understand? I need you to be a man. Right? Got it?" He looked past her, studying the refrigerated case of Mountain Dew varieties and their wild claims of refreshment. "We'll be back home in a few days, and everything will be back to normal," she promised. As she said it, she almost started to believe it herself, the story she kept telling Frankie—this was just a trip to the coast and back, only the tiniest of vacations. She had assumed that Marlon or Dicey or someone would come after them. They had to. She thought about driving slower, making more stops—if it were even humanly possible to do so and still be moving at all.

Tim knit his brow. He looked like he might cry. Tim—poor Timmy!—if only there were some way to make things okay for him, to reach out and touch his curled lashes, push the hair from his eyes. There was a freckle on the side of his nose she was shocked she'd never noticed before. A whitish shingle of skin hinged off his shapely bottom lip. What she liked best, she thought, was to be looking at someone's face up close, so close it was all she could see. She'd looked at Julian this way, spent hours staring at his face, watching the way his mouth moved when he spoke, trying to memorize each movement of muscle, each feature—the kinked silver hairs in his eyebrows, the sensuous curve of his ear, the way his left eye was slightly more almond-shaped than his right. *Tell me everything,* she wanted to say now to Tim. *I want to know everything.* It was this accumulation that she craved, this collecting of details, creating a satchel for each person that mattered. Comparing scars with Rose, paging through Aaron's old yearbooks; love was acquisition. She watched now the flicker of Tim's eyes, studied the ring of gold haloing his cornea. *Tell me everything, Tim. Everything.*

Then he assembled something like calm, reached out his hand, and there in the crowded convenience store clamped his right hand onto Susannah's left breast. (Helen Rosen gasped—had she really just seen that? A handsome young boy feeling up his pregnant girlfriend in the middle of a truck stop! The world was really changing, was really getting scary. She wouldn't be sorry to get home, to settle back onto the couch and watch television and get some knitting done. She wouldn't be sorry one bit.) Susannah flinched. "All right. Cut that out. Come on, let's go." He squeezed a little too hard. She thought she heard someone gasping. She gently pulled free of his grasp and led him outside into the blaring sunlight. She sat him in the backseat. He had forgotten his anguish. She plunked down heavily beside him. He reached over and touched her breast again. She didn't stop him, waited it out. No one had touched her breasts in a long time. They were so swollen and transformed that his touch felt strangely impersonal, as if a child had grabbed hold of a hank of her hair.

She looked at him, but he was staring intently at his own hand, a mystified smile playing on his lips. The thought of Tim touching her in that way made her stomach twinge with mobile, crinkling ickiness, as if dehydrated. But at the same time, Tim was still Tim, still the boy with the chiseled face and noble gray eyes, still the boy who in all his simplicity seemed unusually good and trustworthy to Susannah, for whom things had become complicated so quickly and so often. This would not end well. A state police highway patrol car puttered through the lot, and Susannah ducked low into the seat. Jesus! And where was Frankie? Her sweet little sidekick Frankie—she'd have to remember to keep her in sight. Would Frankie tire of the game, sneak away, call Dicey, call the cops?

But no, here she was. Frankie clambered into the passenger seat of the car, and Susannah took Tim's hand and pressed it softly away. Frankie was saying, "Worst. Bathroom. Ever."

"Oh, no, Frankie, did you go into the boys' room?"

"I told you!" she said, accusingly.

"I know, but . . . can't you be a boy who uses the girls' bathroom? I mean, there might be some not-so-nice boys around in these truck stops, some not-so-nice things happening. And I can't go in there with you."

Tim moved closer to her, petting her arm in mechanical swipes.

Only now did Susannah turn to face Frankie. "Your hair!" A little boy sat in the front seat—a puckish creature with a messy head of close-cropped short hair. "Frankie! What on earth have you done?"

Frankie shrugged. "I borrowed scissors from the lady at the counter. I told her my mom needed them." Susannah rubbed at her temples, put a hand gently on Tim's arm, trying to get him to stop touching her. "Then I went into the bathroom. I really needed a haircut, don't you think?" There was a baldish patch in the back, a longer shock on top. Tim rubbed at Susannah's shorts. She grabbed his hand now (he stiffened) and pushed it away more forcefully and eased herself out of the car. Frankie pulled down the sun visor and examined herself in the mirror. "Much, much better," she pronounced.

"Dicey is going to kill me," said Susannah. Until now, she realized, she hadn't seen this whole thing from Dicey's point of view. Being a tomboy was one thing. But this—it was tiring, it was inexplicable. Couldn't the kid give it a rest for a day, perhaps, for a few hours? Susannah had been an imaginative child—sure, she understood—

whole days of insisting on being a princess, or a dragon. But wasn't Frankie getting to be a bit old for it? Now the child slumped in the passenger seat, kicking her dusty sneakers onto the dashboard, burying herself under her folded arms. "Well, I think I look cool," she said poutily. Tim had reclaimed his spot in the backseat and pressed his forehead against the window.

"Okay," Susannah said, filling her chest with air. "Okay. Okay. Okay."

THE HAND-PAINTED SIGN directed them down a long dirt road snaking up a hill. Susannah stole a glance at Frankie and Tim, then turned off onto the side road. "Detour!" she said in a singsong, trying to channel a teacher announcing a field trip. Her mood had transformed as they slept; seeing their faces, kittenish in sleep, had made her feel terrible for taking them with her and at the same time incredibly grateful to them. She wanted to give them something. An offering, a detour, something fun. "I think you guys are going to love this!"

Neither of them responded. Susannah kept the smile pasted to her face as the dirt enveloped the car. "This is going to be great," she repeated. Tim had been so quiet for so long that she checked the rearview mirror again to see if he was even still in the car. "All right, now," she said. "Don't go too crazy, you guys. I know the excitement is killing you, but just try to settle down."

The church wasn't as famous as others of its ilk, and maybe this was why the road was so perilously rough, cratered with depressions, pocked with ancient tires and tin cans. The building itself was a crumbling adobe edifice fenced off by a few twisted piñon limbs. The doors were propped open. Susannah pulled up and let the car idle outside the entrance. "Eh?"

"What is that supposed to be?" said Frankie without moving.

Susannah stopped the car and got out. "Live a little, Frankie," she said. Tim got out and followed her.

"Haunted Caves?" he said.

"Sort of." Susannah stepped inside the dim space, waited a moment for her eyes to adjust. The doorway was strung with crutches and canes, dangling from the ceiling like broken limbs. "I think you're going to like this place," she told Tim. All she knew of it was the sign she'd seen on the freeway, but something about it had sounded familiar and welcome and right, and anyway, there was no one to tell her not to. "This is a place that heals people," she said authoritatively. "Kind of like magic."

Tim giggled. "Huh."

"Cool, right?"

"Huh." Tim was made timid by the dark and shuffled along beside her, close to her elbow. Past the gauntlet of crutches stood a birdbath of holy water and a confession booth. To their left was a door with a fogged window like an office in an old detective movie, and behind the door Susannah could hear someone speaking softly into a telephone, droning slowly and evenly as if dictating a letter. Directly ahead of them, a single window emitted a beam of light. Their feet were quiet on the hard-packed dirt floor, past the rows of pews. Susannah and Tim slowly walked up the aisle together in a kind of horrible parody, Susannah realized a little too late, of a wedding.

"There." Where a pulpit would normally be was a shallow hole of dirt. Tim squatted down and ran his fingers through it, as if he'd been waiting his whole life to plunge his hands into that very well. He located a clump, held it up close to his eye, and then smashed it with a giggle. Susannah sat on the front bench, watching him. She wanted to see things the way he saw them, and when she concentrated, she thought she could identify the sparkle in the dirt, the possibilities of a handful of filth, the deep, soothing crunch of gravel between teeth. For Tim, things were simpler, more beautiful. The sunlight found his hair.

This earth was meant to heal everything, wasn't it? It could perform miracles, couldn't it? A pamphlet left on the bench explained that long ago a mysterious traveler had arrived one day and the fathers of the church had offered her shelter, that by morning she had vanished, leaving a hollow in the center of the church—that the miracle dirt there had healed deafness, banished smallpox, guaranteed luck in hundreds of ways. Susannah read the testimonials. She couldn't help smiling—the stories of scars closing, of pains dissolving, the hilariously solemn explanations and prayers—but also she wasn't counting anything out, not anymore. She didn't have the luxury of assuming that everything was a scam. Meanwhile Tim was licking a pebble. All right, well. Susannah closed her eyes, dared the miraculous dirt to surprise her.

"You know, it's about a thousand degrees in that car." Frankie stood in the middle of the tiny church's aisle, her arms crossed in front of her stomach. The voice in the office paused, then resumed.

"Here, Frankie," said Tim. "Heh. Here."

She sighed. They had started to treat each other with the impatience of siblings. "What."

"It's magical dirt," said Susannah. "I mean, that's the story, anyway. You're supposed to touch it and close your eyes and rub the dirt over what you need healed. And it heals you. See all the crutches?"

"Those aren't real," Frankie said uncertainly.

Susannah leaned back and folded her hands on her belly. "Suit yourself."

"I mean"—Frankie peered at her—"are they?"

She shrugged. She knew by now how it was with Frankie. Only if she looked the other way and pretended not to be paying any attention at all would Frankie move cautiously toward the hole, put a hand on Tim's thigh to steady herself as she squatted alongside him. "Well, this sure is stupid," Frankie said to no one in particular. Tim giggled, "Yeah," and swirled his hands more vigorously in the dirt.

Susannah studied instead the palms of her own hands, which

seemed suddenly very far away, the lifelines and lovelines as distant as highways on an aerial photograph. Whose hands were those? When had she become *this*? And it wasn't even only that she was trapped, trapped, trapped in this situation—that she had made the wrong decision so many times—but, God, did she miss herself. When she thought of Julian, and of how sweetly he'd tried to make it all okay for her, how wrongly but how sweetly—and of Char and Dicey waking up in the morning and looking for their kids—and of everything that she now had to do, the driving and dealing with Frankie and Tim and the baby, oh, the fucking baby!—she was in so over her head! Why hadn't anyone told her to stop? Why hadn't anyone forced her to? Up came the pavement, the roaring regret. Then she was crying. The tears came from somewhere else, from somewhere deep in her belly, and were accompanied by a strange, guttural hiccupping, an inhuman tar of phlegm rising to clog her throat. She covered her face with her hands, playing peekaboo with the world. She cried and cried and cried. She was horrified, when she thought about it. When she really acknowledged, which she hardly ever did, what was happening, had happened, would happen, she was horrified. The sobs racked her belly, moved through her sinuses, echoed in her vast, empty head.

After a few moments, she felt them gather around closely. Tim stood stooped in front of her, pressed his hand to the crown of her head. Frankie perched on the bench and leaned her body against Susannah's. They sat there for a long time, or for a short time. Frankie rubbed her back, soothingly, like a tiny mother. Tim pressed his hand to one side of her face, then the other. They were sand and boardwalk and shore.

When they got back into the car, Susannah stole a look at herself in the rearview mirror and saw that the children's dirty hands had left streaks on her face and on her pale striped shirt. This made her laugh, a little, that orangey, post-crying laugh, as she wiped at her eyes with her fingertips. She sensed Frankie relaxing beside her and looked over at her. The crotch of her shorts was smudged with the ruddy earth. "Oh, Frankie," she said. "Oh, sweetheart."

"What?" said Frankie, just a snotty kid again.

"Nothing. Thanks. Sorry about that." Susannah reached over to squeeze her small, grubby hand.

Frankie shrugged. In the backseat Tim leaned forward, pawing clumsily at Susannah's hair. "Yeah," he said. "Yeah, sorry about that."

"Yeah, sorry about that," Frankie mimicked back at Tim.

Tim answered, "Sorry about that."

"No, I'm sorry," said Susannah.

"No, *I'm* the sorry one," said Frankie.

"You don't even know what sorry *is,* kid. *I'm* sorry." They were all laughing now.

"Sorry!" said Tim.

"So-rrrry!" said Frankie, waving her hands. "I! Am! Sorry!"

"Yeah," said Tim, "Sorry about that." Why did it seem so funny? They could hardly breathe, they were all laughing so hard.

"No," said Susannah. "No one's as sorry as me."

6

on reconnaissance

There are times when the whole universe seems a vast practical joke, the point of which one doesn't get; times when one suspects that the joke is at nobody's expense but one's own. There are times when possibility breaches the gloom of disaster, when a man allows himself to think, I think I can get through this, yes, I'm sure I can—and then one's child, say, of the unborn variety, absconds with a beautiful girl—the one once held a little too long, that's all, just a moment too long pressed against one's chest, the hand at the back of the hair, just long enough to alarm her, to set her running like a spooked horse. Times when a man knows that the world has become his puzzle to solve, a warped jigsaw with pieces, he suspects, gone missing.

Which is to say, Julian packed the car as if for a long vacation.

Which is to say. Suitcases of breathable clothing. Packable pants guaranteed not to wrinkle, shrugged into themselves like roly-poly bugs. Bathing suits, travel toothbrushes, every map they owned, including maps of Alaska, maps of foreign countries, detailed road maps of Chicagoland. Shampoo bottles swaddled in plastic bags. An inflatable neck pillow. The digital camera and a clutch of batteries. Sneakers, slippers, sandals. A bouquet of dime-store umbrellas. Rain ponchos. Winter parkas. Sleeping bags they had never yet used but kept thinking they might need. Travel journals, ballpoint pens, mini pouches of aspirin, a portable water filter. They packed dress clothes entombed in dry cleaner's cellophane, hung to flap against the backseat window like crinkling ghosts. Julian stuck his laptop behind the driver's seat, wedging it carefully between a suitcase and the upholstery. He thought they'd thought of everything when Kit came out of the building cradling a bumpy armful of sunglasses, visors, sunscreen bottles gone greasy with age, the floppy safari hats that had prompted a tour group of teens from Dayton to dismiss the Forsythes as "fucking tourists" last year in Lisbon. Then Kit thought they'd thought of everything when Julian disappeared, only to reappear lugging a gym bag: nylon shorts and a jump rope and a yoga mat. Julian surveyed the car, clucked his tongue at the way Kit had packed the trunk and the backseat, began to pull everything out to start over. Kit was about to protest this when she remembered something and raced into the building again to retrieve the hardcover novel by her bedside, then was stopped by the framed photograph of the two of them at their wedding looking preternaturally young and happy, though it hadn't been so very long ago, and this reminded her that it might be nice to bring a few photographs. And while she was in the living room digging through pictures, she was confronted by the specter of the uninhabited nursery and the yellow baby blanket that cousin Elizabeth had sent. It didn't need to be said that if they were to find Susannah in the next week or two, it would be just in time for the birth. So she took the blanket and the hospital bag they'd packed weeks earlier, rashy with anticipation.

It was late morning by the time Julian declared the car seaworthy. They sat in the front seat, staring out the windshield. They didn't drive often. The car had been in their expensive garage for weeks without being unearthed. But they hadn't been able to find an appropriate flight at the right time to the right place, and anyway, who could tell where she would be by the time they arrived? So here they were, looking through the windshield. Where were they? How had they gotten there? And . . . neither of them had the keys, a revelation that inspired another reshuffling of the contents of the car.

It burned in their guts like indigestion, the unspoken thingness of it: that they were headed, inexpertly, fumblingly, toward a motel in the desert that Susannah had phoned from hours ago, in the middle of the night, that she was probably long gone from. That they were chasing their baby across the continent. That they had no idea what they were doing, a situation they rarely found themselves in. "Baby," he said, meaning Kit, "maybe we should hire a professional to be doing this after all. Maybe it's a thing for . . . you know, a private eye and whatever. The police at least."

Kit tipped her head back and ground her skull into the passenger seat. "You're right. Unpack the car."

"I was just thinking aloud."

"No! No, you're right! And while we're at it, let's forget the whole surrogate idea. I told you it was a bad one."

"All right."

"I know—let's just go back in time and do it all differently. Now, shoot, where did we leave our time machine?"

"Kitty." Julian looked at his wife. Could she tell that this was all his fault, that he had held Susannah Prue a little too closely, a little too long? His wife looked out the window, gnawing on the inside of her cheek. Her hands rubbed together in prayer formation between her knees, as if she couldn't get warm. He started again. "You don't need to be so—"

"What? So what?"

He reconsidered, studying the dashboard. "Are we ready?"

"Are we ready?"

"That's what I'm asking."

"I'm ready."

"Okay, me too."

"Ready, just totally unprepared."

Julian started the car, which whinnied under the weight of all their necessities. "I love you, Kitty," he said absently, as the car started to move. In the rearview mirror, their building shrank. "I love you, too," she admitted. Then they were quiet for a long time.

As soon as the city diminished, Illinois started to scare them. The suburbs dwindled into malls and then warehouses, mysterious smoke-stacked structures that resisted recognition. What were they? Factories? Office parks? Plants of some sort? Everyone on the highway drove a thousand miles an hour, all of them desperate to get where they were going. As they drove under the McDonald's oasis, a rest stop built over the road like an inhabited bridge, Julian looked up to see, for a split second, a family settling on a table by the window, a child pressing against the glass and waving at cars. Julian fought the urge to wave back. Instead he sped up, passing beneath it, bulleted through toll plazas, cut off family vans and trailers. Kit pressed her lips together but didn't say anything. If they looked back, they could still see the city, the tallest buildings spearing the pall of the sky, but they didn't look back.

Then there was that line you crossed about an hour out of the city, marking the sudden end to its influence. The sun elbowed through the clouds. Kit rolled down the window. The grit of the world adhered itself to Julian's eyelashes and tongue. Fields stretched in every direction; a green tractor chugged on the horizon; a cow ambled sluggishly, close to the road. Kit shuddered.

They made it to Missouri before stopping to eat. Neither of them had ever before been to Missouri, and it seemed to reflect perfectly their quiet, dry-mouthed panic. They would never again be in Missouri, as a matter of fact, and would always think of a run-down Shoney's by the side of the highway whenever Missouri was mentioned. When they met someone from the state, their whole lives forward, they would think that they understood that this person was inhabited by sour longing.

"What will we do," Kit finally said, "when we find her?" They had eaten piles of greasy food and now waited uneasily for the bill.

Julian searched for their waitress. He felt conspicuously like city folk. It made him jumpy. All the waitresses looked exactly alike! He tried futilely to hail one after another. "Christ," he said. "We say to her. We tell her. Listen," and then he was at a loss.

"Good plan," said Kit. She fished an ice cube out of her glass and crunched it between her teeth. A fleck of ice landed on Julian's cheek.

They had sworn they would reach Oklahoma before stopping for the night, and when Julian suggested revising the plan, stopping early, getting some rest there in Missouri—hoping for an instant in the midst of everything that he might fuck his wife on starchy sheets, take a bath on those plastic motel-tub treads, sleep the dreamless sleep of travel—Kit answered with such a meaningful look that he waved the idea away. "All right! All right! I'm kidding. I was kidding. Let's go. Back in the car, Forsythe." A fit was forthcoming, he could see from the way she stared at him, the way her nostrils flared, so he didn't even ask her to take a turn driving, though his back felt as though things had been disarranged: shoulder blades slumped sideways, muscles fisted all down his spine.

They entered Oklahoma under the cloak of midnight, stumbled sleepily into a Red Roof Inn. The clerk eyed them suspiciously. Kit's diamond ring, her pearl earrings, her impeccable "casual" twinset. Who is this woman, Julian thought, seeing Kit through the clerk's eyes for a brief instant, and doesn't she own, like, a sweatshirt? "You don't have a cigarette for me, do you?" Kit cooed at the kid. She thought she was charming him, but Julian wasn't convinced that she wasn't just scaring him. The clerk shook his head no, then offered her a cigarette outstretched from a crumpled pack. Kit smiled and went outside.

"She doesn't even smoke," Julian told the kid for some reason. "Sorry."

Julian still felt like he was driving, felt the vibration of axles churning beneath the scrubby carpet. Out the window, stars termited through the sky, gobbling the darkness. Julian had never seen so many all in one place. In a moment, he decided, he would join Kit out in the motel parking lot, and if they saw a shooting star, it would be good luck. It would be a blessing. He paid the boy for the room and went outside.

"Hey, pretty lady," he said to Kit, hamming it up. He pretended to be delivering a pickup line. "Do you know any constellations?"

Kit smiled slightly and exhaled cigarette smoke. "The Big Dipper? The Little Dipper?"

"I wish we knew more."

"Like the fancy ones," Kit agreed. "Like those ones that don't really look like what they say they look like at all. Like the ones that the chart says are warriors or chariots, but then you look in the sky and it's just a big mess."

"Maybe we could get a book about it," said Julian. "I'd like to get a book about that."

"All right," said Kit. "We will when we get home. Don't forget."

"I won't," said Julian.

When they woke in Oklahoma, they learned that all the dirt had gone red overnight. "Did you know that dirt could be red?" Kit demanded. She got up early, as she always did, had wrenched the curtains open to let sunlight virus into Julian's eyes. He pulled the covers over his head. He had not, he realized, pulled the covers over his head for some time, maybe since he was a child. He liked it. He thought he might stay. Kit transformed into a disembodied voice, moving around the room like a fairy. The polyester bedspread decisively ended the light. Kit tugged at the blanket and won, but Julian retained the sheet. Now it was more like being underwater; he was still protected from light and sound and Kit's energy rocketing around the room. She had been noticing things all morning, things he would never have thought to notice (and this, after all, was what he had first loved about her, wasn't it? the way she made him see things), and she'd been waiting for him to wake up. Now she ticked off her list: "This lovely landscape painting here, the one with all the owls, is bolted to the wall. So don't try to steal it! The complimentary soap has been used. That cigarette made me sick, I still feel terrible. There is no coffee. In fact, there is no one in the office. We should have bought gas last night. Now we'll have to stop right away, and it will feel like we're not getting anywhere. The baby's due date is one week from tomorrow."

Julian peeled back the sheet, like ripping off a Band-Aid.

They drove all morning through Oklahoma, which turned out to be precisely how they had always pictured Texas: lumbering pickups with rusted wheel wells, men at truck stops chewing tobacco and wearing ten-gallon hats, dusty and abandoned-looking towns. Getting to the actual Texas seemed redundant when finally it happened.

"Does a person ever help another person?" said Kit. She had purchased a Slurpee at the last truck stop. Neither of them had encountered a Slurpee in a long time. Just holding it and stabbing the straw farther into its recess gave Kit the look of a memory. "I mean, has anyone ever really helped anyone else without just thinking what's in it for them?"

"Are you talking about Susannah?"

"I'm talking about people."

"You think she had this in mind the whole time?"

"I'm just saying. Like the UN, like the Peace Corps, like those people who volunteer at homeless shelters or give money to UNICEF or whatever, those people who go to Africa on vacation and dig wells for poor villages—I mean, is any of it real? Is any of it purely to help?"

"Do we have to do this?"

"Everyone's just looking for something they want," Kit concluded, facing the window. "People only do things to build this idea of themselves that they like. Why else does anyone do anything? You have the idea that you are a person who helps others, and you help others so that you can justify this strange, stupid, pointless idea of yourself. It's the worst kind of ego."

Julian squinted into the road. An alien-looking something slumped half smashed on the pavement. An armadillo? A dinosaur?

"I think she should be arrested. Don't you think she should be arrested? Aren't there charges we can press?"

Julian sighed. "That would do it. That would make it all okay again."

"I'm not saying *that*, I'm just saying. A person should have to pay for making us suffer like this."

"A person? Why don't you just say her name, instead of pretending that this is all some abstract philosophizing about human nature? Why don't you just say that you're angry with Susannah?"

"I knew we shouldn't have chosen someone so young."

"No you didn't."

"I did. Just because I never said it doesn't mean I didn't think it, you know. And I did. I thought, why would someone so young be willing to do this? There must be a reason why most surrogates are older, already mothers themselves."

"Are they?"

"We've talked about this."

"If we have, I don't remember."

"You should know by now not to admit to things like that." She sucked at the remains of the Slurpee. Her lips were rosy with artificial cherry flavor. Her mouth would be cold. Julian would have liked to kiss her cherry-flavored lips, her still-cold mouth, but not her, not at that moment. He concentrated on driving instead.

"You know what they said at the motel?" he asked.

Kit blinked at him, as if he were a stranger.

"Where she called from. When I called back, I got the desk. It was an old man. He said, Susannah Prue? Who wants to know? Like he was protecting her. Like they were old friends."

"You've already told me this."

"Well? Doesn't it seem strange?"

Kit raised her hands in an exaggerated shrug. "Some crazy guy from Chicago calls your motel in the middle of the night, asking about your guests . . ."

"And when I tried to explain the situation, thinking this would help get him on my side, make him, you know, detain her if nothing else, he went, 'You her boyfriend?'"

"People don't get it."

"Yes, and I explained the whole surrogacy thing, how it wasn't mine and Susannah's but mine and my wife's, and there was this long pause like he didn't get it, and he went, 'Well she said it's hers and her boyfriend's and they're getting back together after it's born.'"

"Isn't he a little worried? I mean, she could go into labor at any minute, and you said they're in the middle of nowhere, right? I mean, doesn't that *concern* him?"

"I don't think they get concerned in that part of the world."

"Oh, come on. Anyway, why would he believe her?"

"Why would he believe me? You have to admit, her story is a little more realistic than ours."

He might as well have punched Kit in the gut. She sat very still and breathed, managing the pain.

THEY STOPPED FOR dinner at a tourist trap in Texas. It was the kind of place where if you ate an oversize steak in under an hour—with salad, potato, and dinner roll—the steak, approximately the weight of a human baby, was free. The entrance was wallpapered with photographs of queasy-looking victors. Giant plaster bulls guarded the parking lot. There was a motel attached to the restaurant. They could spend the night there, get an early start, reach the Thunder Lodge by morning. There was a cowboy-boot-shaped pool. There was a neon cowboy lassoing toward the moon.

Inside, they were seated, and Julian blinked unhappily at the menu. There was some sort of party occurring. Somewhere people were singing. "Let's go someplace else," he said desperately to Kit.

She smiled, tapped a finger at the steak deal. "I'm going to do this," she said.

"No you're not," he said.

She looked upset. "Don't say that. Don't tell me what I'm going to do or not going to do. I don't need that from you right now." She was right, after all. He didn't know why he got like this, or how she could stand him sometimes.

There were fruit-flavored margaritas in plastic glasses. There were waitresses dressed like cowgirls. Julian was afraid he might cry. His wife was a sphinx in a windbreaker, poring over the menu. She had this way of righting herself in public. In the car she would get weepy and desperate. "She's not going to be there by the time we arrive," Kit would say, out of nowhere. "She's been planning this all along. It's a scam. I've heard of these things. I saw a thing, on *20/20* or something. Didn't we see a thing? On *20/20* or something? It's a thing people do." Something would set her off—driving past a schlocky tourist trap or a rambling gas station—she'd go red and sniffling, "How could we have been so stupid?"—and Julian would sigh. That Kit was upset had been established. Did they need to keep going over it? Then they would stop in some cheesy restaurant like this one. And here she was: upright in her seat, chatting with the waiter about how many people had really finished the enormous steak, about whether *he* had ever done it and making him laugh, making this stranger laugh, as charming as can be, as if nothing had ever been wrong in her entire life. Julian nibbled at a stale breadstick. This would be somebody's mother, he thought. Somebody's whole life, this will be somebody's mother. She seemed much older when he thought of her that way. They both did.

Then Kit was saying, "Fine, fine, I guess I'll take the Caesar salad. Julie, you do the steak!"

"Ha, ha." He leaned his chin against his palm.

"Were you checking out that waitress just now?" Kit said.

"Oh, yeah. Definitely."

"Okay. You don't have to get nasty with me. I was just teasing."

Somewhere deep within the restaurant, people were again—or still—singing "Happy Birthday." A woman's voice rose shrilly above the others, attempting harmony.

They sat at their table, not looking at each other, holding hands. Their elbows cradled the bread basket between them. When the waiter finally arrived with their food, they lifted their arms, tattooed with crumbs.

AT THE THUNDER Lodge (as Susannah squinted through the yellowy windshield; as the Forsythes were first seeing the blood-colored earth of Oklahoma), it was Marlon and Charlotte Garland waking up a little later than usual to the overripe sound of Dicey's panic. "Well, now," Char muttered, pulling on a windbreaker over her thin nightgown. "What's this all about?" As if she had always suspected that Dicey was prone to hysterics. Marlon shrugged the blankets higher over his silvery chest hair. Had he seen Tim that morning? Because Tim awoke early, and it was part of his morning routine to come into his parents' room and say hello and inform them that he was going to eat breakfast. It had always been this way with them and never how parents picture it: a child running in, snuggling between them and kissing their faces like a clean and hairless puppy. Tim just wasn't that way. If you touched him without warning, he went stiff and glassy-eyed, enduring your hug until it ended. Though there were shades of affection—weren't there?—in the way he would collect special things for you, or in this morning routine of theirs. Marlon guiltily recalled a morning several months back, when a father and son, passing through on their way to Disneyland, had played catch out in the gravel—how he had watched from the office, aching with jealousy. There they were, normal as could be! Then again, he liked Tim's rituals. He liked routines as much as Tim did. Only this morning he hadn't come in yet. Or Marlon had slept through it or already acknowledged it somehow in his sleep, or the morning he hazily recalled as yesterday had really happened today, this morning, this strange morning with Dicey crying, "Frankie! Frankie!" at the top of her lungs, hollering as if to rearrange all the sand in the desert. Doors slamming. Char sighing, braiding her hair. "I hope she's gone by the time the crafts fair comes to town," she said to Marlon. He sighed back. "Ee-yup," he said. Only then did he realize: Susannah. He had scared her off, set her running. Jesus.

Char padded into the hallway, into the living room, and unlocked the door that led to the office. In the office she flicked on the two televisions as she passed, took a Styrofoam cup from the rickety hospitality table—really a dinner tray on a stand that they had been given . . . when? for their wedding?—filled it with hot water from the ticking samovar, stirred in some Sanka, turned the air conditioner up a notch, clicked on the light, and finally went out into the parking lot, blinking a few times in the sun. The first thing Char noticed was that Dicey's car was gone, the empty spot providing a clean view of Susannah's abandoned junker. When Dicey saw her, she said (voice warbling, like she was trying not to cry), "My car is gone!"

Char sipped at her Sanka. An undissolved chunk popped open on her tongue. "I see that."

"I mean!"

Char nodded, agreeing with her. Dicey plunked down on the

curb, her head in her hands. She was not a pretty woman, and, worse, she was not one of those women who cried prettily. Char imagined Susannah in tears—cheeks flushed lightly, eyes damp. No, it wasn't fair. Even though they were both youngish women with their whole lives ahead of them (though they didn't see it that way, you never saw it that way at the time), it wasn't fair that Dicey would never have been a lovely young woman. Then again (scrutinizing the miserable face, gone red and splotchy around her eyes and neck, the tensed chin, the oversize ears), it occurred to Char that this might be one of those girls who improved with age, who got prettier once she was more settled into herself and had learned to accept her features. And Susannah, when Char really thought about it, had the kind of beauty that was constructed mostly of youth, and health, and might not age well. She would become, in fact, very ordinary with the years— Susannah's grandchildren someday would look at old pictures and exclaim, *But you were so beautiful!*, surprised and a little hurt. Char didn't have much occasion to be around young people—oh, sure, a pair of newlyweds now and then, tired and serious after a long drive; Tim, if he counted—because generally around these parts they were all old, old, old and as parched as the Garlands, mummified by the heat. Now that Susannah was gone, Char suddenly regretted everything.

"You mean to tell me she stole your car?"

Dicey's face had gone bulldog on her, so upset it wasn't sure what to do and just crinkled up like a fist. "And Frankie."

Char placed her cup on the ground, sighed as she lowered herself onto the curb, favoring her slinged arm. She rubbed at her face with her good hand. "And Frankie stole your car?"

"No, Susannah stole Frankie and my car."

"Frankie's gone?"

"That's what I just said."

"You sure she's not anywhere around here, you know, out back or at the Grotto? You know how kids like to play tricks."

"Her stuff!" Dicey shook her head, suddenly done crying. "She *packed* a *bag*. Everything's gone, her overalls and all her things."

Something racketed up Char's spine then, and she hollered, "TIM!" so loudly that Dicey started. "TIM! TIMOTHY!" The office door creaked open. Char turned gratefully to look, already comfortable in that instant when the problem was handed back to Dicey—but it was only Marlon, his big hands hanging uselessly. "Tim's not in his room," Marlon said. "And he's not out back." He looked out toward the horizon. The sky lowered like a disappointed forehead, a heavy, thick blue creased over everything. The heat pressed more hotly against his skin; the highway looked longer and emptier than it had ever looked before. Now he'd really done it. He shouldn't have said anything to the girl.

There weren't all that many more places to look. They checked again at the Grotto. They scanned the horizon for Tim-shaped bumps. Rooms that had been locked for weeks were opened, emitting lonely, human smells. Marlon wondered about going to the gas station, or to the nearest town. Tim adored the Wal-Mart, loved to walk each fluorescent row, letting his fingertips skim along the patterns of packages. "But we've got to call the police," Dicey was saying, wringing her hands. "I mean, we've got to." Char said, "Pffft," and waved her off. "They probably just went on another little field trip of theirs. You know how Susannah's always talking about exploring—the Haunted Caves, all that. They'll probably be back before you can dial the number!" She didn't know why she would display such optimism just then. She did not mean the things she was saying, her voice as insincerely bright as a halogen lightbulb. "I've half a mind to go back to bed," she said, though she didn't.

But what was happening within Dicey was even more painful. She had passed the possibility of denial and knew it in her bones, as it seeped down her spine and toward her fingertips and toes, that Susannah was gone, Susannah and Frankie and Tim were gone, and that this meant not only the usual pain and anxiety and worry for their children's safety—but to Dicey it also meant that things between her and Susannah had not been what she had thought. There had been no spark, no closeness. Dicey had invented all of that. To Susannah she was just a sucker with car. Perhaps this had been Susannah's plan all along, ever since Dicey had arrived. And here Dicey had let Frankie convince her to stay—just one more day, just one more day—allowed herself to be browbeaten, pretending it had nothing to do with her fascination with Susannah. Dicey bit her lip, grinding her teeth harder, harder—she knew she deserved the tingles of pain—clamped and clamped until the tang of blood filled her mouth. But what did she want with the children? Dicey said, "What did she want with the children?"

Char squinted, fisting her good hand to her hip.

"Now, now," Marlon said. He looked at his wife, but she would not return his gaze, so he turned slowly on his heel and trudged toward the office, presumably to make some phone calls, develop a plan, do something logical and productive and male. Meanwhile Char looked straight into the sun.

"I know what she wanted with Tim," Char said.

"Oh?" Something in Dicey bristled, ready to defend Susannah.

"Don't tell me you didn't you see it."

"See what?"

"A blind man could see it."

"See what?"

Char sighed, annoyed that Dicey was being so dense that she would have to actually come out and say it, when she hadn't quite shuffled the *it* into place. She cleared her throat and searched around for something in the pocket of her sundress, and when she didn't find anything, she squinted up at the Thunder Lodge sign and said, "You know. Susannah . . . and Tim. Something about it just . . . wasn't right."

Dicey looked as if she had no idea how her face really looked.

Char cleared her throat again. "I know he can seem like a normal young man. I know he's a good-looking kid, and has"—and again with the throat clearing, until Dicey's throat felt raw just hearing it— "a man's needs. But he can't . . . she . . . it just ain't right. Her teasing him like that. You know he told me he wanted her to be his girlfriend? About to give birth to a bastard child, this strange woman from nowhere, and my son wants her to be his girlfriend. Such taste in women! And as if he could . . . well, you know, have a girlfriend like that—as if he even knew what he really was saying when he said that."

An aircraft chugged across the sky, mechanical and dark, emitting a long white tail. Dicey sucked at the salty wound on her lip, buried her fingers in her hair, pushing fingertips against greasy scalp, worrying off bits of flaking skin. "Well, couldn't he? Couldn't he have a girlfriend?" This wasn't the part of the conversation she'd meant to pursue.

"I guess," said Char stewily, too embarrassed to admit that she had always assumed that Tim would be a virgin till he died, that he would live in the little bedroom off of theirs forever, that such a thing—a girlfriend, a wife, a normal adult life—was impossible because he was what he was: He was simple, he was different, he was *something*. "But I'd think it'd be someone . . . like him. You follow me? Anyhow—I've seen the way they look at each other, in the Grotto, playing around. You've seen it. And . . . it's just not right. It's just not right at all." Her voice cracked. She knew she was getting carried away, but somehow it was better in front of this stranger, better than in front of Marlon.

Dicey shook her head. "I think you're exaggerating. She's just trying to be friendly. I think that's all it is."

"Oh?" Char became suddenly busy again, searching around in her pockets.

Marlon poked his head out of the office. Microwaves of worry radiated from his forehead. "Police say we gotta wait twenty-four hours before filing missing persons. You believe that? 'Consecutively?' I said. 'Yes,' he said. Heh. Um." They did believe it—it seemed familiar somehow, maybe from movies and cop shows. Twenty-four hours, they all understood, was an eternity, undoable. Char shook her head over and over. Dicey rubbed her face in her hands. She could report the car stolen, but it wasn't her car—she'd borrowed it from Monica, with whom things were particularly complicated, and Monica would have to file the report, and that would mean Dicey's explaining to Monica everything that had happened, admitting that they hadn't yet reached Frankie's father's—and when she'd promised to be back within a week!—and it would mean telling Jean that Frankie was missing. Dicey sucked at the bloody spot on her lip, wincing. Marlon sighed, was swallowed back into the office.

"I'm going to go take a shower," said Dicey. "I need to think."

Because Dicey had a way with the unloved. It was her specialty, though she had only recently come to accept this. Her lovers were always pitiable creatures, and she was a salve, a sweet-smelling balm to be applied for a few weeks until the burn stopped tingling. No one had ever burned for her, exactly. She was not someone who could break your heart. But there was something about Susannah. . . . Anyway, she'd thought they'd had some connection, some something. A connection indeed. They had a connection the way rural phone lines do, subject to the whims of weather, the migratory habits of crows. Poor Susannah Prue, abandoned, about to give birth, alone and afraid— just last night Dicey had been thinking about this and had determined to help her. But that was over now. Now Dicey just wanted to leave, if that was going to be the way. She picked up a T-shirt of Frankie's. It seemed impossibly tiny, the shed skin of a baby. She was already behind schedule—drop Frankie off with her father, the cad, then putter back across the south, or no, maybe this time she would take a different route, because she hadn't found what she needed on this one. Or maybe she wouldn't go home at all. Who was to say she had to? Who would miss her? What difference would it make, in the grand scheme of things? From a therapist somewhere, Dicey had acquired the habit of thinking big picture, and she probably took it too far—big picture made her think the earth will keep rotating, the universe will remain intact, even if I lose Frankie, even if I disappear. It was a good way to render everything useless.

DICEY HAD BEEN peeling a length of chicken meat from its bone when the dinner-table announcement was made. Her sister Jean had "gone and gotten herself knocked up," was how their father put it. Some feat, Dicey remembered thinking—that a person could get *herself* knocked up, presumably by sheer force of will, from desire to be bad. That night Dicey had gone out with some girlfriends to steal white lipsticks from the drugstore. It was difficult to remember now why she hadn't gone and comforted her sister, but there it was.

As for Dicey herself, her one great love affair went like this:

She was a quiet and bookish presence at the high school, though *presence* might have been too flattering a word for it. Her younger sister was the wild one, and there wasn't much room for imagination in a small town like theirs, so Dicey's only option was to be bespectacled and ponytailed, sweet and unremarkable, staying late after school in the library. Hers wasn't an exceptional mind, and the truth of it was that she wasn't even that strong a student, but no one noticed. Life was, after all, she'd learned or had heard somewhere, 90 percent costuming.

She was slogging through Cicero, unraveling a string from her cardigan sleeve, when Mr. Decker sat down. It was three thirty in the empty school library. The lone librarian dozed at the desk. Mr. Decker sat with the chair backward, like the reckless teenager in a movie. "Dicey," he said, and she immediately flushed. He taught English and coached girls' soccer, and he was said to be handsome and young, though he looked like any other teacher to her. He had recently shaved his beard, and what Dicey noticed as he leaned closer was that his face looked damaged and discolored, a cartoon character's five o'clock shadow. When he kissed her, it rubbed against her chin and cheeks, and afterward her face felt windburned, raw, like she'd been stuck outside on a very cold day waiting for a car pool that never came. He held her face and murmured in between kisses. She couldn't look him in the eye. There was passion, lust, something boiling beneath his skin, and Dicey had never considered that such a thing might be directed toward her, and the flattery of the thing was almost enough to decide it. By five fifteen the library was closed, and they were hot and heavy in the stacks, legs splayed out, unshelving whole blocks of 888.000–888.999. After a few weeks of this—Dicey didn't need to be told not to tell—she floated down the school halls lit with a private glow, fingering in her pocket the dirty notes he'd slipped into her bookbag, signed "me" (she'd thought it was so sexy, so adult, so intimate, and only later did she realize he just hadn't wanted to leave any evidence); he'd even called her a few times at home, telling her how much he wanted her, needed her, how there'd never been anyone like her, and she'd rush to meet him at, say, the parking lot of the mall, where she'd give him everything, because he wanted her, needed her, because Dicey was finally the star, finally the one doing something dramatic and exciting, finally had a story of her own, and when she was old enough, they'd run away together, et cetera. And then Mrs. Decker moved back in, and Mr. Decker was busier after school, and by the time Dicey had him for Senior Seminar the next semester, he read her name at roll call without a flinch. You know what, Dicey told herself, lacing up her shoes for PE, who needs men?! Her sister Jean was by now knocked up, and Dicey could see that this man business didn't exactly lead to fun and games.

Or that was how she told herself the story, anyway.

Mr. Decker probably told it something like this:

Dicey was one of those very plain girls who was so close to being beautiful that certain lighting could trick the eye into seeing it. She had the look of someone whose sister might be beautiful, which in fact was the case—her sister Jean was the looker, and you could see faint traces of it in Dicey. Dicey, who sat in the front row of his class and wore always-smudged glasses and sucked on the end of her pen and crossed and uncrossed her legs unconsciously, which made it sort of mildly sexy; Dicey was not a girl in a position to refuse the handsome young English teacher, and he needed someone discreet, and besides, he'd already been rebuffed by the gum-snapping Jean.

Maybe one version was truer than the other. It really didn't matter anymore. It only lasted a short time. What mattered was that Dicey played the part of the responsible sister so perfectly that her family believed it, even she believed it, and so when she learned, a few weeks later, that she, too, had gotten knocked up, there was no question of how it would be dealt with. Her parents argued constantly about whether or not they should kick Jean out—Dad bellowing that she was a humiliation and Mom wanting to help with the baby, let Jean finish high school—while all the while Jean snuck out nights to drive around with friends, pilfer a cigarette or a swig of beer, as her stomach billowed out. Their parents would each confide in Dicey, whom they assumed they could trust. No, one more blow would break everything to bits. And Dicey had ideas for herself—things like college, grand plans for travel, a whole uncharted future. She spent a few weeks walking around in a daze. Everywhere she went, the sun seemed to be in her eyes. Finally she—and in retrospect she couldn't believe it, but what else could she have done?—asked Mr. Decker whom to call. And in retrospect it seemed even stranger that he'd had a card handy with the name and number of a woman, a card he'd handed to her without making eye contact. He'd even given her the money, lips pressed thin, calculating (must have been) the cost of Dicey's embarrassment and her willingness to keep quiet. A few days from her nineteenth birthday, a few weeks after school had let out and she'd graduated, marching across the stage, hiding under the rented gown, Dicey had gone to the clinic. She never told anyone about it, not even Jean.

And she was there, a few months later, when her sister's baby was born. Jean'd held the thing for an instant before handing it to Dicey and saying weepily (still painkiller stoned), "You should be the mother, not me! You're the one who should be a mother!"

UPON FIRST SEEING Susannah, Dicey—saddled with Jean's child, as she'd always suspected would happen eventually, the child she'd always thought could be hers, in a way—thought of her own feet, long ago, clearing off the library shelves. When Susannah spoke, Dicey heard volumes tumbling to the floor. And when Frankie had refused to leave, Dicey had lectured and shouted and waggled her finger, then fled from the room, stood outside the door, buried her head in her hands, and grinned as if her face would break.

CHAR REJOINED HER husband in the office, leaving the cup of Sanka on the curb. Marlon hunched on his stool as usual, his teeth jauntily in place. It was any other day. Any day but this one would have worked just fine. Char took her seat beside him, leaning forward to prop her good elbow on the counter. She reached out, turned the sound down on both televisions. A greenish man mimed the weather.

"Someone called for her," Marlon said. He held the pen in his hand as if preparing to write.

"What?"

"Someone called for Susannah. Yesterday morning, early. Or more, in the middle of the night. Night before last."

Char squinted, waiting.

"Said . . . he said . . . he said someone had just called from this number, and I said it must have been one of the rooms. He asked about her—about Susannah Prue."

"You didn't."

"What could I do? Lie?"

"Marlon. We don't know heads or tails of what's really happening here, and it's none of our business, anyway. Why do you think the girl's been here so long? You didn't stop to think she might be hiding from someone?"

Marlon impatiently popped his teeth out and back into his mouth. "You about done?" Char shook her head but didn't say anything else. "He said he knew her. He asked about the baby. Char, he said it's his. I mean, his and his wife's."

Char slowly unraveled her long silver braid, her sling angled stiffly above her head, preparing the kinked strands for a smoother, tighter braid. "Marlon, I know."

"I mean, Susannah's the . . . ah, surrogate. It's not her baby at all's what I'm saying."

Char nodded. "I know. She told me."

"They live out east, in Chicago, like she said. A few weeks ago, she just disappeared, and they've been going crazy, he said—well, I think you can imagine. He wanted to know where we were. He wanted to come get her."

"You didn't."

"What could I do?"

Char considered this. "And how did he know to call here?"

"She called from her room."

"And that's why she left," said Char. "Well, son of a bitch."

"He called again. Yesterday. He said they were coming here to find her. He was asking for directions, that kind of thing. Asking if I could make sure she stayed."

"Marlon."

"I didn't know what to do. What was I supposed to do? I thought maybe it was best to leave the whole thing alone."

"And now she's disappeared." Char shook her head. Marlon didn't say that he had told Susannah. That was more than he could manage. His chest twinged with pain.

The Garlands had never been involved in a real mystery before, and they felt almost galvanized by the whole thing for a few seconds before Marlon said, "And she took our boy, too"—then they remembered about Tim, and their excitement moldered into quiet panic. Tim! Their boy! They were never a team, a united front, a nation of two, so much as when they were forced to rally around Tim. Talking to Susannah the other day had shaken things up in Char, tumbled buried feelings around like bits in a snow globe. It was a moment they didn't talk about often, the visit to the doctor who advised them to give up their unsquirming baby—not that that had been the worst part! No, it had been far worse to decide to take him in at all, to acknowledge that something was not right. Maybe some babies just never cried, Marlon had said. He'd said it like he was asking for permission to believe it. Char had been standing in the doorway, facing out, her back to Marlon and to the baby, who lay swaddled in a car seat installed on the counter. The baby, they'd found, preferred not to be touched. Marlon kept trying. Maybe it was only that it was too hot out and the baby was depleted, the way they all were, by the heat. Char had fiddled with her hair, painting a villain's mustache on her upper lip with the bottom tuft of her braid, staring out toward the horizon. If she stared long enough, she thought, a boy would come running from the distances, a happy, normal boy. She'd nodded. Yes, maybe Marlon was right. She wanted to give Marlon what she could. If she saw anything move, any stirring on the horizon, she told herself, then that would mean their baby was okay, that Marlon was right, that there was no need to worry. She held her breath, waiting. Any stir, any puff of wind, any vehicle in the distance, any shift in the clouds or leap of the tiniest insect, any hint of motion. She gave the world a minute to respond. Then turned around to face Marlon. "I'm calling the doctor," she'd said dully. "I just know that something is not right." Marlon looked up at her, like she'd offered to gut him where he stood. "Well, fine," he said. "That's just fine. There's no harm in calling, I guess."

THEY SPENT THE day perched stiffly at the counter, trying to formulate a plan. "Can't you please turn those off?" Dicey said, looking irritably at the television sets, now both turned up and tuned to news. It was unlike her to be so demanding, but the heat crept below everything, inching beneath her skin like tapeworms. Char glared, lowered the volume. She and Marlon sat perched on their stools behind the counter—Marlon's hands were clasped, fiddling now and then with a pen, his teeth in place—as if ready to receive customers.

"They'll be back," Char said. She sighed and pulled her braid off her shoulders and bundled it on top of her head and then let it drop again. "They'll be back in a few hours. They'll be back by nighttime for sure."

Dicey shook her head.

"What's she gonna do with those two kids for more than a day? Where are they gonna go? You know they can't get far. She's gonna have that baby any minute. I'm sure Tim's giving her hell. They can't get far." Char had already said this a few times by now. Tim! Her baby! "Tim's no good out of his element," she said. "He'll throw a fit about something and drive her crazy."

The office seemed colder and dimmer than it ever had been before. Dicey shivered, pulled up her knees to her chest.

Marlon was saying, "I'm going to call. I'm going to call the parents."

"Susannah's parents?" Char stared at him.

"Su— No, of course not, Char, Jesus Christ. I mean the parents of Susannah's baby. I mean. The man that called here. I told you. He gave me his name, his cell-phone number. I didn't believe him—it didn't make sense—but now . . . I think we gotta call him."

"What can he do about it?" snapped Dicey.

"Well, I don't know. Maybe she's gotten in touch with him? Or . . . I don't know. I just feel a man would want to know."

"She's not going to give them their baby," Char said.

Marlon said, "You don't know that."

"So call him," Char said to Marlon. "Call him already. Tell him his baby's gone."

They were all quiet then and looked at the phone.

THE FORSYTHES HAD never been to this part of the Southwest, had never given it much thought, and upon awakening from a stiff-necked passenger-seat nap the third morning of their voyage, Julian found himself annoyed by the whole thing. "Why is it so hot in here? Where are we? Where's the . . . you know. The fucking cactuses and stuff?"

Kit had taken a turn driving, though in her husband's opinion walking at a brisk pace might have been a more efficient option. It was something they argued about often, with Kit always insisting that she was only thinking of their safety and wasn't it true that she had never gotten a ticket or been in an accident? She was a regular Girl Scout of a driver. And Julian slumped in the passenger seat with his feet pressed against the floor, as if he could will the thing to move just a little faster, at least the speed limit, by God. And he had already said several times, "It's just that time is of the essence, sweetie, and we're so close." He'd even tried it different ways: "A few hours makes a big difference right now," or the more dismal, "She's probably already long gone. At this rate anyway, by the time we get there, she'll be long gone." Kit had said, "Julie, please." She was always brittle, and especially now. So Julian had reclined his seat and faced away from Kit and angrily feigned sleep until it melted into real sleep, and he had a dream about Susannah. He woke up an hour later confused and hot, baking in a crescent of window-magnified sun. The nape of his neck prickled with sweat, the surface of his face gone burny, dried out. The awkward sleeping position had worked a kink into his back. And when he looked around, here they were, in seemingly the exact same spot they'd been in an hour ago. Jesus, Kit was driving so slowly they were actually going *back in time!* Same bland horizon, same scrubby, colorless dirt, same impotent tumbles of brush. So he said, "Where's the . . . you know. The fucking cactuses and stuff?"

Kit glared.

"You know what I mean. The big cactuses, like in the movies, with the three prongs? Like arms . . . ?"

"Saguaros," Kit said. She said it like she was reminding him of their anniversary, like it was something he should have known.

"Well?"

"They don't have those in this part of country, dear. Those only grow in Arizona."

"Oh, really?" Julian scowled out the window, sullen as a teenager. "How do they know they're in Arizona, the saduaros or whatever? Do they stop at the border? There's *none* anywhere else?"

"Julie, don't get mad at me because of where cacti grow. I really had very little to do with it."

"Cute. How do you know so much about it, anyway?"

Kit reached to turn down the air-conditioning. "I don't know. I thought everyone did."

"Oh, really?" Julian turned the air-conditioning back up and adjusted the vents toward his face. "I must be the biggest moron in the world, then."

"Not the *biggest,* dear."

"Gee, thanks. Where are we, anyway? Death Valley?" Semis blew past them now and then, horn-bellowing into the other lane.

"Death Valley? Julian, have you ever looked at a map of this country?"

"Where are we, then?"

"*I* don't know. *You're* supposed to be the navigator, you know, and then you go to sleep! Do I ever sleep when you're driving?"

"You might as well! 'Oh, Julie, oops, that was the turn!' "

"What is wrong with you?"

"Why don't you just let me drive? This is absurd. Kit, you're going fifty-five miles per hour. The speed limit here is eighty."

"Well, but that's just insane."

"I mean, we've got to get there already."

"Do you want to get there smashed and dead?"

"Do I have a choice?"

"I'm stopping at this gas station. I have to pee."

Julian rolled his eyes. "Again? Fine. But then I'm driving."

"You know what your problem is, Julie? You're a control freak. It's unhealthy. It truly is unwholesome."

Julian pressed his feet into the floor again, willing the car through the turnoff and toward the service station. A ramshackle hut leaned away from two antique gas pumps. Beyond it there was nothing but sand. When he got out of the car, the dust flew to his skin, gluey with sweat. A pale slice of moon was printed in the corner of the sky. There went his sweet wife, into the gas station, her hair tumbling behind. How could he be so mean to her, so deliciously crabby, how could he say things specifically to bother her, only to feel faint with regret a moment afterward? Worse was that it was not surprising. They had done this to each other a thousand times, a hundred thousand times, and it had, honestly, only now struck him as strange—was this a marriage? And suddenly *this* struck him as being strange. Whom did they have in the world but each other? Even now he knew he wasn't finished. He knew they would do more to hurt each other before the day was done.

He entered the gas station beneath a sprig of bells.

Kit was standing too closely to the counter and repeatedly ringing the "ring for service" bell. The sound dinged around the room, a frantic little messenger.

"Kit," said Julian irritably, "think you've rung it enough times?"

"It says ring for service." She gestured to the hand-scrawled sign.

"It doesn't say ring *a thousand times* for service."

It was just all so like her, to bluster into a foreign setting and assume she was doing everything right, to assume that the clerk really did want to be informed of their presence as soon and as insistently as possible. Julian sighed. He had meant to express with this sigh his deep displeasure with his wife's behavior. She didn't seem to notice. Or maybe she did—because she sighed back, and there was a quality to the sigh that he didn't quite recognize. Maybe they would just communicate this way for the next fifty years, with these sighs that were the whale songs of the wed.

Kit stood very straight, not looking at him. Julian moved slowly up and down the aisles of the tiny convenience mart, browsing the shelves of unclean packaging. He would have liked to find one thing in this goddamned desert that wasn't dusty and aged. Rows of Doritos packages from two designs back—before everything had gotten BOLD! and X-TREME! Boxes of saltines that resembled a hospital-issue brand. Rows of milk in dim, silent cases. A spinnable display, thrown onto the shelf among untrustworthy-looking auto supplies, of desert-themed key fobs featuring different names. Julian ran a finger across the letters. Bill. Cathy. Juanita. Pedro. He took one of the fobs to examine it and then held it up for Kit to see, clearing his throat to make her turn her head. Molded in flexible plastic was a three-armed saguaro cactus, a sombrero tipped sleepily on one of its prongs.

Kit sighed.

She'd been reading the sign on the counter. The Haunted Caves were free with a purchase of gas. She liked the sound of this and said it over in her head a few times. She liked the idea of a free haunting. This seemed like a bargain. This seemed like a fun thing. She wanted to show it to Julian, to elicit his excitement and praise over the kitschy amusement. What was a few more minutes? And they were by now used to being on the road and had almost forgotten, or she had, anyway, exactly what they were doing here in this parched pocket of the earth. Everything was too quiet, too far away. Kit had the strange sense that nothing that happened here would ever be completely real, or completely connected with the things that happened in cities, in civilized conglomerations of silver spires—no, it was too wild here, and sun-scorched. Anyway, they never went on trips like this. They frequented Classy Joints, resorts that caused people to ooh in appreciation (oh, they had heard that was beautiful). They visited countries in Europe that Rick Steves nasally recommended on PBS. They went beyond England and France. They learned snippets of the languages, how to say "What a beautiful country" in Portuguese, in Czech. They went everywhere they were supposed to go, except that they never got to do anything like visit roadside attractions or explore Haunted Caves or buy plastic souvenirs. Kit wanted to stop at the chapel with the miraculous dirt, to see the antechamber ornamented with crutches from the healed. She wanted to see where UFOs had crash-landed; she wanted to tour ruins and pueblos and tepee-shaped gift shops. They had gotten hard to impress, and this made Kit a little sad, and by the time the sleepy-looking gas-station attendant appeared, his face creased as if he'd been resting on something jagged, she didn't even want to ask about the Haunted Caves anymore—Julian would just pooh-pooh it and make her feel foolish for wanting to go—so she just told the attendant that they needed to buy some gas and use the bathroom, and did he happen to know a place called the Thunder Lodge? As she spoke, she watched Julian select a bottled ice tea. Even on the

sweatiest afternoon, even while their lives were falling apart, Julian—
his white shirt open at the collar and sleeves rolled up, his silvery hair
curling at the temples—always looked so cool.

"You mean Marlon's motel? Sure, sure. Just a little ways yet"—
Julian glanced up—"but you're a bit early for the crafts fair, aren't
you?"

Kit dug in her purse for money for the gas. She saw that her man-
icure was chipped. "Crafts fair? Oh, yes, a little, I guess."

"Smart, though. Every place for miles fills up. You buyin' or
sellin'?"

Kit shoved two twenties at him. "This enough? Can I use your
bathroom? Please, we've got to get going."

The man rubbed at his face and yawned a big, bearlike yawn. "I
hear that." He didn't move.

The doorbells tinkled. Julian had gone out to take the map from
the glove compartment and unfurl it gracelessly over the car's hood,
battling the tight folds as he forced it open. Kit turned back to the
counter. "Oh, please, we're in a hurry."

He nodded. "The Haunted Caves is free with gas, you know.
Quite a thing to see. So spooky we had a lady faint the other day." He
had obviously repeated this fact a few times since then and become
very fond of it. He nodded again, his eyes buggishly magnified behind
greasy lenses.

"All right, no thank you, here," and she pushed the money on the
counter closer toward him.

"Bathroom's around back," he said.

Kit felt that she had never acknowledged her intestines quite so
much; they squirmed around, coiling themselves into sailor's knots.
She went out into the heat, which gripped her in its dry fist; turned the
corner to maneuver her way into the tiny, filthy bathroom. What
would they say when they saw Susannah? She had not imagined it,
could not quite imagine it. She had only dreamed it, and in that version

each time they found Susannah, she was no longer pregnant, she stared at them blankly as if she'd never seen them before, and Kit screamed herself awake, the scream transforming to a colorless grunt on the awake side. She stood on one leg, balancing awkwardly, trying to hold down the flush lever with her other foot. There was nothing in the bathroom that seemed safe to touch—everything peeled, tattooed with nonsensical graffiti. The sink was haloed with a ring of primitive Sharpie drawings: big, happy dicks floating on cloudlike balls. She washed her hands hurriedly and pushed open the door with her side, backed out into the light.

Julian leaned against the car, glaring at the map. A hawk sheared the sky in two. Finally Kit spoke first. "You know, these Haunted Caves are so spooky they had a lady faint here the other day."

Julian imitated a smile.

The gas-station attendant meandered out.

"Over here!" called Kit, tapping at the pump. She hadn't seen a pump like this one in years, maybe ever. She would have more readily trusted a modern station, where all the machinery was hidden. Here things were too out in the open, pieces fastened together by a grout of sand. The gas-station attendant didn't seem to want to rush into anything. He wiped his hands on a rag, stopped to examine a wrench that was laid across his coffin-shaped toolbox, wiped his hands again, and made his way over to them. Julian meanwhile focused all his energy on reassembling the map, discovering the worn creases, returning the folds to their channels.

The gas-station attendant had said they were close, maybe a twenty-minute drive from the Thunder Lodge. Julian insisted on driving.

"So the nearest hospital is on an Indian reservation. An *Indian reservation*." Kit leaned forward, her brow furrowed.

"Kitty. Darling, we've been over this. And it's a health clinic, not a hospital. And it's . . . what? Only a couple hundred miles to Las Cruces? We can probably make it there."

They *had* been over this before. They'd called Dr. Kilgore's office and coordinated a potential future faxing of records and all that, and now it was more like a final dry run, soothing in the way that retelling familiar stories is always soothing to a couple, to a family. The way repeating a story again and again makes a pair what they are. And so: "Julie, remember when we met?"

"Who, us? Nah. Didn't we always know each other?"

He was driving much too fast. Sand and debris spewed behind them, projectiled into two thin channels that Kit watched in her side mirror.

"I was sitting on the park bench, and you walked by me? And then you walked by again and again? Like a teenager trying to decide whether to say hello?"

Julian smiled. "And I thought, 'Well, that's the prettiest girl I've ever seen.'"

"And you asked me the time, and I just didn't get it. I was thinking, 'I can see the watch you're wearing, you creep.'"

"You were dismissive and broke my heart, and I left you to your newspaper, and that was that. We never spoke again."

The sky thickened, lowered.

Kit laughed. "Except that the next weekend Sarah and Dan had that dinner party, and Sarah said, 'Dan has this colleague we think you'd love.' And I thought, 'Yeah, no, I seriously doubt it,' and I almost didn't go."

"But then you heard that your ex was having a baby with his new wife, and you went out of spite."

"Of course not! I went because I knew you'd be there."

"Right. Because you knew you could wave at me with a glass of wine and say, 'Don't I know you? You tried to pick me up in the park!'"

"I would never."

"You would and did, my darling. It was humiliating."

"You were so cute when you blushed."

"What were the chances, though, honestly, that I would find you, the beautiful girl in the park, when I thought I would never see you again?"

"At the dullest dinner party ever thrown."

"It didn't seem dull to me."

A rainstorm punctured the scene. It happened the way it happens in the desert—one moment it's sunny and blue, the next you're battling through sheets of hail, the sky's gone dark, and you hardly know where you are.

"Julie! Slow *down,* my God, are you trying to kill us?" Kit clutched the dash. The highway stretched black and slick ahead of them. There was no one else on the road, and though he'd been driving all morning and two days before that and hadn't been sleeping well, Julian felt wide awake, supernaturally alert; he could hear individual raindrops needle at the roof of the car, he could feel his wife's panic thrumming barometrically though his sinuses, he knew that he had complete control of the car, the road, the weather. He knew that the rain would stop in a moment, that they would get to the motel and find Susannah, waiting to be found. That she would collapse into his arms.

"Slow *down,* will you?" Kit was saying, becoming more and more shrill. "It's slick! Look how slick the road is. Can you see anything? I can't see a thing."

Julian slammed the palm of his hand against the steering wheel, his shoulders hunched up beneath his ears. "Would you just let me drive?" he snapped, and was going to say more, too, was deciding between an *I've gotten us this far* kind of a thing or a *You never trust me to take care of things* sort of tack, when the wheels locked and the car started to hydroplane, drifting toward the shoulder. Things seemed to freeze and accelerate at the same time. The highway roared like an ocean. Kit found time to reach for Julian's thigh, to lay her palm upon

it, while the car lowed slowly (or no, *quickly*) across the road as if mag-
netized to the shoulder—and Julian tried to think (turn *into* a skid—
no, turn *away* from a skid—no . . .) but there wasn't time, and he
yanked the wheel away from the side of the road, and the car went
careening in the other direction (of all the things to die of, it was
unfair that his own incompetence might be one of them, his own
momentary inability to recall this section from driver's ed), and now
was when Kit screamed—Julian in the midst of everything found a
moment to be annoyed and bark "Shut up!" before his reptile brain
took over, that sensible croc led by instinct and fatality, calmly guid-
ing the steering wheel, righting the craft, and in a moment they were
driving down the road again as if nothing had ever happened. Julian
slowed. A semi blew past, honking. Kit sat with her hands over her
face.

"Um," Julian said. His knees and elbows felt melted.

"Stop. Please. Pull over."

He did. They watched the rain sheeting down on everything in
wide white chunks, the expanse of desert turned to mud.

Kit pressed her hand against his thigh again. He started to cry.

"Jules." She unbuckled her seat belt and moved close to him,
snuggled under his chin, stroked his stubble. "It's okay. We're okay."

He had not cried in a long time. It had probably been years, and
now he wondered why. It felt good. The sobs rose hot as burps in his
chest, and he felt his whole body release into it. He would have to try
this more often! Because here he was, an adult, the adult version of
himself, not where he thought he would be by now at all, a man who
had misplaced his child, no, a man who hadn't been able to impregnate his wife, a husk of a man who had dragged her out here when a
more reasonable person would have let police or detectives or an evening newsmagazine program take over, *something*. He had almost just
killed them both. And soon—not now, she was a little too kind for
that, but not so kind that she wouldn't say it all—his wife would say to

him, *I told you to slow down.* So he cried. She let him. It passed through his body like a current, warming his fingertips.

The rain ended without fanfare. In a minute the sun was shining again and the ground had regained its normal color, like a child's face after a tantrum. Julian wiped his face. Kit handed him a hankie, and he blew his nose. "I love that you carry hankies," he told her.

"I know you do." She touched his cheek, then moved back to her seat and rebuckled the belt. "Want me to drive?"

He did, desperately. "No," he told her. "It's fine."

"Are you sure?"

Julian pulled the car back onto the road. Far in the distance, the sun glinted against something that looked like a neon sign. "Sure."

Kit leaned back, gazed out her window. "I told you to slow down."

7

THE BODY BETRAYS
THE MIND

None of them knew the color of the sky. Their eyes glanced level and were fastened on the land that swept past them. The mountains were the hue of slate, except for the tops, which were as white as wave crests, and all of them knew the colors of the earth. The horizon narrowed and widened as the buttes rose and flattened alongside the highway, dipped and rose, and at all times its edge was jagged with distant ranges that seemed thrust up in points like waves.

They hadn't been on the road nearly so long as it felt. Maybe it was the way the land had changed, the way the hour from dusk to dark seems longer than an hour in the afternoon, the way April lasts longer than June. They'd traveled from one landscape to another, and things had gone rocky and rough toward Arizona. Tim had never seen a horizon so pointy, mountains so close, dirt so colorful, streaked as it was with all matter of red, orange, purples, and pale blues, and he stared, rubbing his hands together, trying to summon up in the reaches of his mind the word that might express what this was. *Ouch,* his mind offered. But that wasn't exactly it. He sighed, pressed his forehead against the windowpane, rubbed his hands along his thighs, once, twice, thrice.

The colorless tumble of the Thunder Lodge and its environs seemed like an uninspired memory—a world jumbled together from broken concrete and depleted dust—and with her eyes now dazzled, Susannah wondered why she had ever stayed so long in so dismal a moonscape. Buttes soared to either side, smeared with stone of a menstrual hue. Wispy clouds gave the world its shape. When they stopped (again and again) for Susannah to pee alongside the road, her lungs filled with a silty air—grimy and mineral and wholesome.

Only the car was displeased with these developments. It huffed and strained as they climbed snaking mountain paths in the thinning atmosphere. The engine sputtered occasionally, an old man choking on a length of bone. Now and then a semi blared past, and Susannah thought, If we broke down, would they stop? Whatever would become of us? Frankie had descended into a long, silent pout. Tim had taken to tapping at the window and giggling to himself over some extended joke. When they stopped for gas, Susannah could only lean heavily against the car and will Tim to stop as he bounded toward the gravel strip that inevitably traced the station, searching for pebbles. She had stopped trying to keep him from eating them, though the sound of him grinding sand between his teeth was unbearable. He was insistent, and she was just not feeling that energetic. Frankie had stopped asking about the ocean sometime that morning, and Susannah had stopped mentioning it.

The road signs repeatedly suggested the Grand Canyon, though they were far south of it. They'd pass one of the signs, and Susannah would screw up her energy to ignore it, and then as soon as she'd started to forget it, another would pop up, unhelpful as a nagging parent. ROUTE WHATEVER, TOWARD GRAND CANYON! SCENIC CANYON DRIVE STARTS HERE! Honey, did you know that this was the last cheap gas until the Grand Canyon? She remembered painfully how Aaron had always wanted to go to the Grand Canyon. He had a mania for visiting famous places; he wanted his photo taken in front of monuments, bridges, plaques of all kinds. He had always said it was his proof that he was alive, the way he would know, when he was old and senile, that he'd been on this earth, that he had seen things. Susannah was just the opposite. She wanted to go places no one had ever heard of, to have photographs only of unidentifiable objects, the backs of people's heads, landscapes of chipped paint. Whatever that was a symptom of, whatever that meant, was what had in the end come between them. Well, by now he'd have his snapshots of the Taj Mahal to throw on his pile, and Susannah would have in her glove box a pile of sea glass Tim collected at the shore. Her glove box! She realized now that she had forgotten to clean it out, that back at the Thunder Lodge, in her dead car, were the things she'd been collecting—Char's fork, Dicey's coin. Susannah bit her lip. She'd have to start over again. She reached across Frankie and opened the glove box. Frankie awoke damply. "Whatcha doing?" A neatly folded road map, the owner's manual for the car. Susannah snapped it closed. "Nothing." She sighed.

This, their first day on the road, had been a bad one, long and tiring. They'd taken the wrong turn—the only turn they'd had to make all day, and Susannah had missed it—and backtracked and lost time and moved slowly, and now they stopped for the night well before Susannah wanted to. If they kept up this pace, they would never reach the ocean at all. Frankie tripped off in her swimming trunks to find the pool, which seemed to Susannah like a kind of betrayal. The Grotto had been a good friend to them, and had started to seem, indeed, unlike any ordinary swimming pool, something more . . . well, Grottolike. And here was Frankie, acting like any capricious kid. Well.

It left Susannah and Tim alone in the room, and Susannah stretched out on one of the beds and let her back sink into its own pain. Tim sat on a plastic chair he'd tugged up close to the flickering, bunny-eared TV. He spun the dial gleefully. "Huh," he said. "Huh." His excitement was contagious. After all—watching the sepiaed cop show reflect in Tim's eyes—wasn't this exactly what she liked about him? Okay, he'd been sullen and intractable all day. But ever since she'd met him, there had been that wonder. He was surprised by the world, confused but generally pleased. He found joy in things like pebbles and leaves, in the sensation of earth in his mouth, things Susannah herself hadn't noticed in many years or maybe never at all. And then he turned his head and a lock of hair fell in front of his eye, and Susannah, who had been sitting at the edge of the bed, pushed the hair gently back behind his ear. What a sweet specimen he was—how lovable, how needing to be loved. He wanted to go to the ocean with her, understood its pull, embarked on her little mission without so much as a question. He didn't care why they were going—he was just happy to be going. Here he was, a human at its most stripped down, a person without excuses, without explanations. Just a man, a slip of a boy. God, thought Susannah, how she loved him. She wanted to hug him, to hold him close—even though she knew it didn't make sense—like she'd wanted to hug Julian, to say in that small way, *Hello, I care for you, let's keep each other warm for a second.*

She patted his arm then, and he flinched and in one quick movement slapped her hand away—his face a mask, his body stiff—hitting her hard enough that she cried out. His breath was dusky, mildewy— had he been brushing his teeth?—"Timothy"—had they brought a toothbrush for him?—"No." His eyes were open and unchanged. "No," she said again, unhysterically. He gathered himself up, stood at the bed's edge, his arms swinging guilelessly.

But it had frightened her. She collapsed onto the bed, lay on her side. Something felt loosened within her—her belly no longer felt so screwed to her spine, her hips no longer felt immobile and heavy. The stranger scootched around a bit as if trying to get comfortable, and oh, aha, the baby had dropped, getting ready to be born, dangling himself like a diver preparing for the plunge. Susannah lay there, looking past Tim. Tim stood by the bed without speaking. Then he tightened his hands into fists and punched at his thighs once and emitted a sort of roar. He stalked out of the room, leading with his forehead in a way that reminded Susannah of what? Oh, of Char, his mother, dear God, his poor mother. The door slammed shut behind him.

Susannah rolled onto her other side. She considered crying but couldn't muster the energy. Tim and Frankie should not be left alone out there, she knew this. Tim would wander all night. He would stand outside the motel rooms' windows, grazing on cigarette butts and dirt clods, the world his buffet. He would scare people, or worse. And Frankie, running around the pool—a seven-year-old boy alone in the night. She squeezed her eyes shut and pressed her palm against her belly button. What good could come from any of this?

TIM FOUND FRANKIE at the pool. It looked like the Grotto, which made him feel a bit calmer. Frankie greeted him. With her new hair, she looked so much like a boy that Tim had started to think of her that way, had started calling her "him." He liked her better now, as a boy. He'd always wanted a little brother.

It was dark already, though it hadn't been a moment before. Above them the sign—TUMBLEWEED MOTOR LODGE—in tall, serifed letters, placed beside a neon twist of an old-fashioned car—leaked light across the sky. There were people splashing in the shallow end— a man and a girl and their baby. Tim did not speak. He walked along- side the perimeter of the pavement, letting his right palm scrape against the stucco wall. He was looking for the embedded Virgin—his left hand fisted, nails cutting crescents of bruise into the palm. He in- stead found a spigot, some hooks for towels. In the far corner, a coiled garden hose startled him—he'd thought it was a snake. The man and the girl did not look up at him. He wanted to find something for Su- sannah Prue. Something to say "Hello" and "Thanks." Something that said, "You are nice, and I like you." A beautiful smooth pebble, a shimmery pane of rock. Something to give to Susannah Prue.

Frankie played listlessly with an inner tube some child had left, a flimsy plastic doughnut with a dinosaur's face. It was the kind of toy she had always coveted—Penny Pascalis had one back in Mobile and never let Frankie touch it at the municipal pool during swimming lessons—but now that she had her hands on one, it seemed pointless. It didn't even really carry her weight. She leaped on top of it, and it slowly sank, again and again. The game now was to see how far she could sink with it before her limbs involuntarily flapped. She was disappointed in herself for not being able to sink all the way.

The man and the girl maintained a stoned kind of interest in their bikinied baby, who stood on sausagey legs and swayed slightly, frowning at them. Frankie floated a little closer to them, pretending to stare at the sky. The man and the girl stood in the pool, the water gathering at their waists like skirts. Frankie wanted to overhear something, hoped to glean some secret adult knowledge. But the couple just stood there, giggling now and then with great effort.

Frankie looked down at her lean, flat chest, her swim trunks inflating with water. She wanted to know whether the couple were in love, whether they would stay together forever, whether they really loved their baby or were only pretending because you had to. She wanted to know what real parents were like. But more than that, she wanted to know whether the couple thought she was a boy or not. She was trying it out, performing an experiment, testing her hypothesis. "Hey!" she called out suddenly. The couple turned around, surprised. She knew that behind her, Tim was standing still near the stack of lawn chairs, but she was a little tired of him right now and pretended not to notice. "Hey, can you guess my name?" Frankie said to the couple. She shook her head, hoping to call attention to the boyishly short hair. She slipped the inner tube over her waist and kicked at her legs to maintain her float.

The man smiled and rubbed his chin as if contemplating this. The girl held out one hand absently for the baby to clutch with its fat little fingers. "Rumpelstiltskin," said the man, laughing uproariously.

"Ha, ha! Didja get that, baby? Like that story. Is it . . . Rumpelstiltskin?!" The girl continued to smile indulgently. She was pretty, Frankie registered, but with a face like a mask, makeup slathered over bad skin, and something else, a blankness. "Now, where's my gold?"

"Ha, ha." Frankie floated away from the couple, staring into the sky. Before getting darker, it became deeper, and softer, with the nap of velvet.

But the girl pressed the man's arm as if shushing him and said, "What letter does it start with?"

"*F.*"

"Hmm! Fred? Let me see. Philip? Oh, wait, I guess that's not an *F.* Um . . . "

But Frankie had gotten what she needed—it was working! It really was! They thought she was a boy. She felt a swell of pride. "It's Frank!" she said.

"Ooh," said the girl. "I was going to guess that. Can you guess my name?"

Frankie pushed off the wall in a lazy kicking arc. "I doubt it," she said, closing her eyes.

THEN THERE IS the ocean, written with white and turbid wakes.

Susannah had never seen the ocean, which was probably why it was able to mean so much to her. After all, she had thought (she was already forgetting) that the desert would mean something, too, that geography could be more than a metaphor, could afford some insight into her parched inner state. When Julian had said he'd always wanted to see the desert, it had seemed like a sign. Then the pictures in Tim's room, and what Frankie had said about swimming. Maybe Aaron was right all along. Maybe she was stupid to see everything as a sign. And now she'd stayed in the desert too long, and now it had become a knowable place, human as a city, and she had to keep looking. But the ocean! The seas! She would lie flat in salt water, brined in the world. She would feel the shape of the earth in her palm.

The last time she had really been happy, really and truly happy—unclouded, untortured, decisive, knowing, just *happy* in a way that now seemed impossible—had been at the lake with her friends, or, really, Aaron and his friends—sun cresting on the wavelets, someone's toddler storming toward them in a white ruffled bathing suit fat over its diaper, Aaron rushing up behind and pushing Susannah into the water. Fish and sea glass and minnow. Rocky sand, distant boats. And a few days later, they were breaking up, Aaron was leaving to travel. Just like that, there was no Susannah. She'd gone around her apartment, filling a box with photographs of the two of them together, only to realize that they were the only photographs of herself that she had. Cutting his face out of them seemed silly. All their talk of getting married, their debates over what they would name their children—in the end it hadn't amounted to much. Well, it happened.

She paced around the anonymous room. She was exhausted but couldn't sleep. How was it that there was such a thing as a bed, a television, a window? How was it that these rooms existed, just sitting there and waiting for someone like her to come inhabit them for brief instants and then disappear? The world was so cluttered with junk! That was it, Susannah decided, pacing to and fro, the baby rollicking around inside. There was no way a person could concentrate on a thing in a world so cluttered with junk. The room had its starchy curtains and a round table by the window and a double bed and cot straitjacketed with sheets and glossy bedside tables and a gloppy painting of seashells. Balanced on the television set was a remote control to the cable box, chained uselessly to the stand. How could a person think about anything when there was a remote control chained to a television stand? There were people out there who made these things, who understood how these things were made and what they meant, people whose knowledge of the world was minuscule and complete. People who were comfortable in their own skin, okay with the world. Like her aunt, like her cousins, like the Forsythes, people who believed in facts.

So! She would pace up and down the floor, to and fro, her walk made ungraceful by her heavy front.

When they got to the ocean, it would provide some solace, the answers would come belching up on the waves. But for now here came the children galumphing into the room, Frankie wet from the pool tumbling onto the pillows despite Susannah's protests and Tim moving slowly through the door with his hands clasped in front of him, like a politician trying to look harmless. He kept his eyes on the ground, went to the bathroom, peed with the door open, slouched back head drooping to the squeaky cot, and lay down upon it as if his body were another squeaky cot, just as stiff and as unyielding. Susannah summoned Frankie to the sink, wrapped a towel over her shoulders, set about to fix the choppy haircut. She could at least smooth things out. Frankie chattered away. "And even the people at the pool thought I was a boy! When we get to California, can we buy me some things? I need regular shoes—mine have Dora the Explorer, which is for girls and anyway kind of for kids. You know what I mean, little kids. When we get to ocean, I'm going to find a sea horse and a starfish and a conch shell, and I'll put them in my new room and always remember this summer."

"Baby," Susannah said. "Please hold still. I don't want to cut you."

Frankie shrugged. "Should we call my Aunt Dicey maybe? I mean, we've been gone all day, and she's probably getting worried."

"Well," said Susannah. She pressed gently at Frankie's ears, snipping the stray tufts of hair sprouting unevenly there. Her ears were soft, freckled, furred with yellow hairs. She had that little-kid summer smell of chlorine and sweat and outdoors, of the coconutty sunscreen

Susannah had smeared over her shoulders. Susannah impulsively leaned down and kissed Frankie's ear.

Frankie squirmed away. "That tickles!"

"Okay, okay, hold still!" Susannah said, laughing, and trimmed a clean line across the back. What Dicey would think when she saw Frankie, Susannah couldn't imagine, but at least now it wouldn't look like the kid had been attacked by a barber with a vendetta. Pinkish scalp shone through a spot in back where Frankie had cut too close, but there wasn't much you could do about something like that.

"I mean, I still want to go to the ocean. I think we should get to swim in the ocean," Frankie was saying, trying to hold her head very still. "But I kinda want to call Aunt Dicey. Just to say we're okay. I won't tell on you or anything."

"Tell on me! For what?" Susannah said, almost believing herself. "Anyway, I already called her. While you guys were at the pool. Sorry, I didn't know you wanted to talk to her." She removed the towel, brushed hairs from Frankie's neck and ears.

Frankie shivered and said, "Your hands are cold!"

"Okay." Susannah stepped back to admire her work. "You're done."

"Cool." Frankie shook her head puppyishly. "So can we call back?"

"Well, Dicey said she was happy to hear from us and she was glad we were going to see the ocean, but she said that she wasn't feeling well and was going to bed as soon as she hung up. So I wouldn't want to wake her."

"Oh. Uh, okay." Frankie ran from the bathroom, leaped over a suitcase, and launched herself onto the bed. She kicked her legs up against the wall, two knobby exclamation points.

"Do you guys need anything?" Susannah was trying to sound sympathetic and not at all maniacal, asking the question about twelve hours too late. "Tim?" His eyes moved, but nothing else. She wanted to offer them something to make the night easier, better. She wanted to give them anything they wanted, to make it clear to them how grateful she was that they had come with her, how much she adored them, what a good time they were going to have. "Do you want to . . . uh, watch TV?"

"Yeah," Tim said, his eyes still closed. "Yeah. Probably not." One lanky hand rose in salute. She took the thin woolen blanket from where he'd kicked it to the floor and draped it over him. He squeezed his eyes shut, the corners of his lips still twitching in a poor parody of sleeping. Frankie had curled over to her side, mumbling, "I'm not tired at all, not even one speck. I want to stay up laaaaate." Susannah went back into the bathroom and dusted Frankie's hairs off the edge of the bathtub, washed her hands, and squinted at her dark eyes in the mirror for a moment before going to lie on the bed behind the already snoring Frankie, whose dirty feet were nestled on her pillow. As soon as Susannah lay down, the baby started doing its aerobic laps, hurling itself from one side to the other. She was half asleep and already slogging through honey-thick dreams, dreams where the baby extracted himself like a miniature Houdini, escaping her clutches by morning. Frankie curled up cattishly beside her. Her warmth anchored Susannah to the world—that and nothing else.

MIDMORNING THE NEXT day (while Susannah piloted Dicey's car down a theatrically long and dusty highway), Marlon and Char Garland were joined by two new guests. Char stood at the office window, watching the shiny luxury car slouch into the drive, crunching over the paper cup of Sanka she had abandoned by the curb the morning before. Inside the car gleamed two white faces, even from a distance seeming generally attractive and overly well groomed. "The crafts fair already? Little early, aren'tcha?" Char muttered to no one in particular. Marlon looked up, replacing his teeth and shifting his jaw to shimmy them in. The TVs blared contrasting weather reports. "What's that?" Marlon said.

Char tapped a finger at the glass. "Customers."

"Oh." He gathered the notebook, his pencil. "The crafts fair already?"

"How should I know, Marlon?"

They both knew it must be the Forsythes. Neither of them wanted to say it.

He nodded, pursing his lips.

The couple that hurried up the walk and erupted into the office was clearly not the crafts-fair crowd, who tended to favor shaggier hairstyles, vaguely Native American touches, the color purple. These people were tidy and neat, both on the small side, compactly built, lean and muscular in a vaguely feline way; each gave the impression of being as tightly coiled as a jack-in-the-box. Though they had to have been in the car a long time, as the Thunder Lodge was a distance from anywhere, they struck Char as being unusually fresh and clean—the woman's pretty, if pinched, face was made up, the man's silver-stranded curls pushed neatly back. Char joined Marlon behind the counter as if preparing for battle. Something twisted beneath her ribs. The door opened with such force that it wobbled on its hinges.

The woman: "Have you heard anything?"

"Anything about what?" said Char, and meaning it, but Marlon gave her a look. Wasn't that a funny thing—Julian watched how the man let his wife know, without saying a word, what the situation was. Julian had a deep respect for the coziness of marriage, for the way two people could start to work as a single organism. The woman looked feeble, exhausted, her face creased and brown like she'd been left out in the sun to dry; she had an arm in a sling, which made her appear even more delicate. The man smiled at them, a grin of solid white, a crescent moon. Even at such a time, he couldn't help but try to be the good proprietor, the welcoming host. Julian liked him immediately. Maybe this would be how he and Kit would turn out—wordlessly connected, work-ing side by side. He enjoyed a brief fantasy of running a motel together, out in the middle of nowhere. They would be spectacularly unsuited for it, but still. He watched the way the old man watched his wife with con-cern and thought that he couldn't wait, almost, to take care of shriveled old Kit. Now Marlon was saying, "Nothing new, not since they left. We called the police, of course, and they say they're looking."

Kit uttered a pained little sound. Julian had been saying, "She will have left already—she knows we're coming," and yet something in Kit had believed that Susannah wanted to be found, that she had reached the end of her rebellion and was ready to be caught, to be forgiven, to come clean, like a cat surprised by a mouse clamped in its jaws. "Which way? Where did she go?" Kit leaned forward. She felt faintly ridiculous. What a mess they'd made of things. Julian steadied her with a hand to her back.

"Julian Forsythe," he said, shaking Marlon's hand, nodding at Char, who did not offer her hand but waved hello with her sling. "We spoke. This is my wife, Kit."

"Pleased to meet you," said Kit, narrowing her eyes. "Who's 'they'? You said, 'they' left—who's 'they'?"

Marlon made an ignored offer of water or coffee. He shrugged again, suddenly feeling very tired. "Susannah and . . . well, our son. And . . ." He was trying to figure out how to identify Frankie—*the child of our guest's sister?*—when Kit exclaimed a strange syllable of sound that was not quite a laugh and not quite a word.

Then: "Your son!" She turned to Julian. "So she's run off with an-other man, Julie. How do you like that?"

It took Marlon a moment to register that though her face was still pinched in an angry way, she was teasing her husband, who shrugged and smiled a little. "Kit, I doubt that's what—"

"Oh, I don't think that's what it is. They haven't run off together so much as—"

Kit interrupted, "Come on. Don't you? I mean, that's certainly how it sounds—as if they've run off together. They've run off together with our baby. There it is, her instant family, her new life on the lam." This was to Julian.

Marlon felt his gall rising like a tide. "I don't think you understand. Our son is . . . he's just a boy. He's just turned seventeen."

"Oh, Susannah!" cried Kit. She raised her eyebrows.

"No, no. I mean. And he's, ah, special. You know what I mean? He's a special kid."

"Honey, everyone's kid is special."

"Ah, no, I mean. He's disabled, see. He's mentally impaired."

The smile Kit had been hiding behind wilted, a little.

"You see?"

"We're so sorry, sir, for—" Julian was saying, but Marlon ended it with a wave. It was difficult to concentrate with the TVs blaring. He squinted at the Forsythes through the static of sound.

"Nothing to be sorry about. I just mean to say that it's not what you think. They're not, uh, lovers or whatever you're saying. I don't know why she took him. But he's, not—you know. He's just a kid."

"Of course," said Julian, shooting a look at Kit. "We understand."

Kit turned on her heel and threw herself into one of the plastic chairs. The air conditioner's artificial breeze tousled her hair. She knew how to be polite and charming, how to win people over, but had somehow decided it wasn't worth it here. Here she was snappish, impatient, desperately rude. Julian tried to send a message through the top of her skull: *Keep it together, Kitty! It's hard, but you can do this!*

Char had gone out the back door to fetch Dicey, and now the two of them appeared in the doorway Julian and Kit had just entered. Char brushed past them and again perched on her stool next to Marlon, and Dicey sat beside Kit, introducing herself. Julian stood leaning on the wall facing the doorway, in between the wall with the plastic chairs and the wall with the counter, beside the rickety tray table balancing the coffeemaker and stack of yellowing Styrofoam cups. He felt that if he made any sudden moves, terrible things would happen; he envisioned the boiling-hot pot cascading into Kit's lap, chairs rat-skittering toward the corners, a powder of creamer settling into all their eyes and noses, sifting into crevices like volcanic ash.

"We could call the police again," said Char, looking at Marlon, who nodded thoughtfully and was about to answer when Kit interrupted.

"She didn't leave any clues? You searched her room? She didn't mention anyplace?" Having read too many whodunits.

Dicey spoke then, directing her comment toward Kit, who since her arrival had become the focus, the locus of the most pity—sitting there swiping at her eyes with a paper napkin Marlon had offered (Julian didn't think he'd ever seen her crying in public, and it was awful, awful!)—and therefore the most caution. "Maybe we should start calling hospitals with maternity wards—start that way?"

Kit raised the possibility of a stakeout. The idea was briefly entertained, but after all seemed unlikely to work—how would they know which hospital she might turn up in, how far she might have gotten? Couldn't they report Dicey's car stolen? Dicey pointed out that it wasn't her car, that she would have to contact her friend and explain what had happened and have *her* report it, and oh, that was a call she dreaded, and oh, what was she going to do, they were overdue at Frankie's father's house, and he would be angrily calling Frankie's mother. The women took over, speaking quickly, as if they'd known one another their whole lives. Marlon meanwhile was on the phone with what was presumably the police department, who seemed reluctant to take any information, being on their lunch break, naturally, as they tended to be. Even Marlon, who had always lived in the drowsy Southwest and should have been accustomed to conducting business within a somewhat relaxed time frame, fisted his hand on the counter, tightening it in frustration.

Julian stood looking out the window. And—was there a little boy? A little boy, just standing there in the middle of the desert, the parched expanse of land reaching from the motel to the horizon, just standing there and lifting one hand to wave? No, of course it couldn't be. It would have made no sense whatsoever. Julian rubbed his eyes with the thumb and forefinger of his right hand. He was tired, that was all.

Still, something about what he had seen—no, what he had *imagined*—irked him, crawled through his stomach like indigestion. He had to excuse himself from the increasingly warm office. He passed through Kit's glare, muttered that he'd be right back, stepped outside for a breath of fresh air only to encounter—right, he had forgotten it—a wall of heat, parching through his lungs. Breathing fire would have been just a tad less refreshing. What a place. Julian sat down on the bench outside the office. Burrs of molting paint adhered themselves to his khakis. Everything felt unclean. He looked down the highway one way, then the other. Would his child be a different child for having spent time here? Sand, pastry, seedpods—of what odds and ends were people compounded. Julian squinted at the glazed sky, at the weal of a distant mountain range rising from the earth like a misshapen scar.

The sound of Kit's voice carried above the others, insistent. "No, we called her mother, we called her work—she didn't tell anyone, hasn't been heard from in weeks!" Shrilling above the air conditioner's whir, above the deafening quiet of the place. Julian leaned back, looked up. Some kind of hive had been built in the eaves of the office, smashed lintlike into the tiny overhang. Somewhere a phone was ringing.

He waited a moment to hear them answer it. It took two rings for him to realize that it was happening not in the office but somewhere near him, beneath him, and he leaped up to hunt around for it. A canvas bag lay halfway under the bench, hurled carelessly by a person in a hurry, or maybe forgotten in the lazy heat—Julian seized it (three rings) and pulled out a folded newspaper, a thick old-lady wallet, a cracked tube of children's sunscreen (four rings), and finally a fat, outmoded cell phone, chunky as a toy. "Hey!" he called impotently toward the office, where Kit, he saw through the door's glass pane, was holding forth. "Um!" He looked at the phone: UNKNOWN CALLER. He pressed Talk. "Hello?" he said.

There was a pause. Don't hang up, he willed the crackling pause on the line, don't hang up. There was a moment when he thought how sad he would be when it was a wrong number, someone pushing credit cards. The phone scorched against his ear. Finally a child's voice said, "Hello? I think I got the wrong number."

"Wait, no! This isn't—who are you trying to call?"

Another pause pulsed through his skull before the child said, "Hello?"

"Hang on! Hang on, okay?"

"Hello?" answered the child uncertainly.

It was all so tenuous, the connection, the child's will. The line imitated a flickering campfire, a busy highway. Julian bolted for the door, pushed it open, crying, "Hey, hey, I think it's your kid!" Dicey jumped up and took the phone from him. Julian held his breath as she put the phone to her ear. But she frowned, looked at it, held it out to show him. The call had been lost. The screen door slammed a few times before latching shut.

"There's no towers," Char said.

"Beg pardon?"

Dicey went outside with the phone. Julian watched her sit on the bench, her back curled, as she extended, pitifully, the phone's tiny antennae out into the limitless sky.

"What did you say?" he said again to Char.

"I said there's no towers. There's no cell-phone service around here."

Julian looked to Kit, who said, "Well?"

"But I . . . but it was a kid—Frankie! I'm sure . . . it was someone." He sank into the chair.

"Do you want to lie down a minute?" Char said. Her eyebrows pressed together, her forehead a bed of salt lines and wrinkles. "We could let you into one of our rooms. You people have had a long couple of days."

"You know, I didn't come here . . ." He was about to get indignant, to say that he hadn't come here, you know, to be insulted, to be accused of madness, and he had really just about had enough of . . . of . . . *all* of *this*—but then he saw Kit's face. He *had* just seen a boy dissolving into the desert, after all. Maybe he really did need to lie down. Poor Kitty. She was the pretty stranger on the park bench, staring at him. So often she seemed brand-new again.

Marlon led him into Joan of Arc. He turned on the air, pulled the curtains closed, and shot Julian a worried, vaguely suspicious look before leaving, a look that shook its head and went, *City folk.* Julian closed his eyes. The imprint of the noon sun pounded bluely against his eyelids.

In the office Dicey had rejoined the others. She waved her phone at them. "Can't even get service for a second, not even right where he was. I don't get it."

Kit sighed, clasping her hands primly on her lap. "He's tired. I'm sorry. I don't know what to say." Dicey patted her shoulder sympathetically. The air conditioner whirred, stopped as if holding its breath, then restarted.

Then Char cackled. "To think it's you!"

"I'm sorry?" said Kit.

The air in the office seemed charged now, crackling and combustible as an electrical storm.

"It's just funny how these things go, that's all. If you'd never hired a girl to have your baby, she'd never've run off and come here, and we'd still have our boy, and we'd be sitting here right now all normal, just as quiet as little mice. Ha!"

Marlon appeared behind Char, frowning. Kit straightened her back.

"Oh, so this whole thing is my fault, is it. How fascinating." (Marlon recognized the timbre in her voice, the freaked-out indignance of someone who didn't like to feel foolish, whose default was defensiveness. God, she sounded exactly like Char.) Kit turned to Dicey. "Isn't that fascinating? And here I was, thinking, well, gee, if you all had only listened when Julian called, saying Susannah had phoned from here, that she had our baby, if you had only believed him and understood and *detained* her for a day or two, we'd be on our way home by now! But I see you're right. In fact, I'd go further than that! While we're at it—let's blame my darn uterus for not being able to carry my own baby. That's just lazy, is what that is!" She scolded her midsection. Char watched with a bemused smile frozen on her face. Kit was flushed, she sounded angry, but there was such an air of performance to it that Char couldn't quite see where all this was heading. Meanwhile Dicey tried to pat Kit's arm, only to be brushed off, and Marlon was sighing loudly and trying to interrupt. Kit cried, "Or no, let's see, it was those damn college professors who encouraged me to make a career instead of crapping out ten kids by now. Hey! Let's go find them!"

"You people," Char said, shaking her head.

"You *people*? What does that even mean? I'm sorry—what is that even supposed to mean?"

"You'd have been a good woman if nothing bad had ever happened to you." Char said it quietly. "I want you to know I understand that."

Kit opened and closed her mouth like a fish.

"All right," Marlon rushed in. "We're sorry. Char wasn't thinking."

"It's really my fault, anyway," Dicey said. "They took my car. I shouldn't have left my keys where they could find them. I should have watched Frankie more carefully." Everyone was in a hurry, suddenly, to accept the blame. Kit shrank back into a chair, pushed her fingertips at her eyes. The things that happened. No, they couldn't bear it. No, one didn't even want to get through it, one just wanted it never to have happened at all. She'd had an employee once, a woman who was quiet and unremarkable, who had gotten a phone call at work one day that caused her to wail in pain, to sob in a way that was terrifying, as if she were possessed. Kit had thought of her differently after that. What a capacity for pain people had, what things they were asked to endure. She felt faintly ridiculous for losing it in front of these people, these people who clearly only wanted to help. They had all lost children in the deal. They were all in the same boat. And then, a jolt of panic: What if she made a terrible mother? What if she were just too mean, too selfish, ever to be someone's mother? She felt scraped clean. She was empty inside, wooden, remote, and they could all tell, they could see through her, they could tell she didn't deserve Julian, didn't deserve any of it, that she was cold, that she was brittle. She had to counteract it, to try to be witty and sharp, but when it came down to it, sarcasm was a very meager gift, and she wished she had more to offer.

"Well, what a sorry bunch we are," said Char.

"This isn't very helpful," Dicey agreed. "Let's just try to figure out our next step."

Kit nodded at her.

It was about an hour later when the office phone rang.

INDEED, AS CHAR had pointed out in her usual indelicate way, it was a strange series of events that had connected one thing to another, that had suctioned this motley crew together, an intricate web of things, of one thing, another, the next, that had brought Julian and Kit to Susannah and Susannah to the Thunder Lodge, that had somehow tangled Dicey in the midst. It was the grace of the world or an accident of luck or something, that had led a child to a truck stop with a bank of phones tucked away in the back by the pinball machines; that led the child's temporary guardian to be distracted at that particular moment by an incident occurring in the convenience-mart section of the complex; that led a boy—drowning in frustration and the hideous, hot sounds of the place (the pelting *ding* of pinball machines, the slamming shut of register drawers, a family of tourists arguing among themselves over the cost of plastic sunglasses) and his general confusion, a result of his having been wrenched from the day-to-day to which he was accustomed, that and the teenage blood roiling soupily through his veins, and the heat of the woman always nearby, but never near *enough*—to stand stock-still in the middle of the store and, when the woman reached out and touched his shoulder, start to howl, a frantic, inhuman keen of a shriek, constructing a biosphere of pity all around, but also allowing the child to slip away to make a phone call with the quarters she had found abandoned in the slot of a pinball machine. No one thought about those quarters until later, or maybe never at all, but they had belonged to a trucker whose name was, improbable as it seemed, John Smith, who left them in an Elvis-themed game that twanged out a mechanized version of "Heartbreak Hotel" because John had always been a fan of the King and needed to rest a minute before climbing back into the rig for the next twelve-hour leg of the job. He had been about to play another round when a wiry man in coveralls walked by and nodded, meaning that he'd gotten the message John had left scrawled in the urinal and that they would meet in the truck to complete their sordid affair. So John Smith left the quarters. So Frankie had found them as she wandered along the bank of games, inserting a finger into each machine's cool cavity. She hustled over to the telephones, pushed a low table arrayed with brochures (*The Grand Canyon! The Wild West—in Wax! Enchanted Buttes Horseback Riding!*) close to the wall, and stepped on it to reach the coin slot, called Dicey's number but must have gotten it wrong somehow (a man had answered, then crackled off), hung up, and stood there a moment, thinking. A mom was herding a few rowdy children away from the fracas in the convenience mart. Frankie reached out and tapped her. "Excuse me. Do you know if they have a phone book here?" The mom blinked unfocusedly at her. "Beneath the thingy?" And, in a hurry to follow the children through the door, "Y'know?" So Frankie located the phone book chained to the bottom of the booth, swung its robot arm up to open the book, hummed the alphabet song softly until reaching the *T*'s, yes, the Thunder Lodge. But now Susannah was calling her in a creepy singsong meant to sound normal but edged with panic—"*Fran*kie, *sweet*heart, where *are* you?"—so Frankie coast-is-cleared in both directions and tore the page from the phone book and crammed it into her pocket for safekeeping, along with the remaining three quarters, for the next time she encountered a telephone. Okay, so she felt a hot jag of guilt when she grabbed Susannah's hand and swung it gaily on the way to the car with exaggerated abandon, but she just wanted to call Aunt Dicey was all, and Susannah, who smiled at Tim now with clenched teeth, seemed a little tense today.

They climbed back into the car, coasted out into the wake of the street.

After a few moments: "Hey. Do you see that?" Susannah nudged Frankie. They had gotten a delayed start, disembarking from the Tumbleweed Motor Lodge late in the morning. Susannah had been aching all over, and then Tim had had a fit about her urging him to shower. He had disappeared out back for an hour, only to reappear with a fistful of gathered cigarette butts, and then Frankie had added to the trouble by unpacking all her suitcases and insisting on leaving behind a ruffled confection of a party dress she claimed no longer to need. And now that they'd finally gotten on the road, afternoon light infected the sky. Susannah grunted and shifted in her seat for miles, unsure of how much longer she could stand to drive. Tim sat silent in the back, starting to emit a musky smell, forehead suctioned to the window. They had already stopped once for another of his famous Scenes in Truck Stops. Hopelessness sucked in through the vents. Frankie looked to where Susannah was looking, first in the rearview mirror, then whipping her head around to survey the empty highway, neat as a pencil line, rulering straight back toward the horizon. "See?" Susannah said.

"See what?"

But the car Susannah had seen, had thought she'd seen—following them and closing in and then swerving suddenly into the ditch causing a mushroom cloud of dirt and sand—didn't seem to be there anymore. And here she'd worried! Here she'd thought they were being chased! Really, nothing was wrong at all, nothing in the whole world. Susannah took a hand off the wheel and rubbed at her eyes. "Nothing," she said. "Nothing."

IF FRANKIE WAS beginning to feel uneasy about the situation she now found herself in, it wouldn't have been anything new. Like any child, she was accustomed to disappointment. Here was Frankie, buffeted by the whims of adults, with no control over her life, no explanations for the things in the world that baffled her. She had never felt at home at home, so being exiled to her father's shouldn't have made her feel as funny as it had. But it *had* made her feel funny. It had made her feel rotten, and small, like an accident, like a living bruise. She had been aware from a very young age that the circumstances of her birth had not been happy—she never had that extended period of egoism familiar to most children—she always knew that her mother was a person occupied with her own life.

Frankie would go out playing with the neighbor boys, a rough-and-tumble pair from a boisterously male family, exactly who Frankie had always wanted to be. They went adventuring through the humid forest out behind the mall, launching homemade arrows at each other across the sewagey creek. The older boy threw dirt in Frankie's eyes, crowed with victory. But what Frankie lacked in brute strength she made up for by knowing certain things. In a thicket of reeds, she enlisted the younger. "You are much stronger than your brother," she confided. The sun slanted down, angling into their eyes and mouths. Frankie put a hand on the boy's arm. "I wish I could see you really get him good." The younger boy wanted to prove himself. He trotted off to sneak up into a tree, as Frankie instructed, while she headed around toward the crick. This was something she had learned from watching her mother—the way flattery would make any man pliable as a palmful of honey, even a five-year-old not-yet-a-man with a captured frog bulging in his pocket. So when the older boy again threw the dirt toward Frankie's eyes, the younger boy let fall a thunderstorm of leaves and twigs and pebbles, and the older boy looked up yelping as the younger one scrambled back down the tree. "Victory is ours!" he cried, pumping his fist in the air. The older boy couldn't decide whom to be madder at and so changed gears, went calmly looking for a sword. "Okay," he said, "fine. I'll just kill you, that's all. I'm going to stab out your guts and then put you in the trash can." Frankie sat laughing in the bowl formed by a knot of tree roots. It was so effortless with them, while the girls in her grade struck her as intensely silly, utterly unapproachable.

Later in the afternoon, they resurfaced at the boys' house. The older boy declared himself finished playing with babies and plopped in front of the enormous television in the den. Frankie and the younger boy went to his room. Frankie closed the door and stood in front of it. "Take off your pants," she commanded. "Please."

The younger boy cocked his head at her, like a baffled dog.

"I just need to see something for a second. Then I'll show you mine. Take them off. All kids do this. I hope you're not chicken." She spoke forcefully, without inflection, the way her mother did after she had her first drink but before starting her second.

The boy shrugged at her. His brow furrowed, he fumbled with his shorts. "Okay," he said, already pulling them down.

Frankie put her hands on her knees and bent down to see closer. Like a little grub, it hung limply between his legs, pillowed on tiny testicles. The boy laughed for some reason. Frankie reached out quickly and flicked it with her forefinger. "Ow! Jerk," said the boy, his brow crumpled again, staggering back a step. "Why don't you go home already!" he said.

Frankie left without a word. She walked the long way around the block to get home. Hers was like that but tiny, and erupting at the top of a vagina that was pink and curled as a snail's mouth. Frankie's eyes stung. What *was* hers? When would this be explained to her? She stuck her hand tentatively into her shorts as she walked down the deserted street, cupped the tiny thing, removed her hand, practiced scratching at her crotch in that mindlessly male way of the neighbor boys, of her mother's boyfriend. They didn't even think about it, she guessed. To them it was like breathing. She tried to do it without thinking about it.

She arrived home in the buttery late afternoon to find her mother coiled in front of the television with a glass sweating in her hand.

"Mom," said Frankie. "Mom. Mom. Mom."

Finally her mother lifted her head. "What, sweetheart."

Frankie wanted to say something she didn't have the words for, something that burned under her tongue like a cinnamon lozenge— hot, serrated, too sweet. She felt homesick, for some reason, homesick for someplace she'd never been. She said, "What's for dinner?"

Her mother emitted a long sigh, like a punctured tire. "Je-sus. How do I know?"

Frankie sat comfortably in the crook of her mother's legs. She picked at a loose strand in the blanket. Her mother stopped her with a cold hand. "Macaroni and cheese."

Frankie shook her head no.

"Hot dog."

No.

"PBJ."

Frankie sighed.

"*I* don't know what you want," her mother said finally, crankily. "I can't read your mind, Francine darling."

I know, thought Frankie, but I wish you would at least try.

THE SKY DEEPENED, lengthened, blued in the afternoon. They did not talk. They drove past the buttes and plateaus, through the brilliantly stained rock and sand, the pyrotechnic desert. Susannah's spine and now her entire left leg seared, her extremities swollen as water balloons—no, overstuffed sausages, no, a suburban easy chair—the baby swimming toward the ground, it seemed, as fast as he could. Susannah had invented a game of naming the baby again and again. As in: Abraham. A name with power, distinction. And the game was a life in fast-forward, in which she'd picture his life as an Abraham. He was serious and dark and needed glasses at a young age. "Or Rex!" (Frankie was playing the game, too.) Rex Forsythe-Prue, that was a good one. He was sturdy and fearless, he rolled up his sleeves, he had a shock of yellow hair. He played tennis and went surfing; he invented nicknames for everyone; he went to prep school and summered with school friends in places like Hyannis, Kennebunkport; he married a curator who threw wonderful parties. Maybe that one wouldn't work. There was no place for Susannah in Rex's life, though Julian and Kit might do. No, she shook her head, not Rex. So Michael. Something plain and solid. Michael was dependable. Michael clung to his mother as a child but made friends at school that he kept for the rest of his life. Michael was at the top of his class at the sprawling state university and went on to a sensible, successful, though uninteresting career. But Michael was a tricky one, because he could also be a poet, a drunk, a gambler. Michael would have brown hair and dark eyes, but Michael would be malleable. So maybe George. There was nothing wrong with a name like George. He would be Georgie as a child, cute enough, a sweet but noble boy, and then grow into his name, George, the kind of person who would take being a man seriously. Susannah would be decided for a moment, and then all the kicking and carrying on would start up again and she'd think, What? You don't want to be George? Right, no, you're right, too many President Georges. I'd been thinking more Curious. Okay, let's keep thinking. Julian. Maybe Julian was the name for this kid.

Of course Kit had already named the child something or another. Who knew how he would turn out? Kit had probably chosen some aggregation of syllables that she'd read in a fashion rag or else heard called out on a playground, some already dated name that everyone was thinking was so different but that was already becoming common, something perfect for a person like Kit, who wanted to be original but without any risk. Susannah shuddered. She wasn't sure when she'd started to dislike Kit so intensely. She'd been okay with her, even loved her for brief, intense moments, at the beginning of all this. It was difficult to remember now where things had gone wrong, when the idea of leaving had popped into her mind. She didn't think it had been more than a few minutes before she actually left. She was never good at being impulsive, simply didn't quite know how to do it correctly. She had a knack for being impulsive about the things that were most important, that needed the most thought or planning, that were the worst to be impulsive about, while at a grocery store she'd be struck dumb, numbed by meaningless choices, unable to pick an apricot, one plum, three peaches. If a friend called—back when she had friends!—to ask her to a last-minute thing, a bike ride or a violin concert, she would sputter inarticulately, her brain frozen, unable to say yes or no. And here, with everything at stake, with George's (or whoever's) life at stake, she had impulsively crammed things into bags, turned out the lights, gotten into the car, driven to the desert. God, what a stupid person she was, God, what a terrible person.

"Um," said Frankie.

"There's no one else on the road," Susannah snapped. "I wasn't swerving that much. It doesn't really make a difference."

"No, I was just gonna ask something. I was just gonna ask, how far is the ocean from here?" Frankie furrowed her brow, trying to block the sun from her eyes and failing miserably. Susannah reached out and pulled down the sun visor. It didn't help.

"Not too far," she said. "One more day, I think."

Frankie bounced in her seat a few times. "It's going to be cool," she said. "I have seriously always wanted to swim in salt water, ever since I was a little kid." Susannah smiled at this. Frankie said, twisting her seat belt with her tiny hands, "We will have to look out for jellyfish and sharks."

Tim grunted in alarm. He had been listless in the back since the gas station, his head against the window, moaning quietly now and then. He seemed to be moldering around the edges, going as soft and dark as ancient fruit.

"Yes," Frankie said, turning her head to address him. "We'll have to be careful, because they can really hurt you. Jellyfish, and sea urchins, and electric eels and sea horses."

"Sea horses can't do anything do you," said Susannah.

"Is that what you think?" said Frankie ominously.

SHE WAS STILL wondering whether they'd entered California yet or not—it seemed like you'd know somehow when it happened, that you'd feel somehow different—when a neon sign appeared on the horizon, distant as a star. Relief pouched beneath her skin. She knew they hadn't gone as far as they should've, but she also knew she had to stop driving for the day. She didn't know when she'd ever felt so tired.

Frankie strained against her seat belt. "Is this a good place to stop? I want to go swimming. I'm soooo sick of the car. Are we ready yet?"

Despite having already checked them in to a room in her mind, Susannah scowled. "Frankie, are we close enough to see? It's a speck—do you think I can read it? I don't even know if it's a motel."

The miniature squall had roused Tim, who now leaned forward in between the seats and rubbed his thighs and giggled. "Huh. Huh. Go to the Grotto."

"Timothy," said Susannah. "For the last time. Just . . . not right now." Pain spasmed through her legs. "Fuck." It was the only word that seemed to really express what she was feeling—the curt, plain stab of darkness.

"Look! Can we stop here, please, please, please?" Frankie tugged on Susannah's sleeve, and Susannah yanked her arm free, swerving the car slightly into the oncoming lane.

"What is wrong with you, Frankie?"

Tim joined in now. "Yeah! Definitely, definitely. Go to the Grotto, huh, yeah."

They were getting nowhere fast, and that was that. It seemed they had covered almost no ground at all, that truly, truly, they would never reach the shore, the ocean in all its bottomless beauty, that they were still so close to the Thunder Lodge that Char needed only to reach out her hand to take hold of them by the scruffs of their necks; Char, who must have hated Susannah by now even more than she already had. Char might even—Susannah had a terrible thought. Might the Garlands have called the police? They might have. They must have by now. They certainly had the right to. Of course they had. Because though she didn't *feel* like a kidnapper, she guessed she could see how someone would see things that way. They pulled into the driveway beneath the sign—an electric tidal wave spewing happy neon spray, a looping blue script: THE AQUA CITY MOTEL. Susannah cut the engine, and they all stepped out in a wobbling daze.

"We're home?" said Tim uncertainly, rubbing his hands together and knitting his brow. Frankie shrugged at Susannah. Here they were, right where they'd started: a perfect simulacrum of the Thunder Lodge, laid out the same way in reverse—the office, the row of rooms jutting to its right, the gravel drive along the highway—only that the doors were painted a turbid blue, a blue with a gut of black, and music came coasting from the office's propped-open screen door. In the left-hand distance pursed a ridge of mountain, crimped and dark as a prosthetic alien forehead. A wedge of moon was smooshed in the sky. The desert of the Aqua City Motel was that driest kind of desert—sand cracked into lifelines across the china plate of the terrain. The name of the place must have been someone's idea of a joke, or else part of some ambitious plan that hadn't quite succeeded—a water park rising from the ashy dust, tubes tangling in the air. "Well," said Susannah. "Let's do this, I guess."

She tried not to think of the word *waddle*—so accurate, so unforgiving—as she waddled to the office. Tim was lurching toward the Grotto, toward where he thought the Grotto should be, his hands clasped in that way of his, like praying but more knotted, in front of his heart. He giggled. "The Grotto," he said happily. "Uh," said Frankie, who began to follow him, "Tim, I don't know if they—Hey!" They disappeared behind the office.

Inside, a couple stood behind the counter, apparently in the middle of some debate, and so Susannah tried to let the screen door close quietly behind her, but the woman—beady-eyed, with a whitish bob swaying, swaying because she was gesticulating with bare, ropy arms—clapped her hands and announced, "Ah, hello! See, I told you now wasn't the right time to take lunch." This to the man, a dark fellow with a missing front tooth, who sighed patiently back at who Susannah guessed, from the way he sighed at her mostly, must have been his wife, or someone he had known for a very long time. They seemed an accidental pair—she very white and tidy, in a crisp sleeveless blouse, he lanky and creased, dressed in pilling flannel—but they moved effortlessly together: He handed her a clipboard of forms, and without looking she took it and handed one to Susannah to fill out. They made her homesick, a little, for the Forsythes. Even when she knew that Julian was frustrated with Kit, there would be some minuscule moment between them—the way he opened an umbrella for her on a rainy day, the way he'd mop up coffee she spilled without her even noticing it—offerings that Kit accepted without registering, motions that seemed to Susannah to be exceptionally kind and loving, that made jealousy ricochet through her rib cage like an echo in a cavern. Julian was a wonderful husband, would make a wonderful father.

"Hello," said Susannah.

"Roger, what was I just saying? I told you I had a feeling about today—I knew we'd have a customer." But she didn't wait for an answer, darted around like a perpetual-motion machine, in the process of extracting coffee from a dingy five-cup maker that steamed on a crowded desk behind the counter. Here it was a curtain instead of a door, and it was left draped open, revealing the pleasantly untidy living room.

The man, Roger, leaned his elbows on the counter, staring at Susannah as if bored by her. Another harried young mother with too many kids, he thought without really looking. Her other kids were already making a racket out back. He was glad they'd never had any kids; he was pretty sure, anyway. They made him nervous, always jumping around, always touching everything. Besides, Letty was enough for him, more than enough, Letty and his bike and his poker buddies—he guessed he was busy enough. Right? Right. The mother filled out the form—name, card number, peering outside to get her license plate number—biting her lip, her face bright red, her hair falling all over her face. She was cute, but what a mess. No thanks.

Letty sprinkled nondairy creamer into a dry Styrofoam cup. "Don't you want to sit down or something?"

Susannah did, desperately, but she shook her head no. "Thank you. I just want to get a room for the night. A double. There are three of us, two adults, one kid. I mean, one adult, two kids."

"Need a cot?" said Roger, still not looking at her face. They had that exhaustion to them, these women with too many children. You didn't want to get too close—didn't want to catch it.

"Yes, please."

"They must be so excited," Letty said. She spoke to Susannah like they'd known each other their whole lives. "For the baby!" She poured coffee into her cup and swirled it around as she searched for a stirrer, and, giving up, finally she stuck her index finger into the coffee and drew an O quickly and then stuck it into her mouth. "I guess so!" said Susannah. "They must be!" Roger had never wanted kids, which was fine with Letty. Her girls were grown; they lived far away with their father, a gambler and a cheat whom they preferred over her. That was the way things went with girls: They always blamed their mother for everything. She'd been so happy when she was expecting her own girls, so purely, cleanly joyful, as if those months were all she'd been put on earth for. But this poor girl—she was tired, and here alone with her kids. Letty wanted to wrap her arms around her, to smooth her tousled hair. But you couldn't do a thing like that; you could only push a key across the counter and try to smile very warmly and say, "Do let us know if there's anything you need."

Susannah entered the dingy cell like all the others—two single

beds shoved against headboards that were attached not to the beds but
just to the wall; the outdated phone book lumbering on the bedside
table, like a giant's well-thumbed novel; the cot folded clammishly by
the door; the bathroom paved in peeling laminate, featuring a tub
sandpapery with skids, the requisite overly complex shower nozzle. Susannah dropped her small bag onto the bed. You could travel through
the whole world and here were these empty rooms, waiting for you.
The window yawned open. Heat moved around the room.

"Out back is the pool," the woman had told her. "We call it the
Cove." Susannah left the room and now stood by the pool, watching
the water move. The pool was nothing like a cove. A few potted trees
loitered by the fence. Tim stood very still in the shade of the building's overhang. Chlorine burned in Susannah's nostrils. Toward the
gate where she had entered buzzed a couple of modern vending machines glowing with cinematic images of Cold Refreshing Coke, the
lights looking meager in the slanting afternoon. She saw, a little farther
by the highway, a pay phone mounted to a pole that stabbed up at the
cantilevered sky. Frankie was there, slamming the phone back into its
cradle, shoving a yellow scrap of paper into her shorts pocket before
running back to the motel, tearing off her T-shirt and cannonballing
into the water. She had phone calls to make now, did she? Susannah
closed her eyes, received the splash.

BECAUSE the whole group was huddled in the office
to stay cool, to debrief, to discuss, and because Julian had earlier answered and lost a phantom call, they were sitting right next to the office phone when it rang, when Frankie finally found herself at that pay
phone stalky as a pussywillow alongside the river of asphalt. Marlon
looked at all of them, picked up the phone. "Thunder Lodge?" He
nodded, and everyone breathed out in relief. The whole room lifted,
brightened, weighed lighter on their skin. Dicey stood up and gestured

for the phone, her weight pitched awkwardly forward as if she might try to dive into the receiver itself. "Frankie? Oh, baby doll, are you all right?"

Kit exchanged a look with Julian, who was returned from his rest in Joan of Arc. When she looked away, Julian observed his tidy wife, the way she leaned back on the grungy, scuffed chair, scowling at the mud puddle in the coffeemaker, scowling generally at the room, at its existence. She had no patience for anyone's dramatic episodes but her own just now. It would do for her to behave magnanimously toward these people, kinder, opener, gentler; if only there were a way to communicate this to her without saying it. It was one of the impossibilities of Kit. But then she shook her head in a sudden fillyish way and her hair fell over her shoulders, and there it was—the most beautiful girl in the world. Julian sighed. He wanted to tell her, then, about the boy he'd seen standing outside. He tried to promise himself that he wouldn't, that he never would, because one never knew with Kit—she might be sympathetic, credulous, but she might turn on him with a sneer and use it later to humiliate him.

Kit meanwhile leaned forward, making a *Yes, and* . . . gesture to Dicey. Dicey frowned into the phone, acknowledging Kit without interrupting the frown. Marlon leaned forward, too, from across the counter. He was close enough to hear Frankie's voice squeaking through the lines. Dicey said, "All right. Okay. But you're okay? And Tim's okay? Oh. But before that he was okay?" Char and Marlon froze like rabbits in a yard. Dicey waved at them, shaking her head, mouthing, *Nothing, nothing.* "Baby, where are you now? Well, can you find out? Can you ask someone? Is there a sign anywhere?" Kit broke in, unable to stop herself, "And Susannah? The baby?" Julian and Marlon shushed her in unison, and then Julian shot Marlon a look for shushing his wife. Char stood beside Marlon, popping her knuckles on her good hand, releasing firecrackers of sound into the air. "Yes, Frankie. Hurry, please, okay?" Dicey turned from them, facing the wall, curving in toward the phone. There was a pause of at least fifteen minutes, at least a hundred years or so, or maybe only a few seconds, in which they all seemed to hold their breath as the child craned her neck up at the sign and sounded out the words—"Aqua . . . City . . . Motel"—and Marlon stood, his stool clattering back on the floor. "Tell her!"

"Hold on one second, baby," Dicey said to the phone.

Marlon started again. "Tell her— The Aqua City Motel? We know that place. We know the lady that runs it—motel's even built by the same guy who built ours. Tell her to make sure they stay there. We can get there in a day, by tonight if we leave now. We know that place."

"Their pool is a mess," Char confirmed. "Just terrible."

"The Aqua City Motel," Dicey said. "Frankie, can you make sure you stay there all night?"

AFTer THe CaLL they sat around dazed, a little embarrassed at the heat they had just shared, like a mismatched pair after a one-night stand. Dicey stood rubbing her hands together. "Julian, can we take your car? Does one of you want to stay behind here? I'd like to come with to get them, with whoever's going, if that's all right. In fact, I'll take my things, and when we get to my car, Frankie and I will just continue on our way." Because what else could they do, really? Where else was there for them to go? Though there was now this strange sense that they were all connected, forced to work together, they would of course eventually complete the transaction and go their separate ways. Dicey nodded her head. "Sound good? We should get going as soon as we can."

"Let's see," Kit said, sitting on the chair next to Julian, who had sat down very close to her and grasped hold of her hand, like a husband was supposed to do in a crisis. *God,* it occurred to her, they looked like

a stricken couple being interviewed on a news program, cast in flattering, warm light and interrupted by memory montages, a slow-panning
close-up of the snapshot of Kit and a roundish Susannah, arms linked,
laughing, a shadow behind Susannah's smile that no one had noticed
until now. Julian squeezed her hand firmly, sweetly. "If we all go there,
and once we get there Dicey and Frankie leave in their own car, and Julian and Susannah and I come back here—I mean, with Tim, of
course—would that work? Marlon, Char, are you okay with staying
behind?" They could even do it after the baby. Though a relief had
washed over the room, Kit now wondered whether Susannah might
still refuse to hand over the baby. *Surrender, Dorothy*—it cackled
through Kit's brain, surfacing from somewhere. *Give up the ghost.*
What did these things mean? Where had the spores of words come
from? Susannah had come this far, and she would go, Kit suspected,
further. It was remarkable, how quickly one could go from wanting to
do anything to help a person to praying for the world to crush her.

Marlon and Char had wordlessly commiserated over the plan and
agreed. Marlon had half suspected Char to set her jaw, insist on coming with—but in truth, neither of them could quite bear the thought
of being separated just then. This was a job for the young, they told
themselves, a job for quick-reflexed city people. "And someone'll bring
back Tim?" Char said, nodding, convincing them of it.

"Of course," Kit said quickly. She stood up, her muscles alive and
animal. Some instinct had kicked in, flooded her like a nerve gas.
Nothing mattered but finding the baby, grasping hold of Susannah's
arm and not letting go. They would need to get Susannah to a hospital right away, most likely. Or maybe Susannah would be fine—solidly
pregnant still, the baby lazily resisting birth—and they would have
time to drop Tim off and get Susannah home before the baby came.
The due date loomed, stormish. They would deal with the details
later. Kit headed for the door, feeling frantic, starved. "Let's get going.
Can we get going already?"

DICEY HAD GONE to her room to pack up her things, hurling clothes into her duffel bag, half afraid the Forsythes would leave without her. While she was tearing through dingy St. Catherine like a runaway in a TV movie, a bitterness rose, rich and orange in her throat. Because she had lost the child, and when she'd always thought of Frankie as being, at least partially, her own lost child, as if something of the baby she hadn't had floated through the air and lodged itself in her sister's womb. She'd even suspected—though she wouldn't have said this to anyone—that her child had been a boy, that Jean's had been a girl, that they had somehow combined, intertwined in the uterine muck, and that that was why Frankie was Frankie. Dicey swallowed hard. Frankie! Rubber sandals, hairbrush, half-read magazine. Where was her swimsuit? The shirt she had slept in. She hurriedly zipped the bag shut.

Outside, the day slammed brightly against her. Julian Forsythe stood talking to Char, going over the details again. From his posture, the look on her face, Dicey knew he was trying to be kind. The woman, Kit, leaned impatiently against the car, thin and lightly tan and frowning. Here was the expectant mother. It made Dicey feel like laughing. Kit seemed about as motherly as a shoe. Dicey threw her bag into the open trunk, "So," she said to Kit, but Kit ignored her. A shining RV chugged down the highway, its flank shimmering with a detailed woodland scene, a grave-looking showdown between an eagle and a snake, an American flag canted to one side. A gunshot crackled—no no, the trailer's engine backfired—and they all jumped a little. Dicey opened the back door of the Forsythes' car and sat on the edge of the seat, her feet still in the dust. Kit leaned over and honked the horn.

A few moments later, Char and Marlon stood in the drive, waving as they drove off.

"Well, what is it?" Marlon said. "Kit got your tongue?" He chuckled.

Char took a step toward the office and looked up at the Thunder Lodge sign, seeing in its electrical storm something menacing that she'd never seen before. Marlon looked up, too, and they stood there together, not touching, watching their sign like it was a sunset.

THEY'D BEEN OUT there all afternoon, for hours and hours, Susannah sweating into a plastic chaise—God, but she felt tired, heavy, immobile—interrupting her torpor only now and then to watch Frankie do handstands, when the woman from the office meandered out. "What cute boys you have!" she beamed.

"Oh," said Susannah, "I'm just . . . the aunt."

"Ha! And they're making you baby-sit? In your condition?" Letty winked to show she was mostly kidding. "I'm in kind of the same boat as you, actually."

Susannah was very surprised to hear this. "Are you?"

"Susannah Susannah Susannah LOOK!" Frankie was plunging her fists impatiently into the water. Susannah looked, hard. Frankie did another handstand. It was the same as all the handstands she'd done already. When the wet face emerged, Susannah clapped a few times, raising her eyebrows.

Letty patted Susannah's arm and went to straighten the rows of chairs. "Well, Roger and I are only watching this place for my sister, who owns it. So it's like we're watching her baby."

"I see," said Susannah.

Letty had more to say, too—about the difficulties of caring for a motel, about how they would have liked to do things a bit differently than her sister did but how it wasn't their place to, and so on—and Susannah was listening, really enjoying just letting a person prattle on, realizing she hadn't for some time had the luxury of allowing someone's words wash over her with no more responsibility on her end than an occasional mmm-hmm. It was so *easy*. Susannah's focus flitted from Letty's voice ebbing around her to the flicker-buzz of the Aqua City Motel sign to the glowering heat of Tim in the corner (he seemed intent on braiding his fingers through the chain-link fence and then lining up his eye with one, then another, of the holes and peering through them). So she was surprised, and flinched a little, when she heard the smack of Frankie's body hitting the pavement, and Letty's "Oh!"

Frankie pushed herself up quickly. She'd been running from the poolside toward the bucket of plastic toys she'd spotted near the vending machines. Now she stood and told the ladies, "It's okay, I'm okay," while she inspected the heels of her hands, brailled in pills of skin, sockets welling with blood. "Oh, honey, you're hurt," said Letty, pointing at Frankie's knee, also skinned and reddening, but Frankie shrugged, a little too cavalier. "I'm fine." She made her way gingerly to the pool's edge and sat dangling her legs in. "Stop looking at me! I'm fine!" But Susannah knew that she wasn't fine, that it must sting, or she wouldn't have settled for the edge of the pool. It was unlike Frankie not to dive back in. She stood watching Frankie until she realized that Letty was watching *her*, and so she made her way over to where Frankie sat and then stood there, teetering (she was off balance these days and missed the ability to do things like squatting, sitting on the ground) and reaching awkwardly for Frankie's shoulder but settling for just tousling at her hair, and said, "Frankie, maybe we should go inside. Put some Bactine on those scrapes."

Frankie shrugged. "I'm fine."

"Such a brave boy!" Letty was saying in the background, clapping her hands together. "There's the difference, I guess! My girls would have been screaming and crying at that age."

Susannah and Frankie exchanged a look. Frankie smothered a smile—just another browned boy in shark-print trunks. But the poor kid (Susannah went back to mindlessly exchanging pleasantries with Letty—what a treat it was to converse in a normal, everyday dialogue), the poor kid had only a few years left of this kind of fluidity, of being able to play this game. The thought of Frankie going through puberty, her nipples erupting outward into unmistakable buds, her slender frame staying slim and girlish—oh, the poor kid. Susannah fought the urge to bundle Frankie up in her arms, cradle her like a long-limbed baby—because here she was already, Frankie was fine, she was re-silient, she was no one's long-limbed baby, bounding up, shaking out her hands, wandering over to Tim with the bucket of toys and bossily instituting some sort of game. Letty beamed. "He's such a sport! Usu-ally teenagers won't play that nice with the little ones—what a sweet family you have!"

Susannah shuddered—the night was growing cold the way it did in the desert—and called out, "You guys, come to the room. We should get an early start in the morning. Let's watch some TV and go to bed."

They scowled up at her.

"Ocean," said Tim. "Tidal wave. Deep-sea trenches."

"Right." Susannah stole a look at Letty, who was busy retrieving litter from beneath the chairs.

"Yeah. And we're hungry," Frankie added. "We never even had any lunch."

Tim pressed his eyebrows down.

"Tim, are you hungry, too?"

He released his brow then and made his unsmiling giggle. "Yeah. Hungry, yeah."

Susannah willed Letty to stay back where she was. She liked Letty's image of them as a happy little family and didn't want to have to explain about Tim, to have to explain about anything.

"Okay, you guys, well, our options are a bit limited. We still have some bread and peanut butter in the car, right, Frankie?" Because Frankie had been managing the food, pointing out items at truck stops and convenience stores for Susannah to purchase—loaves of soft white bread, Pop-Tarts for Tim, thin plastic tubes greasy with salted peanuts, now and then a few overpriced waxy apples (for nutrition, she told Susannah). But Frankie's good-sportedness seemed to be fading, and in the face she made, Susannah again saw that sullen kid sulking alongside Dicey. She had thought she'd won Frankie over, that they were partners, but now it occurred to her that this agreeableness had been contingent on factors out of her control. She had not yet had to say no to Frankie. Now she found herself in the midst of a standoff as Frankie shook her head and said, "I'm sick of peanut butter sandwiches. I want to go somewhere." She planted her legs wide, fisted her hands on her hips.

Tim nodded.

"We want to go somewhere," Frankie started again, "and get hamburgers. Aren't we on vacation? You get hamburgers on vacation."

Susannah stepped backward, looking for a chair. "Frankie. Baby."

"No! I want hamburgers!"

Tim punched his thighs. Now he was getting worked up, too, and soon there would be a fit, and all Susannah wanted was to go to bed— Lord, she was so tired, her body hot and full and aching—and Frankie, who had been her helper all along, her teammate, her partner, had suddenly turned against her. Susannah rubbed her face. What would happen to them now? It had always been such a precarious balance.

She jumped a little at the hand on her shoulder.

Letty stood with the bluish glow from the neon sign haloed behind her. "I don't mean to intrude, but, well . . . I could take him. You must be exhausted, and I need to get a bite to eat, anyway. Rog could stay in the office, and Frankie and I could go to town to get some burgers. There's a great place he'd love—fun for kids, you know, a family place—and it wouldn't take us long. He'd be back by bedtime."

Frankie leaped up. "Yeah!" She ran to Letty, grabbed her hand, leaning against her leg. "Please, can we, come on, pleeeease?"

Susannah knew this game, knew that overly saccharine smile of Frankie's, the appeal to Letty's ego, the letting her win—she knew; the flicker in Letty's chest that went, *I know this child like you do not; yes, we understand each other, this child and I.* Susannah would have liked to forgive Letty for this, but it froze halfway up and solidified in her gullet, a hairball of emotion.

Then Letty added, "I could take him, too," gesturing toward Tim, who had crept forward. He stood in the waning sun, a hank of hair fallen forward over his eye, his hands clasped in front of him. Had he gotten thinner since Susannah had known him? Taller? "I'm sorry, honey, what's your name?" Letty said to Tim. There was something of Dicey in her—that willingness to please—that crawled across Susannah's skin. Susannah was too hot now, the baby shifting, her knees going gelatinous beneath her. *I have to sit down.* But no one looked at her, no one helped. Had she said it out loud? How could she make certain to say it out loud? How would she ever work up the energy to make the noises, to push out the right kind of air? Tim looked at her and then back at Letty and giggled—huh, huh. Frankie stepped in front of Letty and said, "That's just Tim—he doesn't want to come with. Oh, take me, let's go, I'm starving!" Letty was watching Tim, and Tim was staring at the ground, his hands fisted at what Frankie had said. It was possible that Letty still thought him to be a normal boy. Frankie tugged furiously at Letty, shooting Tim a look the ferocity of which Susannah had not ever seen from her, and finally Frankie won, and she and Letty were leaving the Cove, trudging into the parking lot. Over her shoulder Letty called, "Should we bring something back?" and Susannah, feeling faint, shook her head no but registered a guttural protest from Tim that she could not translate. "Hamburger!" he finally shouted after them. "Hamburger!" Then he and Susannah were alone by the shifting waters of the chemical-scented pool.

SUSANNAH MADE HER way back to the room. She had never unpacked at the Thunder Lodge despite how long she'd stayed, and now she stood in the room with the lights off and the window open, carefully lifting the folded clothes from her suitcase, listening to Tim hum tunelessly in the bathroom (he had followed her into the room, smiling at her, suddenly sweet again) and to the occasional drone of traffic along the highway. A sweatshirt she hadn't needed for weeks. Her swimsuit. The maternity jeans with the expandable elastic waist. The lovely wrap dress in an expensive-feeling fabric, adjustable to the size of your belly, that Kit had bought her when the third trimester began, that Susannah had never worn. She took these things and settled them into the drawers. At the bottom of her suitcase were a few cotton onesies, patterned in daisies. They had been hers when she was a baby. Her mother had given them to her, despite her protests, despite her patient explanations—but *she* wouldn't be the one to dress the baby; she would save the onesies for when she had her *own* child.

It was something to pass the time, was all. She shook out the dress, the beautiful dress that Kit had bought her, the dress that Kit had (Susannah held it over her front like a paper doll's pulpy frock) probably wanted Susannah to wear at the baby shower. The baby shower she'd missed, ruined. She undressed, standing now in the middle of the room, one hand pressed to the top of the television to steady herself. The dress dropped over her skin, gently clingy. She went back in front of the mirror and brushed out her hair. It had gotten longer and thicker during her pregnancy and now seemed almost inhuman, like a horse's tail, the wig of an antique doll. She wished she had some lipstick or something but settled for biting her lips into redness, pinching her cheeks.

She stood there looking at her reflection, pressing her hands against what felt to be the baby's head. Watching her body in the mirror, she felt distinctly that her own individuality was, and had been for some time, merged in a twoness: that her free will had received a mortal wound and that her mistake or misfortune might plunge innocent him into unmerited disaster or death. It seemed incredibly unjust. Here she was, a woman (she supposed, though she still felt in so many ways like a kid), solely responsible for the little creature's life—for an entire future, maybe, an entire bloodline. Maybe he would grow up to do great things, or maybe he would grow up to do nothing better than make his parents happy. And here was Susannah, with the power over his life. She was more than a living nest. She could carry with her the knowledge that she had helped to create a life, a suitcase of joy she could forever stow in her room, a unique light in the universe, and that was something. That was a starting point. That was hers.

Susannah Prue sat on the bed. Some galloping sound drummed along outside—what might have been a truck pulling a loosely lashed trailer along the uneven highway but wasn't, quite.

Horses. *Horses.*

It was difficult to remember why she had been so intent on seeing the ocean in the first place.

8

It's time for bed soon, ha. Ha. Ha. Hem. Tim guesses it's time for one half hour of music and then Dad and Mom say no more and then bedtime, that's when it's time for bed. The clock at the new motel says ten in red and that means time for bed. Susannah Prue doesn't know he guesses about time for bed but the clock says ten and that's it. He's not sure if Dad and Mom will be mad about bedtime if he is here and not at the Thunder Lodge, the place where they live; here, not at home. He stayed up late at the last place, too, last night! Ha, ha. This is okay but the curtain is too hard and so he doesn't like that. The curtain is hard, like a bad shoe, like too blackish in his eyes, too hard to move. This he doesn't like. No, he doesn't like it. He needs it to be to the side. Yes, push the curtain to the side so his eyes are open enough. He guesses she doesn't know about bedtime.

When will it be time to get more pebbles? Once he collected seventy-five in one day; his mom counted. It didn't seem like many but it turned out it was many, it was seventy-five. There were seventy-six she said but he didn't like that no so she said stop shrieking already she threw one out and said there, seventy-five, and that was nicer, much nicer, because seventy-five is nicer, smoother in your ear, like pebbles. Pebbles feel blue in your hand, feel light blue, just right.

257

Susannah Prue also feels blue, she is many. This is how you can tell if something's good because so much is not good and that never feels blue—loud noises screeching like red or laughing in yellow. Ha! The clock has a ten and an oh and a five! And he is still awake here, ha! It is okay here except the curtain is too hard, and dark. One time when he was at school all the rooms were going dark, dark with noise and it hurt, and that was when he started screeching, screeching red which only made it worse, the whole room a big pile of blood. Oh, well, ha, ha, ha, ha. Oh, well. He has six pebbles in his left pocket. But he really likes them, and what if Susannah Prue takes them away. Susannah Prue doesn't know about ten and oh and oh, and she doesn't know about blue feelings in your hand when things get noisy. In the morning he has two Pop-Tarts still soft and white because this is how they crumble in a way that's good on the teeth. It feels good on his teeth and this is what he likes. In the morning he has two Pop-Tarts and a cut-up orange. Four oranges, then. Because the orange is slick on your tongue, like saying Ha ha ha ha, slick and blue and good. But he does not like the white rind, no, he will shriek if that gets in his mouth, yes.

When Susannah Prue goes to sleep, he can go for a walk. He used to always go for a walk, but then Dad and Mom said no, said go to bed at ten like we do. Because at a walk you see nasty things. He likes to see the nasty things. He likes to walk and peep in the motel-room windows even though they say not to. When you can see the nasty things or a lady's butt it makes it bright, bright, bright in your belly, in your penis, it feels bright and wonderful. It gets tight in your pants and then you can touch it nice and gentle like petting a dog, nice and gentle. But he is not supposed to do it. It's hard sometimes not to do it when you know there are windows full of ladies' butts and everywhere other people are touching their own penises. But Dad said cut it out Dad said just cool it so he has to walk around and take six pebbles in one hand and six in the other and that's how you know you are safe. Six in one and six in the other. Or if it gets really bad and growly in your gut you can try coffee grinds but be careful you don't let them see because they don't like this either. You can put your finger in the coffee grinds all wet and pointy, put your finger in your mouth then, and it's like pebbles in your throat, and if you eat enough your head gets all buzzy and it feels really good, it feels wonderful, blue and smooth. Susannah doesn't watch hard so he can sneak lots of things, coffee grinds and sand on his tongue. This is part of what he likes so much about her.

But before bed he's supposed to have one half hour of music. Music is a CD he got them to order off the TV because there was a commercial all swirling with thumpy music and beautiful ladies shaking their butts and the whole thing was good and so he asked Mom to please please please get him that and she did. It's a mix for a party. It is volume nine and he has no other volume. Also he has never been to a party. He would like to go to party, but when he thinks about it, it sounds like thumps and is probably dark and red so actually no he wouldn't like to go, he doesn't think so, no. He likes to stand in his room and listen to the thumps, the men on the music talking even like how he wishes people would always talk, even and the words all matching, and then the ladies in the background going wooo. But Susannah Prue doesn't know about the music.

Susannah Prue is the prettiest lady and probably wants to do it. He knows just what to do, too, you put your penis in a lady and this he'd like to try. Also you touch her bosoms and her butt. This also he'd like to try. Because finally here they are. The little boy Frankie is away for once, and now they are alone. Susannah Prue is in the bathroom and has been there for a long time. She is wearing a beautiful dress and is all rosy and blue-feeling and good. When she comes out they will do it he guesses, ha, ha, ha, ha. So maybe now Susannah Prue and he will do it. He collects her pebbles and she likes them and she talks to him like she knows about pebbles, like she knows what he means, and she lets him touch her hand sometimes and so now he guesses they will do it.

But it would be good to have a half an hour of the music first. He is doing his counting exercises like how the teachers at the old school asked to please please try to remember instead of screeching. One-two-three-four-five-six-seven-eight-nine-ten, counting like that and not screeching. Sometimes it is hard to remember because everything gets so foggy and bright all at the same time and you can't stop it. But he is trying to breathe and stay calm like when Susannah Prue says there are no oranges to eat. He is supposed to have two soft Pop-Tarts and four triangles of orange. Without these things the morning gets growly and dim, and his head starts going fast, fast, like what is going to happen you don't know but red and red until you can't see. He touches the curtain but yuck, it is too hard, he'd forgotten. The screeching wants to come up from his stomach but he tells it no. Hey, no, he tells it. He sits at the edge of the bed and flicks through the stations but fuck shit shit the stations are all buzzy and making bad sounds so he twists and twists and twists.

Now Susannah Prue comes out of the bathroom. She has wet hair and the big huge wet belly and she is wearing pajamas. Where are his pajamas? The dark red fills in his stomach because he doesn't think he has his pajamas and you need to sleep in pajamas. But he solves this one, see, he can do it, he says to himself, it is all right, you just won't sleep until you get back to your pajamas. Last night this is what he did, he just lay in the bed and then walked outside and then came back in the morning because he did not have any pajamas. This works out good because then you aren't breaking any of the rules about things. Because you cannot sleep without pajamas can you. Heh, heh, heh, now the clock is ten and twenty and he is not asleep and the little boy Frankie has been gone a very long time and it is just him and Susannah Prue, and Susannah Prue is standing near the bed. She is sexy even though the belly. He'll do it with her and then they'll make a baby. He'd like that. He's never seen one real baby only pictures and they look soft and he likes that. He learned at school about touching ladies and babies and all about it. He thinks that must be why they are here. Just like the people in windows do. He is a little worried about the pebbles in his pockets and the curtains too stiff and dark and having missed music time. But Susannah Prue smiles pale blue like an egg, smooth like a pebble, and he loves Susannah Prue, he does.

Only when he starts to get ready to do it to her, pushing at her shirt and reaching for his penis, she starts shouting all mean all loud, scraping and purple and nasty. And by then he doesn't have time to stop it. He really really wanted to do it, and it takes over, even when she's pushing away, even when she's hollering, but he's stronger than her and pushes her down, red, he feels red like love welling up and he can't figure out how to stop it, and he never gets to do it to a girl and it's making him so mad. Why can't he have what it is that he wants. He has so much love for her, filling up his guts, spilling into his arms and making them do things. So he keeps pushing until she screams screams screams so loud it's cutting him, it's hurting him bad, so purple and blackish, and finally he sees in her face the what the meanness and dark feeling and so he has to jump away and what to do, rub his hands together one two three times and then out the door and maybe if he closes his eyes and just keeps running he can escape it. He will run like a horse, like a horse runs away, just running until this starts to feel better, pounding it away, away, away.

9

LOVE AND
EVERYTHING ELSE

They'd spent a long time preparing. Things had been debated: colors, scale. The smaller banquet hall—the Minnesota Room, someone's anniversary party had been there once, or else a bar mitzvah—was booked at the inn. The catering menu was selected: cucumber and cream cheese finger sandwiches on marbled bread, melon salad, cheese plate with strawberries. The Margit twins had duplicitously insisted on champagne, citing the particular pleasures of having a baby shower for a mother who could drink, who could get tipsy and say too much, who could really *enjoy* herself. At their own baby showers, they'd been too *pregnant,* they said, to really *enjoy* themselves.

Decorations had occurred. Hotel employees had strung up giant loops of powder blue crepe, placed tasteful arrangements of yellow mums on the tables, gossiped about the night managers while straightening the tablecloths. Meanwhile the friends were troubling over what to write on the cards that usually they'd scrawl with "Congrats and Good Luck!" It wasn't like Kit'd be actually *doing* anything. There was a general if unspoken sense that she'd outsourced the physical strain because she could, because she didn't want to be bothered with something as messy as childbirth, the way she sent out her laundry for others to do, or always ordered dinner in, or had someone clean her apartment. Kit dirty herself, stress her pretty body? Of course none of this was said—of course they loved their friend or tried to, even though she had the kind of life that made everyone a little jealous, a little touchy—her perfect job, her perfect body, her perfect husband and their enviable relationship. To the naked eye, her friends were all cooing and excitement. Presents were sought out, selected, ordered, or repurposed—stacks of onesies and booties and little blue hats, a car seat and a baby swing and a mobile for the crib. Old friends reminded the new friends of how long the old friends had been friends with the glowing mother-to-be. But for the most part, they were ready, all at home picking outfits, the shower churning dimly in their minds (what was *called* for in such a situation? would the surrogate be there? did they give anything to *her*?), when the manager of the project, one of the oldest of the old friends, a banker named Marjorie, received a telephone call from Kit. Marjorie had Kit's other very oldest friend, Carole, over, and Carole sat there bemused, tangled in the bedsheets, watching Marjorie answer the phone. There had been that shock when the phone rang. Marjorie checked the caller ID—it wasn't her husband, okay—and answered, and there was Kit, tiny on the other end, as if speaking from the bottom of a deep well.

"You're *where*?"

Kit had hoped to get through the call without having to fully explain things. She squinted into the chalky dust, where a scorpion stood delicately waving its paws at her. There was something humiliating in what had happened—a terrific and irrevocable failure, a sad attempt at adulthood squelched first by her own body's machinery and then by the poorly chosen surrogate—and part of her didn't want to admit to what had happened. They'd been made fools of; they'd been taken for a ride. She suddenly understood (there, on the pay phone at a highway road stop, watching Julian as he cleaned the car's windshield) why battered women didn't want to tell anyone they'd been beaten. One wanted to deflect the pity. She sighed and told Marjorie, "New Mexico, somewhere. Or maybe Arizona. I'm not exactly sure. No, no—*New* Mexico. Right."

She held the phone away from her ear a little.

"Yes, Marj, I know. That's why I'm calling. I guess we have to cancel the shower. Unless you want to have it without me. Ha, ha."

Marjorie almost really considered this. It was too late to get the deposit back on the room.

"It's complicated. Julian and I are here. Ah, our surrogate. Is here. I can't really explain it right now. What? Yes, of course we're still going to have the baby. We should be back in town by next week, and I'll call you then, okay, darling? Tell everyone I'm terribly sorry."

Marjorie held up the phone for Carole to see. "She hung up!" Then snuggled back into bed. "Their surrogate's run off. I knew she seemed too young. Didn't I say that?"

Carole kissed her shoulder, sleepily. "You can't trust anyone." Then, "Does this mean I can return the baby swing, d'you think?"

KIT LEANED AGAINST the pay phone for a few minutes. The closer they got to Susannah, to the baby, the farther away she felt. She didn't feel at all like she was about to become a mother, and maybe she wasn't. Maybe that's how they should start to think of things.

The show had to go on, anyway, somehow, the way things always do, even when one feels as abused by the world as Kit was allowing herself to feel—all the while chiding herself for feeling so very sorry for herself. One's husband had to look over quizzically and lasso one back into acting sane. "Kitty, you ready?" Julian was half in the car and half out, cagily leaning toward her. Dicey sat in the backseat throughout it all, still strapped in, snug in the space they'd carved out of the rock face of luggage. This—Dicey's quiet patience, her benevolent stillness—made Kit dislike her a little more in that moment. She sat back down and buckled in, and off they sailed.

"Well, I canceled the baby shower. It was supposed to be tomorrow," she said after a while. Julian shot her a worried look. Dicey uttered a mew of sympathy. The sympathy only irked Kit more. She turned around to face Dicey. "Did she ever say anything to you? I mean, I'm just trying to put it together. Was this her plan all along? To take the baby and run?"

Dicey's face froze in an unreadable expression. "What?"

"I'm just wondering if Susannah didn't have this in mind the whole time. If she wanted a baby and needed the cash and, you know . . . planned the great baby heist."

Julian gripped the steering wheel. "Don't be so dramatic," he said. "Please."

"I'm not being dramatic."

"Just, please."

"Oh, you just please."

Their nattering, as ordinary a part of the day as anything, was transmuted by the smallness of the space in the car and by Dicey's presence: Kit became disproportionately offended; Julian was snappier than usual. What usually sounded to them like teasing or nerves or exhaustion, they now heard alchemized through the ears of a stranger into unnecessarily pointed barbs, and though Dicey hadn't said a word, Kit felt her pity boring into the back of her head. Unmarried people didn't understand, she wanted to tell Dicey. You don't get what we mean, how these words are powered by an engine of love and everything else, even though what we say sounds dismissive and rude. She might have said to Julian, "Shut up already," but what she meant was, *I will never be able to express exactly how I feel about you.*

Julian sighed.

Here was the landscape—barren as a stone. In the distances were mountains, jungle gyms of buttes and crests. Kit kept identifying bits of dead things out the window, gnarled carcasses that turned out to only be brambles. Light spread across the reddish earth in great buttery slabs. The clouds roared into color. A tinkling song faded up from the silence and invaded the car—the calliope-tinged sound track of a two-bit circus, a rubbery idea of happiness—as an ice cream truck sped up behind them, swerving into the oncoming lane and passing their car. A cartoon pair of children on the back of the truck, noses infested with freckles, grinned and brandished their eternal ice cream cones for a few miles before shrinking into incoherence. There were no other cars on the road. Julian squinted into the sun, which rested as squarely in his view as a target, too large and red and quivering.

The whole ride, Dicey had been aware of being not entirely welcome. This probably should have made her angrier than it did, but a kind of exhaustion had set in, and as she leaned against the pillow (it smelled of soap and candle wax, distinctly of someone else's house) and a tower of matched luggage, propping her feet on the sleeping bag crammed under the seat, she gave in to it—too tired to think, too tired to worry. For the first time in days, in weeks, she let herself stop thinking about Frankie. She released into it like easing into a too-cold pool—in an instant the water warms, welcomes your body. She was nothing. She was a child in the back of the car, lazily observing a family vacation, letting the adults bicker and navigate and be in control. On the other side of the backseat was Jean, kicking at the driver's seat. She let her head grow heavy on the pillow, felt her eyelids flutter shut. She may have slept for a hazy moment or two.

"Why do they call it having a baby?" said Kit suddenly, "when it's really having a whole person? Having a human. The thing is, it's going to be an adult much longer than it's going to be a baby. I mean, the commitment you're making is actually to an awkward, pimply teenager—it's going to be a teenager even longer than it's going to be a baby, you know what I mean?—or to some strange adult. Some humorless man in Accounting who clears his throat too much and raises his hand in meetings, you know, who smells musty, someone with a flaking scalp and a comb-over. Or some woman who's thirty pounds overweight and collects angel figurines. They were all babies at some point, and their parents must have thought, 'We are expecting a baby.' Not, 'We are expecting Barry Krebs, the man with a lazy eye who creeps everyone out.'"

Julian sighed, too used to this kind of thing from her, but Dicey laughed, leaning forward between the seats, returning to life, rehydrating, reinflating, because Kit had summoned her to do so. "Because that sounds awful. Doesn't it? It sounds impossible. No one would ever do it then."

Kit laughed, too. She lifted her hair from the back of her neck, and there it was, Julian saw, that something in her that was so easy, so effortlessly feminine, so real, so Kit, and with that smile they were in cahoots all of a sudden, Kit and Dicey. Kit had pulled it together, had decided to gather Dicey from her backseat solitude, draw her close. Dicey laughed, and Kit laughed, and the whole car seemed lighter, quicker. They skimmed along the surface of the darkening highway. The women started laughing about something else—those babies who were born as wrinkled and disgruntled as old men, like tiny presidents—and Julian detached from them, floated away, his mind mumbling. When they finally got home (it felt like they'd been gone for so long that nothing would be the same when they finally returned, as if the climate would have shifted into apocalyptic heat, the lake evaporated, their building crumbled), if they did ever get home and regain their normal lives, Julian wanted to sleep for seventy-two hours, wake up and make love to his wife, and then he wanted to go fishing. He wanted to learn how to fish. Something manly and simple, something one did with one's hands. Yes, fishing! Something one could teach to one's son. He'd lived entirely too much in offices and cyberspace—his hands were too soft, he could see that now—and he would change this when they got home. He had been inappropriate with Susannah, he had been outstandingly wrong, and thank God nothing more had happened, nothing he really had to be ashamed of—thank God he'd never actually betrayed Kit. He wanted to be unimpeachable. He wanted to be a good husband, a good father, as good as he could be; he wanted to make things better for people in the smallest of ways, the way Kit had made things better for Dicey just by drawing her in. Somehow he had to tell Kit how much he admired her, how good she was at being Kit, how he could never think of living without her. Everything would change when they got home. They would be stronger and better; they would take more vitamins; they would call their mothers. He would call Kit's mother, out of the blue, just to talk. Yes! Things were going to change!

Julian flicked on his headlights, illuminating the small world darkening ahead of them.

They would testify later that it was dark, the moon a useless sliver, that Julian was tired from driving all day, that they had been turbined by frustration; and though all of these things were true, it was also true that they would say to each other again and again that they ought to have been more careful, that maybe there was something they could have done—perhaps some magical combination of events that could have occurred: If only Julian had lingered talking to the Garlands at the lodge, if only Kit had stayed longer in the gas station's bathroom to soap up her hands, if only Dicey had taken the time to hunt around for the bathing suit that instead she'd abandoned, if only Julian had driven faster or slower, if only they had gotten there a few seconds later, a few seconds earlier—because there was no such thing as fate, was there, just people bouncing off each other like particles in atoms, like buoys in a lake—perhaps it could have been prevented.

When it couldn't. It wasn't. At around ten they spotted the sign for the Aqua City Motel, a bluish gleam Julian took for a star, then, as they neared, a smear of gold as bright as a lighthouse after a long voyage at sea. Kit was the one who identified it, smacked Julian's arm. "There!" she cried, as if she'd discovered a constellation, and she looked back to Dicey and said, "That's it! We're here!" Dicey smiled weakly—she half suspected that the crew would be long gone but kept this thought to herself. Julian swerved into the right lane without looking, the car swimming too fast toward the turnoff. A quick glance told them the Aqua City Motel was the Thunder Lodge in reverse—everything laid out the same, if dimmer (half the sign's neon burned to blackness)—and they drove toward this mirror world holding their breath, not speaking. The sky had gone black. Kit was twisting in her seat—"Is that your car, Dicey, parked right there? Oh, they're here, Julie, look, that's her car!"—and Dicey had started talking, too, trying to calm Kit, trying to explain, "Now, we have to be careful, we don't want this to become a big scene"—and Julian, exhausted from the driving and the everything, the all of it, was looking up, noting the haze of spirits, or no, moths partially obscuring the motel's sign and therefore wasn't watching the road when something—someone—darted out in front of the car, materializing from nowhere. It would occur to them later, when they sorted out the story, trying to fit the pieces together, that he'd come from the vast unlighted spaces out in back of the motel at the same time as they were pulling off from the highway into the gravel turnoff too quickly, it being difficult after all to go from eighty to ten in a few seconds, with Julian's reflexes rusty from exhaustion and the anticipation and the adrenaline—and something, a deer he (being a Midwesterner) thought at first, ran out in front of the car. The contact made a sickening thud.

"Oh," said Julian. "Oh, God."

Because everything had stopped, gone silent, gone dead. The moths went still near the sign.

Nothing was real for few crystalline seconds, the three of them frozen in the car, willing themselves backward into the moment before the thing had occurred. Because only an instant before, everything had been okay, and they were still close enough to that instant to feel its warmth like a body beside them in bed, to believe that they could reach out and grasp hold of it, reclaim it, like the bed when the body has just left. Nothing was irreversible—how could it be? Maybe they could still undo this.

But something was loud about it. Oh—it was Kit, screaming. A hypotenuse of blood, she pointed out, on the windshield. Then things lurched back into play, herky-jerky as a silent film. Julian still gripped the steering wheel— "What do I . . . ?" The car listed up, slightly, on his side. They were on top of it. Should he reverse? His mind stopped, left him alone in the mess of it. Life had gotten, without warning, gruesome.

"That was a person," Dicey was saying. She said it matter-of-factly. "Uh, that's a person. He . . ." And she got out of the car. For a long time afterward, Julian would wish he hadn't seen the look on her face. Dicey didn't scream, but she closed her eyes and her hand went to her mouth. "Back up," Julian heard her say. "Back up, as gently as you can." He sat in the driver's seat, heat pooling in his face. "Julian! Back up!" said Dicey again, sharply. His hands trembled. It took him a few seconds to guide one of them to the gearshift, one to the steering wheel, to plant his shaking leg onto the gas. Kit sat beside him, chanting, "Ohmygod ohmygod ohmygod." The car descended the too-soft lump with a crunching sound—the collapse of bone—and settled again on the pavement. The fucking car! Julian thought dimly. How could it behave as if nothing had happened?

Dicey disappeared, and when Julian and Kit got out of the car, propelling themselves outward as if escaping a cell, they saw that she had knelt beside the bloody mess. "Call an ambulance," she said, so softly at first that it seemed she was talking to the man, whispering him a final admonishment. "Call an ambulance, go!"

A guttural cry rose from the motel, from someone in a doorway that had been swung open, releasing a long corridor of light onto the gravel drive and settling on Dicey's parked car, vaudevillian as a spotlight. "Tim!" cried Susannah Prue from the doorway. "TIM"—it came shrieking and tearing at them, batted to and fro like a released

kite and finally dissolving in the tackless air. Kit had run to the office
and pounded on the door, her hair lit by the blinking red Vacancy sign
above. Dicey looked up at Susannah, and Susannah looked at Julian
and then slumped against the doorframe in a drunken squat. Dicey
looked from Tim to Susannah to Tim again, before running across the
gravel to grip Susannah's elbow, to pull her up and lead her inside to
the bed.

Meanwhile Tim lay on the pavement. His arms had been pinned
beneath him, his face smashed against the glistening ground. Julian
crouched in low, whispered, "Kid? Kid, are you alive? Please be alive,"
hoping against all hope, though the head looked oblong, and broken,
didn't look exactly headlike anymore, that the kid would be okay as a
personal favor to Julian. He stood up again, because . . . Jesus, but
he'd never seen so much blood, and the body wasn't moving, wasn't
rising in breath, the lungs collapsed inward like rotted fruit.

Then Kit came from the office with a man, while another car
drove up and pulled in behind theirs. Julian looked mournfully into
the car's high beams. The car's back end was perilously close to the
highway, but Julian could not fathom how he would move his car or
where, even when a woman emerged from the driver's side, her face
washed out by the headlights, bleating words at him. A child popped
out of the passenger side. Julian stared at him wonderingly—a familiar silhouette in the stillness, a tiny, elfin boy of perhaps seven or eight
with a mussed head of hair and rumpled swim trunks, brandishing the
remains of an ice cream cone that dripped down his arm. (But how,
Julian found himself thinking, had they gotten that ice cream truck to
stop?) The man from the motel was the one with his wits about him
enough to rush over to the little kid, stand between him and the carnage he hadn't yet seen, walk him quickly toward the office.

"My God," said Letty. "What have you done?"

It's at moments like these that a person most feels at one with the
others around him, most a part of that massive human organism, a

clueless breathing beast clawing its way through the world, vulnerable
and prone to grave errors. Moments of beauty or joy stay deliciously
private, but fear, horror, shock, revulsion—these batten down the defenses, they break through a person's public membrane and seethe
through the air. Together we beat back the void, thought Julian. There
they were, stranded together on this desert island, an ocean of sand
separating them from hospitals, from towns and barrooms and playgrounds and diners, from semblances of life, from people who could
help. No, they stood unprotected on the skin of the earth, the eerie expanse of quiet, the uninvolved glow of stars and, from somewhere, the
keen of a coyote. Julian saw his wife come toward him, watching her
as if from a great distance, understanding but not fully feeling the
weight of her body pressing against his. No one was crying; no one
was speaking. They stood there like lovers at a sunset, watching the
blood leech from Tim's head.

"Shouldn't we . . . ?" Letty started. She leaned in, then stepped
back again. "Try to make him comfortable?"

"I don't think you're supposed to move them." Kit's voice
sounded surprisingly steady, surprisingly calm. Julian looked at her—
how did she know these things? It was like learning that she'd once
been an expert in the ways of the Maori or the Zulu and had never
told Julian of their unusual customs until now. "Anyway, I don't . . . I
don't think he feels anything."

Julian stepped away, pulling back from Kit, running his hands
through his hair. The moths, he noticed, had resumed. They crowded
around the sign, beating their paper wings, willing themselves toward
the light.

THOUGH THIS PARTICULAR part of the country
has a way of seeming deserted to a stranger passing through, really it's
teeming with legions of natives tucked away in tiny towns shrugged

between wide-shouldered mountains, nuclear physicists and half Indians and ex-cons and part-time shamans dwelling peacefully in planned communities off the highway's tributaries, along with tepid expats from the Midwest renting pied-à-terres in the almost-cities of the up-north—Taos, Santa Fe. Susannah wasn't the only one who'd thought a foreign landscape might clear the head, might make it easier to become a better version of herself, a her with a finer, cleaner mind. The land was peppered with such pilgrims, most of whom fancied themselves artists, artisans, or, even worse, connoisseurs, and therefore the annual crafts fair held at the Indian reservation (due northwest from the Thunder Lodge) tended to gather a crowd. It was quite a *happening*— the only see-and-be-seen of the region. The craftspeople prided themselves on attracting not tourists but *travelers,* real *artistes.* And since there weren't many options for lodging nearby, it was the Thunder Lodge's bread and butter, the Christmas in June, the booked-solid-for-a-week of a place that tended to be uninhabited as a nun's womb.

The Garlands were in the habit of avoiding the thing itself—a dusty tableau of tents, a few hundred tables displaying pottery and silver jewelry and hand-beaten light-switch covers in the shape of Kokopelli; a few leathery refugees from the sixties playing acoustic guitar somewhere; wind chimes and whatnot; the smells of the reservation women pushing their roasted chilies and lard-soaked fry bread. The reservation was somewhat depressing when one made the mistake of picturing life there: a bleak little village of decaying adobe homes, sagging beneath matrices of television antennae and satellite dishes; a historic mud chapel dreamed up by a particularly enthusiastic round of Jesuit missionaries, and in the churchyard the sheltered pit, the kiva, where the religious ceremonies actually took place; and off behind the houses, across the dead channel of the river, was a brackish pond believed to be where ancestors lived or some such. Char had taken Tim there every year when he was younger—it was the only time of the year the tribe allowed visitors to the sacred spot, and this was only a grudging concession to the spiritual-minded artists who really would have found a way to it no matter what—because how Tim loved water! How he loved to tiptoe up close and covertly dip a hand in (sunburned by disapproving glares; Char knew that touching wasn't allowed, but she had to pick her battles)—and he always cocked his head and squinted at the clouds reflecting on the diorama-smooth surface while Char told him the story, every year: how the people believed the pond was full of ghosts, swimming with souls. It always made him laugh, the way she described it: transparent old folks splashing around, their arms sleeved in flotation doughnuts, doing the backstroke as the water poured through them, tossing a ghost volleyball back and forth, trying to impress each other with underwater handstands. And according to the story, there was a pond of the exact same dimensions on the other side of the world—a line could've connected them, cutting straight through the core of the earth and out the other end, in the mountains of Tibet or someplace, and they believed that the souls were able to leak from one enchanted pond to the other. Char of course couldn't believe any of this but liked it as a story for Tim, liked the reticulate world in which such things might exist.

This year she wouldn't go. This year she and Marlon sat crunched on their stools, curling over the counter like unwatered plants. The phone seemed to ring constantly. A few nights before it began—before the opening ceremonies with all their boozy good cheer and attempts at grandeur, the traditional spirit singers and the drum circle and the overweight holy men emerging from the kiva in a fanfare of steam, the performance artists rattling out poems rhythmic as idling car engines, the luminarias winking along walkways—this was when people started calling, started checking on their reservations or announcing late arrivals or asking in that familiar breathy rasp was there a room available, by any chance was there one? Each time the phone rang, they'd jump, exchange a look, clutch the receiver for news of Susannah, news of Tim. Marlon touched her arm around 10:00 P.M., spit his teeth into the cup. "I guess I'll go make sure the rooms are all clean," he mumbled. Char nodded, not looking up from the televisions tuned to contrasting news reports.

A pair of artists arrived around midnight, just as the Garlands were prepared to shut off the light and settle into bed—two elaborately dreadlocked students from Colorado who wanted a room with two beds. Char sighed as she handed them the guest register, selected the keys. St. Bernard. "And out back is the Grotto," she said dully, pushing her braid off her shoulder. "Cool! Where's Hugh Hefner?" snorted one of the students.

"It's just a pool." Char glared them out of the office.

In the morning there were a few more. Marlon checked them in after a sleepless night—an experimental flautist toting a case birdlike with feathers, and the wolfish storyteller she'd hitched a ride with all the way from Ontario, who would need separate rooms. Marlon watched through the window as the storyteller lugged a small colony of marionettes from his VW to the room—two handfuls of dangling, lifeless children. Char was talking to him about Dicey's room. Should they clean it? Should they hurl her bathing suit (its pilled bottom thin as new skin growing over a wound) into the lost-and-found box? Would they ever see her again, or Frankie, or Susannah? And then what if they all returned and suddenly had no place to stay because all the rooms were rented? It was difficult to imagine the place now without Susannah. As much as Marlon had thought he was tired of her, she'd become such a part of things that now he (not that he wasn't angry with her for taking off, but she must have had her reasons, the poor kid) kind of missed having her around. But the room, they had to do something about the room. Char was sniping about it; she'd been cranky since the convoy left, understandably so, and Marlon guessed he knew her well enough by now to know that she would blame him until things got better. Oh, she might not mean to, and it might not make any particular sort of sense, but everything Marlon said or did would be wrong until they heard from the Forsythes, until they had their boy back, until everything had gotten back to normal. Char cleared her throat as if about to say something when another van lurched into the driveway. For the first time in twenty years, she looked displeased to be getting the crafts-fair traffic, her dread palpable as a damp washcloth. Marlon peered at her sidelong, popped his teeth into his mouth.

SOMEONE IN ST. CHRISTOPHER needed extra towels, and so while Marlon was checking in the new arrivals (a potter from Rio Rancho and a shaman–slash–creator of premium yoga), he watched out the window as Char made her way down the gravel drive. Nothing had changed in thirty years. Their first night at the Thunder Lodge, Marlon had stood exactly where he stood now, arranging things at the front desk, and had looked out the window to see his wife moving along the gravel, tracing the sidewalk that lipped out from the row of rooms, *their* rooms now—and the sight of the lone woman, braid whipping behind her in the abrasive wind, had caused a longing to well up in the back of his jaw, bittersweet and unnamable. Though he had known it was only Char, looking ghostly and mournful because of the neon light in the woolen darkness, he couldn't shake the feeling that he'd seen a premonition, that he'd seen this all before. That whole first night, he'd had the queasy sense that this place was possessed by something, that they would never leave it, or that someday it would be their downfall. But what good was a feeling like this, when the paperwork had gone through, the down payment made, their new lives plotted? "I just want to be alone with you," Char had told him, "alone in the desert, where we can get some peace." She never said things like that. So they'd left their jobs in Las Cruces—he'd worked the desk at a soulless Comfort Inn in an industrial park, and she'd been doing odd jobs here and there—taken out the biggest loan the bank would let them have, and plunked their lives down into a decrepit roadside motor lodge (Char had liked the hyperbolic, retro sign, and so they'd taken that sign as a sign), and there they were, a happy little family.

Now something made Marlon want to call out to Char, make her turn around and come back to her stack of towels. Watching her walk, he had the terrible feeling that if she passed by St. Anne (the room in the middle), it would be too late, and he wanted to stop her, to bellow into the distance—but the guests in front of him blinked expectantly, and one of them said, "Sorry, how much is the room?" snapping Marlon's attention back, destroying his chances of saving his wife, and he cleared his throat regretfully. When he looked up again, she was gone.

"How much you got?" he joked mechanically. The artists' smiles were like hints. The man paid with his credit card.

In another moment the phone was ringing.

The new guests shuffled their way to their room. Char appeared behind Marlon. His head pounded.

"What?" he said into the phone. "What?" It was too hot in the office, or too cold, or something. Marlon felt that he couldn't hear, even when he pressed his ear against the phone until it suctioned shut. "What? Sweetheart, you'll have to speak up. I really don't think I can hear you." She said it again, and he did hear her, just like he'd heard her the first time, but still nothing fit together exactly right. The words floated alongside each other, separate as chunks of driftwood from various shipwrecks, bobbing saltily in the tide. "A Char accident?" Marlon could not seem to puzzle the words together, to muscle his way through the onslaught of sounds. He shook his head. Char was fine! "Sorry," he said. "I think you're mistaken."

Dicey meanwhile was squeezing her eyes shut, shut, shutter, gripping the phone cord in the office of the Aqua City Motel. The neon tidal wave crackled against her face, weakened by the daylight. It was bad enough that they'd waited this long to call the Garlands, but it had been such a strange night, everyone finding reasons they couldn't. "Marlon. I'm so sorry. I can't tell you how sorry. This is so hard to say."

"Artist's day? Oh, a room for the crafts fair?"

"You have to listen to me, Marlon. I know you don't want to hear this."

Char stepped toward Marlon. His back was quivering. She reached her good hand toward him—she wanted to touch his faded flannel shirt, rub along his spine—but froze a few inches off and returned her hand to her dress pocket instead. He pulled the phone away from his face, looked at it cartoonishly, drew it back, saying, "Jim Isbed? No, no, wrong number, wrong number." He slammed the phone into the receiver. "Wrong number."

DICEY CALLED BACK and spoke with Char, who answered her in modulated tones, jaw set, trying to agree on a plan as if they were coordinating a car pool. Char wrapped her steely braid around her fist like a boxer winding his knuckles with cloth. When the accordion maker arrived (he came every year and prided himself on befriending the locals), Marlon chatted him up with terrifying brightness. "Fine, fine day!" Marlon bellowed. "Couldn't be finer! Two nights? Three? Staying the whole week! Think it'll be a good fair this year? Accordion to you? Ha, ha." Char lowered her brow, pulled the phone with her into the living room, shut the door.

Outside by the Grotto, the new guests were dangling their limbs in the water. The experimental flautist pranced around in bare feet, her flute emitting tuneless gasps. The puppeteer stood in front of the Virgin Mary figurine, cocking his head like a dog on the other side of the door from a party. Char leaned toward the window above the couch, the phone cord straining now as far as it would go, and pulled the pane shut. The laughter and splashing hushed. It was obscene that it should be so sunny, that people should be so happy and carefree; it was disgusting.

The living room was blue, dim. Tim's eroded tennis shoes peeked out from under the couch.

"Bring him back here, I guess," Char croaked. "Bring him home."

There was a long silence. Dicey cleared her throat. "Ah, see. I don't know . . . I'm not sure that's a good idea."

His sweatshirt was crumpled in the armchair, a discarded exoskeleton. A pile of his pebbles mountained on the range of the coffee table. A plastic horse bucked its invisible rider on the shelf.

"Well, I guess we've got to bury him somewhere." That didn't seem real, either. There must have been some mistake. They'd just seen him a few days ago. How could he already be dead enough to be buried? Surely it was all a misunderstanding, and so Char tried to be patient with Dicey until they could figure it out.

"Yes," said Dicey. "But I mean . . . we'd better get a coffin here. Or . . . I mean, I don't think you want to see him like this." She cleared her throat again. "I mean, however you want it. Here, at the hospital, they're suggesting cremation. They could do it here. And we could bring, ah, it back to you. The cremains. I mean, that's what they call it. Char, I'm so sorry. You really . . . you don't want to see him, not like this."

Dicey now understood why people spoke in clichés at times like these. She found it excruciating to think of a way to say these things to the dead boy's mother, and so she borrowed from Lifetime movies, from airport paperbacks. *It's better this way.* (A lie.) *He was killed instantly; he didn't feel any pain.* (Another lie, probably.) *You don't want to see him, not like this.* (Finally, a lie with some truth to it.)

"You people. You people."

"Pardon?"

"You people. You came and caused trouble from the start, and now look, just look, just look." Char's throat filled up with something cementish, and her mouth fastened shut. ("Please, Char," Dicey was saying. "We're so very sorry.") A soaked Nerf ball landed against the window with a *splat,* followed by cascades of giddy laughter. They would be there all day, laughing and drinking and splashing idiotically. Char wanted to blame that, too, on Susannah—that oafish monster of fertility who'd come and hypnotized Tim. Of course he'd been walking around in even more of a daze than usual; he was away from home and probably disoriented and a little scared, because he knew better, he knew *better* than to be running around in the dark, running in front of traffic, because he wasn't that way before Susannah Prue had come and made him act crazy. Because Tim knew better. Tim knew better than to be running around at night, near traffic! It couldn't be true. These fools, they must have gotten something wrong—it was someone else, probably. Or he was sick, he'd been hurt badly, but he was still alive. He had to be still alive. He knew better than to be running around at night.

THAT morning had dawned fair and fresh; the night nurse was relieved, the doctors changed shifts, the lights in the room were turned off as daylight swelled in the windows. "Do you see him?" Julian cried, but Kit just waved him back out into the hallway; though Susannah had gone into labor the night before, the baby's head had not yet crested. Julian haunted the dingy waiting room—blank, scuffed walls hanging emptily around a handful of plastic chairs, stacks of fishing magazines. Fucking fishing magazines! In the middle of the desert! In a shabby county clinic miles from anywhere, a trek even from a parched vein of the Rio Grande. He dug through his pockets, fingered through his wallet. He wanted to go buy a soda, or maybe a paper cup of muddy vending-machine coffee, but of course he didn't have any change, just a single dollar bill so crumpled and torn it looked like a victim. He didn't think he could take the vending machine spitting out that dollar bill at him again and again, so he didn't even try. He slumped in his chair, engaged in a standoff with the fanned-out assortment of magazines.

The police would be in soon to question him. Then Julian would look longingly at the magazines, as if all he wanted in the world were a moment alone with them. Tim had been taken to the hospital in the same ambulance as Susannah, the ambulance wailing down the empty highway. An EMT who had not yet grown his first beard—he looked to Julian to be about twelve years old—had ridden crouched over Susannah, squashed up against the walls of the vehicle, watching through the long ride as Tim—Tim's body—inched toward Susannah with each bump in the road. They didn't know what else to do. They'd waited twenty or thirty minutes for the ambulance. A lifetime. Tim was dead. They had no illusions about that. Julian clung to his wife's hand, bewildered and dumb.

And now, at the hospital, he sat staring at the window. The darkness clung to skin like a layer of mud. Other than a coyote that bayed in the distance, echolocating the universe back to Julian, the world was empty.

In the room Susannah lay miserably on her side, beached on the shore of the bed, Kit's cool hand on her forehead. Now and then a bored nurse stuck her head in the doorway, chomped on a cartilaginous wad of gum, and disappeared again. A shower curtain subdivided the room. Before and after. On the other side of the curtain, an empty bed.

"I'm sorry," was the only thing Susannah could say when she squeezed her eyes shut and whispered. "I'm sorry I'm sorry."

Kit heard herself say, "Hey." But she couldn't figure out how to proceed—because it wasn't true that she forgave Susannah, nor that she wanted her to think everything was okay. Neither of those was really the case. An anger, a pointy indignance, still jabbed around in her chest, in so deep that pulling it out would just expose the wound to infection. So much, so very much, was Susannah's fault. All she wanted was to acknowledge that Susannah had spoken, and so she said, "Hey. Hey there."

The contractions seized Susannah as if the fist of the world had gripped her and given her a good shake. She hadn't expected it to feel like this. She would suffer, and then it would be over. Things were never quite how you thought they would be, now, were they? And oh, aha, only now did she remember it, did the whole thing resurface (as these things tended to, at the oddest of moments)—the summer at the beach with her aunt and her cousins, the sheepy dog galumphing around in the house's yard, pulling its chain out of the ground. Susannah had been the only one to see him escape. She had been so fascinated by his woolly, liquidy movements, by the ripples of his fur in the wind as he galloped down to the sand—he looked like a man in a dog suit!—that she hadn't thought to try to stop him. She'd stood there watching him run, thinking it was glorious to see him running down the boardwalk, feeling so happy for him, so happy to see a dog hurl himself into a pile of dead fish and roll around, so happy to see him snuffle along the shore and bite at the water. Go, Cooper, go, she'd thought, standing there watching. She'd tried to call her mother that morning, and her mother hadn't picked up. She hadn't talked to her mother all summer, for months and months, and she started to wonder whether she would ever go back home, whether her mother even missed her at all. But if Cooper made it down the beach, then maybe her mother would call back. She struck that deal with herself, standing in the foggy morning, sucking on a pink-flavored jelly bean and watching the dog. If Cooper made it down the beach, her mother would call back, her mother loved her, and Susannah would eventually get to go live at home again. Then Becky had run from the house, shouting. Had Susannah seen the dog get away? She'd shaken her head no, studying the remaining jelly beans in her palm. Yellow and blue and black. Which should she eat next? Becky shrieked down the lawn, toward the boardwalk and the shore, and soon Scott and her aunt and uncle all tumbled out of the house (Susannah popped the black jelly bean into her mouth and watched Cooper disappear on the horizon—the moment tasted of licorice, burning in her nose—and an instant later she spit the candy out into the grass), and they spent the whole day walking up and down the beaches, shouting, "*Cooper! Coooooperrrrr!*" Later that night her aunt sat her down and asked was she sure she hadn't been in the yard when the dog ran away, was she sure she hadn't accidentally let him free, and Susannah had said no, no, no, while Becky and Scott cried and made missing-dog posters in the living room—but it all worked out in the end, because soon Susannah was home again. Her mother was as distant as ever, closed up in her blue room most of the time, but at least Susannah was home. And now she thought, What kind of kid was I to do that, to not even care that they'd lost their dog or tell them which way he'd run, to forget entirely that I'd ever seen it happen?

"Push," said the nurse. "Wait, not now. Okay, now." It wasn't pain so much as it was red. It was purple—the varicosed, blackish purple of the last thirty seconds before sunrise. It was the dark bite of licorice; it was the dog disappearing on the horizon. The heat of it enveloped her. So this was what it was to be swallowed by something bigger than oneself. So this was what it was to go sucking into a whirlpool, to be tugged by the forces of nature, unable to protest. Every now and then, she'd remember Tim—she'd remember what had happened to Tim—but it seemed unrealistic, as strange and private and out of whack as a half-recalled dream, and so she shoved it from her mind for later. Because that couldn't be real. Because if it was real, it was another thing that was her fault, another pain she had unleashed. Her mother's closed door, the dog disappearing on the horizon. Oh, people would try to comfort her. *She* hadn't been driving the car. But she'd been the one who had plucked Tim from the safety of his natural habitat, who had secreted him across borders like a nineteenth-century explorer with a kidnapped Pygmy, who had dragged him through truck stops and motels while he clenched his fists a little tighter each time, who had convinced herself that he was an ordinary man trapped in an inadequate brain, a flawless jewel lodged in an inexpert setting, and that she could fix him, she could make it better. She was the one who had flirted with him, let him kiss her hand, changed clothes in front of him, and then, when he tried, when he wanted, when he came toward her with unzipped pants and a gleam in his eye, she was the one who had screamed, who had pushed him away, who had said horrible things, who had let him run from the room, who had not followed him out. And that was why the Garlands no longer had a son, why Julian felt like a murderer. Tim! His boy-pungent smell, outdoorsy and musky and a little bit sour, like unclean hair! He'd already started to seem like the kind of boy who had been doomed—the kind of boy everyone knew would die young and horribly. Up came the pavement.

She would have the baby and release him out into the world, like a greasy pigeon she'd rescued and nursed back to health. Maybe she had always known it. Because she was glad that the Forsythes had finally caught up with her. Because relief now blossomed deep inside, a keyhole of light. Too much had already been lost because of her, and she needed now to redeem herself in whatever small way she could. She wanted to be done with all this. She wanted to get this baby out of her and go home. She wanted to be able to worry about things like bills and shelf space and invoices and trading work shifts and watching television.

Kit offered her sips of water, stroking her forehead without looking into her eyes. Finally she rang the nurse. "I think it's time!" Kit was shouting into the intercom, the timbre of panic reverberating down the hall, and the nurse's hollered response, like a mutated echo: "Okay, dear, we'll be right there." (After all, she was playing a round of solitaire on the computer that she wanted to finish.) Kit poked her head into the hallway, smoothed down her hair, forced a deep, exaggeratedly calm breath. She looked one way—toward the nurses' station—then the other—toward the waiting room where Julian might already be talking to the police, over there in the other part of their life.

Well! Things certainly weren't going as planned, were they? And for Kit things tended to go according to plan. She hated when her assistant scheduled her for a last-minute meeting—one needed time to *prepare* oneself—or when a friend called with jarring news—a divorce, an affair, a spur-of-the-moment dinner party. Kit liked a plan, she liked things to then hew to that plan, she liked (though she knew it seemed simple-minded) that she had gone to college, lived abroad and had adventures for exactly one year, gotten the internship, gotten the assistant position, moved her way up, dated men, found Julian, married him in a wedding she'd sticky-noted and paper-clipped in bridal magazines before they'd ever met, looking toned and fresh and flawless in a confection of a satin dress. She did not like that they hadn't been able to conceive. She did not like that. It lodged in her chest like a lozenge of cancer, bubbling away there, because this, none of this, had been in the plan, and it wrenched her perfect life—not that it had been free, in any sense, or easy; she had always worked so hard for everything!—irrevocably out of whack. And now her husband was down the hall, being questioned by the police. She felt an anxious flutter in her chest, a roar of heat in her gut. Because not only had they had to get this fucking surrogate, not only did her husband seem to be what? In love with Susannah? Kit knew it wasn't quite that but acknowledged that there was something the two of them shared that did not include her, and that was bad enough, honestly—but they had possibly, sort of, no, they *had*—she could try not to think about it for the moment, but there it was, as it would be for the rest of their lives—they had run over a boy in their car. It was a thing that happened to people, she knew this. Just not to *her.* Meanwhile Susannah wailed. Kit understood that it probably wasn't pleasant, but did the girl have to be so dramatic about everything? She knew that she would have been able to do this better. She would have been pregnant better, had the baby better, driven the car better; she would have been better at all of this.

The hospital was unsettlingly empty, as if everyone had been killed off by the listlessness of the staff. Was it Kit's fate to be surrounded by complete and utter incompetence? Now and then there were signs of life—a cry would tumble from the maternity ward, or a nurse would amble down the hallway with what appeared to be a newly born football. Sure, what was the rush? These babies, if all went well, would be alive for nearly a century, per kid, and so naturally the nurses felt no particular urgency, were in no real hurry to get these grubs of people going, to plop them under grow lights and inject vaccines and cocoon them in their first little outfits and send them wriggling into their lives. Sure, what was the big hurry, anyway? Where was the freaking fire? Meanwhile, Susannah moaned, on her back now, melting in the sheets. "Kit!" she cried, not meaning to. Where was Dicey? Where were Marlon and Char? It felt strange, after all that had happened, to be here with this pointy stranger, this woman with impeccable hair. Though they'd seen each other so much in the past months, Susannah still felt nervous around her, unsettled by Kit's confidence or bluster or whatever that was, and Susannah had never quite let her defenses down with her. But now she thrashed and screamed for Kit, as if they were family, or friends, as if Kit were someone she could trust. "Kit! Why is it so hot in here?" she said. Out the window, a wasteland. Kit clasped her hands. Her fingers were shaped like drawings of fingers: tapered and fine. The baby would have hands like hers. The baby would grow up surrounded by perfection and rules, would live in a universe as understandable as a board game, because Kit had that in her—that will to organize, that ability to explain. "Shh," she said now. She was effortlessly competent, locating the thermostat and cranking the air-conditioning up a notch, sweeping back toward Susannah, saying, "Shh, Su. Keep breathing. That's right." She didn't coo like the nurses; she didn't sugarcoat. She didn't pretend anything was other than it was. She didn't tell Susannah that everything was okay, which Susannah appreciated. They were both adults, working together; they could be honest with the fact that everything was certainly not okay. Then the pain swept over Susannah again, painting her whole mind that bluish purple, that arterial red. She was losing her train of thought—what had she . . . ?—but it wasn't about thinking anymore. It was the hormonal surge finding the crevices of her body, shutting off, gently but firmly, her ability to think about things like Kit and her fingers, about Tim's clenched paws—until she was only her body, only animal heat and strength and pain and warmth, fluids crashing around, the tide of the child, the forces of the universe plunging into her spine and taking over, or wait, it was the hockey-stick-size needle the nurse was brandishing. How was it that this happened every day? Everything collided (the nurse chatting laconically to Kit over Susannah's spread legs, words bubbling up now and then, the weather, oh, the heat, did they hear what had happened at the Aqua City Motel?)— Tim, where was Tim? Oh, that's right, she was giving birth to Tim. No! That wasn't it at all. What was it again?

Then a moment of clarity, like a warm spot in a pool, and as Susannah drifted toward it, she grabbed Kit's hand. Urgently: "Hey! I'm still going to get paid, right? Oh, God, I'm sorry, I know I shouldn't've left, and that was wrong—mmph—and I'm sorry. But I can't—ugh—I can't keep going on with this if I'm not even going to be paid for it. I can't. You have to still pay me, right?"

The nurse frowned. "What's she talking about?"

"After all I've done for you!" Susannah was saying things she would never really say, but this childbirth business was turning out to be like drinking—making her unable to catch the things she normally caught—loosening her to say the things she wouldn't normally say. She thrashed in the sheets. The money! The money! She had to get something out of this—something had to make all the pain worthwhile.

Kit glared at the nurse and said, "I told you when we first got here—when you called our doctor to get everything faxed over. Don't you—Oh, whatever. This is my baby."

The nurse blinked politely.

"She's having our baby!" Oh, Kit was so tired of saying it over and over. Meanwhile Susannah clenched her teeth, emitted a growling moan.

"They're lovers, Bess." The doctor blew in impatiently, tugging on his rubber gloves, fingering through his tray of tools. "It's the thing these days. Get hip to it!" He winked at Kit.

"What? Oh, no, no, no—my . . . my husband's in the waiting room." The doctor raised his eyebrows, a slit of a smile on his lips. "No, I meant it's *our* baby—my husband and me—and she's the surrogate."

"Well, why didn't you just say so?" The nurse sniffed. The doctor peered between Susannah's legs, nodding. "And so how'd y'all end up out here? You're from back east, aren't you?"

Kit rolled her eyes (trying to offer Susannah some water that was violently resisted). "We're from Chicago."

"Right, like what I said." The nurse snapped her rubber gloves.

"We . . . ah . . . she ran away." Kit gestured toward Susannah, who answered with an eloquent scowl. "She . . . well, what were you going to do, Su? Keep the baby?"

"No!" The nurse gasped, covered a burping laugh. "Miss Pure!" But Susannah could only glare up at them, as furious and inarticulate as a pissed-off circus animal. Her breath heave-ho'ed in her chest. *Prue,* she would have said, could she have, *that's Prue, you idiot!*

Kit smiled, despite herself. Having these strangers in the room made it possible to say the things she couldn't exactly say to Susannah, the things that needed to be said, that Susannah needed, somehow, to hear. "I think that's what she was thinking. She decided she wanted our baby for herself, and so she took off. But luckily . . . I guess we found her just in time." Susannah tried to sit up, and the nurse and Kit simultaneously pressed her back. It was a nightmare! The way they talked about her like she wasn't even there! The way she couldn't manage to respond! So it had finally happened. She had finally become invisible. So it was true that she was irrelevant, that she was no one's favorite, no one's darling. That was for people like Aaron, like Rose, like Kit—charismatic, beautiful people. Being the surrogate hadn't helped one bit. It had made everything a hundred times worse. The doctor nodded and said, "That's right, now push"—everyone was in such a rush to take the baby from her, she was surprised they didn't just cut it out and leave her for dead. Finally she unclenched her jaw and managed to say, "Julian? Where's Julian?"

"I'm here," he said from the doorway. And there he was, looking small in ill-fitting scrubs, like a child Halloweening a doctor. Susannah couldn't help it—she laughed.

"Thanks," he said dryly.

Susannah felt as happy to see him as she'd ever been, even though he went and stood by Kit, hugging her once tightly to his chest. Meanwhile Susannah was sinking into it, rising under it, the intense pressure in her limbs, the contracting in her torso—if only they would shut up. If only Kit, with her tiny clean hands, her sweatless brow, would shut up for once! Then the doctor was saying, "All righty, kids, I think this is it." Susannah surfaced now and then, trying to keep her consciousness above water, bobbing like a shipwrecked sailor. She clung to Julian's voice as if it were a surfboard of driftwood, carrying her back to the shore. "You're doing great," he said again and again. "Breathe." He and Kit took turns saying it, the way they'd all practiced in birthing class, the class they'd taken at the hospital one million years ago.

A whole hour had passed, gold-beaten out to the ages. Time held long breaths in suspense. Susannah, with a mighty scream, felt a release, as if her whole body had finally dissolved into sand. A cheer rose in the room, followed by a squeal like a kitten's. "It's a boy," said the doctor, unnecessarily, and he lifted up the slimy little creature—Susannah caught a blurry glimpse of a bloody handful, pawing in the air, his bluish cry racketing through the room—and a flurry of happy sounds blew in from where Julian and Kit stood. So that was good-bye, thought Susannah. So long, stranger.

THEN SHE WAS being cleaned, as if she had devolved in her sleep into a gigantic helpless monster of a baby. The room was arctically cold. Julian and Kit had disappeared. Frankie was gone. Dicey had taken her away without so much as saying good-bye, a realization that caused Susannah's chest to seize. Was she having a heart attack? Where were her feet? Where were her toes? The nurse dressed Susannah in a diaper, an ice pack—maybe she really *had* become a big baby—and then she was alone. She drifted into sleep and dreamed of swimming. She awoke. The light was butter melting on a biscuit. Afternoon. Had they left? Had they swaddled their baby, thrown a couple thousand dollars on her bedside table, left her bleeding there like a prostitute? Susannah frowned but couldn't summon the energy for anything else. Again she slept.

When she woke, it was evening, and a pair of policemen were peering into her face. "Oh, did we disturb you?" said the one with a Hitlery mustache and cockeyed hat.

They were here to question her. About the baby? She didn't know! How was she supposed to know! Oh. Oh, about Tim. That was right. Something had happened to Tim.

Susannah sighed, rolled to her side, felt a new bubble erupt and goosh out of her, as if it had been the baby's last breath trapped inside. "Sure, I'm ready," she said into the pillow. It smelled of antiseptic and a sick person's sweat. Of *her* sweat. Her crotch burned and stung, like after the first time only a billion times worse and without any of the lingering pleasure, without the love; her gut felt cramped and grieving, as if it'd been mugged. She wanted to see the baby, her baby. She understood that she wouldn't take it, fine—she didn't really want a baby, of course not!—but the need to see him, to hold him for even just a minute, was keenly physical: a twitching in her arms, an ache in her breasts. Oh, of course, that was right—her breasts were full of milk. Sure, why shouldn't the police question her now? The young one sat uncomfortably on the plastic chair, which squeaked under his polyester pants, making farting sounds every time he moved. Susannah lay in the bed, feeling utterly mammalian, as if she were there to feed him, as if the young one were about to curl beside her in the bed and clamp his teeth onto her nipple. The one with the mustache turned off the TV. Susannah hadn't noticed that it was on, but when he turned it off, the room seemed to settle down. "So," he said, like a cop in a movie. "Where were you when Timothy Garland died?"

FRANKIE, WHO never cried, had her shorn head buried in a pillow in the backseat. Dicey was driving as fast as she dared, plummeting toward Phoenix. They didn't speak.

"Are you crazy?" was what she'd said to Frankie. It wasn't at all what she'd planned on saying. "Getting in a car with some stranger? Buckle up, now. We're leaving." They hadn't said good-bye to Susannah. They hadn't said anything to her at all. In the morning Dicey made her phone call to the Thunder Lodge and then, eyes stained red from sleeplessness, nerves jangling like loose coins, got into the car. When she'd first seen Frankie in those unreal, dim moments just after the accident, she hadn't even recognized her. She'd thought, Who's that little boy?—only to later register with a shock that it was Frankie, that Frankie had cut off all her hair, and how had Susannah let her do such a thing, and oh, God, how was she going to explain this to Skip, to Jean?

"She's not a stranger!" Frankie had shouted, slamming the door shut.

"Well, look what happened," Dicey said as she turned the key in the ignition. Something about the car felt different when Dicey sat in the driver's seat, as if Susannah's temporary possession of it had shifted something, changed the composition of the vehicle itself, so that when Dicey first sat inside it, she got right back out to examine the sides, to check the license plate, to make sure it was even the right car. She spent a long time adjusting the seat, retilting the mirrors. What *was* it? There was a pile of dirt, for some reason, in the glove box. And, "Buckle *up,* I said!"—she extended a hand and slammed Frankie against the passenger seat, much harder than she'd meant to. Frankie cried out—it couldn't have really hurt her, but she shot Dicey an unforgettably injured look—then climbed into the backseat and burrowed in. Dicey drove, not saying what she wanted to say, which was that God Almighty she loved Frankie so much that she could have died of it, so much that she wanted to shove her again, that she wanted to squeeze her until she screamed, that it was not a feeling either of them could survive. Instead all she said into the rearview mirror was, "Jesus, Frankie, put on your goddamned seat belt already, will you?"

KIT STOOD IN the hallway, talking to Julian's parents. The pay phone was just down the hall and catty-corner from the nursery, so that if she stood with the cord outstretched as far as it would go, straining umbilically across the linoleum, she could just see out of the corner of her eye the glass wall, could make out the row of bassinets, the flash of blue that indicated her son. The elder Forsythes had both gotten on the phone and talked over each other, each demanding different bits of information at the same time. Kit closed her eyes—God, but she was tired—and tried to sift through their questions. "Yes, yes, she's fine, the baby's fine, we're all fine. We can leave tomorrow. . . . No, we're not sure, we might end up flying—we haven't gotten that far yet." She couldn't very well say, not to these sweet old voices, that Julian might have to stay there for further questioning because . . . well, they'd done more than had a baby here. She just couldn't get into all of it now, and it occurred to her (sickening as cold rain down a shirt's back) that maybe she never would have to, really—if they never told anyone back home, how would anyone ever know? (Relief seeped through her limbs.) She really couldn't express strongly enough to her in-laws how itchy she was to get home and start the process of suing Susannah, and of course settling into life with the baby; how it was hard to feel motherly yet toward the mewling little tadpole she'd only just met today, not when rage and sorrow and hurt surged through her veins like a drug, when she'd been wrenched from her routine of preparing for the kid, when she'd missed the baby shower and setting up the nursery and all the things that she'd convinced herself would make her feel a little more *expectant* than she was; how she wanted to tell everyone in the world about what had happened to her, about her very sad story. She wasn't sure what this instinct was, but something in her boiled, urged her to climb to the roof of the hospital and scream out into the desert, "I was robbed! I've been wronged! It isn't fair!" She knew that she should be relieved, that she should be thankful, after all that had happened, to have a healthy baby dozing there in an institutional bassinet. Meanwhile the Forsythes cooed, "What's his name? When do we get to meet him?"—and—"Let us talk to Julian!"

But Julian had excused himself, had needed to get some air (forgetting again that the air outside was about as refreshing as a stroll on Venus), and now traced the circumference of the hospital. He had scarcely noticed anything, let alone their surroundings, during the

nightmarish ride the night before. Now, in the brilliant light of the
desert at 5:00 P.M., he saw that the hospital was across the highway
from a series of businesses—or maybe it was the main drag of whatever
town they were in. The signs were all absurdly large, as if signaling to
aircraft passing by: McDonald's, Burger King, Rosa's Chili Hut, Wild
West Pawn Shop, Indian Mike's Trading Post, Taco Bell, and another
McDonald's, the identical pair of yellow arches goal-posting the commercial strip. Along the highway, weathered, hand-painted billboards
advertised a gas station, an observation tower with high-powered tele-
scopes, Wal-Mart. Nearby was a bleak-looking high school, abutted
with dusty playing fields. In the distances the mountains.

What a lovely day, as if it were a new-made world. Julian had noticed that despite movies and television shows to the contrary, the
worst days of one's life were usually the most beautiful—the sky clear,
sun grinning like a beauty queen. He couldn't think but only feel, feel,
feel the tingling of being alive. He walked out back, past the Dump-
sters labeled BIOHAZARD, past the piles of human waste and discarded
body parts and God knew what else, past the service entrances and the
long ruts of truck tracks. He stood facing the desert, visoring a hand
against the dust kicked up by the wind. Here it was, despite everything. The great sullen shroud of the desert rolled on as it had rolled
five thousand years ago, as it would five thousand years from now.
Here was whatever it was he had felt for Susannah, whatever it was he
felt about Tim, about Tim's parents—and a sudden renewal of love
for Kit, his love for his wife like a terminal illness, his lust for her traveling throughout his legs like poison from a spider bite, sometimes
dormant but never subsiding, and flaring up without warning, bubbling rashlike on his hands and neck. How the wild winds blow it. A
vile wind that had blown before and since, through prison corridors
and cells, ventilating wards of hospitals, now came blowing over Julian
as innocent as a breeze. But he had to beware—the anger at Susannah,
the furied indifference toward Tim, this sense of wanting to escape it

all, the inkling that it might be possible to—this wind was tainted. Run tilting at it and he would run right through it.

Already in the corner of the sky, someone had stowed the coming night's moon. The scythe of it glowed in the heat.

10

ALONE ESCAPED
TO TELL YOU

For a long time now, a makeshift shrine has moldered in the concrete wall surrounding the pool, a chintzy roadside saint lodged into the crevice. The blue of her plaster hood blisters, her face worn smooth as if from tides. For a long time now, the thing has been forgotten, or maybe only ignored—the stack of pebbles stowed behind Mary's back, the collection of dead insects gathered at her feet like children waiting for a story. The shrine, like a foreign word or the names of the dead, avoided, unspoken. Time passes.

A boy comes near, peers into the shrine, his face distorted fish-eye style, his breath summer-breeze hot, scorched at the edges from the cigarette he smokes, stubs out, then stows in his pocket. He is lean, gangly, maybe sixteen. He has bad skin through which you can tell he'll be handsome someday. He moves like a puppy with huge, fisty paws. One hand extends, brushes away the debris. Ancient insect shells land lightly on the pavement like petals, like nothing at all. He disappears, only to return in a few moments with a trash bag and a wet washcloth, and he sets to work, humming—bathing the statuette as tenderly as he would a lover. Such attention would stir anyone after so much neglect, would raise the heat to anyone's face, even a dried-out and deserty anyone. The accordioned brow, the straight white teeth biting lower lip, the sweat beading at his temples. It's the way he looks at a thing, the way his attention shapes it into being a slightly better version of itself than it had expected to be. He's become that good a flirt; he strolls through the high-school halls, disarming girls with that grin, that gaze, because he knows it is all about seeing people the way they wish to be seen, that if you can manage that, you can get away with anything.

When the area is clean, he disappears again, returns after a longer pause, armed with a framed photograph of himself—or no, of a boy who looks something like him, hair flopping dangerously over one eye, something defiant in his stare—and a sprig of plastic flowers, a red rubber ball, a tiny mound of pebbles, a square of Plexiglas. The photograph is eased in beside the statuette, facing out at an angle. The flowers are nestled on the other side. He steps back to look, adjusts the flowers. Then one deep breath and there is the glass, a shield against the outside world, reflecting a version of him, of Frankie, slanting into the shrine, making eye contact with the picture of Tim. Frankie wipes his hands together and turns away.

A few children splashed in the pool, but most everyone was out at the picnic tables, which were draped in gingham waxed cloths and piled high with food—plastic dishes of Frito pies, bowls of chilies (hot, hotter, hottest), stacks of fry bread seeping grease onto paper towels. Bottles of pinkish wine, burst-open bags of tortilla chips, constellations of cut fruit going soft in the sun. In a nearby cooler, long-necked bottles of beer sweated into a bath of melted ice. The sun pounded the sky into submission, left it to bruise toward dusk. "Frankie," his mother was shouting, "I need you to reach something for me!" Someone was playing a banjo. Someone was playing a mandolin. Someone was singing. At the table they were laughing, reaching over one other, chattering about nothing in particular. Over by the grove of spindly saplings, a bespectacled couple entwined beneath a blanket, whispering hissing I love you's. A matted-looking dog slurped spilled beer off the ground as a child wearing only a diaper tugged at its tail, shrieking with delight. At the table a red-faced man in a button shirt and tie (but he always wore a tie, it was part of his *thing*) was holding forth about the future of art. "Art that *does* something for once!" he was saying. The girl sitting next to him laughed. "Oh, please! Why does everything have to do something?" She had checked in the night before with a trunkful of handmade wallets.

Because the crafts fair started tomorrow, and they all had high hopes still, they were yet shiny-eyed with potential—because who knew what would happen? Maybe they would sell things and make a lot of money. They had heard about the sacred lake, about the Indians' ceremonies. Who knew how it would play out? Anything could happen.

One of the women who had been singing now sat at the picnic table, squeezing between the man with the tie and the wallet girl. She was breathless and laughing. "Look—they leave it lit up all night and all day," she said after a moment, pointing to the sign.

"I like it," said the girl.

The man agreed. "Old school."

"What's with the zigzaggy thing?"

"That's the lightning bolt! Get it? The Thunder Lodge?"

"Oh!" They all started laughing again, more because they were in the mood to laugh than because there was anything particularly funny.

Farther down the bench, Frankie sat beside the guitar-playing girl, his face lit by a citronella candle someone expecting mosquitoes had brought. "Yep, we were supposed to be on, like, a three-hour tour, Gilligan style," he was telling her. She strummed another C chord and laughed, hid behind her hair. "We were just passing through. But then we never left."

"Who, you and your mom?" She nodded her head toward Susannah, who had come out looking for something. Frankie watched Susannah, her hair pricked with points of light.

"Sort of, yeah," said Frankie. The girl leaned closer to him.

The other woman who ran the motel kept swooping around, making sure everyone was fed and happy, making sure everything was all right, teasing the children, scolding the dog. Sweat tattooed her face. "Everyone okay?"

"Yes, Dicey, this is wonderful, thank you," they answered, again and again.

Frankie accepted a cigarette, and the women appeared at his side. "What's all this?" Susannah said, squinting at him.

"Uh-oh," the guitar girl said, laughing.

"Frankie!" Dicey said. They loomed in front of him, fists on hips. Susannah held out a hand, palm up.

"Busted, kid!" said the girl, and went back to picking out campfire songs. The party parted, leaned away from either side of Frankie. The heat and noise seemed to fade.

Frankie glared at Susannah, his face flushing ever so slightly. "Gee, thanks." He held the cigarette like a branding iron above her palm, miming a burn.

"Not funny," said Susannah.

Frankie shrugged then, stubbed the thing out on the ground, and when he saw that Susannah still stood there with her hand outstretched, he laid the mangled butt along her lifeline. Dicey spun on a heel, marched back toward the kitchen.

"You're going to have to learn to be a little sneakier, pal," said Susannah.

"All right," said Frankie. "I will."

"Don't stay up too late."

"I *won't*."

"Don't drink anything."

An exasperated sigh. The guitar girl by now lost, taken away by a bearded man playing bongos.

"All right, then," said Susannah. She was turning to leave when Frankie grabbed her hand and pulled her down to the bench and hugged her tight, burying his face in her armpit. Whenever he did this (less often lately), Susannah had the sense that her skin had dissolved, that there was no Susannah, only this warm lump of human hugging on the bench, only the places of her that Frankie needed to touch. Frankie, Frankie. She put her nose to his hairline and breathed in his clean smell, the musk that emanated from his scalp, equal parts paper and earth. She patted his back once, absently. "Have fun," she whispered. "And really, no cigarettes."

"All *right*. Je-sus," said Frankie, back to being caustic and teenagerish and male.

Then she went, and Frankie watched her silhouette greeting Dicey's in the office window, sat there thinking until a stream of water drilled into his chest. He looked up in time to see a grubby child wielding a neon plastic AK-47. "You!" Frankie cried, and gave chase, making sure to trail the kid all the way around the circle to the guitar-playing girl, who greeted them, "Well, here comes trouble!"

susannah prue sat on the bench outside the motel's office, strips of moldering paint crackling against her thighs. They had repainted shortly after taking over the motel, after the Garlands announced their retirement, but the desert had done its work on the bench again, and Susannah made a mental note to tell Dicey— they'd have to have Frankie strip it and repaint it. After all, he couldn't just mope around at the Grotto the whole summer, waiting for girls. He was supposed to be working; that had been the deal. If he wanted to stay in his own room at the motel, to move out of the oversize closet he'd used as a kid in the living quarters behind the office, then he had to earn his keep. But of course—so typical—it was impossible to get him to do anything. "I'll go mow the lawn," he'd say, gesturing to the sandy expanses out behind the motel. "I'll be back soon."

It had been tricky, those first few months he'd returned from his father's. He hadn't lasted long there—six months, perhaps. Three-fourths of the school year. It seemed like an age ago, and now Susannah thought, What on earth did an eight-year-old know? Why had Dicey gone to pick Frankie up and come back to the Thunder Lodge, where Susannah had stayed since the baby's birth; why had they moved in together and settled Frankie into Tim's old room, let her restart school as Frank, the boy next door, devoted themselves to their new little son? But they had been young, too, and maybe that was just how it worked. Maybe it made sense that your children were young when you were young, so that you could be foolish together.

Dicey swept by in her long linen skirt, brandishing an empty platter. They shared a smile before she disappeared into the office. Susannah squinted at the horizon, looking for the boy she used to see there, the ghost of whatever, the shadow who'd appear on the side of the road like an unidentifiable but familiar smell. There was no reason to look—she hadn't been seeing things like that in a while. It was as if her brain had straightened out under the influence of Dicey's reliable mind. Dicey had a knack for numbers, appointments, names, a way of grounding Susannah.

"Telephone," announced Dicey now, holding open the screen door.

Susannah looked down the dusty highway in one direction, then the other. She rose from the bench, went into the office. The cool air pressed its tongue to her skin. Who could this be now? Who called and asked for Susannah anymore? Because they had retreated into this life, hadn't they? A life that Susannah's friends and family back home had scratched their heads over before they gave up on her altogether.

She hadn't spoken to any of them for ages—not her mother, not her cousins. She'd lost track altogether of Rose, of Aaron, hardly remembered how any of them could ever have affected her at all. Anyway, she had gotten quieter here; her mind would churn with tumbleweeds of ideas tangling silently together, and she would have a hard time formulating the words. It had a strange effect on people, this internal stammering did, and Susannah found that they waited through the pregnant silence, leaning forward, nodding their heads encouragingly— that people wanted to hear, even more, what she was about to say, as if her silences meant that she was formulating something ingenious— which actually made it harder to say anything at all, because at that point wouldn't whatever she said be a disappointment? Around the Thunder Lodge, people didn't talk much, anyhow. At the new Wal-Mart, cowboys ambled by one another in the aisles, nodding dustily, and even the greeters just watched you come in, their faces hatchet-marked with sun lines, eyes serious and round. No one asked too many questions around here—not about why the Garlands had abruptly abandoned their livelihood and moved away, or what had become of that strange boy of theirs; not about the two women who ran the motel; not about the teenage Frank, who made it his business to woo all the girls of the township high school and yet who had something different about him, something puckish, something almost feminine. They had their places here. Susannah and Dicey and Frankie were just three more characters in the sparse stage play of the desert; the locals knew who they were—those Thunder Lodge people—and that was enough. Even Susannah had gotten so that she didn't ask too many questions. Still, there were these moments—when a clot of traffic moved past and the highway roared like an ocean; when the late sun angled in from the window, dressing Dicey in gold; when a sudden peal of laughter erupted from the guests having dinner or a splash from the pool tinkled through the air sounding golden, golden as Dicey's cheekbones in the sun, golden as the swell in Susannah's chest as she realized who was calling—moments like these when Susannah thought she knew how she'd gotten there and why, when she recognized the unwieldy spool that had connected one thing to another, stringing along moments like a bridge of rocks surfacing in a river, uncovering the way from one side to the other.

"Hey, button," she said into the phone. Dicey smiled and turned to go into the living room. Susannah put out a hand to stop her, but it was too late.

"Hey, Aunt Su," he said.

"How's your birthday, you big boy? I was going to call in a little bit."

"I know. We're not going to be here, so Dad said to call you now real quick. We're going to the movies."

"That sounds like fun."

He considered this. "My friends are coming. Friends from my class and from karate." There was a pause. "Then we're having pizza."

"That sounds real nice, J.T."

He didn't respond.

"J.T.?"

"Yeah, I think we're leaving now. I guess Dad will probably call you a little later."

"Okay."

"Is Frankie there?" But someone was calling, muffled, *J.T., let's go,* or that's what it sounded like. Susannah pressed her ear against the phone, trying to vacuum up all the sound, greedy for bits of it. "Oh, okay, I guess I gotta go." He had called on his own, Susannah thought. Julian and Kit hadn't told him to call at all. Well.

"All right, button. You have a great time at the movie."

" 'Kay."

"You can call anytime you want. You know that, right?"

" 'Kay." A pause. Another voice from somewhere, more impatient this time. "Bye, Aunt Su," he said. And then he was gone.

Acknowledgments

Many thanks are due to my classmates and mentors in the MFA program at the University of Minnesota, especially MJ Fitzgerald and the inimitable Charles Baxter; to Siobhan Adcock and Lauren Haldeman for astute readings of early drafts; to Michelle Mounts and Sara Barron for illuminating conversations about this book and writing in general; and to my agent, PJ Mark, and editor, Sally Kim, who are as wise as they are generous, and who graciously guided this book into the light. To my parents and all the Shearns and the Schutzes for awakening an early interest in words and providing unending encouragement and support. And of course, to Adam Tetzloff: first-reader, cheerleader, inspiration, and life-partner extraordinaire.

About the Author

Amy Shearn was educated in New Mexico, Chicago, Iowa, and Minnesota, and now lives in Brooklyn, New York. Her writing has appeared in *Jane*, *West Branch*, *Salt Hill*, and elsewhere. This is her first novel.